ISBN: 978-0-9907353-1-1
eBook ISBN: 978-0-9907353-0-4

Printed in the United States of America

Second Paperback Edition

# THE INDIGO THIEF

## JAY BUDGETT

# CONTENTS

# CHAPTER 1

COUNCILMAN PLUMB WAS already seven minutes late to the meeting when a whimpering Gracie rubbed her muzzle against his checkered tweed jacket, as if she could smell the acrid scent of death that would soon coat its fabric.

Plumb patted Gracie a final time, chalked her whimpers up to nerves, and shut the door to his room behind him. He jabbed the elevator call button three times and waited for its steel doors to open wide like jaws and carry him to the sixth-floor conference room.

As he studied his reflection in the mirrored elevator doors, he imagined the look that would appear on his son's face when the eleven-year-old saw Gracie's soft chocolate coat for the first time. Shawn had been asking for a dog for years now, but his mom's allergies had always made that impossible. It had been eight months since Abigail passed, however, and Plumb decided a dog would do the boy well.

He'd intended to surprise Shawn with the eight-week-old Lab last night, but the chancellor had scheduled an emergency meeting for this morning—something to do with the Lost Boys—and he'd been forced to stay an extra day away from home. The surprise would have to wait until tonight, when he returned home to Moku Lani.

Plumb glanced at his watch—it was 7:25. Right about now Shawn would be finishing an episode of "Captain Ultimatum's Aquatic Adventures" and slurping milk from his bowl of cereal, corn flake remnants bobbing about like abandoned islands. In fifteen minutes, he'd leave for the station with his six-year-old sister, Sandra, and ride the Pacific Northwestern Tube to Kauai Central Station.

The two would arrive at the Kauai Private Children's Academy at 8:30, and Shawn would start his day with thirty minutes of speech therapy. After four years, his stutter was almost entirely gone.

Thinking of his children soothed Plumb for a happy minute. The elevator's chime interrupted his thoughts; he'd reached the sixth floor.

He hurried down the hall, knocking twice before slipping into the conference room; he prayed the chancellor wouldn't reprimand him too harshly for his tardiness.

Chancellor Hackner, however, ignored his entrance entirely, requested a cup of his favorite Earl Grey, and calmly issued an order.

"Blow up the Pacific Northwestern Tube," he said, patting a strand of his black hair into place. He was well built, with a broad chest and wide shoulders. Thick brows framed his eyes, and his jawline was as sharp as a razor.

He smoothed the edge of his pinstriped suit and glanced around the room, smiling politely at Plumb. Plumb tried to mask his horror, but immediately felt sick.

The other council members nodded in agreement—blowing up the Pacific Northwestern Tube was the only option. The Minister of Defense & Patriotism had already approved the order. The threat needed to be contained.

The Hawaiian Federation would not fall.

Hackner leaned back in his seat. "So, we're in agreement, then? We'll blow it up to stop the Lost Boys? Will someone make a motion?"

Councilman Plumb cleared his throat at the end of the table, drops of sweat forming on his brow. "Mr. Chancellor, with—with all due respect—and I do mean you respect, I assure you, sir—I'm not sure that's such a, uh, good idea." Plumb's voice cracked with his final words.

The other council members spoke in hushed whispers. Disagreeing with the chancellor just wasn't done, and when it was, the punishment was severe.

Hackner cracked his neck to the right, and his vertebrae echoed their satisfaction. "And why's that, Councilman Plumb?"

Plumb's face turned red. More drops of sweat gathered along his knitted brow, joined together, rolled down his cheeks, and landed among the hairs of his bushy mustache.

"M-Mr. Chancellor, I'm—I'm afraid I just don't think it's right. Th-thousands of people ride that Tube every morning. To get to Kauai or transfer to other islands... Maybe blowing it up would make sense if there were more Tubes, but it's the only one from Moku Lani. It—it just wouldn't be right. I wasn't elected to approve something like this."

Plumb held the Moku Lani seat on the council. Moku Lani was a rocky wasteland, bought centuries ago from a private family and renamed Moku Lani from Niihau. If the island didn't hold the headquarters of the Ministry of Nuclear Affairs, it might've been forgotten altogether.

Hackner curled his lip in disgust as sweat coated Plumb's mustache like frosting. "What would you have us do then, Minister Plumb? Let the Lost Boys get away? Again?"

Plumb shook his head. "We could've captured them in Kauai—it was the Ministry that let them get away."

"The Ministry of Health and the Kauai police successfully stopped a raid with no loss of Indigo. If we fail to detonate the bombs, I'm afraid you won't be able to say the same. We have a shipment of two thousand vaccines on that subway, my dear man. It's in your province. It's your responsibility to get it out."

The others council members murmured their agreement. Plumb shoved a finger between his neck and collar, loosening his tie. "Mr. Chancellor, please! I—I just think there's a better way—"

Hackner glanced at his watch—he had an appointment in thirty minutes. Was it Margaret or Savannah this morning? Perhaps April. He scratched his head. Maybe Stacy.

"I'm afraid, Councilman Plumb," his lips curled into a smile, "there is no other option. We'll issue the order and the bombs will go off at 8:15 precisely. Our sources have informed us that the Lost Boys will be on the Tube en route to Kauai Central Station at that time."

Plumb's lip quivered. His breath came in spurts. "We can't do it! You're wrong! There MUST be another way! Something, ANYTHING—"

"There is no other way. These are not regular criminals. They are Lost Boys, Councilman. Terrorists. Enemies of the state."

"But, Mr. Chancellor, there will be THOUSANDS of people on the Tube at that time! Kids, too! Think of the children!"

Hackner was unmoved. "If left unchecked, the Lost Boys will become absolutely lethal. You remember what happened to the United States, don't you? And the rest of the world?"

"I wasn't elected to *kill* innocent people."

"You were elected to *serve your country*, Plumb. Protect the world's last sovereign nation from any and all threats. The Lost Boys have the potential to tear this country apart—"

"They're just *kids*! Are they even old enough to be vaccinated?"

Hackner smirked. "You'd know about kids, wouldn't you? What was your boy's name again? Sh-Sh-Sh-Shawn was it? With the stutter?"

"You're sick," Plumb whispered. "You're so sick."

Hackner thumbed absentmindedly through a stack of papers. "Don't your kids go to school on Kauai? Which I assume requires them to ride the Tube every morning?"

Plumb squeezed his eyes shut. "PLEASE, Mr. Chancellor! Please just let me tell them not to get on the Tube—"

"I'm afraid that won't be possible. We cannot afford to let the plan slip. The Lost Boys might find out. They have eyes everywhere."

Tears mixed with sweat and rolled down Plumb's cheeks. "Please, Mr. Chancellor. I'm *begging* you."

Hackner's throat was parched. He turned to the other council members. "Could someone see about my tea? I'm terribly thirsty—"

Plumb slammed his fists on the table. "THE PUBLIC WILL FIND OUT ABOUT THIS!"

Hackner turned slowly back to Plumb, a slight lift of his eyebrows the only indication that he'd even noticed the outburst. "You don't know what the Lost Boys are capable of. They'll bring this entire country down. We must find them at any and all costs. The public will *not* find out the truth about the Tube."

"THEY *WILL* FIND OUT THE TRUTH BECAUSE I'LL TELL THEM!"

Hackner pushed a button beneath the conference table. Security would be here in seconds. He smiled at Plumb's glittering mustache. "The truth is hardly relevant."

The doors burst open and Plumb's eyes went wild as guards dressed in black and green cuffed his hands. Hackner thumbed through his papers and sighed. "Euthanize him."

One of the guards plunged a needle into Plumb's neck. His eyes immediately rolled back into his head, and his face lost all color. Briefly, a smile floated across his lips. Then his corpse slammed onto the conference table.

Hackner watched the other council's members fidget in their seats as they struggled not to look disturbed. "Councilman Plumb lied about his age and forged his birth certificate. His Indigo vaccine wore off and the Carcinogens ate away at his brain. We'll have Margaret issue a regretful statement to the public about this terrible loss this afternoon."

A guard hovered nearby, clutching a cup of tea in a shaking hand. Hackner stretched himself over Plumb's corpse, grabbed the cup, and sipped the Earl Grey slowly as his face relaxed into a smile.

Per his recommendation, the Council voted to send in the Federal guards after the bombs were detonated. To try and find the Lost Boys. Hackner also suggested turning off the nets and letting the megalodons have at the wreckage a bit. The thought of corpses rising from the corals made him nervous. The Council agreed.

At five minutes to eight, Hackner made his way to the chancellor's chambers. He'd have to be quick to make it to his bedroom in time for his appointment. A green orb roughly the size of a basketball flashed brightly on his desk, a single cord extending from its base to the closet.

The ConSynth.

A cool voice called from the orb's depths—Miranda. "I'm not happy, Hackner. It's been five months and the threats have yet to be neutralized. Five entire months."

Hackner leaned against the desk and stared into the orb's swirling depths. "I'm doing the best I can, but what'd you expect? Half the Council are idiots."

The voice moved from the orb to a chaise lounge across from the desk. "I expected progress, Hackner. Not chicken shit."

The ConSynth never failed to disturb him. It was the stuff of nightmares—formulated by engineers in the days before the Final World War. Mad scientists, the lot of them. A person could drain their consciousness from their body and upload their mind to the orb's processor, allowing them to exist forever in a state of suspended animation, while gaining the ability to project perfect holograms—not fuzzy like those used elsewhere in the Federation—of their old body in the process. The resulting image was eerily real; in the early days of working with Miranda, he'd had to reach out and touch her once or twice, just to confirm that she wasn't really there.

She lay sprawled out across the lounge, her bleached blond pixie cut contrasting with her signature sapphire suit. There was a tightness that spread across her cheeks, making her face look like it had been pulled taut with a paperclip. Her haunting blue-gray eyes pierced him from where she sat.

"Results, Hackner," she said. "That's what I want you to focus on in the coming weeks."

"Miranda, darling," he started, "let's be reasonable."

Hairs stood up on the back of his neck. The chaise lounge sat empty. He heard, but didn't feel, her breathing behind him. "I'm always reasonable, Hackner," she said.

His appointment was in five minutes—he had to get out. Had to pacify Miranda. The woman was persuasive. She had to be. She brought down the whole damn world—started the Final World War, centuries ago. Ended it, too.

He grabbed his briefcase. "We'll talk later. I've got a meeting in five."

She pounded a bony fist on his desk. Her suit flashed green. "Results, Hackner."

She was next to him now, whispering in his ear. "That's all I'm after. Kill Phoenix. Kill the other Lost Boys. And kill half the damned Federation, if that's what it takes. The world almost ended once. It could happen again."

He squeezed his briefcase and nodded. "You're right, Miranda. Absolutely right."

"Three years," she said, her voice returning to the ConSynth's depths. "That's all it takes. Three years and you can wash your hands of this place like the men before you."

She was right. He only had three more years as chancellor. Then she'd promised him freedom. His lips twisted into a grin. "Looking forward to it, Miranda."

Three years could still be a long time.

"And Hackner?" she called as he pulled open his chamber doors. A chill ran down his spine. The ConSynth glowed green. "The megalodons were a nice touch."

He shut the door behind him and steadied his breathing in the hall. He thought of Plumb's white face and his cold, dead hands, and reminded himself that there were things in this world much worse than death.

# CHAPTER 2

TURNING FIFTEEN IN the Hawaiian Federation was a pretty big deal, mostly because it meant there was a good chance I wasn't going to die. Sure, there was always the off chance I'd keel over in the waiting room, die with only moments between me and my Indigo vaccination. But those kinds of deaths were few and far between, and most of us only knew a few kids who that happened to.

I'd made it to fifteen. I could count myself as one of the lucky ones who'd survived to adulthood. One of the sixty-seven percent of kids who beat the Carcinogens, and got to live a long happy life before their euthanization at fifty.

One of the *survivors*.

With a rattle, the subway pulled out of the station and dove into the glass cylinder that was the Pacific Northwestern Tube. The underwater Tubes were the quickest way to go from one island to the other, five times faster than traveling by boat. They carried people between islands like pipes carried water.

Most islands had many Tubes, but since Moku Lani was the least populated, we just had the one—the Pacific Northwestern. It had subway tracks, instead of car lanes, and always smelled vaguely like feet. Charming.

On the Tube, it only took twenty minutes to get to the closest vaccination clinic on Kauai. The Feds hadn't bothered putting any clinics on Moku Lani, since it was essentially just a giant rock. They'd drilled into its core a couple of centuries ago to create subterranean levels, which they now used mostly for nuclear energy experiments and marine research. Otherwise, the place was pretty desolate.

Moku Lani was a quiet place to grow up, but not the greatest. There was a Buster's Burgers, but nothing else really. Some kids sniffed glue for fun. I could hardly blame them. It was easier than wondering which friend the Carcinogens would get next. And if they weren't getting your friends, wondering when they'd get you.

I tried to get Mom to come to my vaccination, but she was too terrified to ride the Tube anymore. She hadn't done it since Dad died. I don't think she was particularly fond of being basically twenty thousand leagues under the sea.

She was more interested in researching sharks—megalodons, specifically (think great whites on steroids)—than transportation. She couldn't appreciate the photosynthetic plankton that glowed like stars beyond the Tube's glass. They were the closest things we had to real stars anymore. The smog and clouds—which had smothered the islands ever since humanity's fall in the Final World War—had darkened the world, exiling the old stars to occasional fleeting glimpses and history books.

Mom always made a big deal out of birthdays. A really big deal. She celebrated birthdays the way most people celebrated weddings., and today was no exception. I'd started my morning by finding approximately two million sticky notes decorating the door of my room, with cheesy messages laced with all sorts of Mom-isms. *"HAPPY FIFTEENTH BIRTHDAY TO MY BABY!" "YOU ARE MY SUNSHINE!" "EVERY DAY YOU MAKE ME PROUD TO BE YOUR MOM!"*

I was pretty lucky to have her. We'd only gotten closer since Dad died.

Screens bubbled at the top of the subway's doors. A news reporter sporting a fearsome unibrow flashed across one. "Good morning," she said, "I'm Priscilla Gurley and the time is eight o'clock. Today's top story: LOST BOYS STILL LOST."

The press got smarter everyday.

Mom might not have been able to come, but she'd sent Charlie with me. That was probably the next best thing. And if I was being honest, it might even have been better. Charlie had also just gotten her vaccination a few months ago.

Charlie pushed a strand of dark brown hair away from my eyes, then crossed and uncrossed her legs. She was antsy. "You nervous?" she asked.

I shook my head. "Nah. I've made it this far, right? I'm one of the winners. Just a couple hours now."

She nodded. The odds were good I'd make it, but I could tell she was scared. Our lives were fragile, and we knew it. The Carcinogens could strike a kid down at any time. The Indigo vaccine was the only thing that kept the adults in our world alive.

*The Federation must not fall.* The Federal government drummed that mantra into our heads as fervently as it pumped the vaccine into our irises when we turned fifteen.

"Plus," I said, "I've got my lucky socks on today."

I rolled up my jeans to show her. They were Dad's old pair. Red with pictures of cheeseburgers printed across the sides.

Charlie smiled and rolled her eyes. "I swear, Kai. You and those frickin' cheeseburger socks."

I grinned and quoted my father: "If a man's brave enough to wear cheeseburger socks in public, he's brave enough to do anything."

I still missed Dad pretty much every day. His euthanization had been three years ago. I was lucky Mom still had two years left. Both of Charlie's parents were already gone.

She smiled. "That's a *cheesy* line, if I ever heard one." She paused, then smirked. "*Bun* intended."

You have to admire a girl who's good with puns. I shook my head, feigning embarrassment. "Lord, just stop. Or I'll quit taking you out in public. The chopsticks are already a bit much. But the puns? Now you're pushing it..."

Charlie had pinned her blond hair back into a messy bun and secured it in place with a pair of chopsticks. She'd worn it like this every day since I'd met her in the fifth grade. The color of her chopsticks was determined by the day of the week. Mondays were maroon. Tuesdays, teal. Wednesdays, white. Thursdays, blue. And Fridays were whatever she wanted.

Today was a Friday (she'd skipped school to come to the clinic with me), and her chopsticks were lime green with margarita pendants that dangled from the ends. Her mom gave her this pair when she was seven. A souvenir from her work trip to Club 49.

I pulled the chopsticks from Charlie's bun and shoved them under my lip. "Walruth," I said.

She snatched them back and shook her head. "So immature, Kai-Guy." I loved when she called me Kai-Guy.

She put a chopstick to her forehead and grinned.

"Unicorn!" I yelled.

An old woman—probably forty-eight or forty-nine—shushed us from the row behind. Charlie shook her head, holding the chopstick in place. "Not unicorn," she said. "Narwhal."

We both burst into laughter. Charlie's laugh was something between a snicker and a snort. She was really beautiful—the kind of beautiful that made guys like me get sorta sweaty hands—but her laugh didn't fit her looks. It belonged to an old woman choking on corn on the cob. It was the kind of laugh that made people wipe their brows, thinking: *Thank god—she's like the rest of us.*

I wiped one of my sweaty hands against my leg. "Narwhals are extinct," I said, "like whales. Like seals. Like lots of things."

"Like your dignity?" she teased and winked. I think she was trying to be seductive—she did that sometimes. But it usually ended up looking like a bug had flown into her eye. Maybe that made it even more seductive. I guess it was just the way Charlie did everything, really. She could've burped the alphabet and my hands would've gotten sweaty at the letter A.

Sometimes it still felt like we were those same two kids who had just met in the fifth grade. Not much had changed. I liked it that way. In a world where we were constantly told we didn't have much time, it was nice to sometimes feel like time wasn't passing.

A picture of a girl with long, dark curls and bright green eyes flashed on the screen.

Green eyes.

It wasn't often we saw those. Most of us had shades of brown, which turned blue after we'd been vaccinated, a side effect of Indigo.

People born with naturally blue eyes died out soon after the Final World War. Scientists theorized that they were genetically more susceptible to the Carcinogens that filled the air after the bombs went off. They thought the weakness might be carried on the same chromosome as the gene for eye color, but weren't able to test it since the corpses were all burned at sea

The green-eyed girl on the screen held her left hand to her head. Her thumb was pressed to her chin, her index finger to the corner of her eye, and her middle finger pointed skyward. The rest of her fingers were pressed to her palm. It was like she was throwing up a gang sign.

The words *WANTED: MILA VACHOWSKI* were stamped across her face in scarlet letters. It wasn't often the press showed us pictures like this. The Federation didn't want to hurt its people—the Carcinogens in the air did enough of that on their own.

I stared at the girl's mug shot and shook my head. "I hope they get her."

Charlie nodded. "They've been looking long enough."

"Wouldn't know."

She teased me with her elbow. "Maybe if you spent more time out of the water than in it."

I grinned. Since there wasn't much to do on Moku Lani, I usually swam. "I held my breath for five minutes and thirty-six seconds yesterday," I told her. "Even saw a megalodon swimming on the other side of the nets."

She slapped my arm. "C'mon, Kai. You've gotta stop doing that. Free diving isn't safe. Those nets are about as reliable as Mr. Hoover."

Mr. Hoover had been our teacher when we were in the sixth grade. He'd had a habit of forgetting what day of the week it was and not showing up to work. Once he came to school in a cape. He thought it was Halloween. It was December.

"Aw, come on, Charlie," I said.

"I'm serious. One of these days, something's gonna happen. The nets'll go down and then it won't be so funny. You really wanna do that to your mom?"

"She doesn't mind me free diving. She thinks it's good for me to get out of my head."

I'd been free diving since Dad died. It was nice to be deep in the water. There was something about the quiet and the cold, being able to clear your mind of all thoughts but oxygen.

Charlie shoved her chopsticks back in her bun. "The nets aren't safe, and you know it. The electrical signals go out all the time. I find it hard to believe a boy with a conspiracy theory about the lunch lady would be so trusting."

Agnes Oldwinski had a lazy eye that spun inward whenever she spoke. She'd be staring you straight in the face—"Peas?" she'd ask—and then her left eye would spin inward. I couldn't trust that.

Charlie pushed a strand of blond hair behind her ear. "How many copies of your birth certificate did you bring? Just answer me that, and then tell me you're not paranoid."

A copy of your birth certificate was required at every annual Federal physical. They made notes on it each year and signed it. We were required to have it signed every year in order to be eligible for a vaccine at fifteen. They had to keep the supply controlled somehow; there were never enough vaccines to go around. Production couldn't keep up with demand.

Each vaccine had a dose of Indigo that lasted for thirty-five years. When a person reached their fiftieth birthday, it expired, and they were euthanized. The Carcinogens affected adults even worse than kids. Kids just fell to the ground, dead, but the adults went insane and died a slow, terrible death. Doctors dubbed it "Madness."

I thought back to the birth certificate copies I'd scanned and printed that morning. "Four," I said. I pointed to my cargo shorts. "One for each pocket."

"None in my purse?"

Okay, I'd lied. I'd hidden an extra copy in her purse that morning. In case I got mugged or someone spilled coffee on me. I couldn't be too careful. The copies were my ticket to a vaccine, and a vaccine was my ticket to life. I couldn't admit my paranoia to Charlie, however.

I shook my head and made a mental note to grab the extra copy from her bag later. "Nope," I said. "Just the ones in my pockets."

"So you're really not nervous, then?"

Her eyes were blue, like the eyes of all citizens over fourteen, but there was something different about hers. They were brighter. Not a normal shade of blue like the others, but a shade I called "Charlie blue." She squeezed my hand, and my palms got sweaty.

"Maybe a *bit* nervous," I said, "but it's nothing to worry about. I'm fine."

I was terrified.

I turned to the screen that flashed with the green-eyed girl's mug shot. A diamond stud decorated her nose.

Charlie rubbed my hand. "You don't need to be nervous, Kai. You went with me on my birthday a couple months ago, and I was fine, wasn't I? I didn't pass out in the waiting room or anything."

I nodded. She was right. She hadn't passed out.

But *I* had. In the waiting room while she was getting vaccinated. The nurses had revived me with promises of dinosaur stickers. I still had a T-Rex stuck to my notebook. I didn't tell Charlie. I wanted her to think of me as a man.

I sighed. "It's just, well, it's the whole needle and iris thing, really. It's not right, watching a needle come straight at your pupil like a rocket to the moon."

"Don't think about it like that. You're numb when they do it."

"I know," I said, "but it's the whole idea of it. I mean, why hasn't someone been able to put the drug in a pill or a mist or, heck, even a handshake at this point?"

"Oh yeah, because an Indigo handshake would be *really* effective."

"I don't know. We've got screens that bubble, right? The whole procedure's a lot to stomach, that's all."

Charlie squeezed my hand again. It was still pretty sweaty. I should've wiped it on my shorts before she squeezed it again.

She grabbed my right hand and put my first two fingers below her cheekbone. "At the appointment, they just have you do the Federal salute, look up, recite the pledge of allegiance—'*The Federation must not fall*—and you're done. You rinse your eyes out with some drops and you leave."

"Oh, that's it? Great, no big deal then, just shovin' a needle in the ol' retina. It's casual."

She poked my side. "C'mon, Kai-Guy."

"You're tougher than me, Charlie."

It was true. Her parents had been euthanized four years ago. They were old when they'd had her—thirty-nine—so she'd always known it was coming. It didn't make things easier though.

The state moved her to from her home in Kauai to Moku Lani to live in H.E.A.L., the Federal orphanage. H.E.A.L. stood for the Home for Emancipated Adult Leaders, but the place had a reputation for doing anything but healing its charges, who had only a fifty percent chance of living long enough to receive their vaccination. They just didn't have the support necessary to make it.

"You think I'm tough?" Charlie straightened the chopsticks in her bun. "The boy who free dives less than a hundred feet away from the megalodons thinks *I'm* tough? Quick! Call the press, this is big news!"

I laughed. "Not big enough. If you want the press's attention, you'll have to find the Lost Boys."

She winked. "If I found them, they wouldn't be lost, would they?"

The bubbling screens signaled we were fifteen minutes from Kauai. Through the subway's windows and the Tube's glass walls, I saw a shadow move among the photosynthetic plankton.

Charlie sighed. "When do you think they'll finish the new Tube?"

The old woman who shushed us earlier lowered her newspaper. "Lord knows, honey." Her voice was husky, like she'd spent her entire life with a cigarette between her lips. False eyelashes lined her eyes like dusters, and a purple scarf was wrapped tightly around her neck.

She cleared her throat. "If the Minister of Transportation & Commerce pulled his head out of HQ's anemone for five seconds, then the Feds might actually finish construction on it one of these days."

I stared at her, stunned. People didn't insult the ministers. Or the government at all for that matter. We lived in a democracy, but most people were too grateful for the gift of Indigo to speak up. The Federation had created a way for us to live, to beat the Carcinogens. Who wanted to argue with that?

The subway car fell silent. The woman shrugged and pulled a wooden fan from her purse. A fiery bird was imprinted along its cloth binding.

Charlie pulled my sleeve. "You're staring, Kai."

I could hardly hear her. I was too mesmerized by the fire that danced along the bird's wings when the woman flicked her fan. The flames ran to the base of its neck, curled around its beak, and smothered the rest of its body with fire.

The woman shifted uncomfortably in her seat. "Don't you know it's rude to stare at strangers? Why don't you look at your girlfriend instead?"

Charlie blushed. "I'm—er—not his girlfriend. We're just friends."

"Yeah." I wiped a sweaty palm against my cargo shorts. "Just friends."

The woman shoved the fan back into her purse and returned to the newspaper.

I stared at the bag. "That's a pretty sweet fan. Where'd you get it?"

Her eyes darted back and forth in the subway car. "You're kind of nosy, aren't you, kid?"

Charlie put a hand on my knee. "He's just a little nervous."

"Why's that? First date?"

"He's getting vaccinated today."

The woman narrowed her eyes. "Pity."

Charlie looked stunned. "What? How is that a pity? He's going to live."

The woman looked at me sideways. "You seem like a nice boy."

I shook my head. "No, I'm not. I'm a rebel." I glanced at Charlie. Girls loved bad boys.

The woman's eyes widened. "Okay, rebel. Whatever happens today, *skip your vaccination*. It's the most important thing you can do. They're not safe right now. There isn't much time."

Skip my vaccination? "Before what?" I asked.

The subway's screens froze for a half second. The green-eyed girl's face flickered across them again before the station cut to a reporter in the studio.

The old woman's jaw dropped. "Too late." She stood abruptly and pushed her way down the aisle. The doors to another compartment whooshed open and then closed. She was gone.

Charlie put her hand in mine again. "What was that about?"

"Dunno. Probably on drugs. Maybe Neglex? Possibly a Fryer?"

Charlie frowned. "That's not something to joke about."

I'd forgotten there were a few Fryers—people who'd been hit by one too many Dummy Darts—at H.E.A.L. A single Dummy Dart was bad enough, it could make you forget the past day, week, or even month depending on its dosage. Too many Darts, and, well, you could kiss your identity goodbye. It was like you were born all over again. A toddler in an adult's body. Of course, the Feds still said Dummy Darts were safer than bullets.

Red sirens lit the aisles. A feminine voice that sounded like velvet spoke over the speakers. "*This is a drill. This is only a drill.*"

Outside the windows, sparks flew as the subway skidded to a halt. Its doors swung open.

"*This is a drill.*"

There was going to be more time until my vaccination. More time for the Carcinogens to kill me.

"Just our luck," said Charlie. "You'll be okay."

A clock blinked on the TV screen—it was 8:10.

Charlie reached for my hand. I wiped sweat on my cargo shorts and then put my hand in Charlie's. My heart was beating hard in my chest. I glanced at my cheeseburger socks. I had to be brave.

"Stay close," I said to Charlie. As if there were many options in a Tube a hundred feet below sea level.

A girl with black, curled hair elbowed her way to the back of the subway, keeping her head down. People hardly noticed her beneath the flashing lights.

"*This is only a drill.*"

The red lights lit the girl's nose. She wore a diamond stud.

A scream caught in my throat. This was no drill. It was a terrorist attack.

The Lost Boys were here.

I squeezed Charlie's hand. "We have to get out right now. Get as far away from this compartment as we can."

Charlie didn't understand, but she saw the fear in my face and nodded. We pushed through the aisle. Screams sounded from the direction in which the girl ran.

Charlie and I pushed out the door and hurried along the maintenance shelf in the Tube's pressurized air. I glanced back. The subway compartment where we'd just been sitting exploded into flames.

"*This is a drill*," the robotic voice droned calmly over the sounds of screams and explosions.

Charlie and I stared at our former compartment in horror. The flames leaped from the car, licking at the Tube's glass ceiling, where cracks began to form.

Charlie buried her face in my chest. Shoulder, really. I wasn't much taller than her—I hadn't had my growth spurt yet. Mom said I came from a long line of late bloomers. I was glad Mom was safe at home.

Charlie sobbed. There had to be something I could do. Something I could say to make her feel safer. Maybe I should kiss her. Uncle Lou said fear went well with romance. Instead, I blurted the first thing that popped into my head. "I think this was a terrorist attack. I saw a Lost Boy."

The screams of a woman next to us pierced the chaos. "IT'S A TERRORIST ATTACK! THE LOST BOYS ARE HERE!"

Another explosion sounded. The cracks in the Tube's ceiling stretched wider. Water began to shoot from them in thick spurts.

The Tube was breaking in half.

# CHAPTER 3

THE TUBE'S LEAKING ceiling groaned and quivered beneath the ocean's smothering weight. A boy dressed in a Captain Ultimatum shirt wept and kneeled on the maintenance shelf as throngs of people raced past him like watery through rapids.

Charlie knelt next to the boy. "Shhhh, it's okay, kiddo. Is your mom with you?" He shook his head, and Charlie wiped away his tears. "Do you want to come with us? It's not safe here."

He pointed to the burning compartment. "M-M-My sister S-S-Sandra is still in there," he stuttered.

Charlie threw me a look. "We have to go back."

I stepped back. "Not now, Charlie. Now's not the time to be a hero."

"You're right," she said. "Now's the time to be a decent human being."

My heart beat faster and my hands got sweaty. Charlie made me a better person.

She grabbed a woman and had her take the boy with her, then pushed through the crowd to the compartment. I sprinted to catch up with her.

Fire raged around us as we climbed back into the compartment we'd just abandoned.

*"This is a drill,"* the voice announced over a loudspeaker. *"This is only a drill."*

"Some drill," Charlie muttered, pushing a strand of hair away from her bright blue eyes.

Another explosion sounded in the Tube. The cracks in the ceiling gave a final hiss and then burst wide open, the water rushing in. The loudspeaker fell silent, and the subway car's doors slammed shut, sealing us in. Charlie, unfazed, pointed to a row farther down the aisle.

A six-year-old girl sat whimpering on the ground. "I think it's broken," she said between sobs. "I'm gonna die in here."

I shivered. She seemed too young to be talking about death. I was reminded again how familiar it was, the threat of it perpetually hanging over all our heads.

The girl looked around. "Where's Shawn?" she said. "What happened to Shawn?"

There was a loud crack—the Tube had snapped. The floor lurched beneath us as the subway car groaned and twisted, breaking free of the Tube's shattered casing. We were sinking.

I offered the girl a hand. "We're gonna get you out of here. Okay, little dude?"

She frowned. "I'm a girl. Don't call me dude. My name's Sandra."

"Er—right then, Sandra," I said, "we'll get you out of here."

Charlie tried to help her up, but she shook her head. "It hurts to move."

Charlie offered her a chopstick. "Have a margarita, then."

The girl smiled and cautiously took the dangling pendant. It was no dinosaur sticker, but it was better than nothing, and seemed to calm her a bit.

Something heavy slammed against the sinking subway car as it plummeted into deep ocean. The world grew dark. Water spurted in through cracks in the doors. Hands pounded against its sealed glass windows. People from the Tube, sinking alongside us, drowning like rats as water rushed to fill their throats.

The compartment began to tilt. It was quickly filling with water, and the remaining pockets of air raced to one side, lifting the compartment vertically. We wedged ourselves in between two rows of seats. My feet dangled beneath me as water lapped at my heels. Sandra held onto Charlie's arm. Charlie held onto mine.

Beyond the subway's walls, shadows sped toward us, growing larger as they approached. Shadows that big meant only one thing: megalodons. Monsters of prehistoric proportions. Another byproduct of the war's nuclear fallout. Creatures born and bred from radioactive evolution. They usually lurked outside Federal waters, kept at bay by electrical nets. But today, of all days, those nets must have failed.

Just our luck.

Charlie squinted out the window. "What is that? What's going on out there? Are those shadows—?"

A corpse slammed against the subway car. The red cabin lights flickered from the force of the impact. We didn't have long before the power reserves ran out or the ocean short-circuited it. Red streams danced in the water outside the windows—blood.

A megalodon's gnashing teeth came into view. It was one thing to be told about them; quite another to see one up close. Seven-inch-long teeth, and its body ran upward of forty feet. It was twice the size of the biggest great whites. It shredded the corpse into bits like paper.

Charlie shut the girl's eyes and rocked her back and forth. The subway's lights sparked and went out. The girl screamed again.

"Hold my hand," said Charlie.

It was pitch black, but we could feel the water rise, and soon we were swimming. The subway dove deeper into the ocean. I kicked my legs to keep my head above the water.

Next to me, Charlie panted, struggling to keep herself and the girl afloat. I grabbed the girl and helped her keep her head above water.

Outside, green and white light flooded the water—lanterns. The Federal guards were here at last.

Charlie sucked in a breath. "You see that, Kai?"

I nodded. "They'll get the nets back on. We're gonna be okay. We just have to get out of here."

A lantern pressed up against a window, lighting the compartment with a green glow. There was now only a foot of air between the end of the compartment and us. Not much time at all.

A guard equipped with a ReBreather motioned to us through the window. A shadow passed and his lantern flickered.

Gone.

His lantern floated away. Blood drifted through the water like leaves on a breeze.

The water in the compartment continued to rise.

Charlie gulped breaths. "What's happening out there? Are the nets back on? Did they get rid of the megalodons?"

An explosion threw us downward, hard, into the water, pushing us all the way to other end of the compartment. There was no air. Hardly any light. Just enough to see that the subway car had broken apart around us.

There must have been another bomb onboard. My body ached from the force of the explosion. My lungs screamed for air—I hadn't taken a last breath.

Charlie.

Where was Charlie?

A green glow—a lantern floating nearby. I snapped my eyes open and ignored the burn of salt water. A shadow swam past me, hurrying away from the sinking rubble.

It might be Charlie. I kicked hard and grabbed the shadow's foot. The shadow turned, startled, and the lantern's green glow caught the waves of curls that danced around her head.

The girl from the screen. The one I'd seen on the subway. The one responsible for all this.

The Lost Boy.

Mila Vachowski.

She slammed her heel against my nose. I fought back tears and held on.

Lanterns filled the water around us with blinding bursts of green and white light. Guards sped in our direction. Mila slapped a button on her body suit. Fins dropped from the fabric, covering her feet in silicon flippers.

I tightened my grip on her ankle. I couldn't let her get away. Not after what she'd done. I glanced around me. The megalodons were gone, disappearing as quickly as they'd come; Charlie and Sandra were nowhere to be seen. The sea around me was empty now, save for the guards and the corpses.

Mila kicked hard and swam through the water. I struggled to hold her ankle. Despite her fins, the guards gained on her, rising with the help of jets. They circled us, and the water bubbled as they fired projectiles at her. At both of us.

They must have thought I was a Lost Boy—a terrorist. That I was partially responsible for killing all these people. And there was no one to tell them differently. No one to explain what I was doing. That I was trying to be a hero, not a villain

Mila dodged the guards' shots left and right. Bullets couldn't be used underwater, I realized, so they were firing darts instead. Something pricked my left leg. A burning sensation rose up my calf.

I'd been shot. My leg was going numb. The lack of sensation rose as Mila swam. Soon I couldn't feel my left leg at all. Then neither of my legs. Eventually, nothing below the waist.

But I couldn't let go. If I let go, the guards would swarm me.

The lanterns continued to rise with us. One of them lit up two shadows hanging motionlessly in the water. Another revealed blond hair and chopsticks shoved into a messy bun.

Charlie. Blood floated around her head.

At last I released Mila's ankle, and she swam away. The numbness ran faster up my spine. I paddled toward Charlie, willing my arms to move, to compensate for my numb, worthless legs.

I knew Charlie couldn't hold her breath like I could—she wasn't a free diver—and by now, even my lungs were burning. Best-case scenario, she was unconscious. I didn't want to think about the other scenarios.

The lanterns' light and the guards followed me. They'd already hit me once. They knew I was the weaker of the two. And now they swiveled their darts toward their single target— me. Bubbles burst by my ears as darts sailed past.

Charlie was an arm's length away. I tried to stretch out a hand, but my shoulders locked up, numb. My lungs screamed for air.

I threw my head to the side and swung a hand forward with the momentum. The tips of my fingers were inches from Charlie's.

A dart plunged into the hand stretched toward Charlie. Euphoria filled me. Intense warmth radiated from where the new dart struck. Uncle Lou had told me this happened when a Dummy Dart's serum recalibrated your brain. He said amnesia followed.

And then there was darkness.

~~~~~~

My eyes burned as they snapped open. The world was blurry. Dark. Cold. Wet?

I fought to remember where I was, and how I'd gotten here, but knew nothing.

Nothing.

Panic crept into the corners of my heart. I gasped involuntarily as my lungs demanded oxygen. Water rushed in instead. White spots floated in my vision.

I was drowning. A green light glowed overhead. I tried to kick, but my legs were numb. My lungs sucked in another breath. Consciousness danced around my head, like the faint memory of black curls and blood.

I stared ahead and saw blond locks floating in the water. Charlie.

Then blackness again, followed by the slow creep of death.

# CHAPTER 4

I WOKE IN a dark room, with concrete walls and no doors or windows. Prison?

A bouquet of red hibiscuses sat in the corner. Not prison. I shut my eyes, and saw a subway's flashing red lights.

*"This is only a drill."*

The Tube had cracked in half. Megalodons had swarmed. Federal guards had tried to kill me. Charlie had floated motionless in the water.

Where was she now?

I glanced down. I was wearing a white cotton shirt that stretched to my knees. My cargo shorts from the Tube were missing. Dad's cheeseburger socks were gone, too.

I slid from the cot I'd been lying in and felt the tingle of cold concrete floor on the balls of my feet. My legs had gone numb, I remembered that, but now I felt them. The dart's paralysis had only been temporary. I did a little dance in the room's corner.

A red dot stained my forearm. I remembered the Dummy Dart, and the euphoria that had ensued. It had been a small dose, but I still remembered water flooding my lungs. Even small doses could prove deadly underwater.

The Dummy Dart's serum could stun, drown, and kill a person by making them forget they were underwater and causing them to breathe. Apparently the dose they gave me wasn't enough to make me forget much else. The Feds had thought I was a Lost Boy, so they probably wanted me to remember everything. I guess I was lucky.

A latch in the ceiling creaked open, and a ladder was lowered into the room, followed by a plump woman in her late twenties. Her hair was short, brown, and curly, and her red cheeks were chubby like a chipmunk's. She wore a sundress covered in painted hibiscuses. It matched the vase of flowers.

"Ooh! You're awake!" She clapped her hands excitedly. "So lovely to finally make your acquaintance. We've been waiting nearly a week." She offered me her hand. "I'm Kindred," she said, "Kindred Deer. Like the animals that used to live in the forests."

I hesitantly shook only the tips of her fingers. She didn't seem to mind my reluctance.

I wanted to ask her a hundred questions. Where was I? Where was Charlie? Was Kindred an enemy or a friend? Was she with the Feds? I'd heard the Federation had odd ways of dealing with criminals. People who'd effectively wasted Indigo vaccines by squandering their lives. I couldn't imagine what they did to terrorists.

I patted my head and felt my black hair tangled in knots. I settled for the first question on my mind. "Where am I?" I asked.

Kindred raised a hand to her face like a caricature and giggled. "Silly me," she said. "Silly Kindred. Let me be the first to welcome you to Texas." She skipped around the room and wiggled her hands above her head like a cheerleader.

I glanced around at the room. Still just concrete walls and a crappy bouquet of hibiscuses. Three flowers fell from their stems as Kindred spun. She raced to stick them back on, inadvertently crushing the rest of the flowers in the process.

"Well, not Texas," she said, "but New Texas. The 'Republic of New Texas,' if we're being politically correct. Though, Lord knows I haven't the head for politics. Don't tell the others," she whispered, "but usually I just call it Texas. The others, however, are particular about that sort of thing. Your safest bet is to refer to it as New Texas or—and perhaps this would be best for everyone—not refer to it at all. Yes, that would be best. Don't refer to it at all. We don't want the," she mouthed 'Feds,' "to find out it, do we, dear?"

I smiled and nodded. Kindred returned her attention to adjusting the flowers.

If she wasn't a Fed, then who was she? If New Texas wasn't part of the Federation, then where was it? But, most of all, who were "the others"?

Maybe I *had* drowned.

I remembered grabbing Mila's—the Lost Boy's—ankle. I'd been holding it when I'd seen Charlie floating in the water. Maybe Kindred knew where she was.

"Excuse me, ma'am?" I asked.

Kindred glanced over her shoulder. Four more hibiscuses fell from their stems. She hastily threw them in her pocket. "Yes, dear?"

"Was anyone else brought to, uh, New Texas? Like a girl, maybe? About my age? One with chopsticks kinda stuck in her hair?"

Kindred rubbed her chin. "Well, now that you mention it, I think I did hear something about a girl."

"Oh?"

Kindred nodded. "Dead."

My stomach dropped, and my heart screamed. I'd been too late.

"Actually," said Kindred, "now hang on a minute. I suppose I was thinking about one of my radio soaps—*Waves of Our Lives*. But I did hear something about you reaching for a girl in the water. But don't worry, dear. That one's alive."

I breathed a sigh of relief. A weight lifted from my chest. "She's here, then?" I asked.

Kindred shook her head. "I'm afraid not. The baddies got her. Keeping her hostage, if I remember correctly."

My heart sank again. The Lost Boys had gotten Charlie and were holding her hostage.

Kindred patted my shoulder. "How about we go up and I get us some blueberries? That'd be nice, wouldn't it?"

"Yeah," I said, nodding. "I think I'd like some blueberries."

"Of course you would, dear." Kindred walked back to the ladder and climbed. "What'd you say your name was again?"

I followed her up. "Kai." I said. "Kai Bradbury."

The name fell from my mouth before I had time to think. I should've given her a fake name. Found out who she was, what her allies wanted from me, before telling the truth. But she just nodded.

We reached the top of the ladder, and I saw that the room above was made from a concrete of sorts, like the basement. I tapped a wall and it echoed—hollow. On one wall was a steel door; across from it, a barred window. Outside, there was a clear view: sunlight sparkling off the ocean waves.

Was New Texas a part of one of the islands? It had to be— Kindred must be using a code name. From the window, I could see that there were no other buildings on the beach. Limited infrastructure. Maybe we were on Kauai? The other islands' beaches were too built up...

Kindred led me to the kitchen. "You can meet the others once you've had something to eat, dear."

I nodded and muttered thanks, wondering if we were in a mental institution. Maybe one of the Ministry of Research & Development's experimental departments. That would explain the barred windows.

Rows of glass cupboards lined the kitchen's walls. Kindred skipped to the fridge. "Don't be nervous about meeting the others," she assured me. "They're all such dears."

I wondered how many more times Kindred would say "dear" in the next ten minutes.

She tossed me a bowl of blueberries and powdered sugar. My stomach growled. I was starving. By the time I'd finished, Kindred's "dear" count was at ninety-seven.

"Nets are down and it's only nine a.m.," called a deep voice from the other room. "Gonna be another long day, Kindred."

She scrubbed another bowl of fruit in the sink. "But I've got blueberries, dear. Freshly picked from my garden. That's got to count for something."

"I thought we finished those at Bugsy's—uh..." the voice sniffed as though its owner were crying, "...goodbye thing a couple nights ago. There's still some left?"

A tall boy, about eighteen, poked his head into the kitchen. His eyes were two spaces too far from his nose, and his top row of teeth jutted from his lips even when his mouth was closed. Stray hairs were scattered across his chin. He looked vaguely like a squirrel.

The boy wiped his eyes and wandered over to Kindred at the sink. I tried not to stare at his sweat-stained shirt and flamingo boxers as I wondered again where I was. I hoped Charlie was somewhere safe.

The boy turned to face me. "Wait a second." He stared at me with his wide-set eyes. "Who's this?"

Kindred clapped her hands and pushed him toward me. I panicked and stuck out my hand for a handshake. He gave me a blank look, staring at my hand briefly before giving me a sort of a sideways high five.

Kindred smiled. "You must've heard us talking about him, Dove. His name's Kai Bradbury. He's the one from the Tube."

"The clinger? The one who grabbed Mila by the ankle?"

Kindred nodded. "The very same."

"Well, balls," said the boy.

"Balls?" I scratched my head.

Kindred patted my arm. "It's just something he says, dear. You know, like 'shoot' or 'wow' or 'crap.' He wasn't talking about anyone's balls in particular."

"That's reassuring," I said. New Texas got stranger by the minute. I shuddered to think what they'd done to me when I'd been unconscious.

The boy's eyes were blue like Kindred's, like everyone's in the Federation over fifteen. Unlike Kindred, however, his were especially blank. Clear like a community pool after what Uncle Lou called a "code brown."

He scratched his head. "Where are you from?"

"Moku Lani," I said. I bit my tongue the second the words left my lips. I'd already given them my name. Now my home. This was too much. It could still be a trap. Something set up by the Feds to convict me as criminal. Maybe some scheme of the Lost Boys.

He tossed a handful of blueberries into his mouth. "Moku Lani?" he asked. "Mostly just the nuclear plant there, right? And the home for the kids?"

"H.E.AL.," I corrected him.

"That's the one," he said. "You an orphan?" Kindred shot him a panicked look.

I shook my head. "I've still got my mom."

Kindred shoved a bowl of berries into his hands. "More berries, Dove?"

He nodded and stuffed his cheeks full of them. He looked even more like a squirrel now.

"So, uh, your name is Dove?" I asked.

"Yep, yep," he chuckled. "Dove's my name—just like the bird. My mom saw one sitting outside the hospital window the day I was born. That's how she picked it."

Kindred smiled. "Isn't that lovely?"

"Yeah," I said. "It's lovely, all right."

He stared out the kitchen window with a smile. "Sometimes I pretend she saw a falcon instead. And my name's not Dove, but Falcon."

"Falcon would have been pretty sweet," I said.

He shrugged. "Yeah, but I guess I was better off than my brother. Mom didn't see a bird outside her window with him."

"What'd she see?" I asked. "A squirrel?"

"A tree."

Dove had a younger brother named Tree. This was definitely a mental institution.

"I sense a visitor in the kitchen," another voice called from the hall. "Are my suspicions correct?" A boy about my age poked his head around the corner. "Also," he continued, "do we still have cornflakes?"

"Good morning, Sparky!" cried Kindred. "Your suspicions are indeed correct. This is Kai Bradbury. And, yes, we still have cornflakes."

"Excellent," said Sparky. He shuffled into the kitchen in his blue silk pajamas. His eyes were large and his ears stuck out to the sides like a bush baby's. Around his neck, a creature with brown fur, big eyes, long claws, and a white face hung like a necklace.

Sparky nodded at me as he passed. "Greetings, stranger."

The creature that hung from his neck turned its head and stuck its tongue out ever so slightly in my direction.

I pointed to the creature. "What's that?"

"Tim," Dove said, plopping another handful of blueberries into his mouth. His big teeth were stained blue.

"Not the kid," I said. "The thing around his neck."

"That *thing*," said Kindred, "is Tim. And he's not a thing. He's a three-toed sloth. Named Tim. Rescued from rainforest destruction. And he's a dear."

I took a deep breath. I had to find out where I was and who I was dealing with, fast. Then I could find Mom and we could save Charlie.

Sparky alternated spoonfuls of cornflakes between himself and Tim. "Where's Mila? Shouldn't she be up by now?"

*Mila.*

That couldn't be right. It must be someone else. It couldn't be the Lost Boy. She'd fled after the Tube cracked. Swam away once I'd released her ankle to save Charlie.

Kindred sighed. "I don't know, dear. She's had a rough few days. With Bugsy's," she sniffed, "untimely... you know."

Sparky twisted his spoon. "I think we've all been feeling that way."

Kindred nodded. "It's not easy. Mila knew him the best out of all of us. She had to. They went on raids together."

Raids. Mila. It was too close. It was the same girl. I sucked in a breath.

Kindred turned. "What's wrong, dear?"

"Nothing," I said. "Nothing's wrong. I just, uh, knew a girl named Mila in a class once. That's all. Thought it might be the same one."

Dove grinned. "I guarantee it wasn't this Mila. Our Mila is the one and only Mila..." He trailed off, his eyes drifting and his mouth falling open.

"Vachowski," Kindred finished for him. "Mila Vachowski."

Dove shook his head. "Right, right," he said. "Sorry. Zoned out for a second there."

I felt sick to my stomach. The kitchen's walls closed, and my heart pounded. This wasn't a mental institution. This was the Lost Boys' den. The people around me were terrorists.

But that meant that the "baddies" who'd gotten Charlie weren't Lost Boys at all, but Feds. She was safe.

Kindred put her hand to my head. "Are you all right, dear?"

"I—I'm fine. Just dizzy. That's all. Would you mind if I—could I use your bathroom?"

Kindred nodded. "Of course, dear. Down the hall, second door to your left."

I rushed down the hall, sped past the bathroom and arrived at a panoramic window that provided a clear view of the ocean. There was a lever on the windowsill. I pulled it, and the bars lifted—I'd found my escape. I would get away from the Lost Boys. I slammed my fist against the glass.

A shower of shards rained on me, and I leaped out the window and onto the sandy beach below. Blood stained my white shirt. My knuckles were bleeding. A cool breeze hit my thighs and I struggled to hold my shirt down. A mixture of sweat and blood coated my face. A piece of glass was buried in my right palm.

Waves crashed on the shoreline farther down. There was no one in either direction. Nobody to call for help. I was confused—even Kauai beaches weren't this empty. I was somewhere else, somewhere... far.

I glanced at the sand around me. Bottles and cans stuck up everywhere. The beach was littered with trash.

Footsteps pounded the hall behind me, no doubt responding to the sound of broken glass. I ran to the ocean and washed the window's glass from my palm in the salty water. From where I knelt, I could see that the shoreline curved back in both directions. The structure I'd been held in was on a peninsula, maybe a small island.

The last time I'd seen a real beach was on a trip to Maui we'd taken back when I was in the fifth grade. Dad was still alive then. I'd just met Charlie, and she'd been nice to me— and I didn't have a lot of friends in those days—so we took her with us.

Maui was mostly towering skyscrapers and floating screens. A place sprawling with people and businesses thanks to its proximity to the Hawaiian Quartile, the largest Federal island. Mom said there was a time when Maui was mostly rainforests, but I didn't believe her, and even if she was right, the installation of the Ministry of Transportation & Commerce headquarters on the island had eradicated them long ago.

Maui did have a few beaches left, however, and all of them were lined with condominiums. On our way down to one of them, Charlie saw a family of snails trying to cross the road. She insisted we carry them across because she didn't want them to be crushed by cars. Dad said Charlie was the rare kind of person who looked at a snail and saw another soul.

I splashed water on my face, curled my toes in the sand, and swished my bleeding hand in the water. Someone grabbed my wrist. A tall boy with blond hair and broad shoulders stared at me with blue eyes that burned in the sun. "Perhaps it's best if we keep the blood out of the water."

He wasn't wearing a shirt. Just pants. And judging by the definition of his abs, I guessed he'd never had a milkshake.

He pulled my hand from the water. "You're not in Kansas anymore."

"What's Kansas?" I asked.

"Never mind," he said.

"Are the nets down or something?"

The boy rubbed his square jaw. "There aren't any nets out here."

"Out here?"

"Outside Federal waters."

I stepped back and stared at him. "You're one of them."

He ran a hand through his blond hair and smiled. "Perhaps."

Behind him, I saw Kindred climb through the broken glass and hurry toward us. I glanced down the beach—nowhere to run. I stuck a foot back in the water.

He shook his head. "Not the best plan of escape. You'd be better off running for the trees."

I waded farther into the water, up to my waist, and stepped on something sharp. A piece of aluminum floated to the surface.

"The whole island's made out of trash," said the boy.

"Trash?" I asked. I took another step and felt something plastic crush under my foot. A bottle floated to the surface.

He nodded. "You're going to want to run."

"Run?"

"In three," he counted, "two, one—"

A massive fin broke the surface out in open water—a megalodon. I ran to shore.

The boy smiled. "Fast learner."

He took my arm and pulled me farther up the shore, and I watched as the patch of sand where I'd just been standing was crushed between massive jaws. Compacted cans and bottles floated in the water as the island's insides poured out. A seven-inch tooth glowed in the sun's gleam, and I saw the monster was tangled in a patch of wire.

It had smelled my blood in the water, and now it was tearing the island apart to get to its prey. More fins rose from the water in the distance—more megalodons smelling blood and swarming.

I remembered the red ribbons that had danced in the water outside the subway car, and felt sick to my stomach. My knees collapsed and my face hit the sand.

There was no running.

There was no hiding.

The megalodons were here.

# CHAPTER 5

CHARLIE'S HEAD THROBBED and her chest ached. She remembered struggling in the water, holding on to Sandra's little hand, and being thrown back by an explosion. She remembered the air being crushed from her lungs and her brain screaming for oxygen. She remembered sucking in a deep breath, and feeling water rush in, followed by a burning in her chest, and then nothing.

She flexed her arms and legs. Everything seemed to be in working order. She felt an IV that had been shoved into the crux of one arm. She propped herself on a pillow. She was lying in a bed.

She guessed she was in a hospital.

Her eyes adjusted to the darkness, and she saw the walls were not white, but gray. Not a hospital at all. There weren't fluorescent lights. No lights at all, save for the sliver that tumbled in from a window in the corner.

Charlie felt her chest. Someone had covered her in a cotton nightgown.

Where were her clothes? She pulled the covers from her legs and carefully touched a foot to the floor.

Concrete. More confirmation she wasn't in a hospital.

"Hello!" she called. "Anyone there?"

No response.

The room was small and cold. Her hair hung around her shoulders, the messy bun and chopsticks long gone. She took a step away from the bed.

"*Movement in cell sixteen.*" A metallic voice echoed in the room. It was the same voice that had announced the drill on the subway.

Lights flickered on, and Charlie saw that a toilet and sink stood next to her bed, across from a steel door.

This was a prison.

A slot in the door slid open. "Charlotte Minos?" The voice belonged to someone young—her own age, maybe even younger.

"Yes?" she said. She walked toward the slot. Her knees were still weak. The slot slammed shut.

"*Identification complete.*"

The room's lights dimmed. She waited by the door, but the slot stayed closed. She returned to her bed, closed her eyes, and imagined the sound of cars outside in the street. An engine rumbled and she snapped her eyes open. The rumbling ceased—it was just her imagination.

She heard a whimper and sat upright in her bed. "Hello?" she said.

No response, but the whimpering continued. She pressed her head against the wall. The sound came from a crack.

"Hello?" she asked again, this time louder.

Still no response.

She had to get their attention with something loud. She stared at the wheels on the base of her bed. If she'd learned anything from H.E.A.L., it was to never underestimate the screeching of rusty wheels. She couldn't count the number of times a new kid had tried adjusting their bed in the middle of the night, only to wake up half the building.

She yanked the bed, and sure enough, its wheels screeched like nails on a chalkboard. Her ears were practically bleeding.

She pressed her head back against the wall. "Hello?" she asked again. "Anyone in there?"

The whimpering stopped. Nothing.

Then, finally: "Yes. I'm here."

Charlie's heart raced. "What's your name?"

"Is that you, Charlie?"

Charlie recognized the woman's voice. She'd known it for a long time. "Mrs. B! Yeah, it's me, Charlie."

She heard Kai's mom sniff back tears. "I—I thought I would die here alone. Have they been hurting you? Is Kai in there with you?"

"No," Charlie said. "He's not right now, but everything's gonna be okay. We'll get out of here and find him, Mrs. B. We haven't done anything wrong."

There was a sharp knock at the door.

Charlie panicked. "Hang on, Mrs. B, I'll be right back." She pushed the bed back against the wall. The screech deafened her again.

"Knock, knock, little boy," called a voice from the slot.

Little boy?

The door swung open, and the room's fluorescent lights flashed to full brightness. Chancellor Hackner, the leader of the free world, stood before her. His hair was slicked back and his suit was tight against his chest. Three guards flanked him, their hair similarly slicked and their suits equally tight. Charlie guessed they'd used ten bottles of gel between them.

The chancellor's grin stretched from ear to ear, his teeth big and white like pieces of gum. "Mind if we join you?"

Charlie pulled the covers to her chest. She'd seen his face before, on bubbling screens, but he looked different in person. His hair was shinier and his teeth a more unnatural shade of white. His blue eyes pierced her like knives. He sat himself on her bed's edge, and she moved her feet so they wouldn't touch him.

"I think," he said, stretching an arm toward her knee, "that we both know why I'm here. So let's cut the chitchat, little Lost Boy, shall we?"

She shook her head. "I—I'm not sure what you're talking about, Mr. Chancellor. I don't know why you've got me here. I haven't done anything wrong. The last thing I remember was an explosion on the subway and taking in a big gulp of water. Nothing else."

The chancellor raised an eyebrow and glanced at his men. "And you expect us to believe that?"

"It's the truth."

"Hardly."

She tried remembering what had happened before the explosion. She'd lifted Sandra out of the water. "Does this have to do with the girl?" she asked. "The little one on the subway?"

Hackner patted his greasy black hair. "I suppose she is smaller in terms of stature. But I certainly wouldn't call her little…"

"With all due respect, Mr. Chancellor, she was scared to death, crying when we found her."

He burst into laughter and turned to his guards. "You hear that, gentlemen? Mila Vachowski was balled up in the back of the subway crying after the bombs went off."

They, too, burst into laughter, though their faces betrayed fear.

Mila Vachowski—one of the Lost Boys. Did they think she had *helped* her? Was that why she was here?

Charlie shook her head. "I—I don't think we're talking about the same girl."

"No?" Hackner raised an eyebrow. "So you don't know Mila Vachowski or Kai Bradbury? Any of the Lost Boys?"

What were they talking about? Kai was just a normal kid, like her. "Kai Bradbury isn't one of the Lost Boys," she said.

His smile twisted into its familiar grin. "So you do know him?"

"Yes." She nodded. "Yes, I do. But he has nothing to do with the Lost Boys."

Hackner smirked. "Just like you, huh, sweetheart?" He stretched a hand toward her leg. She swatted it away.

"You're disgusting."

He narrowed his eyes. "Don't think that we believe your lies for even a second, Miss Charlotte Minos. Or should I say Charlie? Your H.E.A.L. file said you preferred your friends call you that."

"You're not my friend."

"Ah, Charlie," he said, "that's where you're wrong. In time, I think you'll find we'll become quite good friends. You just need more time to think. To clear your head and remember the truth. A bit of fasting ought to do the trick."

"Sage!" he called to someone in the hall. "Would you remove Charlie's IV? She's recovering just fine, but have the kitchen hold her meals. She doesn't seem to have her appetite yet."

And with that, he was gone. A girl's small frame replaced him in the doorway. Sage, Charlie guessed. The light caught her glazed eyes—she was blind. Despite this, she expertly navigated the room.

"Arm, please," Sage ordered. Charlie held out her arm, and the girl withdrew the needle.

"Thanks," Charlie said. Sage pursed her lips and nodded. Charlie admired the girl's soft, straight hair. "Your hair's a lovely shade of brown." She watched the girl's body tense. "I'm sorry. Did I say something wrong? I wasn't even thinking."

Sage wrapped the IV tubing around her wrist. "It's all right," she said.

Charlie watched as Sage straightened the sheets at the end of her bed. From the speed with which she did it, it looked like she'd been doing this job for quite a while.

"How long have you been blind?" Charlie asked.

"As long as I've been working here."

"And how long's that?"

Sage's jaw tightened. "Four years."

Charlie stared at the girl's clothes. She looked like a maid of sorts. She wore a simple baby blue dress and a navy coat. Her straight hair hit her shoulders, framing her round face and accentuating her almond-shaped eyes.

"How'd it happened?" asked Charlie.

Sage shook her head. "We shouldn't be talking. I shouldn't have said anything at all."

"Your hair really is a lovely chestnut," said Charlie from her bed. "It's the shade you get when you mix coffee with just the right amount of cream. My mom and dad used to drink coffee that color."

Sage smiled faintly. "People used to say my mother's hair was a lovely shade of chestnut. Like caramel mixed with coffee." She rubbed her eyes. "My hair was blond when I came here. That was the last time I saw it. I guess my eyesight's not the only thing that's changed."

"No," Charlie said quietly. "I guess it's not." She breathed in deeply and asked the question that had plagued her mind since she'd spoken to Mrs. Bradbury. "Am I going to die in here?"

Sage stared at the floor, and wrapped several strands of chestnut hair around a finger before nodding slightly. "I—I think so, Miss Minos."

Charlie lay back in her bed. "Oh," she said, wondering if the same fate awaited Mrs. B and Kai too.

Sage walked toward the door, then turned. "Miss Minos?"

Charlie sat up slightly. "Yes?"

"Don't believe everything you see, and don't believe *any*thing you hear."

"Why's that?"

The girl chewed her lip. "They—they've been putting hallucinogens in your fluids for the past week. Pumping you full of them while you slept." And with that she left, closing the door behind her.

A pit formed in Charlie's stomach. She called for Mrs. Bradbury.

Nothing.

She called again.

No response.

Mrs. Bradbury was no longer there. Charlie wondered if she'd ever been there at all.

For the first time since she'd woken, Charlie realized she was truly alone.

# CHAPTER 6

THE BLOND BOY yanked me from the sand and threw me toward the building.

"CODE WHITE!" he yelled to its concrete walls. "WE HAVE A CODE WHITE ON THE SOUTH END OF THE ISLAND!"

I tried to remember what Mom had taught me about her research. She and Dad were the leading experts on megalodon behavior, and now I wished I hadn't zoned out when she'd talked about work. The doodles I'd made in my notebooks instead wouldn't help me now.

The thrashing in the water worsened as more megalodons arrived and tore the floating island into pieces. Kindred, Dove, and Sparky climbed out of the broken window and ran toward the beach, guns across their chests. Sparky tossed me one, but the blond boy intercepted it. He pulled another from his pocket, and pointed one at me and one at the monsters.

"We got enough ammo, Sparks?" he asked.

"Negative," said Sparky, "though I admit I'm fairly conservative with my estimates."

Tim wrapped a claw around Sparky's gun and yawned. Apparently the action was a bit much for him.

Phoenix scratched his head. "How is that possible? Meels was supposed to get another shipment from the Tube."

Sparky shook his head. "No, Phoenix. That was Bugsy's job…"

So, the boy with the bulging muscles was named Phoenix. I thought of the bird on the strange woman's fan in the Tube. It had been a Phoenix. I thought back to signs they'd hung at Buster's Burgers in recent months. Pictures taken from security footage showing a blond-haired boy. *PHOENIX McGANN*, the words beneath the images read. *THE FEDERATION's #1 MOST WANTED.*

Phoenix stared at his gun and sighed. The crunch of glass and plastic grew louder. He had to shout to be heard over it. "We have enough to tranquilize at least one."

Sparky shook his head. "Negative. We have enough to maybe make one drowsy, but that's it, boss. The cartridges we do have are expired. If they were people, well, then maybe we could down ten or twelve of them."

"They're not remotely people, Sparks. Where's Big Bertha? She'll have something for this. The tranquilizers aren't enough."

Big Bertha? There was a Lost Boy called Big Bertha? I glanced back at the building, imagining the arrival of a seven-foot she-woman with a blond Viking braid and bosoms the size of Mt. Mauna Loa.

"FOR CHRIST'S SAKE," shouted a voice from the building, "CODE WHITE AT NINE IN THE FRICKIN' MORNING?"

I guessed Big Bertha was near.

"Prepare yourself," muttered Phoenix.

A black leather boot kicked down one of the building's doors.

A petite girl not taller than five feet stood where the door had been knocked from its hinges. She had dark brown skin and eyes, and her lips were curled into a growl. Her short, cropped hair had been spun into braided balls, and her mouth was fixed in a frown, making her look a little like a trout.

Phoenix smiled. "What do you have for us, Big Bertha?"

*This* was Big Bertha? Five-foot-nothing was Big Bertha? Braided balls of fury? A light gust of wind could've blown her away. She rolled her eyes and gave Phoenix the finger.

"Real nice," he said.

She slowly dragged a large black bag through the doorway.

"Perhaps," said Phoenix, "it might be possible for you to hasten your pace a smidge? We do have megalodons swarming the island..."

"PATIENCE!" she shouted.

I had half a mind to run into the water right then. The megalodons might've had teeth, but the Lost Boys had guns. And likely torture. With the megalodons, at least it would be over quick.

I stared at the gun Phoenix still pointed in my direction. I couldn't run, not yet. I had to wait for the perfect moment. Bertha still sorted through the bag. Her black braid balls stuck out from its depths.

I turned to Kindred. "That's Big Bertha?"

She nodded.

"And the 'big' comes from where exactly?"

Bertha pulled out a gun the size of a lawnmower. She yanked the trigger and yelled. "CLEAR!" A ball of static electricity fired fifteen feet into the air.

"Oh," I said quietly.

Kindred nodded, smiling like a proud mom. "She makes most of our guns, dear. The rest we borrow from the Federation."

"You mean you *steal* them from the Federation?" I said.

"No, silly." She winked. "We return all the bullets."

Bertha fired another round into the air.

"Brilliant, Bertha," said Phoenix. "What do you call her?"

"The Paralyzer," the girl said, cradling the gun in her arms like an infant. "She launches an electrical shock capable of inducing paralysis for between ten and sixteen hours, and she's effective up to forty feet away."

"Balls, that's cool," said Dove under his breath.

The megalodons' fins teetered as they tore off more chunks from the island.

"Yeah," I whispered to Kindred, "but can it kill a shark?"

Bertha pointed to me. "Who's the kid? Boy Scout? We're not buying cookies this year, thanks." She cackled at her own joke.

I rolled my eyes. "Boy Scouts don't sell cookies."

She stepped back. "And now he's giving me sass. The Boy Scout's giving *me* sass."

Kindred patted my back. "His name's Kai Bradbury, dear."

"What?" she squinted. "Car Battery? What the hell kind of name is that?"

"Better than Big Bertha," I muttered. I glanced at Phoenix. He was shaking his head. Crashing glass echoed around us.

"I suspect he's got brain injuries," said Phoenix. "So far he's been slow. But he did take a Dummy Dart to the head. I imagine the serum's still wearing off."

"For his sake, I hope so," said Bertha. "We don't need another Dove."

At that moment Dove was giggling and chasing a butterfly.

Bertha sucked in a breath. "Now lemme tell you something, Car Battery—"

"It's Kai Bradbury—"

"You don't *kill* sharks. Or megalodons. Or *anything* for that matter in these waters. The last thing we want is a bunch of blood floating around us in the middle of the ocean. You think a few megalodons are bad? Picture an ocean full of 'em."

Sparky glanced at the shore. "Could we possibly focus on getting rid of them? Maybe? For even the smallest of seconds? They've already destroyed fifteen feet of shoreline."

Bertha sighed and fired her gun at the water. The weapon kicked like a bucking horse, and she had to steady herself against the building's concrete wall. The salt water magnified the electric ball's effects, and a megalodon's frozen body floated to the surface. The Paralyzer had worked. She fired again.

"Shiny!" said Dove, noticing the ball of white sparks. Kindred patted his back.

Another megalodon floated to the surface. For a split second, Phoenix lowered the gun he aimed at me.

I jerked Kindred's gun from her hands and immediately fired twice at his leg. Darts flew out rather than bullets. Tranquilizers, I guessed, based on what Phoenix had said.

Phoenix stared at his leg and smiled slightly. "I underestimated you, Kai Bradbury."

The guns fell from his hands and his knees buckled. Bertha aimed the Paralyzer in my direction. I quickly shot probably thirty rounds at her—my aim wasn't great, but one dart finally hit her neck. I guessed Sparky *was* very conservative with his estimates.

Bertha pulled the dart from her neck. "Well damn," she said, and then fell like Phoenix.

"Oh, dear," said Kindred.

Sparky aimed his gun at me, hands shaking. "We—we will not condone this sort of behavior. Cease your fire at once."

My heart pounded. This was no time to be reasonable. These people weren't my friends—they weren't decent human beings. They were hurting people. Stealing lives. They were criminals, and had to be stopped. I fired darts at both Kindred and Sparky, and they fell to the ground.

Dove looked at me with wide eyes. "Balls," he said, before lowering himself to the ground.

My breaths came in bursts. I'd beaten the terrorists at their own game. They were done. I could call the Federal guards and turn them in. They'd been dysfunctional at best; it was hard to believe they'd evaded the Feds for so long. With their capture, I could prove my innocence—and I could see Mom and Charlie again.

The island shook as the megalodons continued to tear it apart. The Lost Boys lay crumpled at my feet. It was just me and the monsters now.

Crap.

I hadn't thought this through. I ran toward Bertha and grabbed the Paralyzer off the ground, aiming it at the water. "*DNA scan required*," announced a robotic voice from within the gun.

Crap.

I *really* hadn't thought this through. I grabbed Bertha's hand and twisted her limp fingers around the gun. Farther down the beach, Tim inched away from Sparky's limp body. His instincts told him there was danger. It was time to flee.

"*Identity confirmed*," announced the gun. I squeezed my hand over Bertha's, pulling the trigger. It kicked in my hand, knocking me back. A ball of energy sailed through the air. I positioned myself again, this time aiming at the water.

A dart landed in the sand next to me with a hiss. A pit formed in my stomach. There was still one Lost Boy left.

Mila Vachowski.

Another dart whizzed past my ear. I had to move. I dropped Bertha's gun and ran for the other end of the island. A dart sailed past my face, its shuttlecock scraping my cheek. Another whizzed past my throat.

Her aim was getting better. I wondered if the darts she fired contained a sedative or a poison. Probably a combination of the two.

By now, even more megalodons ate at the shoreline. New Texas was slowly disintegrating. Farther out, I saw debris floating freely. The monsters were in a frenzy now, this close to tasting their prey.

I remembered Mom saying that megalodons were incredibly smart for sharks, their intelligence rivaling that of dolphins. Like they'd been bred to attack human prey.

It was strange that such an intelligent monster had developed so quickly. Some researchers said that it was because of the massive amount of nuclear fallout in the ocean: that the radioactive waste that had fallen from the sky had altered the genes of other shark species and transformed them into these creatures of prehistoric proportions. But Mom said their rapid evolution was almost too perfect, too much of a statistical anomaly to make sense. A three-headed shark would've been more reasonable.

A dart stabbed through the loose fabric of my shirt, but didn't nick my skin. I knocked it to the ground, careful not to touch its loaded needle. I kept running, and turned a corner on the island, but the darts didn't stop. There was no escaping. Running like this wouldn't work. The second I was hit, I would be good as dead. Mila would throw my limp body into the ocean, and the monsters would tear me apart, bit by bit.

I circled the building. It was more like a fortress, really, except for the windows. The tall, bare concrete walls appeared to wrap all the way around the island. Clearly whoever had built this place hadn't been concerned with aesthetics.

As I turned another corner, I came upon a section of New Texas where the ocean looked smooth. No megalodons. The water barely rippled.

Another dart whizzed past me. Mila was closing in. My heart beat hard.

I stared at the water. It was the megalodons or the Lost Boys. The megalodons had teeth; the Lost Boys had guns.

The thought of the calmness that filled my chest whenever I swam made my choice. I dove headfirst into the water. The cuts on my hand stung and bled again in the salty water. As I ducked beneath the surface, I saw that the trash-compacted island was only about eight feet thick.

Massive shadows hurtled toward me. Megalodons swarming. One snapped open its jaws as it approached.

No running. No hiding. Something in my gut told me to *just swim*. I kicked straight toward the monster's open jaws and aimed for the back of its throat.

Its jaws clamped around me.

No light. No air. It had swallowed me whole.

The world went black.

# CHAPTER 7

A RINGING SOUNDED in my ears like bells between classes. My fingertips and toes tingled and blistered. Voices echoed around me, whispering my name. I caught only fragments, like wisps of smoke through fingers.

"—should've let him die—"

"—too bold and too stupid—"

"—need bold, stupid, and brave—"

"—worried about Tim—"

"—can't tell him the truth, or he'll—"

"—like Bugsy, just Bugsy. Balls, the poor kid wasn't ready—"

"—well, dear, that's what we'll tell him, then—"

"—putting a damn iris scan on the next one—"

The voices melded together in a symphony of sound. One ran into the next. All of them drowned beneath the ringing.

"—he'll stay. That's final. We need a spark—"

"—Sparky's been asleep for two days, dear—"

"—Bertha's got the bag ready for Newla. We'll leave this afternoon. I suspect he's already awake."

I tried to slow my breathing, but it was too late.

"Unlock his wrists," ordered Phoenix. "On second thought, wait until he's fully conscious."

Kindred sat herself at the edge of my bed. "How are you feeling, dear?"

"Toes," I said. "T-toes and fingers. B-burning."

Cold metal pressed against my wrists—handcuffs. They hadn't been so kind this time. I guessed it was fair, considering I'd tried to kill them.

"Bertha, dear, could you grab some algae and eucalyptus from the stores?"

Bertha grumbled something under her breath and then left. Kindred checked to see if Phoenix was looking before she undid the locks.

"There you are, dear," she whispered. "Our little secret."

Mila stood silent at the back of the room. Her bright green eyes glowed like a cat's.

I glanced around at the eyes in the room. Dove, Phoenix, and Kindred had the familiar blue eyes. So Mila and I were the only ones unvaccinated. I blushed when I realized I was probably the youngest person in the room.

Phoenix caught Kindred pretending to fiddle with the cuffs. "I suppose you can take them off," he said. "In fact, I'll bet you already did."

She smiled innocently. "There we are, dear." She let the shackles fall. "Pardon our precautions. We just wanted to be a bit more—"

"Prepared," finished Phoenix.

I nodded. My fingers and toes still tingled. Why hadn't they killed me? What were they planning? Where were the megalodons? I rubbed the burns on my fingertips.

"So," I said, "what, uh... happened?"

The three terrorists exchanged nervous looks. "What happened," called Bertha as she climbed down the ladder, "is that you shot us up like a moron and damn near killed yourself in the process." She handed Kindred the algae and eucalyptus. "Far as I'm concerned, we should kill you right now."

"Really, dear?" said Kindred, spreading the crushed algae between my toes. "That's how you make friends?"

"That's how *he* makes friends!"

"You're seventeen, dear," said Kindred. "He's twelve—"

"Fifteen," I interrupted.

"You should know better by now, Bertha. I mean, really I thought we'd have a nice day. Silly Kindred thought we'd have a nice, memorable day—"

"*I'll* give you memorable," said Bertha. "Just hand me a gun—"

"You swam into the mouth of a megalodon," said Mila, stepping from the shadows. "I shot the beast with Bertha's gun, and you rolled out like a marble. Another went after you, but I got that one too. They floated to the surface and I filled them with bullets. I grabbed your body away from them. Ran inside and turned on the island's extra engine. A feeding frenzy broke out as we drove away. They devoured each other like rats." She looked sick. "Then I waited for the others to wake up. Only these three did."

"I was already awake," said Dove with a dumb grin. "But the sand felt good on my back."

Kindred patted his hand.

"Sparky never woke up," said Mila. "In fact, he still hasn't."

I pointed to my back. "The one with the—?"

"Sloth?" said Bertha. "Christ, kid. Let's use our words."

I glanced around the room. There were no guns. No instruments of torture, as far as I could tell. Just my bed and the Lost Boys.

What did they want from me? I took a deep breath. I couldn't think about what they had planned. I just had to get through the day—focus on the conversation at hand. "Sparky never woke up?"

Mila shook her head.

The tingling in my fingers and toes now made sense. I'd been inside the megalodon when she'd hit it with the Paralyzer. I'd been electrocuted, though the monster's thick skin took most of the blow.

"Now that I think about it," said Dove slowly, "Sparky hasn't slept in, like, two years. I mean, the rest's probably good for him."

Bertha tightened her jaw. "Doveboat, what have I told you about thinking?"

He stared off into space. "I forget."

"Think, Dove!"

"I thought I wasn't supposed to—"

"*You can think when I tell you to!*"

"I believe," said Phoenix, "we can attribute Sparky's continued unconsciousness to his use of Cafetamines. You can't stay awake for two years straight and not expect it to catch up with you. Batteries only last so long."

"Car Battery is already burnt out," said Bertha, looking at me. "And we didn't even get to use him."

*Use him?* For what? What had they intended to use me for?

I had to change the subject. If they thought they couldn't use me for whatever it was they'd planned, then they might just kill me instead.

"Can I see him?" I asked.

"Who?" said Bertha. "Sparky?"

I nodded.

"Why? So you can try to kill him again?"

Kindred rubbed eucalyptus over the algae. "Maybe he wants to apologize?"

Bertha made a face. "And maybe I want to be chancellor."

"Take him to Sparky," said Phoenix. He was wearing a shirt now, but beneath it his muscles still rippled.

"But he's already got Tim in there," protested Bertha.

"Just take him," said Phoenix.

Bertha grumbled and motioned for me to follow her up the ladder. We passed a room with metallic walls and tables.

"The armory," Bertha said with a smile. "My lab." She pointed to a set of weapons laid out across the main table. "Recent inventions," she said proudly.

I scanned the table. A black pen, a small silver box, a three-pronged projectile jammed into a gun, and a bundle of chewing gum wrappers.

"They're—uh—well, they're something," I said.

She showcased them from left to right. "Laser Pen, Video Loop Fractalfyer, Grappling Gun, and some Gum Wrapper Bombs. Or," she winked at me, "as I refer to the four: oh shit, deep shit, deeper shit, and *holy shit.*"

"How refined," I muttered. I noticed a stack of paper clips also rested on the table's corner. "And those are?"

"I call 'em 'Paper Clips,'" said Bertha, "but they're top secret."

"Let me guess: they have an uncanny ability to hold multiple documents together with ease?"

"Shut up, Car Battery."

As we exited the lab, I noticed a pair of pink flip-flops resting against the wall. "Highly specialized weaponry," I muttered.

Bertha flared her nostrils. "ENOUGH! Time to see Sparky."

She hustled me down the hall to Sparky's room. When we entered, the first thing I noticed was Tim, hanging from a bar beside the bed. He chewed leaves with a mournful expression.

"Tim hasn't slept in three whole hours," said Bertha gravely. "We're really worried about him."

"Poor guy," I said, trying to look concerned. "Three whole hours without sleep... Just imagine."

Sparky had no such problem. His head was propped up on a feather pillow, his cheeks rosy and his complexion clear. His lips were even turned up in a slight smile.

"Doesn't he look just miserable?" Bertha said.

"Absolutely awful," I agreed.

Bertha sat herself on the edge of Sparky's bed. "So you really think we're terrorists?

My heart pounded. This was it. This was when they'd kill me. I stepped back and feigned surprise. "What?" I said. "Why would you think that?"

"Well for starters, you tried to kill us all."

I nodded—it was a fair point.

"Also," she continued, "you muttered 'Terrorists. The Lost Boys are terrorists, Charlie!' in your sleep."

They knew I was on to them. There was no time to play games. "Why don't you just kill me, then?" I asked. "Like all those other people?"

Bertha threw up her hands. "For Christ's sake, I've been TRYING! It's the damn management around here…" She pointed to my shirt. "I see you've been worrying your little skirt about it."

Crap. I was still wearing nothing but the long shirt.

"Maybe try some pants next time, eh, buttercup?"

My face flushed red. I was suddenly more concerned with my modesty than with my life being in jeopardy. "You—you guys are the ones who put me in this thing."

She gestured toward my body. "I sure as hell didn't put anything on *that*."

"Right," I stammered, the word clinging to my throat like peanut butter. "I—I'm gonna go look for some pants."

Bertha stared at me with her brown eyes and nodded. "Try not to shoot anyone."

Wait—brown eyes? Hadn't Kindred said Bertha was seventeen? Her eyes shouldn't have been brown; they should've been blue like the others. Why hadn't she been vaccinated?

I thought about the way Bertha had obliged when Phoenix had ordered her to take me to Sparky. Phoenix was the one calling the shots. He would have been the one to decide whether or when a Lost Boy got vaccinated.

I wandered down the hall. A warm breeze wafted through a broken window and lifted my shirt-skirt. I smashed it down on my thighs. Was a pair of underwear so much to ask for?

"Hey!" called Bertha from down the hall. "I—I didn't mean to embarrass you." She paused. "Well, yes, yes actually I did. But look, I don't think anyone's seen anything except maybe Kindred, and hell, she's been looking at blueberries so long you don't have anything to worry about."

Bertha had just compared my junk to blueberries. Things couldn't get much worse.

"If you want pants," she said, "you'll have to steal them. We don't have extras lying around here. New Texas isn't big enough for that kinda thing."

I pulled down the edges of my shirt. "Then let's steal me a pair of pants already."

She raised an eyebrow. "You don't mind being a thief?"

I shrugged. "I've already been robbed of my dignity. The universe owes me a pair of pants, at least. What's a thief, anyway?"

She grinned. "Then welcome aboard, Car Battery." She walked down the hall to me and offered me her hand. "We aren't terrorists at all. We're thieves: Phoenix McGann and his merry gang. The one and only Lost Boys. Like Robin Hood, but with fewer arrows and more wetsuits. Lots of wetsuits. Like really tight wetsuits. Like really, *really* tight wetsuits. Dove wore one the other day—you know, 'cause he's Dove—and I thought, *Wow! I've seen you naked.* I mean, it's probably good you've been wearing your little kilt the past few days because the second you put on a wetsuit, we're gonna see everything." She paused. "Both your little blueberries."

Phoenix appeared in the doorway. "I think he gets it, Bertha."

But I didn't get it. I didn't understand who the Lost Boys were or who they said they were supposed to be. Nothing made sense. The world was spinning. I wanted Mom and Charlie.

"I get the wetsuits," I said. "But thieves? I'm not really— I'm not following you. So you're not terrorists? You're just... thieves?" Phoenix nodded. "But, like, what kind of thieves? Do you steal diamonds? Guns? Bombs?"

Phoenix shook his head. "More dangerous. We steal Indigo. We're Indigo thieves."

# CHAPTER 8

"INDIGO THIEVES?" I asked. The world was spinning. "You steal Indigo vaccines? From the Hawaiian Federation?"

"They deliver an incredible profit," said Phoenix. "Imagine doubling your lifespan. Beating the Carcinogens a while longer. People will pay big money to escape their own mortality. And the rich can afford it."

"But... how do you do it?"

Kindred joined him in the doorway, giggling. "It's all Phoenix, dear. He's the mastermind," she said. She passed me a brown bag with "Kai" written on it in curly letters. "I wasn't sure what sort of sandwich you'd like, so I just packed you blueberries. Can't go wrong with blueberries."

Bertha rolled her eyes.

I stared at the bag now in my hand. "Are we, uh, going somewhere?"

Bertha shook her head. "Not we. You. With Phoenix and Mila. All the way to Newla, princess."

I felt queasy. Why did they want me to travel with them?

"Newla?" I asked, still confused.

"Yeah," said Bertha. "Newla. You know, New Los Angeles? The capital of the Hawaiian Federation? Home to two million people, all crazy or homeless? Christ, what do they teach you in school?"

"I know what Newla is," I said. "But why me? Couldn't Kindred or you go?"

"Kindred doesn't do so well out in the field."

Kindred nodded. "I'm far too sensitive for that sort of thing."

"Yeah," said Bertha. "Last time she hugged a guard instead of shooting him."

"He looked sad!" said Kindred.

Phoenix stepped between them. "We need another body," he explained, "and I'm afraid you're the only one who fits the uniform."

Mila joined him in the doorway. "Same size as Bugsy," she said.

Kindred's eyes got watery.

"Is the equipment prepped?" said Phoenix.

Mila nodded. "And New Texas is on course. We'll be at Federal Water borders within the hour."

"Excellent, Meels." Phoenix looked me up and down. "And can someone get the boy some pants?"

Bertha threw up her hands. "That's what I've been saying "

"He's not getting pants," said Kindred. "He's getting a skirt, dear."

"Skirt?" I said. "Another one?"

Bertha burst into laughter. "Damn, I wish I was going now."

Kindred put a hand on my shoulder. "I'm sorry, dear," she said, "but it's not safe for you in the Federation anymore. They've got pictures of you now."

"Pictures?"

Phoenix nodded. "We've been intercepting Federal broadcasts for twenty-four hours now. They searched your home, confiscated your possessions. You're a wanted man, Kai Bradbury. Charged with treason and crimes against humanity. Your name's been attached to the bombings on the Pacific North-western Tube. You've been classified as a Lost Boy—an enemy of the state. A terrorist in the eyes of the Feds. Just like us."

The room was spinning again. The ringing returned to my ears. My lungs cramped. My knees buckled.

Bertha slapped me. "Pull yourself together," she said. "We don't have time for you to pass out every five minutes."

I shook my head. Things snapped back into focus. Kindred dropped a stack of clothes at my feet. Among them was a new skirt—and a blond wig. She hadn't been kidding.

"I'm—I'm sorry," I said. "Really sorry. It's—it's just a lot to take in."

The Feds thought *I* was a Lost Boy. If they found me, they'd torture and kill me. There had to be a way out of this. A way to clear my name and turn in the real terrorists—or thieves, or whatever they were.

And then a thought struck me: if the Feds thought I was one of the Lost Boys, what had they done to Charlie? I'd tried to swim to her; they must know she was with me. Did they think she was a Lost Boy, too?

"What happened to Charlie?" I asked.

Bertha snickered. *"They're all terrorists, Charlie!"*

"Your friend?" said Mila. I nodded. "Feds got her. Wouldn't worry about her now. No use. She's a goner."

*The Feds got her.* The baddies, as Kindred called them. But she was still alive, at least. There was hope. She hadn't drowned, and the sharks hadn't gotten to her. There was still a chance I could save her.

Friendship was a powerful thing. In an age where families weren't forever, friendships were our only buoyancy. I had to save Charlie, no matter what the cost.

But there'd be no saving Charlie until I left New Texas, and there was no escaping New Texas without the Lost Boys' help. Not when I was a wanted criminal. So it looked like I'd have to stick with the Lost Boys, at least temporarily.

My breath caught in my throat. What had the Feds done to Mom? She'd been at home when the accident on the Tube had happened. Had they arrested her, too? Maybe the Lost Boys knew. "And my mom?" I asked quietly.

The group fell silent. Mila stared at the ground, and Phoenix shook his head. "I'm afraid they got her too. She's gone."

"The Feds have her, like Charlie?"

Phoenix rubbed his jaw. "Unfortunately, no. She resisted arrest when the Feds stormed your home."

My heart beat faster. "What happened? What'd they do to her?"

He put a hand to his mouth. "I'm sorry, Kai. She—she's dead."

Tears rolled down my cheeks like rain. Mila tightened her jaw.

Kindred, however, fixed me with an odd look and shook her head ever so slightly. She mouthed a silent "no". I was the only one who saw.

Kindred was telling me that Phoenix was lying. I didn't understand why, but at that moment I didn't care: my mom was still alive, somewhere. The Feds hadn't killed her. I could find her. Save her and Charlie both.

But for some reason Phoenix wanted me to think she was dead. I couldn't let him know I knew the truth.

I buried my face in my hands. Kindred rubbed my back.

"I'm sorry, Kai." Phoenix said again.

The liar. Two could play his game.

"I—I can't talk about it," I said. "I'm not ready. I have to pretend. I can't think about it right now."

He nodded. Probably figured denial was the first stage of grief. After a while, I picked up a skirt from the pile. "I have to wear this?"

"It's the only way, dear," said Kindred.

"We leave for Newla this afternoon," said Phoenix. He stared at the skirt in my hands. "That's your uniform. It's essential to our mission. We can't move forward without someone—you—wearing it."

What kind of mission were they running? And why were they throwing me into the field so soon after I'd tried to kill them? There had to be an ulterior motive. Maybe it had to do with why he'd lied about Mom...

Well, Newla wouldn't be so bad. And if the Feds really did have Charlie, that's where she'd be. For now, I decided it was best to just go along with the plan, and not ask too many questions. Phoenix wouldn't have given me honest answers anyway.

"And what if we get caught?" I said.

Phoenix's face went grim. "Then we'll be tortured and killed."

I shuddered. Was that what the Feds were doing to Mom and Charlie? I felt sick to my stomach. I had to save them, and soon.

"No funny business out there," added Phoenix. "Not like what happened out on the beach. If you try to kill us again, then we'll kill you. That's a promise. Or we'll let the Feds do it, and that'd be worse. You'll follow our commands—without question—and you'll stay alive."

I nodded. I'd underestimated them on the beach. They weren't idiots. They knew what they were doing, and with or without my help, they were going to do it. It was only a question of whether I wanted to live or die. And if I was dead, I couldn't save Mom and Charlie. I'd work with Phoenix. And I'd stay alive. For now, at least.

Phoenix turned to Kindred. "Did you get the pills?"

Kindred gave him a blank look.

"The ones we talked about earlier," he said. "In the cupboard? Meels, you remember the pills, don't you? The ones we talked about."

Mila nodded, left the room, then quickly returned with two blue pills, which she placed in my hand.

Great, they intended to drug me. Drug me and take me to largest city in the world. In a skirt.

Kindred saw the pills and laughed. "*Those*," she said. "I didn't realize you were talking about—"

"The Indigo pills," said Mila. "We were talking about the Indigo pills."

"It's in lieu of a vaccination," explained Phoenix. "Little doses of Indigo. If you take two a month, you'll be fine. We're the only ones who have them. A creation courtesy of Bertha. And if you run from us in the city... well—then I'm afraid you won't have much time. If the Feds don't find you, the Carcinogens will. The Indigo pills work just like the real vaccines, but are only temporary. In time, perhaps we'll consider a vaccination—but those come at an incredible cost. Each vaccine we administer is one we can't sell, and we need the money. An island of trash doesn't pay for itself."

So that was why Mila's eyes weren't blue. She took the pills every month, too, instead of receiving the vaccine. The smaller doses taken orally must've prevented her eyes from turning blue. I wondered if she, too, was working to earn a vaccine. As an enemy of the state, I guessed sticking with Phoenix was really her only option to get one.

I swallowed the pills without hesitation. "Thanks," I said. "So about the skirt—"

"It's for Nancy Perkins," said Kindred.

Bertha grinned. "Which is gonna be you, sweetheart."

Kindred pushed me into a chair before I could say anything else. She spread a layer of powder across my face like icing on a cake. "Close your eyes, dear. You're going to look lovely."

"What about Phoenix?" I asked. "Is he wearing a skirt too?"

I heard him and Mila snicker as they left the room.

"Not possible," said Kindred. "He's six-foot-two and built like a god. He'd never pass as a forty-nine-year-old woman. Chin down, dear. Stop flinching."

"A forty-nine-year-old woman?"

Kindred pulled a card from my bag and read it aloud. "Nancy Perkins, forty-nine years old. Former executive assistant to the president of Renzo Enterprises. Resident of the Maui province. Visiting Newla to celebrate the last night of her life in Club 49." She paused. "The three of you will collect her identification cards and proceed to Club 49 this evening."

Dove smashed the blond wig on my head and traced its edges along my scalp before adding glue. "Can't have it flying off your head on the dance floor," he said. "It'd blow your cover."

When Mila and Phoenix returned, they were already dressed in full costume. Mila wore a black velvet cocktail dress with an open back, her curls hidden in a tight bun. She puckered her lips, applied a coat of red lipstick, and slid on a pair of large silver sunglasses. Phoenix was dressed in tortoiseshell spectacles, a black suit, and a thin tie. He'd covered his blond hair in brown goop and had it slicked to the side.

"Ready?" asked Mila. She slid the tube of lipstick into my hand and winked. "For you, Ms. Perkins. If it's any consolation, you make a pretty girl."

"It's not," I muttered, "but thanks anyway."

It took me ten minutes to put on my blouse and skirt, then another five to get my bosoms on straight. Yes, they made me wear bosoms. Bertha especially enjoyed that.

Kindred applied a final layer of powder to my face before stepping back to marvel at her creation. "You look wonderful, dear!" She glanced over at Bertha. "The bosoms were a nice touch."

In the kitchen, she briefed me on Phoenix's and Mila's respective covers. They were Parker Chester, a recent university grad, and Maria Lalone, a travel writer from Kauai, respectively. I wondered again how I'd gotten stuck being Nancy.

"The Wet Pockets are ready, dears," Kindred called to the others. "Meet at the main dock in ten minutes. And don't forget your lunches! It's going to be a busy, busy night."

At the dock, I learned that Wet Pockets were four-foot-long pouches made of military-grade cellophane wrap—the kind that was, ironically, used by the Feds to catch criminals. Upon seeing the Pockets in person, I realized they were just clear, thin bags sewn together by Bertha. Propellers had been strapped to their tops, and they were pumped full of air.

I'd seen sturdier sand castles.

Dove pushed us toward the contraptions. "Come on, little sardines," he said gleefully. "Into your cans you go!"

The Wet Pocket wrapped itself around me like... a wet pocket.

Phoenix and Mila hopped into the pouches next to me. I sucked in a deep breath as Dove rolled us into the water. The Pockets sank immediately, weighed down by their heavy propellers. Water spurted behind us as the propellers fired up. Through the clear plastic casing, I saw Phoenix's Pocket lead the way. His must've been armed with a tracking device— maybe even a GPS.

The Pockets dove down fifty feet. Schools of fish scurried in fear from our paths as we shot through the water. We turned sharply, and my Pocket slammed against a rock. Its jagged edge ripped my Pocket's cellophane seam. Water immediately began to stream in, and mascara ran into my eyes.

Crap. Kindred had put on mascara.

I grabbed the Wet Pocket's edges as they tore and fluttered apart, their seam undone. Water slammed into my face. I squeezed my eyes shut. My skirt billowed in the currents. If I'd been on land, at least it would've felt breezy.

My fingers slipped, and the cellophane fabric danced along the tips of my fingers. I wasn't going to make it to Newla. Not this way, at least.

Dorsal fins hurried past my feet. A school of fish, I figured. Large ones, by the feel of it. I squinted my eyes open. Rays of sunlight broke the water.

Suddenly something stabbed my shoulder hard, plunging into the deep tissue. Had I not been holding my breath, I would have screamed. Whatever stabbed me lodged itself in my flesh and yanked me upward. The Pocket's tattered remains flew from my hands as I was pulled toward the surface. Blood from my shoulder poured into the water.

I grabbed at my shoulder, trying to dislodge whatever had pierced the skin. My fingers probed the wound, and I felt a sharp prick as they encountered a barbed piece of metal sticking out of the skin.

A fishing hook. And I was being reeled in.

More fins brushed against my legs, this time larger ones. I swallowed hard, reminding myself to remain calm. The fins didn't belong to fish at all.

They belonged to sharks.

# CHAPTER 9

THE HOOK IN my shoulder pulled me up in spurts. Each new pull yanked me farther from the swarm of frenzying sharks, while simultaneously dousing them in blood.

Blood.

There was blood in the water. The smaller sharks were here—hammers, tigers, great whites—but where were the megalodons? They should've been here by now. I realized I must be back in Federal waters, and for once the nets were working.

I was pulled rapidly upward. The hook's line went slack as I surfaced. I gasped for air.

A bald, old man with the wrinkled face of a mastiff stared at me from the deck of a medium-sized fishing boat. *"The Retired Lobster"* was painted along its side in faded letters. I clambered over the side and threw myself onto the ship's deck.

The old man shrieked and fell backward. I grabbed his fishing pole and yanked the line loose.

My vision went spotty. I was going to pass out. White patches moved everywhere I looked. I lay on my stomach to keep the blood flowing to my brain. My back was warm with blood. I wasn't going to save Mom or Charlie.

The old man stood, catching his breath. "You scared the bloody hell out of me."

"Can't say getting stabbed by a giant hook did me a lot of good, either."

He nodded. "I can see that."

My breathing slowed to wheezes. "You should probably get a bandage or a towel or, uh, something."

"It'd have to be a hell of a bandage," he muttered. He moved his fingers along my shoulder, examining the hook's entry and exit points. "Old Jimmy never fails to do the trick."

"Old Jimmy?"

He poked at the hook in my shoulder, and I winced.

"Old Jimmy sliced the head straight off a shark once," he said. "Like a little bloody guillotine."

He pressed his weight against my back, then in one swift motion, yanked out the hook.

I screamed.

The old man joined me. "Ah!" he sang. "Isn't it great to be alive?"

"I'll let you know, if I still am in a few minutes." The spots in my vision melted together. A storm of white gathered from all directions. I took a deep breath.

The man doused my back with rubbing alcohol. "Bollocks," he said. "Old Churchill will have you up to snuff in no time, miss. Can't let a beautiful woman like you die on me."

I'd forgotten I was still wearing the wig. Most of the makeup had surely washed off in the water, but the wig was still stuck to my head like glue—good old Nancy Perkins.

The man draped several cloths over my wound. "Right as rain," he said. He glanced at my legs. "God, you're hairy."

"Because I'm a man," I said. I pointed to the wig. "It's a disguise." Churchill stared at me blankly. "I swear I can explain."

"You're a strange creature," he said. "Over the years, however, I've found that if we are to truly understand one another, we must not think of ourselves as a species apart from the rest. We must think of ourselves as ugly monkeys." He smiled. "Really ugly monkeys with guns and knives and hooks and all sorts of shit. Then everything makes sense."

He seated himself in a red lawn chair, and began reattaching Old Jimmy to his line. "How about a cup of tea?"

"Thanks," I said, still breathing heavily. "I'd like that."

"Oh, I wasn't offering *you* one," he said. "I was asking you to make *me* one. I *did* just save your life. Pulled the hook from your shoulder and all that."

"*You* were the one who put it there! You should've just left me to the sharks."

"Probably would've if I hadn't needed Old Jimmy back."

"You're insane. You're absolutely crazy and insane."

His eyes flashed. "You think I'm a lunatic? Just some crazy bloke on a boat? I'll have you know I have incredible wit and lightning-fast reflexes." He snatched something from the air and held it between two fingers. "Lightning-fast reflexes," he said again. "I just caught a fly. Out. Of. Thin. Air. Look at the fly!"

"I'm not looking at the fly."

"LOOK AT THE BLOODY FLY!"

I squinted hard at his hand, but didn't see anything. "You didn't really catch one, did you?"

"Of course I didn't! The buggers are damn near impossible to catch, and look at me—I'm ancient. I'd be lucky to catch regular bowel movements at my age."

I stared at him for a while. He jabbed a finger into his ear, and then wiped the wax he found on his pants.

I sucked in a breath. "So who are you, then?"

"Churchill," he said. "Churchill Wingnut. And don't you say a word about me being a wing nut, you bugger. The great Wingnut Clan joined the Caravan generations ago. We were one of the last families to flee the fallen English empire."

"The Caravan?"

He gave me a look. "You can't be serious."

"Never heard of it," I said. "Is it a neighborhood in the Suburban Islands?"

He scoffed. "It might as well be Manhattan, if you really don't know."

"Manhattan?"

"Christ, you're dense," he said. "The Caravan is a bunch of bloody boats that circle the Federation and send old buggers like me out into Federal waters to fish for food. Tuna, turtles, and, it seems, the occasional tourist." He cackled at his own joke.

"So it's like a boat club? You all have yachts or something?"

"It's practically another nation, my boy! A world unto itself!"

"But the Hawaiian Federation is supposed to be the last—"

"*Sovereign nation.* I've heard the rubbish before, and I'm sure I'll hear it again."

"Does it—the Caravan—have anything to do with the Lost Boys?" The question slipped before I'd had time to think. I prayed Churchill was too mad to recognize me.

His voice grew grave. "What do you know about the Lost Boys?"

"Nothing," I said quickly. "Nothing at all."

"Liar! You think me a fool? Tell me the truth right now or I'll feed you to the sharks." He grabbed Old Jimmy and sliced the air with the edge of its sharp hook.

"I'm one of them!" I said quickly. "One of the Lost Boys! Sort of..."

He pushed me in the chest. "Go to hell." I stumbled onto the deck, and my back burned as it slapped wood. "If that were true," he said, "Feds would be focusing their snipers on this boat right now."

"I know Phoenix," I said quickly. "And Mila and Bertha and Dove and Kindred and everyone else on New Texas and please don't slice my head off with Old Jimmy."

Churchill cocked his head. "You know New Texas?"

I nodded. "Just left there ten minutes ago."

He clenched his jaw. "So you *are* one of them, then." He glanced in either direction. "Get in the cabin. Quick. Before I change my mind."

~~~~~~

The cabin's walls stank of rust, and its floors were stained red. A wooden desk stood parallel to a gray steering wheel. A potted bird of paradise stood wilting in the corner.

"Where are the rest of them?" asked Churchill.

Could I trust him? I guess I didn't have much of a choice. "On their way to Newla," I said. "They should be there by now."

"Shit," he muttered, "how in the bloody hell did they manage that?"

"Wet Pockets," I said. "I had one too, but it ripped."

"*Wet Pocket*? What the——? That's the dumbest name I've ever heard. Must be Bertha's invention. She was always terrible with names. Well, I can get you to Newla—help you join the others."

"You can? Into the harbor? That's where they said the Wet Pockets would drop us off."

He shook his head. "Not the harbor. The Navy would capture me. Then torture and kill me, if they discovered I was a Caravite."

I still wasn't entirely sure what to make of the Caravan. It didn't seem real. Like the Federation's very own Narnia.

"But I do have something else that might get you there," he said. "We've gotta be quick though. The others won't be able to wait long once they're on the mainland. And if you're without Phoenix for too much time, you're as good as dead."

"That's reassuring."

"What can I say, it's the truth."

"Look, I don't even know where I'm supposed to go."

"They didn't tell you?"

"They barely told me I was wearing a skirt."

"And for good reason." He paused. "Have you been to the city before?"

I shook my head. "No. I'm from Moku Lani."

"Christ," he muttered. "The bloody boondocks. Never been to Newla myself, but I've an idea where you ought to be going. You ever heard of the Skelewick district?"

I nodded—it was the city's oldest district. We'd briefly gone over its history in the eighth grade.

"You'll want to go to the Morier Mansion," he said. "That's where Phoenix will be, I'm sure. The Caravites have a base there. I've heard it's a big house at the end of the street. You can't miss it."

"Do you have its address?"

"*Do I have its address?* I've been out at sea my whole bloody life! I wouldn't know an address if it looked me in the eye!"

So, Churchill expected me to wander into the world's busiest city, a wanted terrorist nonetheless, with my only direction being "a big house at the end of the street." I was a dead man.

"How fast can you swim?" he asked.

I pointed to my back, wrapped in bandages. "Not fast enough, apparently."

Churchill rummaged through his desk and pulled out a metallic cylinder the size of a vase. Then he pulled out a knife. "Give me your arm."

Reluctantly, I stuck out my arm. Without a word of warning, he sliced a patch of skin from it. I yanked it back. "What the hell is wrong with you?"

"We need bait," he said. "Thank me later." He stuck the skin to the cylinder's edge and motioned for me to follow him to the deck. He pushed a few buttons, and then tied the cylinder to a fishing line before tossing it into the water.

"When I pull it out," he said, "I'm gonna need you to grab on to the shark and squeeze like hell."

"Excuse me?"

"Three loud beeps is your signal to let go. It should place you at the south sewer's entrance. Crawl through the pipe, then swim until you get to a fork. Take the left path—it'll smell far worse—and swim until you find a tent pitched on an inspection platform. There'll be a man there named Reggie. He'll have horrible halitosis and be in a miserable mood. Tell him you're with the Lost Boys, and he'll help you find your way to the Morier Mansion. It's a long shot, but it's your best bloody bet."

It was too much at once. I took a deep breath. "Could you, uh, maybe repeat that? Like one more time? I could write it down or something? It seems like a lot—"

"No time," he interrupted. The line next to him quivered. He yanked the rod, and an eight-foot-long shark thrashed at the water's surface. The cylinder had attached itself to the monster's side, just below its chest.

"That's your ride, lad," said Churchill. "Remember: let go after the three beeps." He pushed me from the deck. "Or you'll blow yourself to pieces!"

"To pieces?" I yelled.

"Quick, lad! Grab the beast now! It's just a little great white!"

I wrapped my arms around its thrashing body. Its gills pulsed frantically and its beady eyes twitched.

"Safe travels!" Churchill shouted. "May God have mercy on your SOUL!" He cackled loudly. "Just kidding! I'm an atheist."

He sliced the line, and the cylinder moaned in the water as it fired up. The shark's skin rubbed me like sandpaper as we throttled off through the water.

Toward Newla. Toward Phoenix. Toward Mom.

Toward Charlie.

# CHAPTER 10

I TIGHTENED MY grip as the shark snapped its snout back and forth. The muscles in my arms burned. The cylinder—a torpedo—yanked us effortlessly through the water. I wondered why it needed to be attached to a shark at all. Probably just another crazy idea of Churchill's—he seemed the type to go for the theatrics.

We cruised ten feet below the surface. Again I was grateful for my large lung capacity. The cylinder beeped once, twice, and then three times as we sailed through the water. I loosened my grip on the shark. It darted from my arms. The cylinder beeped several more times, then shot off the shark's skin and burst apart at the surface.

A metal shard from the explosion drifted past me in the water. I grabbed it and shoved it in my skirt's pocket. It was a far cry from being well armed, but it was better than nothing.

Farther ahead, I saw the rocky edge of the Hawaiian Quartile. HQ was the Federation's largest island, and Newla was its largest city.

At the surface, I saw the remains of a partially submerged pipe, not wider than my shoulders, blown apart by the cylinder's explosion. The device had managed to track and destroy the sewer's entrance. The explosion's noise, however, would undoubtedly draw the attention of the sewer's personnel. I had to move quickly to avoid detection.

I lifted myself from the water and into the pipe. Immediately, my eyes stung—its entrance stank like tuna, eggs, and milk left in the car on the hottest day of summer. A brown liquid trickled through the pipe like melted manure. I crawled on all fours, and my hands were caked in the sludge within minutes. Things literally couldn't get crappier.

After five minutes of fetid crawling, I reached the pipe's end. If I moved any farther, I'd fall into open air, but I had to keep moving. I heard water rushing below.

I threw myself from the pipe's ledge and splashed into a putrid canal. My wig was heavy, saturated with the brown sludge; I tore it off and scrubbed my face to remove the rest of the makeup.

The canal's current pushed me through a dark, narrow cavern. A metal sluice divided the canal into two distinct forks. Its metal door split the water between the left and right paths, diverting it with precise ease. Remembering Churchill's advice, I aimed left.

But the current's force grew stronger at the sluice's gate, and as I grew nearer, the left gate closed. I was pushed right, missing Churchill's exit. There was no turning back. Forward was the only option.

There would be no Reggie, no Morier Mansion, no meeting up with the other Indigo thieves. I was on my own. But at least I'd be in Newla. The city where Charlie was likely being held prisoner. I had to find her and Mom, and save them both.

A distant rumble echoed through the sewer's damp chambers. I stretched my arms out to the sides, and realized I could touch both sides of the canal now. It was growing narrower, and the current moved faster. The walls became sharper and steeper. Climbing out was impossible; I was at its mercy.

The canal was no longer lit by dim bulbs, but bright fluorescent tubes. My eyes burned from the sudden change in brightness. The distant rumble became a roar as the narrow channel led into a massive cavern. Floodlights glowed overhead, and the canal snaked around a thick metal column.

A man in a white biohazard suit and hood passed directly over my head on a suspended walkway. Along the walls, yellow hazard triangles warned: *"DANGEROUS CONDITIONS— KEEP PANTS ON AT ALL TIMES."*

Vats of green, yellow, and pink chemicals vibrated along the canal's sides. A pit formed in my stomach. This was no normal sewage canal. It was a route to the treatment facility.

Overhead, a sign read: *"Newla Advanced Sewage Treatment Facility—NASTF."*

They should've come up with a catchier acronym.

In the fourth grade, we were shown a documentary about the Newla Advanced Sewage Treatment Facility. The NASTF reclaimed ninety-eight percent of the water that entered the Newla sewage system, through a series of fire-heated sand filters and pressurized pumps, which pounded the toxic matter into oblivion.

If I reached the pumps, I was dead.

I clawed at the canal's walls, but it was no use—they were too steep. The facility's blades churned in the cavern's center column, roaring as fires started and stopped within its compartments.

I pressed my thighs against the canal's walls in an attempt to slow myself down. The metal shard I'd grabbed earlier jabbed my leg from within my skirt pocket. I'd be at the central column in seconds. Ground up in its blades like grass in a mower. I tossed the metal shard toward the churning blades, praying they'd jam.

Miraculously, they did. The blades ground to a halt, buzzing furiously as they fought to dislodge the metal. It wouldn't last long, though. I quickly grabbed one of the frozen blades and lifted myself from the water. The blade sliced my palms like a knife through butter, but I ignored the pain. Standing tall on the blade, I was just able to grab on to the metal walkway stretched overhead. I pulled myself up just as the blades clicked and spun once again, the jam dislodged.

My knees quivered as I straddled the thin walkway. A white suit wandered over, probably searching for the cause of the stoppage. He spotted me and waved a furious finger in my direction. Blood from the blade's cut had pooled in my hand. I rubbed my face with it and lowered my head. I stared at the white suit and screamed.

He fell in terror. My cue to run.

I ran to the cavern's edge. A red exit sign glowed next to another row of the colored chemical vats. I dove behind them, then looked back. Other white suits had arrived, but they weren't aware of me yet; they hurried to help their fallen comrade.

I sprinted to the exit and found a tunnel lined with familiar dim lights and walls carved from rock. These walls, however, eventually gave way to white plaster ones oddly reminiscent of a stale office building. The dim bulbs, too, were soon exchanged for their fluorescent brethren. The sewage smell was likewise replaced by the soft scent of lemon. Wherever I was headed, my sopping, smelly clothes would not be well received.

Farther down the tunnel—now hallway—a glass case housed a red fire extinguisher.

Over the past two hundred years, there'd been many eras of innovation. The red fire extinguisher had avoided every single one.

Another white suit emerged from a doorway just ahead of me. I ran for the extinguisher, elbowing him aside as I passed. He fell with a grunt.

Wrapping my hands in my skirt's fabric, I smashed through the extinguisher's glass case and yanked it out. I aimed the extinguisher in the white suit's direction, pulled the pin and prepared to spray while he pulled himself from the ground. He yanked his hood off, and snarled at me with beady eyes that burned like cigarettes. Then he lowered his head and charged.

"HA!" laughed a voice from a room he charged past. "LOOKS LIKE TONY HAD THE CHIMICHANGAS FOR LUNCH!"

He stopped in his tracks. "Excuse me, *Lenard*, but there's actually an intruder RUNNING DOWN THE HALL AS WE SPEAK—"

I squeezed the fire extinguisher's handle and coated the hall with a flurry of gray haze. Tony keeled over, coughing, the debris filling his lungs. The thick smog all but hid the fluorescent lights that lined the walls. The dull shadows cast as a result made it look like a bomb had been dropped.

"FIRE!" someone yelled, and co-workers joined the coughing Tony in the hall. More screams sounded. Boots beat against the concrete flooring. The crowd fled for the exits. Thunder echoed.

They were stampeding in my direction.

# CHAPTER 11

THE EXTINGUISHER'S DULL haze smoldered in the fluorescent lights overhead. White suits threw on their hoods as they ran. I squeezed the extinguisher's handle again. Only feeble wisps of white smoke trickled out this time—empty. I hadn't thought this through.

I tossed it aside and ran again toward the exit signs that glowed overhead. My footsteps were lost among the others as the white suits closed in. The haze that hid my presence thinned as I ran farther.

At the hall's end, a concrete door was marked with a glowing escape sign with a picture of stairs. To its left was a red handle covered by two layers of glass. A thin metal rod hung beside it, and above that, text read: "IN CASE OF EMERGENCY, BREAK GLASS AND PULL."

I broke the glass and pulled. Sirens sounded and red lights flashed. A robotic woman's voice echoed pleasantly over the intercom. "*CODE RED. Please evacuate the facility immediately. This is not a drill. CODE RED. Please evacuate the facility immediately. This is not a drill.*"

The sound of rushing water emanated from the ceiling. Along the walls, panels slid into pockets, revealing pipes with openings the size of grapefruits. Stale water gushed from the pipes. The building was flooding itself. Trying to douse the "fire" from the inside out.

I hurried up the stairs as water poured down the steps, rivers running to douse a fire that didn't exist. The angry stomp of boots quieted, replaced by sloshing as the white suits trudged through the rising water.

My lungs burned as I climbed. I'd gone up six flights and still hadn't seen a single exit. Farther up the stairwell, I could see light splintering in from a window, breaking the twilight cast by the red lights. I climbed toward it.

Below the window was an exit door. I pushed it open and ran out. The setting sun blinded me. I stepped into a patch of grass.

I was standing atop a cliff that overlooked the ocean. Streaks of red and orange soared in the sky over the sea. A portrait of color, kindly painted by the Carcinogens that so desperately sought to kill us. I looked down, and saw ivory hoods bobbing at the ocean's surface at the base of the cliff—suit-clad men pushed out by the rushing water.

At least the suits were buoyant.

I ran from the cliff toward the city's urban sprawl, passing rows of cars that hung suspended from racks in the parking lot. The racks were common on HQ, maximizing the use of precious space—one thing that was always in short supply.

The Feds were trying to reduce the space shortage by engineering synthetic volcanic eruptions each fortnight. Over time, these eruptions would slowly expand HQ. The Council promised that in another decade the space created from the eruptions would double HQ's current size and answer the space scarcity question once and for all. In the short term, however, all they did was render half of the island uninhabitable.

Newla's bright lights loomed ahead. The city buzzed to a beat all its own. Its flashing lights made people forget the horrors that had come, and those that had yet to come. The clouds that descended after the war had made the world dark. Dad had always said that the people who moved to Newla were trying to hide from the darkness in a city of light. I always figured it was cheaper to just buy a lamp.

The city's towering skyscrapers welcomed me like open arms. Some towers shined clear like diamonds; others sported green vines that devoured their spines.

A homeless girl doused in freckles begged drunkenly for money on a corner. Above her, an advertisement for pharmaceuticals bubbled on a screen. It showed a woman weeping at a child's funeral. The ad then cut to her swallowing a handful of pills. A respectable nurse in a white turtleneck replaced her on the screen.

*"A child's death is unbearable,"* said the nurse. *"So why should you have to bear it? Where there's death, there's Neglex—the pills that help you forget people you've met!"*

The weeping woman appeared again, this time laughing with a group of men. She held up a bottle that read *"NEGLEX"* and winked. I felt sick to my stomach. The homeless girl below the screen stared at me with dull eyes. I didn't have any money, so I tore a piece of fabric from my skirt and offered it to her.

"I'm really sorry," I said, "but—maybe you could sell this. It's all I have." She accepted the gift.

I wandered farther into the heart of the city. It was divided into districts, and each section had its own distinct culture. The buildings around me were taller now, more opulent. One skyscraper had an infinity pool on its highest floor that poured over the edge and down the building's side like a waterfall.

I peered up at another glowing white tower. A man's smiling face erupted from its light. Bills of money rained from the sky onto the street surrounding the tower. Holograms.

*Montesano*, the building flashed. *The World's Finest Investment Firm.*

My clothes dried in the heat generated by the city's many lights. Holographic actors danced on the window ledges of the city's many skyscrapers, flickering every so often from static charges.

*"Nothin', nothin', nothin', nothin' like Miss Marsha's Muffins!"* sang a trio of men in top hats on one ledge, their skin flickering blue.

*"YOU GOTTA GET YOURSELF SOME GOLD FIGURINES!"* screamed another hologram from a different ledge. *"YOU'RE GONNA LOVE 'EM BABY, OR MY NAME ISN'T MARTY VAN SCHNAUZER!"*

A blond hologram in a tight red dress beckoned to me from a building's roof down the street. *"Feeling naughty?"* she asked. She traced a heart in the space between her breasts and collarbone. Her dress burst into flames. *"Then go to CHURCH!"* she screamed, her holographic hands clawing the air as she fell into the building's depths. *SIXTH DAY ADVENTIST CHURCH* flashed in silver letters across the space where she'd been standing.

I stood there in the square, dumbfounded, the buildings flashing around me. Massive screens displayed news stories, and holograms advertised wares hidden in buildings. They promised goods of quality, horror, luxury, delight.

We didn't have anything like this in Moku Lani. The closest thing we had to luxury was Buster's Burgers. And even that place smelled like feet.

I squeezed my eyes shut, grateful to be free of the Lost Boys and the megalodons, if only for a second. A breeze rushed through my hair—I was also grateful to be rid of the wig.

There were so many people here that I melted easily into the crowd. I stood with my arms spread wide and eyes closed.

Maybe Phoenix was wrong about me being wanted. Maybe he'd lied to me about that too. Maybe I was still a free man.

Murmurs broke the city's deafening roar. "Call the police!" shouted someone.

I snapped my eyes open. A crowd had formed around me in the square. The people stepped back, keeping their distance as I turned. On the screen behind me, my dumb grin smiled back.

Red words were stamped across my face: *WANTED: KAI BRADBURY. ENEMY OF THE STATE.*

Sirens wailed. The police had been called. I broke free of the crowd, my feet beating against the city's brick sidewalks. I glanced at the buildings around me and watched as my picture followed me on their screens. The advertising holograms had all ceased hawking their wares; they now turned their damning fingers to me instead.

*"CATCH HIM!"* they shouted. *"CATCH HIM! CATCH HIM! CATCH HIM! FIND THE LOST BOY!"*

# CHAPTER 12

SAGE PENDERBROOK WANDERED the cold, concrete halls of the Light House's kitchen an hour before dawn. She made her way past the freezer's big brass doors and braved its arctic temperatures to steal a slice of frozen sourdough bread. Carefully, she wrapped the bread in the caramel cashmere cloth she'd brought from her room.

She expertly navigated her way through the basement to the sixth floor's lobby. Soft snores sounded from behind the desk—Barry was working. He'd continue his nap, as usual, until the second shift came on.

Sage reached through the desk's glass window and pressed a red button by Barry's hand. The doors to the back room slid open. She typed a code into the keypad, listening to its beeps as she pressed its buttons. Then she put her eye against the room's retina scanner and whispered "Sangria Penderbrook."

"*Identity confirmed,*" announced the retina scanner. The doors to the prison slid open. Sage made her way to cell sixteen at the end of the hall. The door's slot screeched as she pulled it open.

"Excuse me, miss," she said.

"Wha—?" The girl in the cell woke with a shake. Charlie, she'd heard the chancellor call her. She guessed the starvation pangs had kept her awake most of the week.

Sage shoved the cloth-covered bread through the slot. "I brought something for you."

"Somethin'?" said Charlie, still half-asleep. "For me?

"Yes, for you, Charlie."

Charlie took the wrapped package from Sage's hand, and Sage heard her peel open the cloth, corner by corner. She squealed when she found the sourdough.

"All of this?" she said, like Sage had brought her a turkey instead of a slice of frozen bread. "For me?"

Sage nodded. She wished she could've stolen fresh bread, but those loaves were monitored more carefully by Cook's watchful eye.

Charlie's stomach grumbled its thanks. "I, uh—gosh, I can barely think—I wish I had something to give you. You know, in return for the bread."

She put her hand through the slot and pressed it to Sage's face, rubbing her cheek with her thumb. Sage jumped, her cheek tingling where she'd been touched. "I'm so sorry," said Charlie. "I didn't know that would hurt you."

Sage shook her head. "No—I'm sorry," she said. "It's just... uh, well—you're the first person that's touched me, well, in a while... Since I got here, actually."

"I thought you said you'd been here for four years?"

Sage's chin trembled as she nodded.

She'd been here a long time. She remembered watching sunsets with her mom on the Kauai beaches. Running along the sand with their yellow dog, Max. Tossing him a Frisbee for most of the day. He'd been a stray when they found him, and somehow, that had made him all the more hers. Two wild hearts that found one another.

The memories were distant and fragile now; they clung to the corners of her mind like cobwebs. She was just as much a prisoner as Charlie. The kind words Miranda offered her each month were never enough. The warmth of Charlie's hand on her cheek made her realize the frost that had settled on her heart and the numbness that had enveloped her since her mother's death.

She shoved the key into the cell's lock. The door opened with a hiss. She put a hand on Charlie's shoulder. It was bony, hard, like the porcelain sinks in the kitchen. She felt hairs tingle along her spine. Charlie was warm.

Charlie patted her hand. "You all right?"

Sage straightened her dress. She'd worn it every day for the past three years. "I'm sorry, miss," she said, catching her breath. She shouldn't have come in here. Or stolen the bread. She'd be beaten if the guards found out. "Sorry, Charlie."

Charlie laughed. "Like I haven't heard that one before."

It had been so long since Sage had heard laughter.

"What are you even sorry for?" Charlie continued. "You brought me food. I think I'll be okay if you touch my shoulder for a minute. It's a bit bony, though. Starvation and all that junk."

Sage smiled and put her hand back on Charlie's shoulder. It was odd, but Sage didn't mind. She'd been alone too long to be bothered by strangeness. She didn't have any peers or any real friends.

The closest thing she had to regular interaction was the stories she'd tell to the occasional mouse. She'd find them hiding in the kitchen's cracks. She usually pretended they didn't talk back because they were good listeners who really liked her stories. After being yelled at most of the day, it was nice to have someone just listen.

"I talk to mice, sometimes," she said finally.

Her face burned red. She could've slapped herself. Charlie was the first girl her own age she'd met in five years, and this was what she said to her? Maybe it was good she didn't talk to people much.

"I've found they're quite good listeners," said Charlie.

"The best," agreed Sage.

"Besides," Charlie continued, "there aren't a lot of options around here. At least from what I've seen." She was right.

There weren't a lot of options. "I'd get lonely too, if I lived here for four years. And animals are always so willing to listen. I know it sounds crazy, but once I helped some snails cross the street..."

Sage laughed. Maybe she wasn't so odd. Maybe she was normal. She felt herself get bold. "And I can burp the alphabet," she announced.

"That's pretty great," said Charlie, laughing. "A little odd, but still great."

Well, maybe she wasn't normal, but maybe it didn't matter. She promised herself she'd teach Charlie how to burp the alphabet.

Someone banged on the cell door across from Charlie's. The prisoner in fifteen had been moved to fourteen earlier in the week. The chancellor was worried the inmate's behavior would disturb Charlie's "progress."

Sage pulled the door shut behind her. It was just her and Charlie now. She worried Charlie's eyes might have wandered across the hall. That she might ask questions. Questions Sage wasn't prepared to answer.

The chancellor had been kind with his punishments for Charlie thus far, despite her resistance. If she held out until the end of the week, however, Sage wasn't sure she'd be so lucky. Starvation was humane by the chancellor's standards, and far better than the methods used by the Minister of Defense & Patriotism.

Minister Zane had less than a year left before his fiftieth birthday and euthanization, and the faster his own death approached, the more quickly he brought others to theirs. Sage had heard rumors of his experimental methods involving dogs and nuclear waste from the Moku Lani reactor. He said it helped enemies of the state remember things more "willingly." By the time he was through with them, however, Sage guessed they would confess to anything.

"Sage?" Charlie said quietly. "I need to get out of here."

Sage's stomach sank. She'd heard this before. From the others.

"I've got someone out there—people. People who need me—people I've gotta see, you know? People I care about. *You* have people like that, right?"

Sage shook her head. Since her mother's death, she'd had no one. Nobody cared about Sage Penderbrook. Not even Charlie. They all just wanted to use her. Even the mice did, if she was being honest.

"You'd have to come with me, of course," said Charlie. "I couldn't leave you behind. You've been so kind to me. The bread meant a lot."

Sage smiled. The other prisoners always told her they were going away, leaving this place forever. But they never invited her to go with them. That was the sort of thing friends said to each other. Sage hadn't had a friend in a long time.

She nodded her head. "I think I'd come."

Charlie hugged her. She tingled all over. *Friend*, Sage repeated to herself again and again. She'd finally made a friend.

"Brilliant!" said Charlie. "We're gonna escape this place. But first, I have to ask you, have others tried running away? Getting out of here? Has anyone *ever* gotten out of here?"

Sage nodded. They had. The determined ones always found a way.

Charlie clapped her hands. "They made it? They got out?"

Sage nodded again. During her time at the Light House, she'd walked into many cells where prisoners had found their way out.

Charlie leaned close. "How do they get out, Sage? How do they escape this godforsaken place?"

Sage gritted her teeth. She couldn't lie to Charlie. Not now that they were friends. She had to tell her the truth.

"They escape," she said quietly, "with a rope around their neck."

A week after the torture began, it was Sage's job to leave a rope in the prisoner's cell—death's quiet calling card. Then the guards would tie a noose in it and hang it above the bed.

If the Federation couldn't crack a nut, they helped the nut crack itself.

Yes, all the prisoners eventually escaped their cells. But unfortunately for Charlie, they never escaped alive.

# CHAPTER 13

POLICE POUNDED THE streets behind me as I raced through Newla, spurred on by the heckling of the holograms that shouted obscenities from window ledges. My heart raced and I panicked as I sprinted along the bustling streets of a city I didn't know. Back home we'd only read about Newla's different districts. Now I was seeing them first-hand, but not the way I'd ever imagined. The Upper East Side, the Lower West Side, North Atlantic, the neighborhoods raced by, on and on...

I swerved off the sidewalk and into the street. Cars slammed their horns. A taxi driver scarfing down a hoagie lowered his window. "YOU SOME KINDA FRYER?"

Farther down, another smashed his horn. "WELCOME TO NEW LOS ANGELES, MORON! NOW GET THE HELL OUTTA THE WAY!"

The police didn't evade traffic nearly as well as I did. They tumbled to the curbs like toddlers learning to walk. The chaos unfolded behind me, but I kept going. I had to. Stopping meant certain death—or worse, torture.

A dark alley caught my eye, and I turned sharply and sprinted down its length. A boy a few years younger than me was sprawled out behind a trashcan, a toothy grin plastered across his face below glazed eyes. He popped another pill as I passed. An empty prescription bottle rolled by his arm, the bright yellow packaging giving it away—Neglex. I guess it worked as well for kids who'd lost they parents as it did for parents who'd lost their kids. But it seemed like the vast majority of people wandering the streets were kids.

The alley exited into a neighborhood that replaced skyscrapers with gothic buildings lined by wrought iron gates. A rusted sign towered over the street: *Welcome to the Skelewick District*.

There were few lights in the district, and the smaller—though still large—buildings sat in their neighbors' monstrous shadows. The only real light trickled from the bronze streetlamps that lined the barren streets. They glowed eerie and yellow. A perpetual twilight.

There were no holographic actors. No bubbling screens. Just pavement, pedestrians, and yellow pallor glowing from the lamps.

I hurried along, keeping my head down. People didn't seem to notice. They just stared at the lamps, hypnotized by the glow of twilight.

It seemed I'd lost the cops. For now. But I had to find Phoenix and Mila if I was going to stay alive.

I approached a street corner where a man in a trench coat stood on a crate, hawking watches that hung from the seams of his jacket. A streetlamp stood in front of him, and he stared at it with unblinking eyes.

If I was going to find the Morier Mansion, I needed help. I covered my face with one hand—a ridiculous "disguise," but really my only option at this point—and sucked in a breath. "Excuse me, sir. Could you—do you know where the Morier Mansion is?"

"Lost?" he asked simply. He picked a watch from his trench coat and pressed a button on its side. Its metal casing flicked open, and white light glowed from its face, lighting the man's eyes.

"Uh—well, a bit."

I prayed he wouldn't turn his attention to my face. He kept his eyes focused on the watch's brilliant light, nodded slowly, and pointed to a house at the end of the street. "Banyan tree in the front," he said without looking up.

"Thanks." I glanced at his coat. "Good luck selling the, uh, watches."

"They aren't for sale," he said. "They're for the lost souls."

"Er—right then." The man was clearly insane. "Well, uh, good luck anyway."

I hurried away. Uncle Lou always said it was best to run from things you didn't understand. Mom disagreed—she said the things you didn't understand were the things you should spend your time looking at. Maybe she was right. I glanced back over my shoulder to look at the man, but he was already gone.

The banyan tree loomed at the end of the street, a tangled mess of twigs and trunks. The Morier Mansion lay hidden in the yard behind it. Through patches in the tree's many trunks, I saw lights flicker inside the mansion. A pointed black gate marked the entrance to the property.

I hopped the fence and landed silently on a patch of moist moss. I raced past the magnificent tree, marveling at the way its roots stretched from its branches to the ground. It was as sprawling as the city itself.

I pounded the brass ring against the black wooden front door. Its knock echoed through the mansion, and the front room's lights flickered out. As I waited, I glanced back. Outside the gate, I could see police officers searching the street. Perhaps I hadn't escaped them yet.

The mansion's massive door cracked open. "Come in, Kai Bradbury," whispered an old woman—mid-forties at least. "Hurry in before they see you."

I didn't need to be asked twice. I slipped inside and the door shut behind me.

The woman shook my hand fervently. She had gray hair bundled atop her head like a dust bunny, and her eyes were hidden behind a pair of purple horn-rimmed glasses with emeralds encrusted in the corners. Several shawls in shades of scarlet were wrapped around her neck.

"How do you do, Mr. Bradbury?" she said warmly. "We've been expecting you for quite some time."

Behind her, Phoenix and Mila stood on the steps of the grand staircase. Mila took one look at my torn skirt and stifled a laugh. "Staying classy, I see."

Phoenix shook his head. "You've been all over the news. What were you thinking? Flooding the sewage treatment facility? Wandering through the city streets like a Neglex-snorting lunatic? Tell me, Kai: Were you intentionally trying to get yourself killed, or did you not believe us when we told you that you were on the 'Most Wanted' list?"

*Both*, I wanted to yell back, but instead I shrugged. "Bertha's device didn't work. It crapped out in the middle of the ocean. You're lucky I made it here."

Mila pulled a knife from her pocket. "*We're* lucky?" she said. "*You're* lucky to be alive."

I laughed nervously. "Well, uh, I mean—you should try getting around in this sort of thing." I shook the skirt. "Was pretty breezy though... Maybe you could wear it tonight?"

Phoenix stroked his chin. "With the police on alert? I'm afraid we won't be going tonight."

The woman in the scarves stamped her foot. "Oh, you're going tonight. Everything's set up, Phoenix, and it wasn't easy. Nancy Perkins is the only cover we've got. She has to wear her Daisy *tonight*."

"I'm not so sure," Phoenix replied. "Not with all those Feds out. And Kai has no idea what he's doing."

"The shipment of vaccines will be moved from Club 49 after tonight," the old woman insisted. "We have no choice. We must act now if the raid is to be successful. And don't be so shortsighted, young man: I remember you making a worse mess of the city, and not so long ago. If anything, this boy should only remind you of your own foolishness."

"Well, in his defense," I said, pointing to Phoenix's bulging muscles, "he's a bit more capable."

The woman sighed. "I do apologize for the disagreement, Mr. Bradbury. Allow me to introduce myself. My name is Madam Revleon, and the Morier Mansion is my home. A land base of sorts for the Lost Boys, as well as for the Caravites. They can't do *everything* from that floating island of rubbish—"

"New Texas," said Mila.

"Yes, yes—New Texas, that's right." She rolled her eyes. "A bit smaller than the old Texas, I think, but never mind that. Though you'll only be here a short while, please don't hesitate to ask if you need anything, Mr. Bradbury. I'm sure we'll see each other again very soon." She turned to Mila. "Miss Vachowski, would you be so kind as to lead Mr. Bradbury upstairs to rest? You both have a long evening ahead of you. I think a moment's rest is in order."

Mila dragged me up the steps of the grand staircase, which fanned out at the bottom then spiraled tightly up to the top. The walls along it were decorated with scarlet tapestries. I pressed my fingers against the velvet words written below one of them: *Veritas vos liberabit.* Above them, a gold knight stood atop a sea of fallen corpses.

"Don't touch that," snapped Mila.

We moved through the mansion's left wing, stopping at a room at the end of the hall. A bed covered by a gold canopy stood in its center. Mila plopped herself on its covers and tossed a pillow onto the floor. "You get ground," she said.

I sighed. The wooden floor didn't exactly look welcoming, and my back still burned where Churchill's hook scraped it. I ignored Mila's instruction and instead moved to an armchair with plush, satin cushions. The sharp face of a bird had been carved into its clawed wooden feet.

Mila's slow, steady breathing started in a matter of minutes; the soft bed quickly lulled her to sleep. I was exhausted from the day's ordeal, but unable to get comfortable in the chair. So I got up and wandered out into the hall, admiring the brass light fixtures that lined the black wooden walls.

Phoenix and Madam Revleon muttered something at the foot of the stairs.

"...*megalodon researcher, really?*"

I strained my ears to hear their hushed whispers, but they soon moved from the staircase. I shuffled down the hall, poking my head into the various rooms. Bedroom. Bedroom. Bathroom. Billiard parlor. Bedroom. A room lined with barred glass windows. All of them dark.

At last I reached the room at the end of the wing. Inside, a reading lamp had been left on, lighting a walnut desk. Papers and open books were sprawled across its surface. I thumbed through a few of the papers. They looked like copied pages from a handwritten journal.

One sheet caught my attention—the cover. I ran my fingers over its title: *The Indigo Report*. The name of a single individual was printed beneath it: *Dr. Harper Neevlor*.

Below that, someone had sketched a bird on fire. I knew that image: the woman on the Tube with the fan. The bird had been covered in flames when she flicked her wrist. It was the exact same image. A Phoenix.

Phoenix McGann.

Was it the Lost Boys' symbol? I flipped through the rest of the pages. Excerpts caught my eye as they turned in my hand.

> *Yesterday, I began testing Indigo with aquatic subjects. The fish had thrown themselves from the tanks by noon. Out of a hundred subjects, there were no survivors. The Indigo appears to have been tainted. Perhaps genetically altered.*
>
> *I do not venture to make a formal hypothesis at this point. The data is far too limited. On a personal level, however, I begin to suspect something has been done to my sample of vaccines. Something horribly wrong.*
>
> *Colleagues mock me for pressing on with the research. They tell me the vaccine is*

*foolproof. That quality control measures do not allow for tampering. But I am unconvinced. I will continue my experiments with these samples and present my findings to the Ministry at the study's conclusion.*

From there, the pages were out of order. I scanned the remaining documents as best as I could.

*—my sample of vaccines remains unstable. Continued use on subjects results in certain death—*
*—located an irregularity in the samples. Possibly a bacterium? Or a virus? It remains dormant at the time of vaccination, but continued injections cause the strain to multiply—*
*—abuse potential is great. The laboratory can no longer contain—*
*—Ministry has warned me about the study's continuation. They fear it is not safe. The results could be capable of dissolving the very fabric of society—*
*—Burned the lab. The data is lost. The experiment has been labeled a failure. The Ministry revoked my access to the laboratory. The last remaining charts now exist only in the pages of this notebook. I have decided to call it the Indigo Report—*
*—they are coming to kill me in my sleep. They want the results. The study was conclusive. The findings contained in these pages are undeniable—*

The papers slipped from my hands onto the floor. I cursed under my breath and hurried to pick them up. Madam Revleon and Phoenix might learn I'd been here. That I'd seen the report.

Who was Dr. Neevlor? What had been done to his sample of Indigo vaccines? And what sort of substance had they been tainted with?

By now he was surely dead, and his secrets buried with him. In my hands, however, I held a fragment of the truth: the Lost Boys were doing something terrible to the vaccines. Meddling with them in some way.

They weren't thieves; they were something else. Maybe full-blown terrorists. The Federation had always been right. The Lost Boys had lied to me. About Mom dying, too. And now, I was certain. She was alive. I could save her.

I'd seen pieces of a plan to pull apart the entire empire, to destroy the Federation itself. I scanned the study's rich wooden bookshelves—antiques built to hold antiques. You never really saw these old, static books anymore. Pretty much everyone just bought a single book and then downloaded stories onto its pages, the text refreshing itself with each new novel.

The books on the shelves weren't novels, though; they were textbooks. Had this once been Dr. Neevlor's home? Did the Lost Boys and Madam Revleon steal it from him? The denizens of the Skelewick district would probably have been too dazed to notice if they had.

I ran my fingers along the spines of a few of the books:

*Optometry & Infectious Diseases.*
*Microbiology: a Clinical Perspective.*
*Pharmacological Design & Operation.*
*Physics and Structures of Clinical Viruses.*
*Understanding Viruses.*
*Evolution of a Synthetic Molecule.*
*Synthetic Viruses, Ailments, & Other Macrobiotic Apparatuses.*

The black parade of titles continued forever. The seeds of revolution just chapters away. I pulled one book at random from the shelf. *Engineering an Epidemic*, its cover read. It was dog-eared in several places.

The floor creaked behind me, and the book fell from my hands.

"What exactly are you doing, Mr. Bradbury?" Madam Revleon snatched the book from the floor. "*Engineering an Epidemic?* Heavy reading for a boy who should be getting his rest, don't you think?"

"I—well—you see the thing is—I just thought it might be fine if I—er—just looked around?"

She traced the book's blue spine with a bony finger. "I admire the occasional sleuth. It's not often one is offered the truth. At least, not readily."

Her eyes flashed to the disheveled desk—she knew. "Phoenix is waking Miss Vachowski. You'll leave for Club 49 within the hour. You don't have long before midnight. You'll need to be in the club by then, at the latest." She looked at my soiled outfit and grimaced. "Grab a new gown from my closet. Wigs are in the cupboard across the hall. Though I expect you've already found those, too." She dropped a ball of something that felt soft like velvet in my hand. "Synthetic skin," she explained. "You'll need it again for tonight—the wrinkles and all that. Mila will do your makeup when you're done."

"Madam Revleon?" I asked.

"Yes?" She slid the book back into its place on the shelf.

"How long ago did you buy this place? I—I think it's really nice."

She smiled and straightened the pages I'd spread across her desk. "Oh, I didn't *buy* this place," she said. "It was given to me by an old friend."

# CHAPTER 14

CLUB 49'S BRIGHT lights flashed on the gold pavement. The golden road ran from the city's center to the nation's most in- famous nightlife destination. Club 49 was a nightclub, euthana- sia clinic, and mortuary all wrapped up into one.

Its slogan—*People Are Dying to Get Into Club 49*—flashed across its main entrance in silver letters. Throngs of people waited outside its grand doorways, vying for a chance at entry, eager to see the forty-nine-year-old volunteers—victims—who awaited certain death and spectacle.

I wondered what sort of person would choose this flashy building as the place to spend their final moments. I suppose it offered people without families an opportunity to claim their fifteen minutes of fame.

I glanced at a clock by the club's entrance. It was only elev- en.

"The club lifts off the ground at midnight," explained Phoenix, when I asked what happened inside the club. "Eu- thanasia is administered to the forty-nine-year-old guests turn- ing fifty tomorrow via their Daisies—glowing necklaces with thick white beads—at exactly midnight. The crowd then lifts their corpses to 'Heaven'—a white conveyer belt lowered at 12:01—in a process called 'Rapture.' After Rapture, you'll be moved on to another conveyer belt, where an attendant will check your pulse to make sure that you're dead. From there, management disposes of the bodies in an incinerator. Some are even turned into little green wafers."

I must have looked worried.

"I'm kidding about that last part," he said, chuckling. "And don't worry—we've sewn a tracking device into your new wig, so we can keep an eye on you at all times. The building's blueprints are highly confidential, which is why we need a body—you—on the other side. Sparky can hack the system remotely once the signal's been moved into the nightclub's classified areas. We'll intercept you once he's secured your coordinates. Before you hit the incinerator."

Mila smiled. "At least that's what we're aiming for."

"Are you ready?" said Phoenix.

I nodded, but my shaking hands said otherwise. I curled them into fists. I wished I had on my cheeseburger socks. Now wasn't the time for nerves.

Mila straightened my wig. "You'll be fine."

Phoenix nodded. "We wouldn't have brought you with us otherwise."

"Where exactly in the club is the Indigo supply?" I asked. "You're sure it's here? Why would they even have it here?"

I felt sick to my stomach just talking to them about Indigo. I knew now that they didn't want to simply steal it and sell it—they wanted to *manipulate* it. Put some sort of virus in it, then redistribute it. I wanted to run from them right then. But I didn't have a choice if I wanted to save Mom and Charlie. It was stay with the Lost Boys or die. And a dead Kai was slightly less useful than a live one.

Slightly.

"Don't be afraid," said Phoenix. "You swam into a megalodon's mouth. Club 49 is kindergarten in comparison."

I chewed my lip. "They don't kill kids in kindergarten."

The two winced. They thought I was being difficult. Either that, or they *did* kill kids in kindergarten. And I highly doubted it was the latter.

Nancy Perkins had scheduled her euthanization at Club 49 for tonight. She'd intended to enter the nightclub through its side entrance—the one reserved for Daisy wearers—and enjoy the copious amounts of attention lavished on her as a result of the necklace. Celebrate both her fiftieth birthday and death. The last night of her life.

But it wasn't Nancy Perkins who'd be entering Club 49's side entrance tonight and given a Daisy. It was me. Celebrating a fiftieth birthday instead of a fifteenth birthday, thinking all the while that I was far too young to die.

"Bertha made you a device," Phoenix said as he slapped a metallic sticker to my neck. "It emits a signal that will neutralize the euthanasia at the time of the Daisy's injection. It's a simple device, really. It can't fail."

*Just like a Wet Pocket*, I thought. I winced, thinking of the pain I'd felt in my shoulder. Madam Revleon had rubbed one of her many odd healing creams on it, and the burning had since subsided, but the failure of Bertha's previous invention didn't exactly fill me with confidence.

"Neutralizing euthanasia injections," I muttered. "So simple."

Phoenix ignored my remark. "We'll join you before long," he said. "We have to wait in line at the grand entrance. Only you can use the side one. We'll meet you inside."

Lucky me.

I patted my face. The synthetic skin was remarkably real to the touch, but in my head I knew I was still just wearing a glorified pancake.

A host smiled at me as I approached the side entrance. His hair shined with a sheen only possible after being smothered in gel. "Good evening, miss," he said brightly. The preferential treatment started early. "First and last name, please."

I cleared my throat, raising my voice an octave. "Nancy Perkins," I said. For once it wasn't so bad being a late bloomer.

"Welcome, Miss Perkins. If you'd be so kind as to place your eye against our retina scanner—standard protocol to verify identity, of course. I'd be more than happy to hold your sunglasses."

I blinked hard behind my polarized lenses. Phoenix hadn't said anything about a retina scan. I wasn't vaccinated—if the glasses came off, the game was up. My eyes were brown, not blue. And my retina signature certainly wasn't Nancy's.

There had to be another way.

A woman with red hair wrapped in a sparkling bun leaned against the retina scanner at another station. She wore orange horn-rimmed glasses and didn't take them off for the scanner. It beeped loudly and flashed green. Her host ushered her in.

*Like kindergarten,* I thought. Phoenix was right—this wasn't supposed to be difficult.

"It's not fair," I whined, pointing toward the woman. "She wore her glasses for the scanner, but I can't? That ain't right."

"But, madam, her lenses weren't polarized—"

"*Madam?* Are you going to call me Grandma, too?"

"Miss!" he said quickly, covering his mistake. "I meant 'miss,' of course. That woman's glasses weren't polarized. They're not like yours—they're not colored."

I felt the imaginary Nancy's blood boil. I stepped back. "So that's what this is about? We're back to judging things by *color?* BY COLOR?"

The other hosts frowned. Mine grew increasingly flustered, beat down by his colleagues' angry glares. "Er—I'm sorry madam. I mean miss, definitely miss—but your glasses—"

"I know." I raised my voice. "IT'S THE COLOR! COLORED ISN'T GOOD ENOUGH FOR YOU—"

The host ushered me forward without another word. The retina scanner beeped its objections, but he knocked it to the ground, muttering something about it being defective. The other hosts looked on.

"Enjoy your stay, miss," he grumbled.

*Stay.* People who came through these doors didn't leave.

I wandered into the victims' grand foyer, an oasis of gold. It adorned the walls, the frames, even the floorboards. King Midas would've crapped himself.

The ceiling, however, was a starry abyss. Walls melted into nothingness, and specks of light broke the darkness. Stars, looking just like the real ones. The ones we could see before the war. Buttons of light swaddled in black cloth.

"Lovely, aren't they?" A small woman in black stood beside me, her eyes turned to the ceiling. Fine lines traced the cracks between her lips. She turned, and her blue eyes stared back at me beneath a head of mousy brown hair.

"Quite." I nodded. In one hand, the woman held a book. "Fancy a bit of reading this evening?" I asked. "You haven't got much time."

She laughed gently—if such a laugh were possible. "Oh, no," she said, "it's not mine at all. It's my daughter's."

I walked with her to the back of the gold foyer. Two young women ushered us forward with warm smiles.

"Are you seeing her tonight then?" I asked. "Meeting up with her in the club?"

"Not in the club," said the woman, "but after."

Her daughter was dead. She'd been in the group that didn't make it to fifteen. I put a hand on the woman's shoulder, and she smiled sadly. I thought of my own mom and the notes she'd left for my birthday, wondering when I'd see her again. Or if.

The two women retrieved our Daisies from glowing boxes. The devices wrapped around our necks with a click and began to glow. They weren't really necklaces at all, but collars. We were dogs. Trapped. There was no escaping death.

The two of us wandered into the club's main ballroom— the place where younger visitors (not victims) were allowed to enter. Bright lights flashed over deafening music, but our Daisies' glow rose above it all, like little suns. People stared, drawn to the pearly light that was rivaled by none in its brilliance.

We moved to the ballroom's edge to avoid further attention. Along its perimeter stood a row of massive vaults.

"Indulgence Rooms," explained my new friend quietly.

One was red and covered in round beds sporting moaning patrons. I felt sick to my stomach. Another—deep blue—was filled to the brim with food, drink, and gluttonous victims. The Indulgence Rooms continued along the perimeter, each one catering to its own particular human vice.

The woman with the book grabbed my hand and held it. We stood there for a while, hands locked, and watched strangers dance, ignoring the stares of people who longed to look at the Daisies. We were like idols and victims both. In a way, it was nice not to be so alone.

"What's your name?" my new friend asked finally.

"Nancy," I said quickly. "Nancy Perkins."

She nodded and stroked the back of my hand with her forefinger. Her skin was soft like velvet—a byproduct of old skin that hung loose from its bones.

"And your real name?"

My eyes widened—how had she known?

She noticed my surprise, pinching my hand's taut skin between two fingers. "Not the skin of any old woman I know. A boy, perhaps? Your secret is safe with me. I only want to know your name. I haven't met a young person in—in such a long time."

The creases that lined the corners of her eyes reminded me of my mother. Her bright blue eyes were the same. "My name is—Kyle," I said finally. I couldn't give her my real name. It was still too dangerous.

"What a lovely name," she whispered. "Too nice a name for you to kill yourself tonight."

"WHAT?" I shook my head. "I'm not—I couldn't—listen, I'm not gonna kill myself."

But she wasn't listening. She had a faraway look in her eyes, and she stroked her book's spine. "My Marie told me the same thing the night she did it, too."

Her daughter hadn't died from the Carcinogens—she'd killed herself. Probably the only thing worse.

"My sweet Marie," the woman continued, eyes watering, "she—she didn't know what she was doing. She didn't know stepping in front of that train would change so many things."

I wrapped my arms around her. "I'm so sorry." My shoulders grew wet with her tears.

"You had your whole life ahead of you..." Suddenly she pulled away and slapped me. "You shouldn't have done this. You really shouldn't have done this." She raised her voice. "WHY ARE YOU DOING THIS? YOU SHOULDN'T HAVE TO BE DOING THIS!"

She thought I was trying to kill myself. Thought I'd dressed up as a woman and snuck into this club to die.

"It's not real," I said. "I'm not really doing this! I'm—I'm with my friends. They're here—somewhere. We could find them."

She slapped me again. "You fool! Your friends aren't *here*," she pointed around the club, "they're *here*. INSIDE YOUR HEAD! You have a mental illness. Just like my poor Marie. *Oh, Marie!*" she wailed.

She was hysterical. A few people on the dance floor stopped and stared at her—us. Security would be here in seconds. They'd test my eye with their retina scanners, and then I really would be dead. The clocks chimed quarter to midnight. I was running out of options.

"I'm on a mission," I hissed. She looked like my mom. A poor, broken version of my mom, but my mom nonetheless. I could trust her.

"I'm with the Lost Boys," I explained. "It's gonna be all right. I'm not gonna die."

She fell silent. "The Lost Boys?" she asked, wiping away her streaked makeup. "They're here tonight? You're—you're not going to kill yourself?"

I shook my head. "This is all part of the plan."

"Oh," she said quietly. "Wait—cross-dressing is part of the plan?"

My face flushed red. "It's a long story."

She pointed to a clock. "We don't have time. I'm—I'm... glad you're safe. Listen—could you hold my book for a minute while I go to the restroom?"

"I could go with you," I said. "Make sure we don't get separated—you know—so you have someone with you at the end."

"Go with me to the *women's* restroom?" She made a face. "No, I don't think so."

I guess she had a point... but I couldn't help but feel that she was acting strange as she left. Was she going to tell someone else? The dampness on my shoulders from her tears, however, said I could trust her.

I scanned the crowd for Phoenix and Mila. A waitress in a tight cocktail dress approached me with a tray. "Care for a drink, miss? I have beer, wine, nectarine..." I started to wave her away. "...And the house specialty, the 'Triple C'—Cotton Candy Cocktails," she finished.

Cotton Candy Cocktails?

I was fifteen—old enough to vote and drink—an adult by Federal standards. I grabbed a cocktail from her tray and tossed it back, thinking about how Mom would laugh and giggle when she'd had a few glasses of wine.

God, it really did taste just like cotton candy. I waved down another waitress and had two more. My arms felt warm and tingly.

Where was my new friend? I hadn't even gotten her name, just her daughter's. There hadn't been enough time between the shouting and the tears.

"Three minutes until midnight," announced the DJ over the speakers.

The crowd went wild. Lights in the Indulgence Rooms flashed, then glowed crimson. My Daisy flickered, counting down the seconds until midnight. My whole body felt light enough to float.

"Kyle?" My new friend grabbed my arm.

I smiled and started laughing. "FRIEND!" I said, bursting with enthusiasm. "My new friend! What—what was the hold up, ya silly goose?"

"Long line," she said. "I guess a lot of women have to *go*... before it's time to go."

I laughed so hard I knocked down a fat lady in stilettos. Whateva.

"God, you're funny!" I squeezed her arm. "You're so great. You're really great, did you know that?"

Her eyes darted from side to side—she was so silly. "So," she said, "mind if I ask you what's—uh—going to happen?"

"Anything could happen!" I shouted. "You hear that, world? ANYTHING COULD HAPPEN!"

"I meant with your plan," she said. "With the Lost Boys. What's happening with them? You said you weren't going to die like the rest of us."

The DJ's booth glowed white. "SIXTY SECONDS," he announced.

"SIXTY SECONDS!" I shouted. "SIXTY FRIGGIN' SECONDS! I GOTTA *DAAANCE!*" The blue Indulgence Room caught the corner of my eye. "SOMEBODY SAVE ME A TURKEY LEG!"

"Focus, Kyle." My friend grabbed my arm. "Answer my question."

She was being a little bossy.

"I dunno, OKAY? I'm prolly just gonna drop like the rest of ya... TO THE FLO'! ALL THE WAY DOWN TO THE FLO'!" The Daisies ceased blinking and faded to a dull white. "What the—?"

The woman grabbed my face. "*Then* what's going to happen? What are you going to do after that?"

The rest of the club's lights went black, and the Daisies burst into the brightest white I'd ever seen.

"ARE YOU SEEING THIS? HOLY CRAP! ARE YOU SEEING THIS?"

She dug her nails into my arms. "Tell me."

"Ouch! I—I think I get lifted by the crowd to Heaven and the others meet me there. Have you seen my friends? Muscle-y and cool and all that stuff? Have you had a Cotton Candy Cocktail? They LITERALLY taste just like cotton candy. I could've drank like fifty of 'em but they cut me off... whateva."

The ground shook as the Daisies glowed brighter. People gathered along our sides, waiting to lift our bodies once we fell. My legs were wobbly like jello. JELLO!

"And then what happens?" shouted the woman over the crowd. "What happens next?"

Her eyes grew large. She was on the edge of her seat—she couldn't get enough of the plan and its details. I had to make it bigger, better.

I grabbed her arm. "A—silver—car," I said dramatically as the cocktails twisted in my stomach. "A silver car will pick us up in front of the club once the mission's accomplished—after we've broken into the vaults and stolen the Indigo. There'll be horses, too. Black ones. With fiery manes and little flower baskets on their saddles in case we get hungry on the way home and stop to pick up snacks. And then a big blue bus will race past with the horses and that'll be our cue to—"

"TEN, NINE, EIGHT—" the crowd chanted as the clock counted down.

The woman whispered into the collar of her blouse. "Did you get all that?"

"SEVEN, SIX, FIVE—"

"THE HANDS!" she shrieked into her collar. "CHECK THE HANDS! HIS HANDS GIVE HIM AWAY!"

"FOUR, THREE, TWO—"

She'd set me up. This woman who reminded me of Mom had set me up, and I'd been too drunk off Cotton Candy Cocktails to notice.

"ONE!"

Midnight.

The entire club shook. Chandeliers swung overhead as the jets resting under Club 49's foundation fired up and lifted the club off the ground.

Rapture had begun.

The Daisies glowed their most brilliant white yet, blinding employees and patrons alike. I was glad I'd been wearing my sunglasses. I pushed away from the woman and the crowd. Cotton Candy Cocktails still danced in my head. My limbs felt light.

"STOP HIM!" the woman yelled over the din of the crowd. Suddenly the room fell silent, save for the weeping of those who would lose their loved ones tonight. Then a few people shouted last words, and the room once again became a cacophony of sound.

I ran toward the gold room where I'd been given my Daisy, past patrons who stood dumbfounded by its brilliant white light.

Where were Phoenix and Mila? Why hadn't I seen them in the club? Was there something wrong with the plan? Had they even made it in?

A gold light flashed in the grand foyer. There was a final burst of screams, then a click.

The Daisy's needle plunged into my neck.

# CHAPTER 15

CORPSES SLAMMED AGAINST the floor like thunder—death's symphony. My body was no exception—my legs crumpled beneath me, numb.

Adrenaline surged through my veins, flushing away the drunken stupor left behind by the Cotton Candy Cocktails. I was completely lucid when hands grabbed my limp body, knocking my sunglasses to the floor.

I was alive; Bertha's device must've worked after all. The euthanizing element contained in the Daisy's injection had been neutralized, though the muscle relaxants they'd added to ensure the bodies fell in union obviously remained in working condition. Bertha had probably intended it to work that way, to ensure that I fell at the exact moment as the rest of them.

Still, I tried to wiggle my legs and arms, but met with little success. I guessed the relaxants would render me numb until Rapture was complete and I'd been lifted to Heaven.

More and more hands lifted me on either side. It was like I was body surfing. The people were surprisingly gentle.

Across the room, a group of drunkards dropped a woman's body and cursed under their breaths. Security raced to lift her back up. Not that it mattered to her—she was dead—but still it was bad PR for anyone who saw it. I prayed my own group wouldn't be as clumsy. I doubted the synthetic skin stretched across my face was strong enough to survive if it happened.

Somewhere in the club, someone hummed. The rest of the patrons joined in. It was almost spiritual. A shining conveyer belt slid from the ceiling, glowing white from within.

Heaven.

Corpses were placed on the conveyer belt's bottom and floated, one by one, up into the ceiling. When my own turn came, my eyes were blinded by the light as I rose. I imagined a room decorated with white furniture, plush carpets, and glowing fixtures waiting for me at the conveyer belt's top, all earthly gold exchanged for shimmering crystals.

Then the conveyer belt jolted to a stop, and my body bumped against the corpses on the lift. When it started up again, and I passed the bright light, my eyes adjusted to my new surroundings.

The walls around me were unfinished concrete. There was no sparkling room with white furniture. Just an ordinary conveyer belt that pushed us along like cars on an assembly line. The heavenly white light had all been for show.

Farther down the line, a fat worker yelled. "Just look at the hands, and then push the body forward!"

"No shit, Sherlock," his skinny friend scoffed, and rolled his eyes. "You call the Feds yet? Reckon the chancellor'll wanna hear 'bout this."

How could I have been so stupid? I'd given away the whole plan. The Feds were on their way, and Phoenix and Mila were nowhere to be found. I was a dead man.

The fat man jammed a finger in his nose as he searched the corpses for gold or valuables. "Can't believe they quarantined the club over something like this. Does it even *matter* if we find him? He's headed for the incinerator either way."

The skinny one slapped the fat one.

"What was the hell was that for?"

The feeling was returning to my fingertips and toes. I tried to scoot myself farther back on the conveyer belt, away from the two men, but I still couldn't move.

"'Cause you're stupid! You really think the chancellor wants the kid to burn?"

The fat man belched loudly. "Uh—yup."

"Cheese and crackers... You're dumber than a frickin' squirrel chasin' a dishwasher. It's like my Grams used to say: Easier to kill a fish in one hand than shoot two birds in a barrel."

"What the hell are you even saying? Hey—where's Stevens? And everybody else?"

I was getting very close to the two men now. Any minute they'd check my hands, and I'd be caught. But just as my body slid past them on the conveyor belt, the lights flickered. The fat one grabbed my foot. I tried to kick him, but my toes barely wiggled.

Then the lights went out, and he let go. The sound of splattering liquid echoed, and the sharp stench of gasoline rose from the floor.

The skinny one sucked in a breath. "What in the name of turkey tots is goin' on 'round here?"

Someone struck a match. A single flame hovered in front of the two men, lighting the face of the man behind it—Phoenix. "Don't move," he said. He dropped the match. The floor around the men burst into flames, trapping them in a ring of fire. Mila stood nearby, a canister of something—gasoline, I guessed—held in her hands.

"HELP US!" screamed the two men. "ANYONE, PLEASE! THESE SHIRTS ARE *HIGHLY* FLAMMABLE!"

Mila turned to the conveyer belt. "You in there, Kai?"

I tried to move my tongue, but it caught in my throat.

"No use asking," said Phoenix. "He's still paralyzed."

"We're just letting him burn in the incinerator then?" Mila shrugged. "Fine by me."

Phoenix pulled a gun on the two screaming men. "How do we turn it off?"

Their faces went cold.

"We'll never tell you," said the fat one.

Mila shook the gas canister in her hand. "Really? 'Cause I think that'd be in your best interest."

The skinny one laughed. "Go ahead. We're already dead as a doorbell after this screw-up. Besides," he shook his head and narrowed his beady eyes, "the longer you stand here, the closer the Feds get to the club."

Mila snarled and dropped the canister, then began yanking corpses off the belt. I was already fifteen feet away—there were at least forty corpses between us—and getting farther from Mila every second. I'd never be pulled off in time. Ahead, a mechanical arm sliced Daisies from the necks of corpses, and beyond that roared the incinerator.

Phoenix glanced at his wristwatch. "It's 12:20."

Mila nodded and kept pulling corpses. Phoenix fired his gun at the fat man's foot. He fell, screaming. The skinny one cackled.

"You're next." Phoenix winked. "And I'm aiming for your groin."

The skinny man fell silent, and the fat one moaned.

"Three seconds," said Phoenix, aiming his gun.

The mechanical arm sliced the side of my neck. My Daisy dropped to the floor with a clunk.

The skinny man crossed his legs to shield his groin. "Back wall to the right," he blurted. "Code is 5257."

The incinerator's heat burned my toes. I had only enough feeling in my legs to twist my ankles away, shielding them behind a corpse.

Phoenix kept his gun trained on the skinny man as Mila tried the code. The conveyer belt screeched to a halt. It felt like the bottoms of my feet were burning. Mila yanked body after body to the floor. The men in the circle of fire sobbed.

I flapped a wrist hard against the conveyer belt. Mila ran to where I lay.

"You all right there?" she asked. I nodded yes. "Can you use your voice yet?"

I let out a low groan.

She tossed me over her shoulder. "Right, then." Either she was strong or I was really light. Probably a combination of the two.

Phoenix lowered his gun. "Let's go."

There was a bang against the room's steel doors, and the men in the ring of fire burst into laughter. The Feds were here. We were surrounded.

Phoenix tossed a couple of small packages at the foot of the doors as the sounds of marching feet echoed from beyond them, and then his eyes darted to the ceiling. It was twelve feet high and unfinished. Metal air ducts hung above wooden planks.

Phoenix yanked several belts from the waists of corpses and tied them together. The marching beyond the doors grew louder. He tossed his makeshift rope toward the ceiling and over a wooden beam, then secured it with a knot.

He motioned for Mila to climb. "I'll take the kid."

Mila pulled herself up the rope and swung her feet over the beam, then motioned for Phoenix to do the same. He threw me over his shoulder like a rag doll and shimmied up the rope with surprising ease. When he joined Mila on the beam, he pulled up the rope behind him and patted my back. "You all right?"

I nodded and curled my toes and fingers. "GUH!"

The room's doors burst open, and immediately the sounds of marching echoed throughout the space. I tried to plug my ears with my fingers, but my elbows were still numb, and my hands just shook a little at the wrists.

Phoenix pressed a button in his pocket, and bombs exploded at the doors.

"Gerr pacca-juhs!" I shouted. "Guh berhms ger da paccajuhs!" *The packages. The bombs were the packages.*

Chaos broke out below us. The fat and skinny men in the ring of fire of fire screamed and babbled something about corpses' belts leading toward the ceiling.

116

Phoenix tossed me over his shoulder again, then leaped through the rafters, jumping from beam to beam as Mila followed.

We stopped at some metal vents just above the incinerator. The vents' metal tubing curved around, carrying on past the incinerator toward other rooms.

Phoenix pulled a pen from his pocket and pushed a button on its side. A red beam shot from its end and he sliced a square out of the vent's metal sheath. It hadn't been a pen at all, but the laser I'd seen in Bertha's lab. At least *some* of Bertha's inventions worked the way they were supposed to.

Mila crawled into the vents first, and Phoenix pushed my body in behind her, then joined us in the vents' metal tubing.

Thin wisps of smoke rose from behind us. These vents weren't used for air conditioning—they were used as a chimney, to carry smoke away from the incinerator and out of the nightclub.

Phoenix held a hand to his ear and nodded. "Sparky just radioed me the Indigo's coordinates. It's farther back in the club. We can get there through the vents."

We crawled on our hands and knees, making our way through the vents as Phoenix barked directions. I was slowly regaining use of my arms and legs, but still, Phoenix had to push me along, and for the most part I just slid along like a limp rag.

Suddenly, there was a *whoosh,* and a wave of smoke and wall of heat lunged at us from behind. The incinerator had been turned back on, and its fires filled the vents with smog and heat.

"Shit," muttered Mila before a coughing fit overtook her. The vent's temperature was rising quickly. Phoenix sliced a hole in the top of the vent with his laser, diverting some of the smoke and saving our lungs for that much longer.

"Keep moving, Meels," he said, urging her forward. "Once the smoke floods the incinerator room, they'll know we've sliced a hole in the vent and are moving through the ceiling. We'll have to go quickly if we want to secure the Indigo."

She nodded and covered her mouth to prevent another coughing fit.

Phoenix was smart—a real mastermind. I guessed he had to be to have escaped the Feds so many times.

We crawled onward with Phoenix slicing a hole in the vent every few feet to provide us with some respiratory relief. Smoke billowed out through the holes, but traces of it still clung to the vents' metal sides and fought to smother us. It stank like rotten eggs, like burning flesh.

It *was* burning flesh, I realized. They were burning the bodies. I felt nauseated and crawled faster. I was finally able to move myself forward without Phoenix's help.

Then Mila stopped abruptly. We'd reached a dead end.

She shook her head. "We've gotta go down, Phoenix."

"Perfect—we're here," he said, and sliced a hole behind us. The vent, however, must have suffered from one too many cuts, because it chose that moment to collapse beneath us. We fell to the ground—the shock was enough to jolt the last bit of paralysis from my limbs, and I stood.

Clear plastic cases filled with blue vials lined the walls of the room—Indigo vaccines. We'd landed in the club's stronghold. Between the cases, I figured there had to be over five thousand of them.

Phoenix ran to the small room's door and melted its lock with his pen. "What time is it?" he asked Mila.

"12:50," she said. "Ten minutes before Big Bertha's show time. Did Sparky send her the new coordinates after they moved the Indigo from the safes?"

Phoenix nodded and pushed a stack of vaccine cases to one end of the room.

Gunshots sounded in the hall, followed by screams. There was a sharp bang on the door, then more gunshots. An alarm sounded. Red lights flashed overhead.

"THIS AIN'T NO DRILL!" yelled a breathless voice over a loudspeaker. I recognized it as the skinny man. "WE'RE IN FRICKIN' LOCKDOWN! SEEK THE NEAREST AREA

OF REFUGE AND AWAIT FURTHER INSTRUCTIONS! THIS AIN'T NO DRILL!"

Mila and Phoenix pushed the rest of the Indigo cases against the wall as smoke flooded the room, pouring from the broken vent above. My lungs burned like fire.

"Give me your face," Phoenix said, grabbing the side of my cheek and pulling hard. The synthetic skin peeled off in his hand. He tore it into three pieces, keeping one for himself and tossing the others to me and Mila.

"The synthetic skin has enough microfibers to filter out the air's impurities," he explained, pulling the skin taut and wrapping it around his nose and mouth. "I know it's a bit of a *stretch*," he winked, "but give it a go." I did as he instructed, and the burning in my lungs quickly ceased.

The door flew off its hinges. Mila raised her gun, and Phoenix peeled off his suit jacket. Beneath it he wore a silver vest with a red blinking light: dynamite. In one hand, he held a button.

Nine Federal soldiers stormed the room in a V-formation. They had guns. Big guns. Almost as big as Bertha's.

"FREEZE!" shouted the one in the center. "BY ORDER OF THE MINISTER OF DEFENSE & PATRIOTISM, YOU ARE UNDER ARREST."

Phoenix stepped forward, shaking his button. "Unfortunately, gentlemen, I'm afraid arresting us is not in your best interest."

Mila tightened her grip on her gun, and I just stood there, sort of waving my arms like I was protecting myself from a stray dog. I glanced around the room, searching for a loaded weapon, a rusty pipe, something. But there was nothing. Just a lone paper clip sitting on a case of Indigo.

Briefly, I imagined myself shaking it at the Feds as they cowered in fear. The image was comical—it was better to have nothing. I spread my hands into flat palms and leaned forward in the only stance I could remember from fourth-grade judo.

"Jesus, Kai," muttered Mila. Maybe I had the stance wrong.

"ONE MORE STEP AND YOU'RE ALL DEAD," shouted the same soldier. The officer in charge, it seemed. The men aimed their guns at Mila. "TELL THE GIRL TO DROP HER WEAPON!"

Phoenix pressed and held the button with his thumb. Lights on his vest beeped and flashed—it was a dead man's switch.

"I told you," he said, "that that wouldn't be in your best interest. Shoot any of us, and I lift my finger from this button, detonating the three tons of dynamite strapped to my chest. We'll be dead, and the Indigo will be gone."

The officer thought for a second. "Hold position, men," he said. He lowered his weapon slightly and stared at Phoenix through narrowed eyes. "You don't have enough to blow this place."

Phoenix smiled and stepped forward. The lights on his vest flashed again. "Guns down, gentlemen," he said to the others. They hesitated, unsure. "Don't make this more difficult than it is has to be. Chaos begets chaos, my friends. And wouldn't we all like a bit of peace?"

The officer shook his head. "You're crazy."

Phoenix flashed him a dazzling smile. "Ah, excellent detective work, my friend. You ought to get a medal."

The officer mouthed a silent curse before sighing loudly. "Stand down, men."

"And the guns?" said Phoenix. "Please slide them to my associate, Ms. Vachowski, immediately."

The soldiers crouched to lower their weapons.

"WAIT!" shouted the officer.

Mila glanced toward the ceiling and then looked at Phoenix. "It's 12:59," she hissed.

Phoenix stared calmly at the soldiers and moved to lift his thumb. "Three tons of dynamite, gentlemen. The choice is yours."

The soldiers elbowed their leader aside and pushed their guns forward. Mila quickly wrapped them in a steel cord and secured them to her waist. A soldier muttered something into his shoulder—he was calling for back-up.

"Really?" Mila examined the guns. "You brought a rocket launcher?"

A soldier's face flashed red. "Uh—well, you never know—"

She fired it at the ceiling. The soldiers ran for cover. A massive hole smoldered where the roof had once been. Through it, I saw night sky.

Phoenix pointed to the cases of Indigo. "Paper clip!" he shouted.

Mila grabbed the paper clip and tossed it at the soldiers. It melted, midair, into a thick gold gas. They coughed and yelled as it smothered their lungs. It had no effect on us, apparently unable to penetrate the synthetic skin masks we had stretched across our mouths.

More marching feet thundered in the hall—reinforcements had arrived. The thunder was soon drowned out by the sound of whirring blades roaring overhead. Through the hole in the ceiling, I saw a helicopter hovering over the nightclub.

"Twenty seconds!" yelled Mila.

The bottom of a rope ladder dropped down through the hole.

"Climb!" shouted Phoenix.

I hurried up the ladder, and Mila followed, guns swinging from her waist. I glanced down below, and saw Phoenix lift his thumb. I braced myself for impact.

Nothing.

The bombs strapped to his chest had been fakes. The soldiers had never been in any real danger. It had just been a ploy on their psyches. A small but brilliant piece of Phoenix's master plan.

"TOSS THE GRAPPLE!" shouted Mila as we reached the helicopter's cabin.

A five-prong hook fell from the sky, secured by a steel cord to the copter. Phoenix grabbed the grapple as it fell, and wrapped its hook around the Indigo cases in a knotted bunch. Gunshots fired again.

"Keep climbing," shouted Mila. "It's one a.m."

"What happens at one?" I asked.

The nightclub roared as the massive jets that held it airborne sputtered and died. The show was over. The corpses had been lifted to Heaven and burned. Rapture was finished. Phoenix's face stared up at us with a look of fleeting horror.

Club 49 plunged to the ground.

# CHAPTER 16

I RACED INTO the helicopter's cabin, followed closely by Mila. Bertha sat in the pilot's seat, and Dove in the co-pilot's to her right.

"Where's Phoenix?" Dove shouted. "Jesus, Bertha. Could you turn it down?"

Bertha flipped a switch and the copter's drone quieted. In the old world, helicopters had been loud, noisy things, but technology had since progressed to the point where they could be turned almost noiseless in situations where stealth was considered an advantage. I guessed Bertha usually kept the blades roaring at full volume because she liked the dramatic effect.

Mila wiped sweat from her forehead as her lips shook. "Ph-Phoenix was—he was still in the club when it dropped."

Dove waved away her concern. "C'mon," he said. "It's Phoenix. He's gotta be out on the cord."

I peered out the window. Sure enough, a dark figure teetered on the edge of a stack of dangling Indigo cases—Phoenix. "Dove's right," I said.

Mila strapped herself to a jump seat. "What's the SA, Big Bertha?"

Bertha tightened her grip on the controls. "Club 49's on the ground," she said. "Feds have been circling it for nearly an hour, waiting for it to plunge after Rapture. There's at least a dozen squadrons on the case. Sucked Newla dry for the forces, then called the rest of HQ for backup. No troops in the sky just yet, but we're waiting. And something strange has been happening with traffic—they've stopped all silver cars in a three-mile radius."

"Silver cars?" said Mila. "What the hell? How'd they even know we were in there? I thought everything was under control?"

My face flushed red, praying she wouldn't figure out I'd revealed the plan with the help of some Cotton Candy Cocktails.

Bertha stared at me through the windshield's reflection. "If I had to guess," she said, "I'd say Car Battery spilled the beans."

Sweat gathered on my brow. "Well, I just—"

"Really, kid?" Bertha turned in her chair. "You had the simplest job: shut up and look pretty. And you still couldn't keep your mouth shut?"

"But—"

"And ten bucks says you didn't take the 'Paper Clip' seriously—I even showed it to you *in my lab*." She threw her hands from the controls. "For Christ's sake, I'm working with a bunch of squirrels."

"Huh?"

"I like squirrels," said Dove.

Bertha rolled her eyes. "You're all nuts."

I snorted. "Because your inventions work oh so well."

She flared her nostrils.

Mila moved between us. "Hands on the controls, Bertha."

Bertha shrugged. "The sky's clear."

Dove pointed ahead. "Balls," he said, "I'm not so sure about that."

Seven copters dove from the clouds, cutting through the smoggy sky. Their weapons were aimed at us, the barrels of their guns already glowing red.

"GET THE CORD IN!" shouted Bertha. "We need Phoenix and the vaccines in here where they'll be safe. The Feds won't fire at us if they know we have Indigo."

The Feds fired.

Bertha yanked at the controls, and we lurched to the side. I found the cord's winch and pressed a button on its side. The copter's door swung open again and the cord began to coil. Outside, Phoenix and the vaccines rose in the air.

"They're getting close," said Dove. "We gotta move."

The winch moaned as it grinded to a halt. Sparks flew from its gears as it burned out. Several feet of cord still hung in the air.

"The winch is down!" I shouted.

"Shit," muttered Mila. "Hang on!" she yelled to Phoenix.

The Federal copters fired again. Bertha jerked the controls, and we soared upward into the clouds. The copter's blades went into overdrive, screaming as they sliced through the clouds' dewy wisps.

"Limited viz up here," said Bertha. "We're practically flying blind."

Patches of sky flashed around us—gunfire. Outside, Phoenix covered his head. We had to get him inside if we were going to survive.

I pulled at the cord with my bare hands, but it wouldn't budge. We darted through the clouds. What was Bertha's plan? The worried look plastered across her face told me she had none.

Mila unhooked the stolen guns from her waist and tossed me one.

I handed it back to her. "I have no idea how to use this."

She shrugged and passed it back. "None of us did when we first started."

When they *started?* Who *were* the Lost Boys? What were they even trying to do?

I didn't have time to think about all that now. Those were the sorts of questions you could only afford to ask when your feet were planted firmly on the ground. If we were going to make it out alive, I had to put my wandering thoughts aside and *do* something. I had to get Phoenix inside.

"Drop us, now," ordered Mila.

The copter lurched forward, and we fell from the clouds into open air. Three Federal copters hovered nearby, waiting for us. Their guns glowed red as they opened fire.

"Hang on to me," said Mila. I wrapped my arms around her waist, and she leaned out the open doorway. Her rocket launcher screamed as she fired three shots. One shot flew past the Feds, but the other two hit their targets. The helicopter on the right was knocked from the sky in an explosion of fire. Shards of metal fell like rain.

The left copter fired three shots back. Bertha swerved, but one round nicked the cord that still dangled from the cabin. Phoenix and the vaccines rocked back and forth. The steel cord sparked and twisted as it began to untether.

My hands grew sweaty from the pressure. I wiped them against my pants—er, skirt. I had forgotten I was still wearing the skirt. Dear god, how many people were going to see me in a skirt?

I searched the cabin for something, anything to pull Phoenix from the open air… maybe even a paper clip. Remembering Phoenix's trick back at the club, I checked for belts: Mila was wearing one, and Dove too. Bertha was the deciding factor.

"I need your belt," I said to Mila. She gave me a confused look, but then tossed it to me. "You too, Dove." He passed it back. "Are you wearing a belt, Bertha?"

She was silent.

"If you are," I said, "can I have it?"

"I'm *trying* to fly a *plane*—"

"Balls," muttered Dove. "I thought this was a helicopter."

"—and you want me to *stop* to give you my *belt*? There is NO WAY IN—"

Mila held the rocket launcher to Bertha's face, her finger poised over the trigger. "He needs your belt, Bertha."

"And it's comin' off." She tossed me her belt, glancing nervously at Mila.

I tied the belts together like I'd seen Phoenix do earlier, then tossed one end out the side of the copter and wrapped the other end around my arm. I couldn't help but notice that the cable from which Phoenix hung was now down to just one metal thread.

The Feds fired again. Sparks flew. The cord snapped. The vaccine cases fell from the sky.

Phoenix was gone.

The belts yanked at my arm, hard, just about pulling me from the helicopter and cutting off circulation to my hand all at the same time. I looked down, and saw Phoenix hanging from the rope of belts with one hand. Mila grabbed my waist, and together we reeled him in.

"He's in!" shouted Mila.

Bertha nodded as the Feds fired again. We slammed the door shut and Bertha jerked the controls once more, sending us sprawling as the helicopter shot back up into the clouds.

"We lost the Indigo," I said quietly.

Mila shrugged. "But we got Phoenix."

The two hugged. Dove joined in. Bertha rolled her eyes, but cracked a smile—I could see that they were a family. A ragtag, dysfunctional one, with plans to likely destroy the free world... but a family nonetheless.

Shots whizzed past us from beyond the cloud cover. The celebration was short-lived.

Phoenix hopped into the copilot seat. "Where have we positioned New Texas?"

"Sparky's got its engines idling a mile east of Maui," said Bertha, "but there's still six other copters in the sky."

"Not safe to go back yet, then," said Phoenix. "And the Caravan?"

"Three miles south of Newla's port."

"So that's where we'll head."

Outside in the clouds, a shadow leaned toward us. It materialized into a Federal copter and slammed directly into our side. We were knocked into a spiral, dropping from the air as we spun toward the ground. Then another copter slammed us from the left. Bertha's controls flashed red.

"We're losing altitude!" shouted Dove.

"No shit," said Mila.

Bertha pulled at the controls, but they sparked in her hands. "My controls have shorted!" she shouted at Phoenix.

He yanked at his, and the copter rose in the sky. "I've got it, Big Bertha."

Next to me, Mila lay unconscious and bleeding. We'd both been slammed against the wall when the Feds rammed us, and I guessed she must have taken a shot to the head. Sure enough, I spotted a blue bruise already forming on her temple, and a series of cuts pooled blood by the corner of her left eye.

The copter's right door had been totally crushed in—our only exit now was the door on the left.

The Feds fired again, but Phoenix evaded the shots.

Bertha flared her nostrils. "I told you we needed guns on this thing."

"You said we needed them on our toaster, too."

Bertha squinted. "And I still stand by that claim."

Phoenix pushed the controls down, and we dropped a few feet before hovering again. The Feds sailed past us. Bertha mashed at the buttons in front her, but they merely blinked red and sizzled. The Feds spun around in the sky, training their weapons on us. Four other copters dropped from the clouds, rejoining their comrades. All of their guns glowed red as they charged.

"I need someone on the rocket launcher!" shouted Phoenix.

I shook Mila, but she was still unconscious. I glanced at Dove, but he merely stared out the window and whistled.

"Mila's down," I said to Phoenix, "and I don't know how."

The Feds were racing toward us. Their pilots had finally caught on to our evading maneuvers.

Bertha crawled over her seat, grabbed the rocket launcher and swung the left door open. She fired a round each at the two copters that led the formation, and they both fell from the sky. The others quickly shrank back into cloud cover.

Bertha stroked the gun's trigger like a lover, then winked at me. "We're clear."

Phoenix nodded. "Heading south toward the Caravan. Skies should be clear all the way now."

A third copter slammed into us, this one from directly above, jamming our rotor blade between its landing skids. Our engine groaned as it fought to free the blades from the skids.

"TURN OFF THE ENGINE" roared Bertha, "OR THIS THING'S GONNA BLOW!"

Phoenix slammed a button. Our engine fell silent, but our rotor blades were still stuck between the Federal copter's landing skids. The Fed copter pushed us down, out of the sky—a suicide mission.

Bertha grabbed five orange backpacks from the back seat and tossed one to each of us before hurrying to strap one to the still-unconscious Mila's back.

"Parachutes," she explained. "We need to jump while we still have altitude."

Phoenix glanced out the window and shook his head. "We're above land," he said. "The Feds will shoot us from the sky, or grab us in the city when we land."

"Then what the hell do you propose we do? Let them slam us into the ground?"

"I'm thinking."

"Think faster, Phoenix."

I strapped the parachute pack to my back. "I've got an idea."

"Car Battery's got an idea?" Bertha hurried to the door. "My cue to jump!"

I ignored her comment. "We need to get over the ocean water, right?" Phoenix nodded. "Dove, can you climb into the copter above us?"

A look of terror flashed across Dove's face. "I'm scared of heights."

I had to think simple. Dove wasn't the brightest bulb in the box. And he was gullible—he listened to everything Bertha said. I had an idea.

I shrugged. "Well, what does that matter?" I said to Dove. "We're not even that high off the ground."

"Yeah, hardly!" snorted Bertha.

"Really?" Dove's wide set eyes shined bright. He looked out the window. "It looks like we're pretty high…"

"We're really not," I said matter-of-factly. "It's an optical illusion. You know—pollution in the air. Chemical reactions. Ionic molecular bonds. Basic stuff, Dove. They make it look like we're really high, even though we're not."

Bertha raised an eyebrow. She'd guessed what I was up to. "Yeah, Doveboat," she said. "It's basic science. We're probably only a few feet from the ground."

Dove narrowed his eyes. "Then why haven't we hit the ground yet?"

Bertha pointed out the window. "LOOK! A BUTTERFLY!"

His face split into a dumb grin. "WHERE?"

"You could totally climb into the copters above us," I said quickly—we were still losing altitude. "Then all you'd have to do is stun the men and jerk the controls left toward the water."

"And maybe you'll see the butterfly," finished Bertha. She winked at me.

God, I hoped this was dumb enough to work.

"I'll do it!" Dove eagerly crawled out the open door and onto our roof, like a squirrel up a tree. We heard him fire at the Federal copter's window, then we waited. I imagined him crawling through the broken glass, punching the confused pilots, and jerking the controls left.

We hovered in midair, briefly, and then we darted left. Amazingly, the plan had worked.

Dove leapt back into our copter as we shot out over the ocean. "The copilot had a monarch tattooed on her neck," he said with a smile.

Bertha's eyes widened. "Well, I'll be damned."

The three of us looked to Phoenix for further instruction. "We need to direct ourselves toward the water as we fall," he explained. "Dove's given us the time we need—now we just need to aim ourselves west to avoid the city. If we're lucky, we'll hit water and catch a current that'll take us to the sewers. From there, we can go to Madam Revleon's and wait this whole thing out until things settle down."

"And if we're *not* lucky?" I asked.

"We die," said Phoenix.

"At least we have options!" said Dove gleefully.

Phoenix glanced out the window. "We have enough altitude now to have a shot at making it to the coastline." He pointed to the tattered steel cord still stuck to the winch. "We'll use this to stay together until we're ready to pull our chutes. That way we don't drift apart. We jump as a team."

Our copter was still darting forward, and we were in cloud cover now. The four of us suited up, with Phoenix strapping Mila to his chest and Bertha strapping Mila's string of stolen guns—plus a few guns of her own—to herself.

Phoenix secured the cord to our waists. "On my countdown," he said. "THREE, TWO, ONE!"

We leapt from the copter. Clouds raced by my face as we fell. We were in a line now— held together only by the cord Phoenix insisted we use.

Newla's edge loomed beneath us. We were lucky it'd been built so close to the ocean years ago. The chancellor at the time must have wanted a view.

As we fell, Mila's eyes finally flew open. A look of fear flashed in them before she promptly passed out again. Bertha rolled her eyes so loudly I could practically hear her muttering, *Sissy.*

We plummeted through the cloud cover and past the remaining Federal copters. We fell so quickly, we probably didn't even hit their radar. I hoped.

But we weren't so lucky. One of the Federal copters plunged downward, and two dots launched themselves from the metal body of it as it fell—pilots abandoning ship, coming after us. The chase was far from over, I realized. I tried to tell the others, but the words caught in my throat as the air rushed by—we were falling far too fast.

Phoenix and the others angled their bodies to steer us over open water. At last, Phoenix nodded and put a hand to his mouth—the signal he was about to cut the cord. We prepared ourselves to open our chutes. He sliced the cord several times with his laser pen, and we pushed ourselves apart in the sky.

The plan was for Phoenix to pull his chute first, as Mila's weight would cause them both to drop faster, so they'd need the extra time. His aim was also best—he was the only one with a reasonable chance of landing where he wanted, and thus if he came down last, he could join up with those who had already landed.

He yanked his cord, flying back into the sky above us as his chute—created using a special cloth invented by Bertha to be invisible to the untrained eye—caught air. Dove went next, and then it was Bertha's turn.

She yanked her cord.

And yanked her cord.

Her chute was dead.

She was still plummeting toward the water. I swam toward her in the sky, a drunken frog in the air. She wrapped her arms around my chest.

"Just pull the damn chute," she muttered.

There'd be a time for gloating, I was sure.

I pulled my cord, and my neck jerked back. My shoulder screamed where it had been stabbed by Churchill's hook, and whiplash knocked me forward.

We floated in a pocket of air caught by my parachute. Not falling, just floating. Held by the breeze's warm floating hands.

Gunshots sounded overhead. A round whizzed down past my ear, and my parachute hissed—shot. My heart pounded with fear and my limbs tightened from shock. Bertha slipped out of my arms, and dropped toward the ocean like a rock.

Air pressed through the bullet holes in the parachute, driving its ruthless tendrils through and stretching the holes wide. In seconds, the chute's fabric was completely torn to shreds.

I was free-falling now. Fast and hard.

Like our copter, like Bertha, like Club 49, I plunged from the sky.

# CHAPTER 17

MIRANDA COULD STILL remember the night Hackner was elected to the council and appointed chancellor. She always remembered the appointment nights.

He'd been forty-five—the traditional age of one's election to the Council. He would serve his five-year term, like the other council members, then receive his euthanization at its completion. There were no re-elections. The dead couldn't run.

His had been a particularly boring election season, Miranda remembered. He'd won his island's seat in a landslide victory by charming the hearts of the people of Newla, the city that carried most of HQ's vote due to its massive population.

It'd come easily to him, too—he was a natural manipulator. The press sat like puppies in the palm of his hand, their pens scribbling, tails wagging, eager—always eager—to please. He was handsome, charming, persuasive, and—most importantly to Miranda—stupid.

It took the other council members two whole minutes of deliberation to select him, among themselves, as the next chancellor. It would've happened even faster, but Councilman Birch was struck by a coughing fit that lasted nearly a minute.

Of course, the deliberation was merely a formality. In the history of the Federation, there'd never been a single chancellor appointed from any island other than HQ. Sure, several fools had tried over the years, but the zealous bastards always disappeared or died mysteriously during the deliberation—and in the end, HQ's councilman reigned supreme once again.

Miranda remembered watching Hackner enter the chancellor's chambers for the first time, the night he'd been appointed. He'd dropped his boxes in the room's center and plopped himself proudly on the chaise lounge like a fat boy who'd discovered a lolly.

*This is it,* he likely thought. *This is my moment. I have arrived. I am the most powerful man in the world.*

The fool.

Like every man before him, he'd had no idea that the chancellor was merely a puppet—a doll to be used for Miranda's own entertainment. Though, in his defense, the rest of the council never learned of this.

It had taken Hackner longer than the others to notice the glass of champagne resting on the corner of his new desk. He lifted it in the air, sniffed, and swirled it before returning it to the mahogany without a sip.

Then he reached for the ConSynth's cool, glowing glass and rubbed its side, the oils from his fingertips leaving a thick, filmy residue. Disgusting. It was, however, an improvement over the previous chancellor—that one had shaken the ConSynth like a snow globe.

She appeared to Hackner then, in the doorway, with a glass of champagne in her hand. *Cheers,* she said.

She wore a fitted red dress that wrapped her body like cellophane and had a wicked neckline that plunged far past her breasts. She had a feeling Hackner was a man of insatiable desires. The way he plopped himself on the lounge. The smug smile. The touch of his fingers on the ConSynth's glass.

A man starved for power and control. He was about to lose both. All it took was a glass of champagne.

He grabbed his glass. *How did you get in here?*

She smiled coyly. *The better question would be how you're going to get me out. This dress is too tight—stifling. You look like a strong man.* She winked. *A man with power.*

*Power.* The word danced on her tongue. One of the few lovers she'd ever known. She smiled and raised her glass again. *To your continued success.*

He nodded eagerly and slid the champagne down his throat.

Poison. A slow-acting variety, of course. Harmless at first, but the compounds contained within it multiplied over time in vicious fashion. Without an antidote, he'd be dead in a month. And only Miranda, with the help of her blind assistant, knew how to create the antidote. It had never been written down. There was no recipe in any book. Just the one she kept in her head. Even the blind girls didn't know what they were mixing.

And so she maintained her power with each new chancellor.

They fell for it every time.

The mysterious woman in red. The plunging neckline. The not-so-subtle ego stroke she gave through her toast.

And thus, the men who craved power were, without exception, ruined by it. This was the way of things in the Federation, as had it been in the United States, the United Kingdom, China, Russia, even the ancient Greeks and the Romans. Power corrupted all.

But not Miranda. Perhaps—she often mused—because she'd been corrupt in the first place.

Miranda shook her head free of nostalgia. This was not the night of Hackner's appointment. It was not night at all. It was the first of the month—the day Sage came to visit.

She ran her fingers along the desk's mahogany edge. Her fingers never really touched the wood—seeing as they weren't really there—but she liked to imagine they did. Her form was nothing more than a holographic projection of her own consciousness. But it was a damn good one.

A small hand rapped against the door to the chancellor's chambers.

"Come in, Sage," called Miranda.

The door cracked open and Sage slid in, pushing it shut behind her.

Miranda stepped toward her. "How are you, my darling?" she asked.

She was always careful around the girl. She needed to be close, but not too close. The girl wanted to hear her voice nearby—the general echo of the ConSynth disturbed her—but Miranda couldn't get too close, lest the girl reach out and try to touch her. Then the game would be up. Because Sage would realize she wasn't really there—that she was only a projection.

The ConSynth couldn't reproduce a body. It could only sustain a person's consciousness, their mind, their soul, and even this small task required the machine to use energy from a very particular source.

Miranda called them "batteries."

It sounded nicer that way. A silly euphemism. Less sinister for everyone involved. Made them forget the screams of the victims as they were strapped down, as the ConSynth's core was jabbed into their veins, as their eyes went blank.

It was a real shame the batteries only lasted a month. A pity the human body contained such a small amount of usable energy.

"I'm all right," Sage said finally. Her eyes were blind, glazed over, but they still bore directly into Miranda.

Miranda hated when the girl stared. Like she knew what had happened to her. What Miranda had ordered done to her—the blindness, her mother's death, all of that silly stuff. The girl had no way of knowing, of course. And she was too dim to make her own accusations.

Miranda smiled. "I'm so happy to hear that, sweetie." The last word stuck to her tongue like an expired cough drop. She faked a yawn. "I'm quite tired, darling—you know where the materials are. Today, I'd like you to start with the beaker farthest to the right."

Sage nodded and moved behind the desk. A lab table there had been set up with nine beakers. Hackner needed his monthly antidote for the poison, and Miranda was the only one who could give it to him. But she couldn't touch anything, of course, so she used Sage to mix it. And since the girl couldn't even see what she was doing, the antidote would remain known to only Miranda. And subsequently, she would remain forever safe and in power.

Miranda had to stifle a laugh at the thought. She, the most powerful leader in the world, needed the help of a blind girl. It was almost too rich.

She'd tried using sighted girls in the past, but it had repeatedly ended in disaster. One girl had revealed the antidote's mixing formula to the man who was chancellor at the time. He'd threatened to pull the ConSynth's plug and free himself from Miranda's curse. Fortunately, Miranda had been able to have them both killed. But the incident had made her all the more cautious—paranoid.

Yes, it was better for everyone if her assistant was blind. The current system worked like oiled clockwork.

First, Miranda would have the chancellor lay out nine different ingredients in nine different beakers and vials, in nine different sequences. Then, he would leave, and the mixing girl—Sage, currently—would come in. Miranda would tell the girl the precise vials to pour into the precise beakers in the precise order. The ingredients and the compounds used to create the antidote were highly unstable. Failure to follow her instructions exactly resulted in the girl creating poison, rather than antidote.

And without his monthly antidote, the chancellor would die a slow, horrible death. It would begin as a cramp in his toes, then move to his calves, his hamstrings, thighs, on and on…

Eventually the cramp would make its way all the way up to his brain, and then it would hit his heart, which would relax, sending him into cardiac arrest. Then the cramps would begin again. His muscles would cramp without end before, finally, he died—not from physical injury, but from insanity that brought him to a fit of seizures.

Miranda knew the poison well—she'd designed it to work this way. If any chancellor attempted to create a new antidote, his muscles would cramp almost instantly from the toxic compounds' double dosage. Miranda had learned that people who craved power didn't like to die. She used this fact to her advantage.

Through this method—the poison and the antidote—Miranda had assured her own existence for the rest of time. She was, for all intents and purposes, immortal. So long as the ConSynth had a battery, she had a life. The chancellors would die, one after another, every five years—but not Miranda. Miranda was forever. A ghost. Not living, but certainly not dead. Every bit herself, every bit as powerful.

This was enough for her. The power was always enough.

Sage held up a beaker; she was done. She'd followed Miranda's instructions. The solution was complete.

"Show it here, sweetie." Miranda peered into the beaker and frowned. "That's wrong. I'm sorry, darling, but that's not right at all. The mixture is still blue." She turned to the lab station. A vial of gold liquid sat unused in the corner. It wasn't like Sage to make mistakes. Miranda clenched her jaw. "You forgot the third vial to the right," she said. "I told you to pour it in after the vial farthest left."

Sage immediately grabbed the vial and poured it into the mixture, which changed to a dark blue.

Miranda flared her nostrils. "You can't just add it at the last second! Have I taught you nothing? The solution must be mixed in the proper order. What's gotten into your head?"

Sage tucked her arms in close and started shaking. Miranda reminded herself to make sure the next one was less easily frightened.

Miranda smoothed her pants. It was important she maintained control—she must always have control. "It's all right, sweetie," she said. "You can come back tomorrow and mix a new one. The chancellor will survive another day without his antidote."

At least Miranda hoped.

# CHAPTER 18

THE WIND THUNDERED in my ears as I plummeted toward the ocean below. Behind me, strips of parachute fluttered, only slightly slowing my descent.

In ten seconds, I'd hit the surface. I pointed my toes, clenched my stomach, and plugged my nose. Years of cliff jumping in Moku Lani had prepared me well.

My body hit the water with a sharp sting. It felt like shards of glass buried themselves into the arches of my feet and dug deep into my veins. My legs burned as I plunged farther into the ocean's depths, slowed only by the tattered remains of my parachute.

I cracked open my eyes, and the salt water offered its customary burn. In the distance, I made out a blurred figure.

Bertha?

I tore off my parachute and swam toward the shadow. It spun gracefully in the water like a sparrow in the sky. It froze as I approached, widening its mouth and showing the teeth embedded in its jaws. Small and rounded, they were unlike the shark teeth I knew so well.

They belonged to a dolphin. *A dolphin.* The creature before me was an actual, living dolphin. I opened my mouth in a silent scream. Bubbles flew from the corners of my lips.

In school, we were taught that dolphins were extinct, like most other large marine mammals. Killed by the nuclear fallout that settled in the ocean, and by the radioactive beasts that had emerged as a result.

The dolphin before me was, in short, a real miracle.

My parents had told me stories about them as a kid. Sailors would fall overboard during ocean storms, and dolphins would appear out of nowhere to save them. The angels of the sea.

As the dolphin teetered in the water, I realized why it had appeared: to save my life. It was going to be my angel.

I kicked softly in the water. There was no need to worry anymore—the dolphin would swim me to the surface like it had done for the sailors in the tales I'd heard growing up. I would wrap my arms around its neck, and it would kick its flippers hard against the salt water, launching us to the surface. I imagined the look on Phoenix's face when the dolphin leapt from the water, my arms wrapped around its neck.

I reached for the dolphin, my fingers tingling. Already feeling the mystical bond between us that would surely form when it carried me to the surface.

It gave me one look with its big blue eyes and hurried away.

*It will come back*, I told myself. The dolphins in the stories always came back.

Thirty seconds passed. It didn't come back.

I swam toward the surface on my own. If I saw a mermaid, I'd keep swimming.

I sucked in a breath when I broke the surface. Two hundred feet away, a parachute drifted down to the water—Dove or Phoenix, I guessed.

Where was Bertha? She had to be nearby. I hadn't been shot down long after she'd slipped from my arms. She'd fallen fast—too fast to land safely, even with perfect form.

Something plastic floated past my arm—one of Bertha's guns.

Where was she? Had she survived the impact? Had she drowned? Was she hurt? I didn't see any blood in the water. I had to keep searching. I stuck my face back underwater and started to paddle.

My head slammed into the side of something hard. "Oww," a voice moaned.

I lifted my head from the water. It was a body—Bertha. Her eyes were closed. I shook her hard. "Bertha!" I said. "Bertha! Can you hear me? Please, wake up!"

She coughed but kept her eyes shut. "I think I hit a dolphin."

"You hit a dolphin?"

She pursed her lips. "Landed on it—BAM!" She started laughing.

She was delirious. She must've hit her head. Her impact with the water had likely been tremendous.

"I was flapping my arms," she said, moving her elbows. She held a waterlogged gun in each hand. "And then finally my parachute flew out of my pack, slowing me briefly 'til good ol' Wet Willy saved me."

"Wet Willy?"

She stuck a hand on her head like a fin. "Wet Willy."

"You mean Free Willy? Like the whale in that really old movie?"

She moistened a finger in her mouth and reached for my ear. "Wet Willy's comin' for ya." She moved her arm and winced. "Oww," she said, holding her elbow in one hand. "I think I broke it. Or maybe my whole body."

She'd lost it. The impact had given her a concussion.

"Take me home," she shouted. "TO NEW TEXAS, BABY!"

I grabbed her feet and pulled her in the direction of the fallen parachuter. We had to find the others. And soon, or the Feds would be on us.

Fifty feet away a green flare shot into the sky. Phoenix was sending us a signal. I swam hard in its direction, dragging Bertha behind me.

"Whee!" she cried as I dragged her by her feet.

But the water was empty when we reached the flare's source.

"Phoenix!" I called.

My legs shook, and my breaths came in short spurts. I was tired. Pulling Bertha hadn't helped. I wouldn't last much longer in open water.

"Phoenix!" I called again.

Something yanked my ankle, pulling me under. It was too late to scream. Phoenix hadn't set the flare off at all—it'd been one of the Feds. The green should've given it away.

The soldier pulled me deeper and deeper. His grip tightened around my ankle as we sank. I tried to kick, but he held on that much harder. My lungs screamed—they needed air, and fast. I hadn't had time to breathe before he'd pulled me under.

A shadow swam behind us, followed by a flurry of bubbles. Suddenly the soldier softened his grip on my leg and a cloud of bubbles shot from his mouth. His corpse fell slowly into the ocean's blue depths. A shiver ran down my spine.

*He is not your enemy*, I reminded myself. *The Feds are not your enemies.* It was hard not to think so when they fought so desperately to kill me.

The shadow swam toward me. Did it have a similar plan in store?

Before I could decide whether or not to flee, the shadow grabbed me by the hand and pulled me toward the surface—Phoenix. He'd saved me again. Air flooded my lungs when my head broke the surface at last. I squeezed my eyes shut and laughed.

Bertha floated next to me, spinning and giggling in the water as waves passed. "I think I'd like some breakfast," she announced.

Phoenix was silent. He stared up at the sky above and clenched his jaw. A hundred parachutes filled the sky—armed men with weapons slung across their chests. Feds.

"Their bullets won't work in the water," I said, "and moisture will ruin the guns."

"BANG! BANG!" Bertha pretended to fire her waterlogged weapons.

"They don't have bullets," said Phoenix. "They know those won't work underwater. They've got Dummy Darts—a lot of them, by the looks of it."

"What if," giggled Bertha, "they weren't Dummy Darts, but Gummy Darts? And they just fired Gummy Bears at us and we collected 'em and ate 'em and then had a picnic."

Phoenix turned to me. "What happened to *her*?"

"Concussion."

"PERCUSSION!" shouted Bertha. "Somebody get me some drums!"

A hum sounded over the crashing waves. On the horizon, a boat sped in our direction. The Feds were coming at us from all directions. They might not have been my real enemy, but they'd try to kill me nonetheless.

Phoenix jumped in the water and waved his hands at the boat to signal to it. "Yell," he told me, before screaming as loud as he could.

The boat swerved in our direction.

I yanked his arm. "*What are you doing?*"

"OVER HERE," he yelled, ignoring my question. "HEY, OVER HERE!"

The waves broke faster as the boat sped toward us. I kicked hard to stay afloat and saw Phoenix do the same; his muscle mass made him heavy in the water. Bertha, however, floated along on her back with ease.

The parachutes were only a few hundred feet above us now, decorating the sky like polka dots swaying in the breeze.

As the boat came closer, a figure leaned over the boat's deck and pulled something up from the water. I recognized the red writing printed along the boat's starboard side: *The Retired Lobster.*

It was Churchill Wingnut.

"CHURCHILL!" I yelled. Phoenix looked confused. "He helped me when the Wet Pocket broke," I explained. "He was the one with the hook and the blood and the shark and... yeah."

Phoenix nodded, as if it were the most reasonable thing he'd ever heard.

"OWW!" Bertha cried out in pain. A thin yellow dart was protruding from her stomach. "What the—?" She looked around, startled. "How the hell did I get in the middle of the ocean?" She threw both arms back, then cried out in pain when she moved the injured one.

"Dummy Darts," said Phoenix.

Waves crashed on either side of us as the *Retired Lobster* finally reached us and slowed to a stop. Just in time—the Feds were only twenty feet from the surface now. They began to cut their parachute cords and drop into the ocean like swollen raindrops. One Fed cut his chute directly over the boat and landed on its deck with a splat. Churchill quickly chucked the man's limp body overboard.

Dove stood on the deck's other end. He raced to my side and pulled me from the water. My legs shook when they hit solid ground, unfamiliar with the feeling after having treaded water for so long.

Dove and I then helped Bertha into the boat, and she shook her head as she yanked the Dart from her chest. "Some serious shit going on around here," she muttered, still looking confused.

Together, Dove, Bertha, and I pulled Phoenix from the water. Churchill continued to toss overboard any Feds who suffered the horrible misfortune of slicing their chutes directly over his ship. As if having your body crushed against the ship's hard wooden deck wasn't enough.

One soldier managed to grab the railing as Churchill pushed him overboard. Churchill promptly brought "Old Jimmy" down on his hand. The man cried out in agony as the hook's sharp edge pierced his skin. Blood swelled and rolled down his arm before he fell into the ocean's basin of churning salt water.

Churchill held his rusty hook high in the air and roared. "OLD JIMMY!"

Bertha's eyes widened. "And I thought *I* was intense."

A massive fin broke the water. Federal soldiers screamed as the incoming megalodon tore them apart with ease.

Phoenix grabbed Churchill's arm and shook him. "You got blood in the water!" he said. "You should've known better. You should've known the nets would be turned off."

He turned to Dove. "You know how to drive a boat, right?"

Dove nodded.

"Think you can manage this one?"

Dove ran to the ship's helm while Churchill stood silent.

The soldiers in the water screamed as the megalodon shredded them into bits like paper. The water grew redder by the second. Soon the whole ocean looked like it was ablaze.

But more blood meant more megalodons. And sure enough, in the distance, several fins broke the surface. As the megalodons swarmed, the remaining soldiers clawed at the ship's side, crying for help.

I felt sick to my stomach. This wasn't right. The men in the water weren't villains—they were just men doing their jobs. They weren't the Lost Boys. They weren't terrorists. They weren't real villains. They weren't real trouble.

I watched Phoenix stare at the bloody water with a blank expression. And it was at that moment that I realized: I was one of them. A Lost Boy. One of the people responsible for the deaths of all these men.

A particularly desperate moan erupted from the water. I ran to the ship's side, and threw my hand to a man not much older than myself. His bright blue eyes burned into my soul—a lovely blue, the color of water when the sun breaks on it just right. The same color as Charlie's eyes. Not one of the typical shades of Indigo blue, but something brighter: Charlie blue, I'd always called it. His fingers were inches from mine. I stretched my arm a little farther, knowing his hand would soon fall into mine.

There was a kick and a splash. Salt water stung my eyes. His fingers slipped past mine and he fell back into the water. Bright green eyes replaced his—Mila. She'd tossed the man back into the water, and now she put her hand into mine.

Before I could pull her on board, the ship's engine revved, and I squeezed her hand in my own. The boat shot forward, pushing past screaming corpses. My body lurched against its railing as Mila's was dragged through the water, my grip the only thing keeping her from becoming a megalodon snack. A massive fin shot up beside the boat. Following Mila—food.

Phoenix sprinted to my side, and grabbed Mila's other hand. Water poured onto the deck as the megalodon launched its face from the water, its teeth glistening in the scattered sunlight. Mila's bright green eyes were filled to the brim with frozen fear.

The megalodon gnashed its teeth, its jaws heading straight for Mila's legs, still dangling limp in the water like worms.

# CHAPTER 19

THE MEGALODON'S TEETH dripped blood, and a pair of black and green pants were lodged between two of its teeth—undoubtedly all that was left of a Federal soldier it had consumed only seconds before. I silently gave thanks that it was only a pair of pants. It could've just as easily been a bloody arm or leg.

Despite having jaws large enough to swallow their victims whole, researchers had found that megalodons were particularly fond of tearing their prey to shreds. The scent of torn flesh seemed to satisfy their insatiable blood lust, however briefly.

The *Retired Lobster* groaned as it raced forward, its rusted engine no match for the megalodon who easily kept pace. Having already left the soldiers to its mates, it wasn't about to give up on us, its last chance at a meal. Its wide jaws were easily large enough to tear apart not only Mila, but the tiny boat itself. My heart beat hard in my chest, and my knees felt weak—if it killed Mila, the blood frenzy would sure lead it to kill and eat us, too.

Phoenix and I fought to pull Mila up on deck, but the force of her feet dragging in the water drew her even closer to the monster's mouth. If we pulled too hard, I worried we'd dislodge her arms from their sockets. The clash of the megalodon's teeth, however, told me this would still be the preferred option.

Mila didn't scream, but gritted her teeth and squeezed her eyes shut to avoid the salt water's sting as it sprayed. She was tough. Tougher than most girls I'd met. Maybe even as tough as Charlie.

Her fingers were slowly slipping from mine. My hands became more slippery by the second, and Phoenix's grunts told me he was experiencing the same problem. If we didn't do something, we were going to lose her, and soon.

I yelled for help. Churchill grunted and swung his arm back. A piece of steel flew from his hand and over the deck. Its jagged edges did tilted somersaults as it sailed through the air. It spun past Mila, and toward the megalodon, burying itself in the monster's massive snout. The beast fell back into the water, its fin trembling before it disappeared.

The monster was gone.

Bertha ran to our side, and with the added help of her uninjured arm, we were finally able to pull Mila from the water. Her feet collapsed beneath her, and she shook uncontrollably. We kneeled down beside her on the deck. Bertha leaned against the railing. "Hate these sharks," she muttered. "Hate these damn mutant sharks…"

Churchill, alone, stood in salute. "Old Jimmy's gone," he said mournfully. "Found his final resting place in a megalodon's snout."

To us, it might have been an old, rusty hook, but to poor Churchill Wingnut it had been something more. I got up and stood by his side, joining his salute—it was the sort of thing Charlie might do.

Mila broke the silence with a breathless laugh. She shook her head and looked at me. "I can't believe you swam into the mouth of one of those things."

I wanted to tell her that, at the time, I had thought she was going to kill me, so the megalodon was really just the lesser of two evils, but I figured it was best for everyone if I didn't mention that, so I just shrugged.

Dove poked his head out of the captain's cabin. "We're out of Federal waters now," he said. "Not that it matters much with the nets down." He turned, apparently noticing Mila for the first time. "Whoa... what happened to you?"

Mila stood, wincing as she stretched her shoulders. "You drove off without me, Dove."

"What?" He gave her a blank look. "But you're in the boat..."

"But she wasn't at the time, Doveboat," said Bertha, rolling her eyes.

He looked confused. "But she is now? So did she, like, teleport?"

"Oh, for Christ's sake—"

"Where's New Texas?" Mila interrupted. "And Kindred and Sparky?"

"Meeting us at the Caravan," said Phoenix. "Dove, did you put in the coordinates?"

"There's no GPS, boss. We're flying blind."

"Don't need any bloody GPS," said Churchill. He scuttled into the cabin and came out holding a bronze and wooden device. "This is what I use," he said. "Old-fashioned telegraph— Feds don't have anything like it. The Caravans have one on their end." He typed out a message and put on a headset. "We'll need to go three miles south to join it. Tell New Texas to meet us there."

"You already got their response?" I asked. "That was fast."

"Well," said Churchill, slightly embarrassed, "they haven't actually responded yet... I just feel it in my bones, lad. So that's where we'll head."

"Er—right, then." I nodded skeptically.

Dove, however, had no problem accepting Churchill's "bones" as a perfectly reasonable navigator. He moved to retreat to the captain's cabin before Churchill stopped him with a raised hand.

"I'll drive," the captain said. Then he looked around and saw Phoenix massaging Mila's shoulders, and Bertha nursing her own arm. "And don't worry, there's a medical bay on the Caravan," the captain reassured them.

I leaned on the ship's bow and watched as the ocean breathed fast and slow: a living entity in and of itself. In the span of a few short days, I'd traveled outside Federal waters twice, nearly died several times, lost my mother, my best friend, and my own innocence in the eyes of the state.

I vowed I'd find the last three again.

The Lost Boys had saved my life, over and over again—but why? What did they want from me? They'd lied to me: Mom couldn't be dead. She was innocent. Charlie, too, with her bright blue eyes and chopsticks. They had to be alive, of that I was sure. The Federation would keep them that way, if only to get to me.

*We steal Indigo. We're Indigo thieves.* Phoenix's words echoed in my mind, coupled with the cases of Indigo vaccines that had fallen from the sky. Mila had shrugged when I'd mentioned it. Thousands of kids wouldn't get their vaccines because of that loss, that failed theft. They could've been sold for millions. Somewhere, rich venture capitalists would pay for Indigo, for life itself.

But I knew the Lost Boys weren't thieves. In that arena, they'd proven themselves to be incompetent at best. And yet, by attacking Club 49, they'd created fear in the city of Newla. Fear was what they were after. Fear and terror.

It was strange to think how nice they'd been. Kindred, with her blueberries, didn't seem like the sort of person who'd strike fear in the hearts of millions. And they'd already saved my life twice. Why me? Me of all people?

It didn't make sense. None of it made any sense. The Pacific Northwestern Tube exploding overhead, the water rushing in, the nets being down, the megalodons swarming, the green glowing lanterns of the Federal guards racing toward the wreckage, Mila retreating toward the surface. None of it made sense.

*The nets being down.*

The nets had been down on the day of the attack on Tube. They'd been down today, too—just in time to unleash the megalodons on the swarm of Feds. That was just too convenient to be a coincidence. Did the Lost Boys have control of the megalodons?

Phoenix put a hand on my shoulder, and I jumped. "You okay?' he asked. I nodded. In my mind I could still see the soldiers' blood floating in the water. In a few years, that could've been me. Or Charlie.

"We'll arrive at the Caravan soon," Phoenix said, leaning against the railing next to me. "I know everything's happening really fast—probably faster than I could've handled at your age."

"Were both your parents dead when you were my age?" I asked. It was better if he thought I didn't know Mom was still alive. Otherwise he'd realize I was on to their game.

He gritted his teeth and stared out over the railing. "They died when I was twelve."

"I'm sorry to hear that. I didn't realize you'd been at H.E.A.L."

"I wasn't," he said, his face hard. "Never got on the train to go. My parents weren't euthanized. They were murdered."

*"Murdered?"*

He nodded. My chest tightened. I couldn't imagine my own parents being murdered—the very thought of it made me sick. Death was always present in the Federation—on the minds of children and adults alike. The Carcinogens in the air made sure of that. Our lives revolved around death. Murder, however, was rare.

"Yes," he said quickly, clearly wanting to change the subject. "And I didn't go to H.E.A.L. because I couldn't leave my city."

"Newla," I said. This was how he'd known it so well. He'd wandered the streets. Probably lived on them for a time. One of the kids who slept behind the trashcans—addicted to Neglex or worse. "You lived on the streets."

"No," he said with a small smile. "I *slept* on the streets. I *lived* between the pages of books. You ever read *Peter Pan*? How'd you think I came up with 'the Lost Boys'?"

It made sense—explained how he was so smart. I wondered if his parents had been booksellers, maybe professors. My own dad hadn't liked English so much. He used to say that when it came to novels, you only had to read the first ten pages and the last ten pages. He told me fiction was like an ice cream cone: if you looked at it too long, it'd melt. I guess there were a lot of things that melted if you looked at them too long.

I figured it didn't hurt to ask.

"What—what did your parents do? Before they—yeah."

"Farmers," said Phoenix.

"What? I thought you said you lived in Newla? Isn't the Ministry of Agriculture on Molokai, next to the Suburban Islands and not much else?"

A worried look flashed across his face.

"I—er—meant they were writers. They wrote books and stories. Liked English and literature."

"That's the whole story?" I asked. "They were writers and they were murdered?"

"In so many words, yes."

"And after that you had to live on the street? They didn't leave you anything?"

"They left me books," said Phoenix. "Books and a brown leather journal."

"And that's the truth?"

He raised a brow. "Truth?" he asked, and I nodded. "Why wouldn't it be the truth, Kai? Do you think there's something I'm not telling you?"

"I—er—dunno," I said. "Just seems like there's parts of the story missing. What was in the journal?" I thought back to the report I'd found in the Morier Mansion's library—the way Madam Revleon eyes had lingered on the copied pages. "I mean, did you read it?"

Phoenix nodded. "I read it."

"Then, what did it say?"

Phoenix's mouth smoothed to a flat line and his brows sank under the weight of my question. "Nothing of great importance."

I threw up my hands. "Secrets, then," I said. "It seems like everything's a secret, and they're chewing at me from the inside out."

Phoenix stared out at the ocean. "Secrets gnaw at the soul, piece by piece, but the truth devours you whole," he said quietly.

"So there are secrets?"

Phoenix smiled. "Just trust me, Kai. That's all I ask."

I thought about Mom and Charlie locked in Federal prisons somewhere. "Well, trust is a lot to ask," I said. "And it's awfully hard to give without the truth."

Bertha stomped her foot against the deck. "I see it!" she yelled.

We joined her at the ship's starboard side. In the distance, I made out a line of boats. There had to have been at least a hundred, all draped in shades of blue fabric. If Bertha hadn't pointed them out, I could've mistaken them for the crest of a breaking wave, or the space where water met the sky.

And then there was a flash of light, a mist rose from the ocean, the sky grew hazy—and the Caravan was gone. Mila's eyes locked with mine, and I realized she was just as frightened as I was. The others, however, stood unfazed.

"Nothing to be afraid of," said Phoenix, noticing our faces. "The Caravan's got spotters circling at all times. If they see a ship, they give a signal, and the fog pours out. There are plates underwater that heat the ocean into steam to make it rise into fog. If it weren't for them, the Feds would've gotten the Caravan a long time ago."

"Yeah," muttered Bertha, "and the nukes they've got don't hurt, either." Phoenix shot her a look.

Churchill Wingnut rolled out another square box resting on a table. He placed a black circle roughly the size of a plate on its surface. "Record player," he said when he caught my eye. "I'll bet none of you blokes have ever seen one of these babies before." He dropped the device's metal hand onto the surface of the black plate, and music erupted from a horn on its side. Trumpet solos roared, and guitars rang out in time. He danced a little jig. "Mariachi music," he explained. "It's the signal."

Bertha tapped her foot to the music. "The signal?" she asked. "It wasn't like that before."

Churchill nodded. "We have to switch things up every once in a while. Mariachi music's been the signal for the past two months. Before that was polka."

"Ah, yes," said Bertha, smiling. "I remember the polka."

We cruised forward in the calm water. The mist dissipated just as quickly as it had appeared. There were boats on either side of us now, and they formed a spiral canal of sorts. The Caravan was a town wrapped around itself like a coiled snake—a single train that, when bunched together, formed a spiral. From the inside, the boats didn't look like boats at all, but houses lined up along a canal. Bridges stretched across the tops of the homes, connecting the houses that lined the external border with the ones nestled in the center. The spaces between the boats were nearly nonexistent—they were pushed together like adjacent compartments on subway trains. Bright reds, yellows, and greens glowed on the fabrics that adorned the internal walls—colors that were a sharp contrast to the blues we'd seen before.

Churchill Wingnut spread his arms wide and threw his head back. "Welcome to the Caravan!" he said. He lifted the hand from the record player, and the music stopped. "The last free nation outside the whole bloody Federation!"

There was a piercing sound, high-pitched like a mosquito, but perhaps even shriller, and hands hurried out from wooden windows, yanking the colored fabrics down before closing the shutters with a slam. A low rumble emitted from the boat at the forefront of the Caravan—the locomotive of sorts, I guessed.

Churchill ran into the cabin muttering, "*What the hell?*" as mist swirled. The locomotive hummed loudly, and then hurtled forward. All around us, the Caravan's spiral city unfurled, and the wooden bridges that hung across the boats' roofs snapped.

Phoenix pursed his lips, and his face grew hard: something was wrong. This was clearly not the welcome he'd expected.

"The bloody boats think they're under attack!" Churchill yelled again.

"Listen," said Bertha, jabbing a finger in his chest. "I get that all the Caravites are—" Churchill dug a finger in his ear and pulled out a stack of yellow wax like honey. "...Strange," she continued. "A bit loony from saltwater fumes going to your brains, and all that. But there's no way those boats think that *this* little thing"—Churchill winced at his ship being called little—"pulling up into their harbor means they're under attack."

Dove grabbed Bertha's shoulders and turned her to face the expanse of ocean behind her. As the last few Caravite boats unfurled amid the rush of rising mist, a shadow, roughly the size of a football field, lurched toward them in the water.

Bertha snapped a hand to her face, and groped her waist for the one of the guns she'd lost in the ocean. Dove flew past her and hurried to take the helm of the ship from Churchill, who—like Bertha—stood in awe of the towering shadow.

We were on the run again.

# CHAPTER 20

*THE RETIRED LOBSTER* groaned as Dove yanked it full throttle. The ship's bow lifted and its engine sputtered, and we shot forward to join the ranks of the Caravan's last few boats.

Bertha eyed the Caravan. "One hell of a ship," she muttered sarcastically as the small craft groaned again. The dull buzz of its failing engine rang in our ears. "Next time, I'm signing up for The *Perky* Lobster."

I glanced back at Dove, who spun the ship's wheel with his familiar blank look. "Maybe something a bit bigger than a lobster next time," I said.

"Good point, Car Battery." She grumbled something about wanting to drive, then disappeared into the captain's cabin to push Dove away from the wheel.

Churchill sat huddled at the back of the deck. I joined him. "You okay, Wingnut?"

His teeth chattered from the breeze that rose from the ocean. He smiled weakly and gave me a thumbs-up. "Peachy." The wrinkles that caked his face quivered in the wind. I'd have guessed he was decades older than fifty, if such a thing were possible.

Mila stole a blanket from the cabin and wrapped it around his shoulders—her way of saying thanks. She owed the man her life. I guess we all did.

"Hey, Kai!" said Dove, tossing me a pair of binoculars. "You've probably got better eyes than me—younger and all that junk." I realized he probably had no real grasp of the concept of aging. He didn't know that a couple of years didn't really make a difference.

"Whaddya see back there?" he asked.

I pressed the binoculars to my face, but it was useless: the fog that sprayed from the Caravan left the ship that raced behind us in shadows. "Visibility's bad," I said finally. "Can't see a thing."

"Afraid that might've been the case." He turned to Phoenix. "Looks like we're running blind, eh, friend?"

A small smile stretched below Phoenix's hard gaze. "Wouldn't be the first time." He threw Dove a playful jab.

The two had known each other for a long time. They looked about the same age—maybe friends in another life, before they both became orphans. Before everything that happened to them, happened.

*The Retired Lobster* plowed forward, and Dove leaned against the metal railing. "Hey, Dove?" asked Phoenix. "If you're out here, who's driving the ship?"

Mariachi music blasted from the cabin, and the boat swerved in the water. A wave shot over the railing, and broke on the deck as Bertha's booming laughter erupted from the helm. Mila cursed under her breath and Churchill scrunched his face: Bertha had found the record player. A trumpet solo blared, and she danced behind the wheel.

Then a muted boom sounded off to the ship's side, and a plume of water shot skyward, twisting in time to the music— an explosion.

There were bombs in the water.

*The Retired Lobster* rocked in the rough waters. Crashing waves tore at the fog that hung around the surface. Through gaps, I saw men throw packages from Caravan boats into the water: mines. They had seen the shadow that had towered behind us and recognized it as a threat, and they were determined to stop it at any and all costs. They'd blow us up too, if they had to.

The mines continued to burst, and we drove right through them, desperately chasing the Caravan. Another patch of water went skyward. Waves even bigger than the last batch crashed onto the ship's deck. Water poured in, racing past the *Lobster's* wooden railings. The ship teetered back and forth.

There was another explosion. Another wave. More water. We were drowning in water, even aboard the ship. Still the mariachi music thundered on.

"Where's your lifeboat, Wingnut?" I shouted to Churchill. More waves rolled across the deck, and I could see the Caravan pulling farther ahead before it disappeared behind fog and explosions.

"DON'T HAVE A BLOODY LIFEBOAT!" he shouted. "JUST ME AND THE OPEN SEA!"

I grabbed a bucket and began bailing gallon after gallon of water off the ship. For every bucket I tossed, ten more splashed on. It was hopeless, but it was still better than doing nothing. Better to die busy, I figured, than to die bored. Another symphony of explosions sent six streams of water skyward. The ocean rocked, absorbing the force of the explosions as the streams fell downward, snapping like lightning as they struck the water.

A massive wave formed from the shocks erupting from the explosions. Ropes of surface tension yanked the water that covered the deck, pulling it toward a huge tidal wave that was gathering in the distance. *The Retired Lobster* dropped low as the massive wave pulled us into its trough. A frothing crest loomed overhead, and the boat quivered as its engine gave a final shout.

Bertha ran out onto the deck. "It's dead!" she announced.

"Thanks for clarifying," I said, and she rolled her eyes. "With engine performance like that," I added, "I'd have thought *you* built it."

"You better hope we die," she said, shaking a fist in my direction, "or else I'm gonna kill you."

"If you're half as bad at murder as you are buildings things, then I won't bother to worry."

Phoenix grabbed the deck's edge, and I did the same. *Brace yourself,* he mouthed, and I nodded as the wave's crest curled over us. For a brief moment, our ship hung, suspended, in a shimmering tunnel of blue. And then the wave crashed upon the ship, and light danced in the corners of my eyes. I felt my body yanked from the deck, crushed between salty tendrils. I tried to let myself go limp as the wave tossed and pounded me like a baker with a ball of dough. My neck snapped from side to side, and water forced its way into my nostrils to drown my lungs.

Then my back was slammed against something solid, and I felt sand in my palms. I moved my fingers, and felt a plastic bottle, and then an aluminum can. I pushed my feet down and I felt land, or something like it.

New Texas.

I hauled myself out of the water and onto the beach. I rubbed my eyes and saw Kindred waving to me in the distance. Then a hand slapped itself across my face, and my ears rang.

"Don't insult my inventions again," said Bertha in a husky voice.

I watched her outline as she hiked toward the fortress, then I turned and ran toward Kindred, who was now leaning over a limp body at the ocean's edge. As I got closer, I recognized the face: Churchill. A clump of seaweed covered his bald head.

Kindred raised a hand to her cheek. "Oh, dear," she whispered, "I think he might be—oh gosh, I really think he might be—"

"Dead?" I offered.

She nodded with pursed lips. Sand crunched behind us— Sparky was running across the beach, a wrapped syringe and a beaker full of black fluid in his hands.

"Hey, KB," he said, nodding in my direction before kneeling next to Churchill and filling the syringe with the black fluid.

Tim poked his hairy head over Sparky's shoulder and started reaching for the crumpled wrapper Sparky had torn from the sterile syringe.

I stared at the black liquid in the beaker. "What is that exactly?"

Sparky tore open Churchill's shirt and plunged the needle into his chest. "Cafetamines," he said. "A chemical cocktail of my own creation, consisting of caffeine and amphetamine salts." He stared at me for a second, and his left eye twitched dangerously. "I use them every day," he explained.

"Well, that can't be good for his heart."

"Nothing is bad for a dead man's heart, and I'd guess we could both agree that a bad heart is better than a dead heart."

Tim gained momentum in his quest for the crumpled wrapper, but then Sparky saw and snatched it away. Tim frowned—if such a thing were possible for a sloth. I'd never seen an odder couple.

Churchill shot upright, screaming. "JESUS CHRIST, MY CHEST!"

"He's seen Jesus!" said Kindred, clapping her hands. Tim yawned, and Kindred turned to me. "Tim's a Jewish sloth," she explained.

Churchill panted hard. "It feels like my heart's smashing against my bloody chest."

"Excellent," said Sparky, his eye still twitching slightly behind his glasses. "That's how it's supposed to feel."

Kindred patted Sparky's hand. "We're going to have to talk about this later, dear. You've got a problem. An addiction, I'm afraid."

Sparky narrowed his eyes. "And what would you call your obsession with blueberries, then?"

Surprise flashed across Kindred's face. "Well, I—er— they're very *healthy*, you know!"

Churchill propped himself on his elbows and scanned the horizon. "Where's my ship?"

Kindred bit her lip. *The Retired Lobster* had, well, retired.

"And the Caravan?" he asked.

"We—well, we lost sight of it... what with the tidal wave and the fog," she explained. "And then you guys washed ashore and—there was a lot of pressure, okay?"

A horn sounded offshore, and with it, the fog surrounding New Texas dissipated, revealing the Caravan, coiled around the island like a snake around its prey. Someone gave a signal, and the red and gold tapestries we'd seen earlier were spread out again. The blue must have been hanging on the opposite side, I thought: they hadn't surrounded us to attack us, but rather to hide us. We were now in a world apart. Away from the rest of the ocean. Away from the Federation. Alone.

A thin line of boats formed a bridge between the island and the surrounding ring of the Caravan. Phoenix walked to where the line met the shore, ready to meet the Caravan's leaders. His hair glowed gold in the scattered sunlight. You'd never have known he'd just had the crap beaten out of him by the tidal wave.

"Ah, the Caravites," said Kindred. "They've got their own little clans, they do. The vagabonds, the exiles, the thought-to-be-lost-at-sea-men, the Irish, the—"

"Founders," interrupted Churchill. He thumped a fist to his chest proudly.

"The English," said Kindred, rolling her eyes. "Few bolts missing in those ones, if you ask me."

Phoenix lifted his left hand to his head and rested his thumb along his jaw. His forefinger was pressed to the corner of his eye, and his middle finger pointed skyward. It was a strange salute, but I remembered the explosion in the Tube by Moku Lani when Mila had done the same thing on the screen. It was an obvious departure from the standard Federal salute. It was one they could call their own: the Lost Boys' salute.

Three men emerged from the first boat's cabin as its bow struck the beach. They walked single file at first, but, upon seeing Phoenix, the first two broke formation and stood shoulder to shoulder, protecting their beloved leader.

Phoenix muttered something, his hand still held to his head, and the guards returned the salute before parting. A man with a thick beard, a captain's hat, and two bushy brows like patches of wool stepped forward. The two guards dropped a ladder from the bow, and the three of them climbed down to the beach.

Churchill waved a hand. The guards, their leader, and Phoenix approached us, whispering among themselves. Whatever they were talking about, the bushy-browed man appeared to grow increasingly concerned. The guards pulled Churchill to his feet, and their leader offered me his hand.

Kindred motioned for me to take it.

"Uh... hi," I said at last.

"Name!" he barked. I almost fell backward—here was a man used to giving orders.

"Kai," I said, still startled. "Kai Bradbury. And you are?"

"Vern," he said with a nod of his hat.

"*Captain* Vern," Churchill corrected him, and he looked mildly irritated. "The great captain. A man who needs no introduction... except for this one."

"That'll do," said Vern, nodding. He was man of business, not civilities. The titles, the formalities, they were a nuisance to him. He gave Kindred and Sparky curt nods, which were returned with a curtsy and an excited headshake, respectively.

Tim stuck his tongue out and extended a claw, but Vern ignored him.

"Shall we board?" he asked, already turning and walking back toward the boats.

"Come on, Captain!" said Churchill, jogging beside him "Don't you care to stay a minute? Flex your feet on solid ground?"

"I prefer the wooden slats of a ship's cabin. Solid ground makes me feel woozy after all these years."

"Uh... well, of course, Captain... I feel the same way... with the woozy..." Churchill flexed his toes in the sand several times before boarding the ship. Phoenix and I followed.

The first boat's insides were bland at best. A black table and chairs rested in the room's center, and the windows were covered in thick, dark drapes. A single glass light fixture hung overhead. The room was clean but simple. A piece of curved glass served as its only décor.

Captain Vern offered us seats. "Come sit," he said. He turned to Phoenix. "Where are the others?"

There was a knock at the door, and a guard pulled it open. Mila and Dove climbed inside. The guards glanced at Vern and he nodded ever so slightly. They snapped cuffs around Mila's wrists.

Phoenix rose from his seat. "I thought you wouldn't do this," he said, staring at Vern.

Another guard ran toward me. I tried to dodge, but Vern grabbed me, and the guard snapped the cold metal cuffs around my wrists.

Vern smoothed his bushy brows. "You know the rules, Phoenix," he said coldly. "You know what must be done."

# CHAPTER 21

SAGE CLUTCHED THE corners of her ragged dress as she walked. It was midday, and she was supposed to be in the kitchen, but she'd planned to meet Charlie. So she'd snuck out without telling Cook.

The paneled wooden walls told Sage she was approaching the chancellor's chambers, and ahead, she heard his raised voice. The door must have been cracked open.

"...Don't put this on me. How the hell should I know how they got it? You're the one who let it get this far... We should've nuked the damn club when we had the chance."

Sage stood outside the door and heard Miranda's voice echoing in the chamber within. "You really are dim, aren't you, Hackner? I hope the next chancellor has at least a quarter of a brain stem. It'd certainly be an improvement."

"You can insult me all day, Miranda, but it won't solve anything."

"Why don't you just drink? Or have you not got that charley horse anymore? Such a pity about the cramps, really..."

"Damn it, Miranda! I shouldn't have to wait so long for my antidote."

"Not my fault the girl screwed up. At least we know the poison's working, right? I find it reassuring, anyway. And if you talk to me in that way again, I'll have your throat slit. Or perhaps make you wait a *week* for the next antidote rather than a day... We'll see what you think of your little charley horse then. I've got a meeting for you with the chairman scheduled at two-thirty. He's traveling in from Oahu."

"The chairman? Of what board?"

"My dear Hackner, he's traveling in from Oahu—it's the chairman of the Indigo Reserve Board."

"Right, then... Howey? The one with the—the water-works?"

She laughed. "He's always been a bit soft, hasn't he?"

"Like melted chocolate." Sage could almost hear the smile on his lips. "What exactly are we discussing again?"

"The supply of Indigo. There's simply not enough any-more. Not with all the attacks. We've got to raise the age—increase the lottery pool's size."

Hackner snorted. "You want more dead kids? That's what this is about, isn't it?"

"Not at all. It's about the Lost Boys and the Caravan. The buzzards are circling us like we're a carcass."

"And you wouldn't nuke the nightclub."

"If I wanted to throw this nation into chaos, I'd let the buzzards do it."

"Then what would you have me do?"

"Meet with Chairman Howey. Tell him to raise the vaccina-tion age to sixteen. Have him make an announcement to the public that the vaccine supply is simply too low to keep the eligibility age at fifteen."

"And how exactly will that stop the Lost Boys?"

"Because," said Miranda slowly, "the people won't just see them as thieves who steal Indigo anymore. They'll see them as thieves who steal *children's lives*. The children who die as a result of going another year without a vaccination and having further exposure to the Carcinogens. And when more children die, the people themselves will take care of the Lost Boys... We'll just sit back and watch the chaos unfold." She paused. "The meeting's at two-thirty, Hackner—that's in ten minutes. Don't keep Chairman Howey waiting. Lord knows he'll start crying."

Sage heard Hackner grabbing his things, and she hurried on down the hall.

"Hey!" he shouted behind her, and she knew his face would be full of contempt. She could feel his rage pulsating toward her like a heartbeat—after all, she was the reason his antidote had been delayed. "What are you doing around here?"

Without stopping, Sage turned her head and put her fingers just below her right eye, giving him the Federal salute, then deliberately walked right into the wall ahead of her. "I'm so, uh, sorry, sir," she said, trying to sound out of breath. "It's just—well, sometimes these halls get confusing, what with not being able to see—"

She stepped back, turned, and then strode forward, slamming into a different wall, even harder this time. Hackner burst into a fit of laughter. His footsteps trailed off down the hall, wandering off to his meeting, still chuckling. He always fell for her poor little blind girl schtick.

Sage hurried toward the prison. By now, she'd be late for her meeting with Charlie. Not that the prisoner had anything else going on, or even a watch to measure time with for that matter, but to Sage it was the principle that mattered.

On the way into the prison, she grabbed a bundle of rope from the supply closet. As she entered the cell area, Eddie, the two o'clock guard, sighed. His voice cracked as he spoke—too many cigarettes. "That time again?" She nodded, knowing he was looking at her rope. "Shame," he said. "This one's real purty."

He handed her the keys. The retina scanner beeped green as Sage whispered her name, and then she raced down the hall to cell sixteen and pulled open the door. "Sorry I'm late," she whispered.

"You shouldn't have told me," said Charlie, laughing. "It's not like I've got the time in here."

Sage dropped the bundle of rope onto the floor. She heard Charlie kick it under the bed. "I've been thinking..." Sage began.

"That's good," Charlie said, nodding. "Thinking's always good."

"I think we should leave the day after tomorrow—two days' time."

"What?" Charlie grabbed her arm. "You're sure, Sage?"

Sage nodded. Her hands were still sore from where she'd held the white rope. She'd never seen it, but she knew it was white—the prisoners had told her. "Positive. Things aren't great around here. I overheard the chancellor say he was raising the vaccination age."

"That—that's not possible. The people wouldn't allow it."

"Too many attacks by the Lost Boys, he said. They're hurting the supply, and making shortages worse. "

"Where do they even get Indigo, anyway?"

"The Ministry of Research & Development." Her glazed eyes stared straight ahead: she didn't like to talk about the Ministry of R&D, but she'd talk about it with Charlie. "Headquartered in Kauai," she continued. "They manufacture it in the labs there. It's a long process—very labor-intensive, and there's not much yield from what I've heard. Plus, demand's always too high."

"You lived there," said Charlie. She must have heard the certainty in Sage's voice. "In Kauai? That's where you grew up, isn't it?"

Sage nodded. It was so long ago.

"That's where I grew up, too."

"But the guards said you were from Moku Lani."

"The Feds moved me to H.E.A.L. after my parents passed. That's where I met Kai. He used to visit the kids there with his mom, Mrs. B. They'd bring in gifts for kids on their birthdays. His mom loved birthdays. Mine was only a week after I first got there."

"Who's Kai?"

168

"No one," Charlie said quickly. "Just this—friend. Well... I mean... you know?" She sucked in a breath. "He's just a really good friend."

Sage leaned against the bed. "Do you think he'd be my friend, too?"

"Of course," Charlie said, laughing. "Kai would be lucky to have you as a friend. You'd both be lucky. He's a great friend."

Sage sat on the bed, and felt the rope brush against her ankles. "I've been thinking about how to escape," she said. "And I've realized, there really is only one way to get out."

"With the rope?"

Sage nodded. "Around your neck."

Charlie swallowed hard. "I was afraid of that."

"But we can fake it," Sage said, grasping Charlie's hands. "We can make them *think* you're dead. I could carry you down the hall in a body bag, and then, once we're out of sight, we can run away. They won't figure out we're missing until it's too late. I can get us out of the Light House, and then you can get us the rest of the way. Back to home."

"In Kauai?" asked Charlie.

"There's still rainforest left there," said Sage, nodding. "They'd never find us."

"You really think it would work?"

"Of course it will." She hoped Charlie wouldn't hear the uncertainty in her voice.

Deep down, she wasn't sure at all. But now, since they'd made her bring the rope to the cell, she knew it was the only option. Things were about to get much worse for Charlie. Starvation was nothing. The things that were in store for her now...

Sage had brought the rope to cell fourteen last week. Sometimes the screams echoed into the hallway late into the night. Minister Zane visited that prisoner twice a day now. Sage was allowed to bring food to a cell again whenever that happened—when they moved on to real torture. Because at that point, they wanted to make sure the prisoner stayed alive. Or at least, that they could only die by choice.

"I'll try to stop back again before two days' time," Sage said, standing. "I can't be in here much longer, or Cook will come looking for me."

"Wait," said Charlie. "Are you sure you have to go?"

Sage nodded, but an unfamiliar feeling burned in her chest. It was a new experience—the thought that someone *wanted* her there. "One of the guards will be by tomorrow," she said. "He'll tie the rope above your bed."

Sage felt Charlie wrap her arms around her, and her heart lifted from her chest. She felt joy. It was strange after so much despair. When she left, she turned the key in the lock, then practically skipped to the end of the hall.

It was a good day. They'd all been good days since she'd met Charlie.

But her joy betrayed her, and Sage, usually so cautious, didn't notice the man standing in the hall—the man who'd been standing outside Charlie's cell door. Sage hadn't heard the heavy breathing of a man still fuming; a man who'd heard their entire plan.

# CHAPTER 22

I BIT DOWN hard on the regulator and sucked in another breath of cold, compressed air. *Scuba diving*, they'd called it as we'd been suited up with the gear. In the old days, people wore all this stuff to breathe underwater—the only way they had of exploring the ocean depths.

Now the Caravan used it as a test of strength and mental resilience—a test everyone had to pass before they were allowed aboard. Over the years, the Caravan had seen many castaways, and they couldn't take them all. So they only took in those people who could contribute to the movement—whatever "the movement" was, exactly. The test we were about to undergo would determine our ability to contribute. If we didn't pass, we died. It was that simple.

*Rule number one of scuba diving*, the man who'd helped us suit up said, *is don't hold your breath*. That was a hard rule for me to follow. After all, we were only going down eighty feet. I'd dived this deep many times before on a single breath from the cliffs of Moku Lani. *That's how most of them die*, he'd explained. *The compressed air expands in your lungs as you surface. Forget to exhale and—pop! You've lost a lung. And there's no room on the Caravan for people with only one lung. The Medical Bay's pressed enough as it is.*

The metal cage they lowered us down in was even more surprising. The cage was for our protection, they'd told us. In the past, sharks had attacked too many men during the test. Of course, the cage wouldn't do a thing against the megalodons. So if you cut your finger on the way down... well, the Caravan cut you loose and left. It couldn't afford to be caught near a feeding frenzy.

The crank groaned as we descended farther into the water. I sucked in a breath from the regulator, watching as bubbles burst from its sides when I exhaled. It seemed like a horribly inefficient way to breathe underwater. The ReBreathers we now used seemed so much more advanced.

Mila grabbed my hand. I flashed her an OK sign, and she nodded and did the same. I was glad for her company—it had been her first time on the Caravan too, and at Phoenix's suggestion, they'd allowed us to do the test together.

The Caravan's fog plates rested eighty feet below the surface, and—having been crafted from stainless steel, among other things—were constantly in need of a good polish. Without it, they'd never last forever. I couldn't imagine doing the polishing alone; it would be hard even with two people.

In Federal waters, the whole process wouldn't have been a big issue. People could dive down in the open and polish the plates without much thought. But outside Federal waters... well, things were different. The slightest cut or the smallest scratch could cost someone their life. Any hint of blood, and the megalodons would be upon you—and when that happened, you were dead. One of the Caravites had even advised against peeing in the water. Too close to blood, I guessed.

The Caravan had used the plates heavily, and they were in dire need of a good polish. The Caravites couldn't afford to let them rust. They were frankly lucky we had arrived as firsttimers; otherwise, they would have had to risk the lives of their own men rather than "test" some strangers.

We had until our oxygen ran out to complete the polishing. If we failed to finish the set of plates by then, we would be deemed unfit to join the Caravan. Each new Caravite was a new mouth to feed, and they could only afford so many crazy fishermen like Churchill. Those who were deemed unfit were left, abandoned, floating in open water. A death sentence, in their minds. If you couldn't pull your weight below the water, the Caravites doubted you could above.

The crank's groans stopped when we reached depth, and I studied the black abyss sprawled out beneath us. There was light at our depth, but only just. The Caravites had given us flashlights and brushes to scrub the plates, and that was it. I could've used a goody bag, with maybe some pretzels as a snack.

I switched on my light, and it shined beyond the cage, bouncing off the plates' shimmering metal and reflecting back at me. Mila nodded, and I pushed the cage's gate open and kicked hard. Salt water seeped into my eyes through the corners of my goggles. I gestured for Mila to join me outside the cage, but she just shook her head, pointing behind me.

A megalodon floated next to the plate, having swum up when my back was turned. Its beady eyes ogled the plate and the glow that shined off it as a result of my flashlight. The monster didn't appear to notice me; it seemed transfixed by the allure of the mysterious sheet of metal. I kept my hand still, and my flashlight poised in the plate's direction, but my body sank in the water as I fought to maintain buoyancy. The light flicked away for a split second, and the megalodon gnashed its massive teeth, its beady black eyes still greedily gulping in the light. It apparently hadn't noticed the flicker.

My lungs demanded oxygen, so I breathed deeply and rose in the water. The light began to move from the plate yet again. The megalodon's black eyes turned to the light source and me as I rose. I froze, reminding myself not to move—movement meant certain death.

I floated higher in the water, bending only my wrist to keep the light focused on the plates. I rose higher, then let out a breath to sink farther down. The regulator bubbled as pockets of air shot out from the sides. The megalodon swam forward, away from the plates, and toward the bubbles that now floated upward, its eyes still focused on the light.

Clanking metal echoed in the water, drawing the megalodon's attention. Mila had crawled out of the cage, pulled off her oxygen tank, and banged it against the metal bars. She pushed herself from the cage, leaving her oxygen tank bubbling on its metal bars. The monster raced toward the source of the sound and bubbles, its jaws wide. It chomped down on the cage, which collapsed beneath its bite's crushing force. The air tank slipped loose and plummeted into the abyss below, and the megalodon hurried after it. For all its strength, it lacked intelligence. Evolution had offered it pure bloodlust instead.

With the megalodon gone, Mila reached for my regulator. I passed her the mouthpiece, and she sucked in breath after breath. We hovered there in the water, hands wrapped around one other, when I felt the brush strapped around her waist.

Brush. Polish. We were running out of time—we had to polish. The megalodon wasn't the only monster that hung like death in the water: the Caravites and Captain Vern were floating overhead.

We rested our hands on the rusty plate next to us. It was three feet in diameter—a perfect circle—and there were two others nearby. We needed them all polished by the end of the hour.

The groan of the crank buzzed in the water as the shattered cage was lifted to the surface. The Caravites and the Lost Boys would soon learn we'd been attacked.

Mila and I took turns passing the regulator and the brush back and forth. While one breathed, the other scrubbed. Soon the rust was gone, and the plate sparkled even brighter in the beam of our flashlights, nearly as mesmerizing to us as it was to the megalodon.

We moved on to the next plate, scrubbing furiously to rid it of the caked-on rust. Before long, it, too, shined under the glint of our flashlights. By now, water had crept in through the corners of my wetsuit and the wrinkles of my goggles, and my teeth were chattering. Luckily, the last plate's rust came off quicker than the rest.

I pointed to the surface above: it was time to go. The plates were clean, and we were almost out of time.

But before we could rise, a shadow sprang up from the abyss. The megalodon. Having been fooled by the oxygen tank—perhaps having eaten it by now, for all I knew—the livid monster was now in search of heartier prey. Its beady black eyes wandered again to the shining plate. Freed from its coat of rust, this plate was now far brighter than the last one the beast had seen. The monster put the glowing plate tentatively between two massive teeth and bit down.

My hand trembled, and I struggled to keep the light's beam still. I'd seen more megalodons in my lifetime than most, but their broad faces still terrified me. Mila cautiously stretched a hand toward the regulator; she was out of oxygen. Unfortunately I'd wrapped its cord around the wrist of the hand that was holding the flashlight. Freeing the regulator would mean moving the light—and that meant certain death.

But she needed air, and she needed it fast. She pointed to her throat, and looked toward the surface. I shook my head—it was too far, too great a risk. The megalodon would see her move through the water, and she'd be dead in less than a minute. And if Mila died, there'd be blood in the water, and the rest of us—including, perhaps, those up above—were dead too.

I wondered what Charlie would do in this situation. The kind of girl who looked at a snail and saw a soul.

Mila looked up again, stretched her arms high in the water, and crawled toward the surface with her legs trailing limply behind—she was afraid to kick and move the water, I figured. Afraid of death. A trail of her own bubbles followed her to the surface.

I held my hand steady—I couldn't move the light. It had to be still; I was too close to the megalodon. And I couldn't breath, either; it would hear my bubbles. Above me, Mila blurred from my view, and I imagined her face breaking the surface, her arms beating against the waves as she swam toward the boat.

*Well, one survived,* Vern would say to Phoenix. Then he would turn to Mila. *I should hope no spots were missed—for your sake.*

The megalodon still hovered near the plate, chewing its edge, strangely mesmerized by its brilliance. My chest felt tight: I had to exhale. I let out a quick, short spurt, and bubbles trickled from the regulator's corners.

The megalodon's snout jerked up toward me. I flicked my wrist, and hit its beady eyes with the light. It gnashed its teeth in response and raced toward the surface, following the bubbles, the force of its flicking tail swirling the water around me.

Suddenly the polished plate glowed red, then rocketed upward, slamming into the monster's stomach, burning its skin while lifting it right out of the water. I kicked hard to the surface, screaming, as bubbles shot from my lungs like bullets. The megalodon flailed at the surface above me, the plate continuing to burn its stomach.

My head broke the surface just in time for me to see a burst of light smash into the monster's snout. Its suddenly limp body rolled off the plate and floated, motionless. I glanced up and saw Bertha standing at the ship's edge cradling the Paralyzer. Mila was in the water beneath her, swimming toward safety.

Fog triggered by the plate's launch gathered as I swam after Mila, grabbed a ladder and climbed aboard. Kindred greeted me with a towel. Mila was huddled on the deck, shaking, her hand wrapped in a white bandage. I found out later that she'd cut it along the edge of her suit. It was her blood, not the flick of my wrist and my bubbles, that had drawn the megalodon to the surface.

Kindred rubbed the length of my arms. "You're shaking, dear."

"Th-the plates," I said, fighting to catch my breath. "Th-they were under th-the water, but then—then they floated up. T-to th-the top."

"There's a switch," said Phoenix, glaring at Vern. "That brings them up."

"And turns them right on," Vern said sharply. "Try polishing the damn things while they're up, and they'll burn your hand right off—it's no use."

"Better burned off than bitten off," Phoenix said. "Wouldn't you agree, Captain?"

"I wouldn't be too worried about a bite. The monster would've swallowed them whole."

"Come now, Captain." Phoenix rubbed his hands along Mila's arms to warm her. "I think we both know that some monsters like to play with their food before they eat it."

"You'd know more about that than I would, wouldn't you, old chap?" Vern smiled slightly. "How's Bugsy, by the way?"

Phoenix's jaw tightened. "He's dead."

"You're—you're sick!" spat Mila as she coughed and rattled water from her wet lungs. Her lips were blue now, like Indigo.

Vern adjusted his cap. "You just remember whose boat you're on, honey. Remember who runs this ship."

"And you remember who's stealing you all your s-stupid Indigo," Mila shot back.

Kindred moved between the two. "I've made us all muffins! Cinnamon apple walnut with an almond drizzle, mmm! Doesn't that sound delightful?"

Mila shook her head. "We don't have walnuts on New Texas."

"We don't on New Texas," said Kindred. "But the Caravites do. Intercepted a shipment of them from the Federation last week. Wonderful, huh, dear?"

Mila moved into the cabin. "Yeah, it's something all right," she muttered.

Kindred and Phoenix followed her, and I alone was left on the deck with Vern and his men. He looked me up and down before offering his hand. "Welcome aboard, son." I shook his hand hard. "It's a pleasure to have you with us. You'll enjoy your time here, I trust."

"Thank you, sir," I said with only slight hesitation. "I—I'm sure I will."

But I was anything but sure. The way he'd looked me up and down... it was like he was sizing up a threat, an enemy. He'd let me aboard, sure—he sort of had to—but I wasn't on his team. I would never be on his team.

Whose team *was* I on?

I thought of Charlie's chopsticks and the balloons Mom brought to the kids at H.E.A.L. when we visited on their birthdays. *They* were my team. *They* were the ones I was fighting for.

But how would I find them? And would they be alive when I did?

# CHAPTER 23

THE CARAVAN BOATS were wider than Churchill's, with long walkways lined with smaller rooms along the sides. The boats were grouped by function—one cluster served as a kitchen, another made garments, the last five made the medical bay, and the list went on and on. Each boat featured a small spiral staircase leading to the lofts above, which contained the minuscule Caravite homes.

"Not a bad climb," said Sparky as we rounded a staircase. "Hardly tiring at all. I'm barely perspiring." Tim was asleep along the crook of his back, his head resting on Sparky's shoulder. We paused at a landing.

"One more flight," said the woman in front, a Caravite who'd introduced herself as Sadie. Her brown hair was piled in a messy brown stack, and she wore a white ruffled shirt that hung around her shoulders. A black vest was cinched around her waist. She'd told us that her ancestors had been among the Caravan founders nearly three generations before—fishermen out at sea when the bombs were dropped on the rest of the world. Bertha muttered something about them actually being pirates, but Sadie ignored her.

Sadie pulled open a door that led to a roof garden and we stepped out into a sea of flowers, all shades of blue, circling a series of glass panels that gazed at the sun.

"Solar panels," Sadie explained. "It's how we power the Caravan. All the boats have them up top."

I glanced at the mass of clouds that always hung over the Federation. Onshore, I guessed it was raining. "There's hardly any light."

"I think you'll find we make do with the little light we're given. And with the hope that someday there'll be more sun."

I leaned against a patch of flowers. Each blue petal was painted with a single yellow stripe—irises. Mom had showed me pictures of flowers like these once, but they were too expensive to buy in Moku Lani. It was strange seeing so many growing at once.

As Sparky and I left the roof and wandered along a hall with glass windows that displayed rows of pastries—the bakery, I figured—a part of me wondered if he was mad at me for shooting him with the Darts. I knew *I* would be.

"Have you been here before?" I asked, hoping to break the silence.

Sparky nodded vigorously. He seemed to do everything vigorously. Kindred had said the Cafetamines kept him awake at all hours of the day and night. "Twice before," he said, his lips quivering as he spoke. "Once when I first met Phoenix, and once a few months ago."

"And did they make you polish?"

"Affirmative. Though they weren't entirely successful."

"What do you mean?"

He grinned. "I shorted the Caravan's power supply. The plates drifted up like ice cubes in a glass of water. Nearly wrecked their whole IT system. Vern had to let me aboard to fix it."

"So no megalodons?"

"Oh, there were megalodons," he said, chuckling. "There always seems to be megalodons when people polish." He jumped from one boat to another, and I followed. "Why do you think I shorted the power? Had to get out of the water somehow—I'm certainly not equipped to handle one of those monsters. I can hardly brush my hair." His bundle of curly hair rested atop his head like a tumbleweed.

Sparky was smart. Strange, but smart. Like the other Lost Boys.

We crossed one boat that Sparky said was the Caravan's bazaar: a marketplace where people bought and sold goods seized from Federal ships. The ceiling was higher here, and vaulted—the boat had no loft. The spiral staircase here went straight to the rooftop garden. As we pushed through a crowd of buyers and sellers, people lowered their heads whenever I met their gaze.

They were afraid of me. But why?

We emerged at the bazaar's other end, and found the next boat to be quieter. Seamstresses sat at windows with needle and thread, but they, too, dropped their heads as we passed. I wondered now why Sadie of all people had shown us kindness.

"Why do they look down?" I asked.

Sparky frowned as his body tensed. "What—what makes you say that? What makes you think they drop their heads?" I pointed to the seamstresses, and he sighed. "I suppose you've noticed things aren't great between Phoenix and the captain."

"Sort of hard to miss."

Sparky pointed to a clear spot at the edge of the next boat, and we sat, kicking our feet out over the open water. "I suppose they see different futures," Sparky said. "Not that one is right or one is wrong—they just want two different worlds."

"What's wrong with the world we have now?"

"Well," he said, chuckling. It was hard to believe he was about my own age—not sleeping must have aged him. "That's a whole 'nother discussion. One I'm sure you'll have with Phoenix, or maybe Mila, in time. Not my cup of tea. Not even my *type* of tea. Not my anything at all."

I liked Sparky. He didn't give me smoke and mirrors like the rest of them. He probably didn't get enough sleep to *have* smoke or mirrors. "So what kind of world do they want? One with more ministries? Less ministries? Flying cars, maybe?

"They tried those a hundred years back," he said, "and they were a disaster. If you thought a pileup on the Tube was bad, you should see one in a skyscraper. All it took was one person to go a bit slow on the brakes and you had the whole airway piled up halfway through Montesano Tower."

"Then what kind of world do they want?"

Sparky stared at the floating island of New Texas in the water behind us. "Phoenix wants a revolution. He wants to start over. He wants the Federation to fall."

I was right—the Lost Boys *weren't* just stealing Indigo. It wasn't about the Indigo at all—it was about war. A war Phoenix was determined to start.

"And Captain Vern?" I asked.

"Vern wants to run. He doesn't know where, and he doesn't know how far from Federal waters they could even make it. They can only grow so much food, and the rest of the rations they have to steal from Federal ships or fish from Federal waters. You know what would happen if they fished outside Federal waters…"

I nodded. The gnashing teeth of hungry megalodons were unforgettable.

"But he knows they have to do something. They've gotten too big, stolen too much. They're no longer just a freckle on Chancellor Hackner's face, but a mole. And moles turn into cancer."

"What about Bugsy?" I asked. "What was Vern getting at with Bugsy?"

Sparky leaned his head into his hand as Tim yawned, crawled over his shoulder, and seated himself on his lap. "Bugsy joined us three months ago. He was a year younger than you. He wore this pair of brown glasses all the time— called them his spectacles, thought they made him seem more distinguished. And he was always waking up early to watch the sunrise, before going back to sleep. His parents died in a car crash—the Feds told him it was suicide, but he knew better.

He met Mila on one of her raids a couple months after their death. He'd been living with an aunt on one of the Suburban Islands, but he'd begged Mila to take him. Said he had to get away from it all."

People passed on the platform behind us, jumping from boat to boat as they headed to their own lofts for the night. Sadie had told us that the Caravites went to bed earlier than most in the Federation; she said they didn't want to have to waste the energy on lights after dark. Better to rise and fall with the sun instead.

Sparky stood. "It's getting late."

"Did Bugsy ever come on the Caravan?"

Sparky nodded. "Affirmative."

"And did he have to polish the plates?"

"The first and only time he came, he did. Polished them all by himself, and Captain Vern had a fit. He didn't want Phoenix taking in any more kids. He thought the Lost Boys were big enough." Sparky glanced in both directions and then whispered. "I think he figured if we got too big, Phoenix would start the war himself. Vern liked us at the size we were."

"And then I came along," I finished.

"Affirmative. You came along, KB. Like clockwork, Bugsy was out and you were in."

"Tick, tock," I said, smiling weakly, but feeling sick to my stomach.

We headed back toward the pastry shops—we'd been set up in bunks above them. I was surprised to see Sparky heading for his loft.

"I thought you didn't sleep? Not with all your Cafeta-mines…"

He shrugged. "Yeah, but sometimes it's nice to close my eyes and lie down. Gives the mind a minute to slow down."

There wasn't room for us all to bunk together. At least that's what they told us. I guessed Vern just didn't want us congregating—probably saw it as scheming in his very midst. So they put us in separate boat lofts, in separate bunks, two by two. Sparky was with Dove, Kindred was with Mila, and I got stuck with Bertha.

She slept with a red mask plastered across her eyes, and her snoring was so loud that, at some points, I could have sworn she'd swallowed a chainsaw.

I wrapped a pillow around my ears, which dulled the snoring to a quiet roar, but it remained a roar nonetheless. At last I gave up on the possibility of sleep, and crawled from my bed and down the stairs.

The cabin's sole light was cast by a waxing moon's white tendrils, peeking out from behind a curtain of black clouds. The boat's wooden floors creaked as I stepped, but the sound was lost beneath the thunder of Bertha's snores.

I hopped from boat to boat—it was lucky the Caravites left their doors unlocked—jumping through the bakery and then the bazaar. Farther ahead, I saw a stout cylinder standing like a tower—the Captain's quarters, I guessed, and the Caravan's locomotive engine of sorts. I wondered if that was where Phoenix slept. It made sense when I thought about it. There, Vern could keep a closer eye on him.

I continued to leap from boat to boat, and as I moved up the line, the rooms grew stranger, the halls wider, the ceilings higher. Wood paneling now ran along the walls. As on the rear boats, the halls here were lined with doors, but these boats lacked windows: there were no pastries or garments on display.

I stopped to examine a door dressed with a beautiful velvet tapestry. *Veritas vos liberabit*, it declared in gold. I ran my fingers along its letters, and the velvet fabric felt soft beneath my fingers like peach fuzz.

I opened the door, and wandered into a library lined with mahogany shelves too similar to Madam Revleon's to be a coincidence. Now that I thought about it, the tapestry, too, had seemed familiar—a twin. A lone chair had been pulled from an old desk's grip, and a narrow slit in the wall—it could hardly be called a window—let in the soft glow of moonlight. My eyes flashed to books sprawled across the desk on their spines. It was beginning to feel like an unattended library was a prerequisite for plotting conspiracies. I grabbed a book from the desk and held it in the thin beam of moonlight.

The cover read: *"The Megalodon: a Magnificent, Marvelous, Malevolent Mutation of the Great White"* by *Bill & Mary Bradbury.* Dad's name had been crossed out with black ink, and Mom's had been circled in red.

My heart grew tight in my chest, and I leaned against the desk, my head woozy. They'd done something to Mom. They'd circled her name.

Where was I? Who were the Caravites? And what had they done to Mom?

She could be on the boat, I told myself. She could be staying here, on this very boat. The Feds had Charlie—that much I knew for sure—but the Caravites could have Mom. They could've gotten to her before the Feds did. That could explain why Phoenix was so eager to have me think her dead: he didn't want me to find her.

I returned to the hallway, and began opening other doors. Behind one I found a room filled with filing cabinets, behind another I found a public restroom. I opened door after door, and they fluttered on their frames like the heart that beat in my chest.

Then I saw a soft white light, eerily similar to the Daisies in Club 49, slipping from behind a door at the hall's end. Entering the room, I saw a lone bulb lighting stacks of square packages. I grabbed a package, gently peeled back its wrapper, and found a plastic bubble filled with fluid. I held it up to the bulb; inside the bubble was a small, thin, curved piece of plastic with a blue iris printed on it.

I covered my mouth to stop the screams that swelled in my throat. What *was* this? Who *were* these people? What were they trying to do?

The floors creaked—someone was in the hall. I slid shut the door and pressed an ear against it. It looked ornate, but its wood was thin, built light to lessen the weight of a fast ship.

"I'm not going to argue with you," said a voice I recognized as Vern's. "There's certainly no denying there's a chance—but that's all it is, a chance and nothing more."

"It's not a *chance*," Phoenix's voice echoed back, "it's a window—"

"Well, we've got plenty of those around here, if that's what you're looking for."

"—of *opportunity*," Phoenix finished.

"I think I'm looking for more of a door, really."

"Could you just *listen* to me for a second, Vern?"

"I'm listening, and I've been listening all night, damn it! I've heard about your plan. I know all about the virus. But you know what? I still don't think it's going to work. It's already over, Phoenix. Trust me when I tell you that. There was never going to be a war. That's a good thing: war fractures the soul."

"There are some causes worth fighting for—until we are beautifully broken."

"You're a fool."

"Just one more raid, Vern. Just give me—give *us*, the Lost Boys—another chance. That's all I'm asking. Just help with one more, and then that's it. I'm out of your hair forever, gone. All it takes is help with one more raid. That's all."

"That's *all?*" Vern sneered. "Help with one more raid, and *that's all?* You and I both know that won't be enough."

"You don't think we can do it?"

"Oh, I think you can do it, all right. You'll do it and get one of yourselves killed. Like you did with Bugsy."

"Damn it, Vern. I told you to quit bringing him up. You know we all cared about the kid. We just weren't ready. They knew we were coming."

"And they won't know this time?"

"It won't matter if they know this time. I'll be on the ground. This time they won't have a chance."

"You've got a lot of confidence in yourself."

"I could say the same thing about you."

"And the new boy? Dr. Bradbury's son? A *great* addition. Far smarter than Bugsy... or is he? Do you plan to bring him with you?" He paused. I guessed Phoenix nodded. "Then you're a fool. Look what happened to Bugsy, and he had three months to prepare—"

"Bugsy wasn't right. You and I both know that. Something was wrong with his head... he just wasn't right."

"And this kid is?"

"He jumped into the mouth of a megalodon."

"So he's crazy, too? Or just a fool? God, you really know how to pick 'em, Phoenix."

"You know who his mother is. The kid's not stupid."

"Well, you're operating under the assumption he's anything like her, and I don't operate under assumptions. I operate under facts. Dr. Bradbury's research is what could save our cause, not another raid."

"But the raid won't hurt. So you'll help us then?"

"On one condition."

"Of course there's one condition."

"Kill the boy."

My stomach did somersaults in my chest. It was getting harder to breathe. I could've used a Cotton Candy Cocktail.

"I—I can't do that."

"You can," said Vern, "and you will. You've done it before, haven't you?"

"I don't know what you're talking about."

"Ah, but I'm afraid you do, my friend. We both know you had a feeling that day on the Tube. There was a reason you stayed back, wasn't there? Let Bugsy and Mila go ahead without you. You didn't want to get caught in the crossfire, isn't that right?"

Phoenix was silent.

"But," Vern continued, "you had to get the shipment of Indigo, didn't you, Phoenix? So you let Bugsy go in your place—even though you knew he wasn't ready. That he'd probably die. But hey, no sweat off your back, if it saves the shipment. I know you too well, boy. You'll kill for this cause, and not just the Feds. What's another boy's life to you? If the

Feds get him, he's dead anyway. If he dies for you, at least it'll spare him the torture."

Phoenix was still silent.

"We don't know where his loyalty lies," Vern said finally. "We don't have the resources for another mouth to feed."

Phoenix wouldn't do it, would he? He'd already saved my life twice. Why go through the trouble, if he was going to kill me in the end? There had to be a reason he was keeping me alive. He couldn't just kill me now. He'd told me about his family—no, there was no way he'd do it now. He might even think we were friends.

After a long pause, Phoenix sucked in a breath. "I'll do it," he said. "If you help us with the raid, then I'll kill Kai when we're done. I promise you he'll be dead by the end of the mission."

# CHAPTER 24

I LAY AWAKE for hours while Phoenix's words rang in my ears. He was going to kill me. There'd be no finding Mom, no saving Charlie, not if Phoenix had his way...

There was a deafening bang, and the sharp crack of shattering glass pulled Bertha from her sleep. "Get up, Car Battery!" she shouted, slapping a pillow across my face. "Jesus, get out of bed! We've gotta get off this boat and back to New Texas!'

Another bang sounded, and flames flickered on the spiral staircase from the roof above. It sounded like bombs were being dropped on the rooftop gardens. The shattering sounds must be the solar panels, splintering into millions of pieces.

Bertha dragged me along the stairs as flames raged on either side of the boat—both the front and the back were on fire. She pushed open a shop's door and stuffed her mouth with three pastries from a glass display case, urging me to do the same.

"Umph uh umph uhh umph'll uh!" she shouted.

"What?" I asked, eyes darting around the room as I searched for an exit.

She tossed me a cinnamon roll and swallowed her pastries. "It might be the last meal you'll get for a while. Eat up."

She stuffed her mouth with three more pastries and pointed toward the window before grabbing a chair in the corner and smashing it against the glass. New Texas loomed not far away. We dove headfirst and swam toward the island. Around us, boats lit the sea with their roofs of fire. New Texas was trapped in a circle of flames.

Bertha pulled herself onto the shore. "You wait for the others. I'm firing up the engines."

"But we're surrounded."

"Just wait for it," she said as she ran toward the fort. "The Caravites just need a minute..."

I scanned the water for other Lost Boys, and saw someone leap from a boat's fiery roof. Another window was smashed open, and two more shadows dove in. I wondered when Captain Vern would order the Caravan to unfurl and run.

Kindred and Mila swam to the shore, followed by Phoenix. All three hurried past me and ran toward the island's center.

"Shit," muttered Mila as she ran past.

"Oh, dear," Kindred whimpered behind her. "Oh dear, oh dear, oh dear!"

There was a siren, and then the boats shot apart, forgoing their single-line formation and instead launching individually into the night. The Caravan disintegrated in front of my eyes. Its boats' flaming roofs raced off to distant corners of the ocean, flickering like the stars we'd once had in the sky.

As the Caravan crumbled, I saw flashes of Federal boats firing bombs in the distance. Somehow they'd found us outside Federal waters, in the middle of the ocean, and it looked as if they'd brought the whole naval fleet. The mammoth ships sat like sleeping giants, stirring only with the occasional cannon's flicker. The pastry ship where Bertha and I had slept sank in front of me. It was lucky Bertha's snores had frightened the boat's usual occupants into other lofts for the night.

Helicopters launched themselves from the decks of the Federal ships and raced toward us as two more shadows dove from the roof of a sinking Caravan ship. Dove and Sparky, I realized. Soon they reached the shore, clawing at the beach's sand and aluminum cans with spread hands.

Sparky panted, Tim clutching at the side of his face with hooked claws. "Not as easy as it looks," said Sparky, shaking his head. I pulled Tim off his face, and the sloth paddled his arms and legs in the air.

"What'd you expect?" I asked. "I bet the poor guy can't swim."

Sparky shook his head. "Negative. He can swim fine. He just lacks the motivation."

I shrugged. What'd he expect from a sloth?

Copters buzzed overhead, and a couple of bombs fell on the island, shooting up sand clouds like fireworks. If we were hit too many times, I worried New Texas would dissolve like the Caravan.

Dove smacked Sparky's butt. "Get in there, already." Sparky hurried toward the fort.

"Is he the only one that can drive?" I asked.

"Sort of." Dove shrugged. "I drive the boats, mostly, and Bertha flies the planes. Sparky drives the island."

"So there's no one else who can drive this thing?"

"Well, Bertha thinks she can do everything... But trust me, you don't wanna see her try."

More bombs fell from overhead, and pieces of the island splintered off into the ocean. Then thunder roared—actual thunder—and it began to rain. The few flaming Caravan boats that remained flickered as the raindrops doused their fires.

The island lurched forward, and I fell to the ground. Dove threw me a hand. The look on his face told me Bertha was driving. Then I heard it: mariachi music roaring over the thunder, trumpets blaring and guitars strumming over loudspeakers. The Federal copters hovered in the air, clearly confused.

"Crap," muttered Dove. "She snuck out one of those too?"

I raised an eyebrow. "She's been sneaking stuff out all day," he explained. "Every time we go to the Caravan she takes as many things as she can, and paddles them back to New Texas. Did she make you take some pastries?"

"She tried."

"Figures."

The island's engines groaned as we hurtled past the Federal ships. Waves crashed in our wake as the copters buzzed overhead, no longer stunned by the screaming loudspeakers, and eager to drop more bombs like lightning. Dove pulled me to the fort and up a spiral staircase.

"Control room," he explained, his chest shaking as he fought to catch his breath.

We found Bertha reclining in a rolling chair, her fingers clacking furiously at a keyboard while she stared intently through a panoramic windshield that circled the room. Holographic widgets cluttered her vision, and Sparky stood beside her, tapping them with worried looks. Phoenix stood in the back, his brow furrowed, and Mila sat hunched in the room's corner. The group seemed oddly casual, as if it wasn't a big deal that Feds were circling us with guns and bombs.

Mila glanced up at us as we entered. "Kindred's making muffins."

Sparky snapped his head around to face her. "Chocolate chip?" he asked.

"Nah, blueberry."

Bertha slammed her fists on the keyboard. "Damn it!"

"What's wrong, Big Bertha?" asked Phoenix, worried.

"We've had frickin' blueberry for the past two weeks, that's what wrong!"

Sparky echoed her sentiments. "Affirmative."

Mila rolled her eyes. "Give me a break."

"And give me some damn chocolate chips," added Bertha, fingers still clacking against the keyboard.

A widget blinked furiously on the screen as Sparky tapped a hand to the glass.

"What's wrong?" said Phoenix. He'd yet to acknowledge my existence, and the promise he'd made to Vern still loomed fresh in my mind.

Sparky glanced at the screen nervously. "Uh... low gas."

"How is that possible?"

"Er... well, you see... the thing is, actually... we were chasing the Caravan for quite a while, you know?"

"You went whale-watching again," said Phoenix. "Didn't you? You wasted our gas looking for whales."

"It was all Kindred's idea!" said Sparky. "She thought it might be nice to see them. Tim wanted to, too!"

Tim smiled and stuck out his tongue ever so slightly.

"Nice work, Slothy," said Bertha, shaking her head.

Phoenix yanked her away from the keyboard. "I need you to go into the armory and get us the biggest guns we have. If we can't outrun the Feds, we're going to have to shoot them down."

Bertha hurried down the staircase, and Phoenix pushed Sparky into the now-vacant captain's seat. "You drive," he said. "And figure out to how to turn off that damn music."

"Yeah—of course!"

Phoenix turned to Mila. "Help Bertha with the guns. You too, Dove." They raced down the stairs. He grabbed my shoulder. "You all right, Kai?"

I shook off his hand. "Peachy."

"Not peach-y," he said, smiling, "but blueberry."

He might've had the muscles, but god, he lacked the jokes.

Bertha returned from the armory, breathless. In one hand, she held an assault rifle; in the other, three black orbs. "Bombs," she explained.

Kindred appeared in the doorway. "Blueberries!" she called. "Blueberry muffins!"

"We don't need blueberries right now," said Bertha, shaking the orbs. "We need bombs."

Kindred pursed her lips. "Oh, dear." She offered me a muffin and whispered in my ear. "Someone didn't get all nine hours of her beauty sleep."

"I'M BEAUTIFUL, DAMN IT!" shouted Bertha.

Kindred hurried from the room, leaving the muffins on the table. Mila and Dove appeared in her place, bullets strapped to their chests. They tossed Phoenix a gun. "Let's go."

"You stay here with Sparky," Phoenix said to me before hurrying down the staircase.

Sand flew in bursts on the beach as more bombs were dropped. I watched out the window, eating my muffin, as the four Lost Boys raised their weapons and fired at the sky. A copter burst into flames.

"Hand me a muffin," said Sparky from the controls. I tossed him one and he swallowed it in a single bite.

A familiar voice cracked over the computer's radio. "Captain Vern to the Lost Boys," it said. "Lost Boys, do you read me? Over."

Sparky pointed to a mic left of the desk, and I pressed a button on its side. "Uh, roger that," I said. "Lost Boys here. Over."

"You boys still in the fire? We've still got a couple of birds around our neck. Trying to take care of them as we speak. Over."

Birds? Did he mean helicopters? Bad guys? What was he talking about? Birds were close enough to helicopters, so I just went with it. "Uh, yeah," I said. "We've got a couple of falcons on our tail here, too." Another copter skidded onto our shore, bursting into flames. "The falcons are on fire. Over."

Silence on the other end. "Uh... what was that last bit?"

If this man wanted me dead, I figured I deserved to have a little fun at his expense. "Falcons on fire," I said again. "Flames and fireworks, too. Looks like a big bad blueberry muffin, if I had to guess. Whiskey. Hotel. Alpha. Tango. Over. Do you read me, Sarge? I SAID, DO YOU READ ME, SARGE?"

Sparky covered his mouth to keep from laughing.

"Uh... come again?"

"Roger that, Vern. Base to Vern. Delta. Alpha. Kilo. Blueberry, pumpkin-pumpernickel-strudel-peach pie. Over."

"Err... what? There must be some static, or something bad with the connection. We have no idea what you're trying to say—"

"ALPHA, KAPPA, FALCON, FAHRENHEIT. OVER."

"We've contained the threat," Vern said, grunting—obviously tired of my charades. "They must've known where we were. There's a rat, I suppose. No other way they could've found us in the middle of the Pacific. Maybe they caught one of our fishermen—I don't know. We lost four of our floats. The rest are free-floating at sea. We'll be lying low for a while now."

He sucked in a breath. "And who exactly am I speaking with? Over."

I jabbed Sparky in the arm. "Sparky," he shouted. "You're speaking with Sparky. Over."

"Right, then, Sparky, tell Phoenix you're clear for the raid. The safe house in the Suburban Islands will host you. Be nice to Gwendolyn for us, won't you? Over."

"Roger that," said Sparky. "Over."

"That's all from the Caravan, then." Vern paused for a second. I could still hear him breathing on the other end of the line. "And Sparky?"

"Yes, Captain?"

"Tell Phoenix I expect him to honor our promise."

My chest felt tight, my head dizzy, and sweat gathered on my forehead.

"And what's that, sir?" asked Sparky.

"Just give him the message. Vern and the Caravan signing off. Over."

The speaker buzzed as the radio searched for a signal. Sparky turned to me. "You know what he promised?"

I shrugged. But inside, the weight of Phoenix's promise hung heavy on my shoulders. No, not my shoulders—my neck. Phoenix's promise hung around my neck like a noose. It was hard to breathe when I thought about it. I reminded myself again of my mission. My own promise to myself to find Mom and save Charlie.

If Phoenix thought he'd kill me, I'd make sure *he* died first.

# CHAPTER 25

CHARLIE STOOD AT the edge of her bed with a rope wrapped around her neck. Its soft white coils caressed her throat's flesh, beckoning her to step forward. Just a little step. Her arms dangled at her sides, and she prayed Sage would soon come. Her stomach snarled; the food they'd given her had been spoiled and putrid. When she touched her cheeks, she could feel the hollows that had formed.

Here, alone, she'd had a lot of time to think the past few days. She thought mostly about her home and the other kids back at H.E.A.L.

Claire's front tooth had been loose for a week the morning she left with Kai. "I'm sellin' this for a grapefruit," Claire had declared, flicking the tooth between two fingers. Charlie tried to explain you couldn't sell a tooth for grapefruit, but Claire didn't listen. She said her mom told her lemons were pieces of the sun, and that if you ate one, it warmed you from the inside out. Charlie asked why she'd wanted a grapefruit, then.

Claire shook her head. "If lemons are pieces of the sun," she said, "then I think, maybe, grapefruit are pieces of the sun's heart. They're yellow, too. And bigger. And pink on the inside." Claire said that if she had a piece of the sun's heart, she could give it back to him—and in exchange, he could give her a piece of her own heart back.

Charlie asked which piece, and Claire said her mom.

Charlie remembered the days when she'd wished for her own mom—actually, she still did. But time had smoothed the gaping hole left by her mother's euthanization.

She thought about Kai, too. The boy who could hold his breath for nearly three minutes yet still insisted on wearing a pair of cheeseburger socks to feel brave. She missed his caramel brown eyes, warm like cocoa, not the cold Indigo blue irises of adults. She missed the way he played with her chopsticks, and his hands got sweaty when he talked to her. The way he tried to wipe them off on his pants and probably thought she didn't notice. The way he looked at her and listened, like everything she said was important. Most people just couldn't listen like that.

There was a hard rap on the door, and Charlie shut her eyes tight, wondering if she should let her tongue hang out. She'd never seen a corpse before, and thought their tongues might hang out.

The slot slid open.

"Bed checks!" Sage called. Charlie breathed a sigh of relief.

"Bed checks!" she called again. Charlie stood silent. It was all part of the plan. The door swung open with a screech, and Sage walked over to her bed. *You okay?* she mouthed.

"I'm fine," Charlie whispered.

"I NEED A BODY BAG FOR CELL SIXTEEN," Sage shouted. "WE'VE GOT A PRISONER HANGING FROM THE RAFTERS."

Heavy footsteps echoed in the hall, and Sage's arms wrapped around Charlie's legs. "I've gotcha," she whispered, and Charlie stepped off the bed as the rope's pressure tightened on her throat, held off only by Sage's arms lifting her slightly from below.

It had to be done this way. Her face had to look a bit purple. The guards wouldn't believe it otherwise. Eddie, a guard with a bad knee and a birthmark on his face shaped like a turtle, wheezed outside the doorway. He held his knee in one hand, and a body bag in the other. "Jesus," he said, cracking it open. "Already? I thought this one had more fight in her."

Sage shook her head. "The pretty ones always go fastest. Like flowers, the bigger the blossom, the sooner it wilts... You got the scissors, Ed?"

He shook his head, and Charlie heard his footsteps trudge slowly down the hall. What was the rush, after all? She was already dead, and he was paid by the hour. She made a sputtering sound, and Sage lifted her a bit higher in the air. Sage was stronger than Charlie would've guessed.

The drag of Eddie's footsteps echoed in the hall as he returned. Charlie heard him fiddle with the rope above her. It snapped when he cut it, and she fell onto Sage, knocking them both to the floor. She bit her lip to keep from panting, but her lungs screamed for more oxygen.

Sage stood quickly, grabbed the body bag, and threw it over her. "To the furnace?" she asked Eddie.

"Nah, computer says this one goes to the mortician."

"Right, then. I'll bag her and bring her down there."

Eddie moved toward Charlie. "I'll help," he said. "Nothin' better to do, 'cept maybe get my yogurt from the fridge. The missus made it for me."

Sage wrapped Charlie's torso in the bag. "Really, I've got it," she said. "I can drag her down just fine on my own. Besides, I heard Rhonda's been eating other people's stuff from the fridge. Might wanna check on your yogurt." Eddie hurried down the hall.

"You okay?" Sage whispered to Charlie.

"F-fine." Charlie sucked in a series of breaths. "Th-throat just hurts. Hard to breathe."

"That's understandable."

"W-where do we head now?"

Sage pointed to the bag. "Lay down here, and I'll drag you."

"You're taking me to the mortician?

"No, the garbage chute. There's a column that runs along the edge of the building. It'll take us to the first floor. Then we'll get out."

Sage wrapped Charlie up in the bag, then dragged the bag down the hall, past the desk, and into the corridor. She hurried across the tiled floors before reaching the room with the chute. After exchanging a few words with a custodian dumping bags of trash, she was left alone with Charlie and the body bag.

Charlie peeled herself from the bag, and Sage pointed to the chute. "You go first," she said, tearing the bag into two pieces. "Take one of these. It'll help break your fall."

"Uh... how, exactly?"

"It's a straight drop. If you hold the bag above your head, it'll flutter and help slow your fall."

Charlie peered down the black chute. "Is it high enough for that to matter?"

"Dunno," said Sage, shrugging. "Didn't take physics. Just sounds like something they might do on TV."

Charlie took one of the strips and peered into the chute's black abyss once again. "Should I aim or something? Maybe try and move once I land?"

"Good idea," said Sage, nodding. "Probably wouldn't work out so well if I hit you when I fell."

Charlie stuck her feet into the chute's opening and straddled the edge for a second. She breathed deeply and grabbed the edge of Sage's torn bag.

It was now or never.

She leaned forward and plunged into the darkness. After a surprisingly short fall, she bounced off of a cloth net, out of the chute, and onto another floor, where she landed on top of three bags of trash. She was in a room identical to the one she'd just left, but perhaps one floor down. Sage, too, bounced off the net and landed next to her with a thud.

Charlie tucked a strand of hair behind her ear. "That was some kind of dumpster?"

Sage's face had gone white. "There wasn't supposed to be a net. Someone knew we were coming."

Marching feet thundered in the hall, and Sage grabbed Charlie's hand, yanked open the door, and ran.

Charlie's legs felt wobbly beneath her, and she realized for the first time just how weak the lack of food had made her. "What's going on, Sage?"

The marching grew louder as Charlie's own feet slammed against the wooden floors. Her lungs clenched in her chest, begging her to slow down even as her legs sped up. Paneled cherry wood lined the walls, and Sage pointed down the corridor.

"I know where we are. There's a door up there on the left. Hide in there," she panted. "The chancellor's chambers will be empty at this time of day, and you'll be safe. They won't think to look for you there." The stomping grew louder behind them. "I'll lose these guys, create a diversion, and find you in there after."

Charlie nodded. Sage must have realized she was too weak to keep running. "Good luck, Sage," she said, before running toward the door. She ran a hand through her tangled hair, wishing she still had a pair of her chopsticks, and turned. "You're a great friend!" she yelled, and the girl beamed.

The chamber's doors creaked as she opened them, and she quickly slipped inside and shut them behind her. She stuck her ear to the door, and held her breath—muttering a quick prayer for Sage as the stomping thundered past. She'd escaped. Well, sort of. She'd been lucky the door was unlocked. She figured she could probably hide in the shadows of the chancellor's chambers for a while, and eventually, Sage would return and find her.

Charlie looked around the chambers, but the room was dark, and she didn't dare turn on a light. The only thing she could see was a lone object: a glowing green orb on the corner of the chancellor's desk. Swirls danced in its depths. Charlie had never seen anything like it.

Entranced, Charlie stroked her fingers across the orb. It felt like glass, and was surprisingly warm to the touch. She pressed her palm against it and felt something that reminded her of a pulse. Energy. Like a beating heart.

Her eyes were gradually adjusting to the dim light, and now she could see that a thick cord stretched from the orb's side, running across the floor and underneath the frame of a black door in the corner. A coat closet, perhaps?

Charlie twisted its handle.

Locked.

She gently tugged on the thick, rope-like cord. The cord glowed faintly green, and a surge of electricity ran from her fingers to her chest. Burning. Pain. Her heart skipped briefly in her chest, and she released the cord. It had shocked her.

There was a noise from the hallway just outside; someone was fumbling with the door. With nowhere else to hide, Charlie quickly ducked under the room's desk, curling her legs beneath her. She had to hold her knees with her hands to keep them from shaking.

"We've got it back," called a voice she recognized as the chancellor's. "The Indigo Report. And Neevlor's dead."

A woman's voice responded. It sounded like she was right next to Charlie. "Excellent," the woman said. It was a soothing voice, the way a lemon menthol drop felt on a sore throat.

Charlie's heart pounded. The woman was clearly standing right next to the desk. Someone else had been in the room the whole time. And Charlie had missed her. How had she missed her? She heard the quiet crack of lips as the woman's mouth spread into a smile.

"Someone's here to see you, Hackner," said the woman, in her soothing voice. "She's under the desk. You were right about them using the chute. The net worked like a charm." The woman paused, then laughed. "Come on out, Charlie Minos. We promise we won't bite."

Charlie's heart rose and fell in her chest. She peeked her head out only to see the chancellor charging at her from across the room. He wrapped his hands around her throat.

"Should I kill her?" he asked someone.

Charlie's vision disappeared in specks, then in patches. Finally it faded into a dull black. *This is how Sage sees*, she thought.

"That won't be necessary," said the woman. "The people will do it."

"And how's that?" asked Hackner.

Charlie felt her body fall limply to the floor. Her vision came back slowly, in cross-hatched patches.

Across from where she lay, a woman in a blue suit had sprawled herself across a chaise lounge. Their eyes met, and Charlie felt she could almost see a chill run down the woman's spine.

"Oh, oh god," the woman said.

The chancellor stepped toward her. "What is it, Miranda?"

Miranda shook her head. "Nothing. It's nothing, you idiot. Forget I said anything. But tell me, Hackner," Charlie felt Miranda's eyes bore into her soul. "How's her hair?"

Hackner roughly yanked at Charlie's hair. It came out in clumps.

Miranda clucked her lips. "I'm afraid the blond just won't do. And it's already so thin. If only it were black..." She paused. "I suppose, actually, that bald might work better for our purposes. Yes, I think bald will be all right."

The chancellor looked confused. "What are you talking about, Miranda?"

"Without her hair, a girl's hardly recognizable. We'll have her head shaved this evening, Hackner. The press will be drawn to her bald, glowing head like flies to a light bulb."

Miranda crossed the room and knelt next to Charlie, then whispered softly in her ear. "Ah, *my darling*, have we got plans for you..."

# CHAPTER 26

THE SKELEWICK DISTRICT'S wrought-iron streetlamps threw their hauntingly familiar yellow glow across the streets. I pulled my cheeseburger socks halfway up my calves. Kindred had washed them, and insisted I wear them.

"Put on your cheeseburger socks," she'd said with a smile. "For good luck, dear."

Or perhaps for my funeral.

For some reason, I wished she'd come with us. Sparky, too, with Tim lazily napping on his back. But it was just me, Mila, and Phoenix. Phoenix had called us the "recon" team. I suppose Bugsy had once been a part of it too.

I wondered if the others knew what would happen to me after the mission. Did they know I was going to die, and that Phoenix would kill me? I guessed they didn't. Kindred, especially, seemed too soft for that sort of thing. Phoenix would probably tell them it was an accident. Blame it on the Feds, like he'd done with Bugsy.

I wondered if Bugsy's death had been an accident too, or if Mila had killed him. She seemed like the type who might.

Didn't show her emotions. Wasn't visibly upset when he died. Might be a sociopath.

She sharpened her blade against the light pole, smiling slightly when it screeched loudly.

Definitely a sociopath.

The denizens of Skelewick didn't seem to mind the noise. They wandered the streets in their trance-like state: pupils dilated, mouths half open. Zombies beholden only to the light.

I remembered the man hawking watches on the corner. *For the lost souls*, he'd said mysteriously, as he pointed at his wares. But *all* the souls in this district seemed lost. Probably why he stocked so many watches.

Phoenix yanked Mila from the light pole. "Let's go," he said, muscles rippling as he walked.

I glanced at my own biceps. They belonged to a girl scout selling Thin Mints.

We hurried toward the Morier Mansion's gates, dressed in all black, our faces covered by gray scarves like gypsies. No one in the city had looked twice at our disguises. We were fortunate Newla was such a bizarre place.

Two days ago, the other Lost Boys had shot down the Feds in copters using Bertha's weapons. They'd spent the next day scanning Federal waters, and then Phoenix had insisted we return to Madam Revleon's before launching the raid. He said he had a few things he needed to discuss with her.

Of course now, more than ever, I refused to believe a word he said. The truth might as well have been a dead language to him—like French, not spoken in a hundred years.

Bertha busied herself by preparing another set of Wet Pockets. She'd gotten to use her rocket launcher during the Feds' attack, so she was in an extraordinarily good mood, not even saying a word when I insulted her last batch of Pockets.

We'd come across an abandoned speedboat earlier in the day. Phoenix guessed Federal ships had killed its owners on their way to raid the Caravan, but I doubted this, and guessed instead that it was Phoenix himself who'd killed them. It seemed too convenient that a boat would magically appear the very day we needed a lift to Newla. But there it was, and we used it. Kindred sewed us the gray scarves, and we'd arrived at the city by nightfall.

A crow screamed from the banyan tree's gnarled branches as Phoenix rattled the mansion's gate. He'd radioed Revleon before we left and told her we were coming—the gate was supposed to have been unlocked. This wasn't a good sign.

Phoenix continued rattling the gate as I threw a leg over the fence. Mila sharpened her knife against the iron rods one final time, and then she and Phoenix followed me.

Phoenix rapped the mansion's brass rings hard against the massive door. There was no response. He slammed them again. Nothing. Mila pounded the door with closed fists, and the crow called from the tree. Madam Revleon was clearly not home. I walked the mansion's perimeter.

"Where are you going?" asked Mila. I shrugged and kept walking. A shutter on the manor's left wing swung back and forth on rusted hinges in the cool night breeze. I lifted my face to the window's edge. The screen had been torn open, and its mesh covering ripped to shreds, made transparent like a spider's cobweb in the moonlight, framed by fragmented glass.

Someone had broken in.

I pulled myself onto the ledge, ducking past the shattered glass before rolling into the room. A coffee table sat sprawled on its side like a fallen soldier, a casualty in a war it didn't know it was fighting. I could hear the brass ring clang against the door. If someone were here, they'd have run by now. I wondered again where Madam Revleon was.

The rest of the mansion was in similar disarray. Pictures were knocked from walls and glass cabinets lay shattered on the ground. There'd been a fight—that much was clear—but who'd won? I wasn't even sure who I was rooting for. I twisted the front door's lock and opened the door.

Phoenix stood in the doorway, confused. "How did you—?"

"Window was open." I pointed down the hall. "Left wing."

"Shit," Mila muttered, eyeing the glass shards that littered the floor. "What the hell happened here?"

The foyer's chandelier hung lopsided and rocked back and forth like a metronome. Tapestries had been torn from the walls, and lay sprawled across the steps of the grand staircase. Phoenix held his head in his hands. "Have you seen her?" I shook my head no.

"Probably hiding." He pointed to the stairs. "Library."

We hurried up the steps. Mila got there first, and stopped in the library's doorway. "Oh my god." She was hyperventilating. It was the most disturbed I'd ever seen her. I pushed past her.

Madam Revleon's corpse lay bleeding in the room's center. Blood pooled on either side of her limp body, and fallen bookshelves lined her torso, flanked by books spread on their spines. I felt sick to my stomach. I pulled my cheeseburger socks high on my calves and tried to slow my breathing. *Be brave*, I reminded myself.

Phoenix kneeled next to Madam Revleon's body. It looked like the intruder, or intruders, had buried bullets in her chest. Her eyes were frozen wide, relics capturing her final moments of terror. The killers must have followed her into the room after a scuffle, maybe even forced her in here.

The arm of her sweater had been torn off, and the words *"The Federation will not fall,"* had been carved into her forearm. The bloody words shined in the room's dim light. Feds had been here. Looking for Lost Boys—and maybe me—but they got her instead.

It was my fault that she was dead. And more innocent people would die if I didn't *do* something. I shut my eyes and tried to remember the pages of the report I'd found earlier in the library. The Indigo Report...

They'd created some sort of contagion for the vaccine, and the Feds were trying to stop them from spreading it, from infecting all the vaccines they stole. It was an evil plan. I couldn't be distracted by my own guilt right now. I had to think about stopping the Lost Boys, turning them over to the Feds, and freeing Mom and Charlie. Those were the only things that mattered now.

I tried to keep calm. If I blew my cover, Phoenix would kill me now, rather than later. I breathed deeply and scanned Revleon's body. "*Neevlor*" was scribbled in black ink across her forehead. The name was familiar, but I couldn't quite place it. Her right arm was positioned across her chest with two fingers pressed just below her right eye in the Federal salute. Her killers had made sure to arrange her corpse like this after she'd died.

"Check the desk," Phoenix ordered Mila. "You know which drawer she kept it in."

Mila tore open the drawers while Phoenix put his palm against Revleon's head, shutting her eyes. He ground his teeth, and a lone tear rolled down his cheek, caressing his square jaw before sliding along the curve of his neck. He wiped it away when he saw me look.

"Anything, Meels?"

The drawers squeaked as she dumped their contents. "Nothing. I think they might have gotten it."

"Shit," he muttered, staring at the cold body. "We should've had her make more copies."

"C'mon, Phoenix," said Mila. "We talked about this. Dr. Neevlor agreed it was too risky."

*Neevlor.* I stared at the name scrawled across Revleon's forehead. I'd seen it before—in the Indigo Report. "Dr. Harper Neevlor" had been typed across its front page. He was its author. But why had the Feds scribbled his name across a dead woman's forehead? A dead woman and an eccentric gypsy, at that. The gray scarves we'd worn around our heads would've looked normal in her closet.

This Morier Mansion must have been Dr. Neevlor's house. It was the only explanation. He must have bought the property from the Morier family some years ago and lived here until his death. Or until the Lost Boys and Madam Revleon came in and killed him, adopting this place as their own. The denizens of the Skelewick district would have been too dazed to notice. They didn't notice anything, really.

I stared at Revleon's pale body and felt a pang in my heart. Blood had poured from her rosy cheeks into a puddle on the floor. Her words echoed in my head: *It is not often one is offered the truth.*

The truth. But what *was* the truth? What was the connection between Neevlor and Revleon? There had to have been *something* more between them for the Feds to have written his name across her forehead. Impulsively, I grabbed paper and pen from the desk and scribbled down the two names. Phoenix sat huddled over the corpse, and Mila continued to search for the Indigo Report.

Neevlor and Revleon. I traced the two names I'd written on the page with a finger. What was the connection? I wrote the names again, this time with space between the letters.

Then it hit me. They were the same.

The two names used the same letters. I rearranged them on the page. Revleon was an anagram for Neevlor. A perfect match. Dr. Harper Neevlor wasn't a man, but a woman. The very woman sprawled across the floor of the library. This gypsy woman had been the author of the Indigo Report.

"It's gone," said Mila finally. Her curled black hair covered her face. "They must have found it and taken it with them."

The Feds had stolen the report and killed its author. I tried again to remember the excerpts I'd read. Something about Indigo vaccines being tainted with viruses. Contaminated samples. Dormant poisons. What had Madam Revleon—Dr. Neevlor—done?

The truth was a mirage. The more I learned, and the closer I got, the farther away it seemed. I remembered Sparky's words: *Phoenix wants a revolution.*

Phoenix wanted to contaminate the vaccines, and infect the Indigo supplies with a virus to make the Federation fall. And Dr. Neevlor had been helping him. Phoenix didn't want just war—he could've used the guns for that. It would've kept things much simpler, but he didn't want simple. He wanted

control. *Power*. That's what he was after. And that's what Vern
didn't want him to have. Vern wanted peace, and Phoenix
wanted power. More Lost Boys meant more power. That's why
Vern wanted Phoenix to kill me—and after he was done using
me for whatever sick purpose he'd planned, that was why he'd
do it.

I couldn't breathe. I couldn't think. My feet dragged me out
of the library and into the hall. There in front of me was a
framed picture of a family. Three women in suits, staring at a
camera. The picture was creased in its corners, and its colors
had bled out and faded on the photo paper. I could just barely
make out the navy color of the suits. The one in the middle
was the prettiest. She sat with her head cocked to one side and
had a cleft pressed in the center of her chin. All three had gray-
blue eyes. I wondered if they'd always been that way, or if
they'd been blue, and the photo had faded. Someone had
scribbled names over their faces in cursive. *Myra, Miranda,
Mary*. Beneath that: *The Morier Sisters*.

Farther down the wing, a TV mumbled in the master suite.
I wandered over to investigate.

The bedspread on the master bed had been folded over, its
covers neatly tucked. A reading light glowed white from a bed-
side table—it seemed Dr. Neevlor had been preparing for bed.
She'd found eternal rest instead.

I plopped myself on the bed's edge and stared at the screen,
wanting to feel numb. To let the television's mindless drone
wash over me. Forget what I'd learned, and become a true denizen of the Skelewick district. Be a lost soul rather than a Lost
Boy. Maybe the man on the street could give me a watch.

A news report bubbled across the screen. "LOST BOY
FOUND" flashed in brilliant red letters. "Fat chance," I muttered, laughing at the irony. The police probably caught some
poor soul drunk off Neglex and liquor, then propped him on
the screen to hide their own ineptitude.

"Mila Vachowski," read the reporter with the fearsome
unibrow, "was found earlier today in the city of New Los Angeles. A member of the Lost Boys, Vachowski has been at the

top of the Federation's Most Wanted for multiple months. She now awaits trial, slated to begin tomorrow, with a verdict to be reached later this week. Analysts estimate she'll be executed by next Tuesday."

They cut to a clip of the defendant's mug shot, and my heart exploded in my chest. The bombs were dropping around me, but this time from the inside out. Soon the walls would close in. There'd be no numbness left to wash over me. The shaved head shown on the screen wasn't Mila, and it wasn't a drunken stranger.

It was Charlie.

# CHAPTER 27

GUNSHOTS FIRED IN the mansion's courtyard finally tore my eyes from the screen. The news broadcast suddenly cut to a clip of the Morier Mansion, surrounded by blue and red lights that broke the Skelewick district's usual yellow twilight.

"BREAKING NEWS," the screen read in scarlet letters. "LOST BOYS FACE POLICE STANDOFF IN SKELEWICK DISTRICT." The men that had broken in through the window must've still been here when we'd first arrived. They must've run to get reinforcements when they'd heard us coming.

I had to get out. If the Feds caught me now, I wouldn't be able find Mom or save Charlie. Or tell the courts they had the wrong girl. Maybe they knew. Maybe they didn't care. It didn't matter. I had to save her before time ran out. It wasn't her fault any of this ever happened. I should never have chased Mila.

"Kai!" Mila called my name from down the hall. It should've been *her* face on the screen, not Charlie's. She and Phoenix were the real killers—the real terrorists. Charlie was the kind of girl who helped snails cross the street, while Mila and Phoenix let men die in megalodon's mouths. But at the moment, the terrorists were my only chance of getting away. I swallowed my pride and ran back down the hallway.

"Where were you, Kai?" asked Phoenix.

I didn't look him in the eyes. "I felt sick," I lied.

"Death can do that," he said, nodding as if it made perfect sense. As if I were so blissfully unaware of his deception that I didn't know he was going to try to kill me.

"Which window?" asked Mila.

Phoenix pointed down the hall. "Third guest room on the left."

The room was remarkably similar to the one in which Mila and I slept during our last visit. She pulled back the window curtains and snapped opens the shutters, her face stern. Past the banyan tree blue and red lights still flashed, and police copters circled.

Phoenix cut the screens and grabbed one of the tree branches that extended overhead. He wrapped his hand tightly around it and, without warning, leapt from the window. Mila ushered me forward, but I stepped back.

"Come on," she said. "Just grab hold of the branch. Haven't you ever used the monkey bars?"

I stared at the ground, a good thirty feet below. "This is different."

"You're right," she said. She pushed me onto the windowsill. "You don't get killed if you don't make it across the monkey bars."

Phoenix swung his leg over the branch and disappeared into a mess of twigs, roots, and leaves.

"Hiding in a treehouse won't help," I said. "If we're dead, we're dead."

She slapped her hand against my back, knocking me forward. I bounced from the balls of my feet and grabbed the branch, which shook from my weight.

"Go on," Mila urged. I swung my leg over like Phoenix, and climbed up. The branch felt solid beneath my feet. I ran ahead, twigs slapping me in the face, wondering how Phoenix had made it look so easy. I spat out the leaves that gathered in my mouth, then heard Mila's footsteps behind me over the sirens' drone.

If the Newla police force were here, then the Feds would soon be here, too. Probably already were, for that matter. Probably grabbed tacos down the street to make it look less obvious that they'd already been here on a mission to steal the report. Wanted to wait to make it look like *we* were the ones who'd done this to Revleon. That *we* were the ones being caught red-handed.

Phoenix leapt from one trunk to another, and I did the same. Gnarled roots hung below my feet like branches, an odd trait characteristic of banyan trees. I wrapped my hands around another branch and followed Phoenix, who was headed toward the main trunk in the center—though it was more like a series of trunks. In the center, each individual trunk was indistinguishable from the others; they were wrapped around one another like tangled threads.

"The mother trunk," said Mila as she pulled herself behind me. Splinters had buried themselves in my palms, but too much adrenaline surged through my veins for me to care. We were swinging nearly thirty feet in the air, and falling from this height would kill or maim me. Failure to move assured the police would do the same. Splinters were the least of my worries.

Finally, Phoenix landed on the mother trunk. "Down the rabbit hole," he said as I joined him. A mass of trunks rested below our feet, curving inward before spreading out to feed other trunks. Together, they formed a wide platform. One trunk that bled into the center stopped abruptly along the curve of another, its dark wood different than the rest. Phoenix ran his hand along the branches that lined the tree's widest trunk, his brow furrowing as he searched along its spine.

There was a soft click, and then the dark trunk in the center lifted slightly upward. Mila ran her fingers along its seams and pushed up.

It wasn't a trunk at all. It was a chute. One expertly disguised with painted lengths of wood, but a chute nonetheless.

Phoenix was right: down the rabbit hole we would go. Mila lowered herself down the chute first, disappearing into the tree's dark depths as she urged me to follow.

The police pushed forward, battering the wrought-iron fences down before them. Men with black shields and guns charged the mansion, firing a round of bullets as they ran. The mansion's remaining glass windows shattered.

Phoenix stuck his head into the tunnel. "You sure you set it, Meels?"

"Five seconds!" she yelled back.

A wall of fire burst from the mansion's depths, and the house's insides were devoured by flames. Mila had set a bomb. Their way of ensuring the Feds didn't get their hands on Revleon's remains—or the other secrets that likely lay hidden inside the mansion's walls. Flames burned through the same halls I'd just walked. I could still see Charlie's face frozen on the screen.

*Analysts estimate she'll be executed by next Tuesday.*

If I didn't save her, she'd be dead in less than a week.

Phoenix pushed me forward. "We need to move, Kai."

I joined Mila in the chute. There was no light, I realized, only darkness. With the Lost Boys, there was never any light. Maybe fire, but no light. With the Lost Boys, there was only darkness.

# CHAPTER 28

MY BREATHING ECHOED in the tunnel as I climbed farther down the banyan tree's hollowed center. I lowered myself along the metal slats that had been affixed to the wall, forming a ladder.

Phoenix read my thoughts. "The Morier Mansion was built before the world fell—it's the oldest building in the Skelewick district, which, of course, is the oldest district in Newla. The yellow lights give it away. The district runs on a different electrical circuit than the rest of the city. The council never figured it was worthwhile for the district to switch, I suppose. That, or they like laughing at the people lost in the yellow light. This tunnel was built shortly after the mansion, and goes deep into the island's core, eventually connecting with the sewers and maintenance tunnels."

Somehow it didn't seem strange that a Skelewick denizen was crazy enough to erect such a tunnel. Maybe they'd been searching for a way to escape the district's hypnotic glow.

"What is it about the yellow light that people find so hypnotizing?" I asked.

"Nostalgia, I suppose," said Phoenix. "The yellow lights are antiques—remnants of a world gone by. I don't imagine it's the light itself that's hypnotizing, but the past. The thing that hangs in the hollowed eyes and heavy hearts of lost souls."

It made sense. *For the lost souls,* the man with the clocks had said. People searching for the thing that evaded us all: time. Wondering how to get back the time they'd lost, searching for a way to change the past. School taught us that people used to live to a hundred, but I didn't believe it. Fifty seemed old enough.

Mila's feet splashed in a puddle at the base of the ladder. At the bottom of the chute was a tunnel about six feet wide and six feet tall. Phoenix had to duck his head just to walk. Mila cracked something in her pocket, and the tunnel was flooded with light.

"I wondered if you still had a few glow sticks," said Phoenix. Mila patted her pockets. The glow stick's light caught the corner of her jaw and lit her cheekbones in silhouettes.

"Always," she said, smiling. She ran along the tunnel, and Phoenix and I followed. Echoes rang as our feet splashed in puddles that had formed over the years. The air stank of stale water, and the tunnel felt humid and hot, like it'd been filled with steam in a past life. The air felt thick and foreign in my lungs, like I was breathing in molasses. The glow stick's light danced in the air with swirls of moisture.

"Where—uh—where are we?" I asked, moisture pouring into my mouth as I spoke.

Mila groaned. "Why'd we bring him again?"

Phoenix ignored her comment. I think he liked explaining the way the world worked—using the stuff he'd read in books. "Old lava tube," he said. "That's why the air's so warm. It's been abandoned for years." He pointed ahead, down the tunnel where the glow stick's light gave way to black. "They say it goes all the way to the Light House's cellar."

"The Light House?"

"You know," said Mila, "the place where the chancellor lives. Big government building. Council meets there. Ministers, too. It's even got a little prison. Shit—what do they teach you in school, anyway?"

Charlie could be in the Light House—in its prison, I thought. I might even be able to get the Lost Boys to take me. Her face was still frozen in my mind. Her bald head, her impending execution. The Feds had known she meant something to me, and they were using her to force me out of hiding.

I thought of the words carved into Neevlor's forearm. *The Federation will not fall.* The Feds, it seemed, would do anything to stop the Lost Boys. At first I'd understood—they had a nation to protect, after all—but now, their methods were starting to seem... sinister. *Too* sinister. If they would do anything to stop the Lost Boys, then didn't that make them just as bad?

I shook my head—I couldn't think like this. Maybe what the Lost Boys were doing was intentional. They thought they could earn my trust by putting me in dangerous situations and then saving my life. That's probably what they'd done to Bugsy—waited for him to trust them and then finally revealed the truth of their evil plans, swallowing him whole. Maybe that's what Phoenix intended to do me before he tried to kill me.

No, I couldn't focus on the Lost Boys' lies, or even the Feds' lies. It was all too much. I could hardly even tell the difference between the lies and the truth anymore. I had to focus on what I knew to be true without a doubt: Mom and Charlie. Saving them was my only real chance at redemption.

I sucked in a breath. "The tunnel goes straight there?" I asked. "All the way to the Light House?"

Phoenix nodded. "We think so, but there are walls and rubble in the way. Been there as long as anyone can remember, and there's no way around it. I'm afraid it's probably just an urban legend. My guess is that that branch just leads straight to the sewers."

I wrinkled my nose in disgust. The acrid stink of sewage still clung to hairs in my nostrils from my previous escapade. "We almost there?" I asked. Mila nodded and shined the light toward a fork in the tunnel. We turned right.

"Left was the Light House," I said. It was more of a question than a statement. Phoenix nodded slightly, but Mila raised her eyebrows. "Or a dead end," she reminded me. "Whether or not we could make it past the walls, the only thing that would be waiting at its end is death."

"But you haven't tried?"

Mila rolled her eyes. "It's enough we know where the Feds are. We don't need to serve ourselves up to them on a silver platter."

"You don't think they knew about the mansion? How did they find Madam Revleon, then?"

Phoenix tightened his jaw. "We should've been more careful. We shouldn't have let her get so comfortable. She should've known to keep the lights off and the curtains closed in that old house."

"You can't just put someone in the shadows and expect no one to find them," I said. "You can't expect to hide people simply by turning off the lights—it doesn't work that way. It's only good for so long." I thought of Mom, and how the Caravites might be hiding her, and waited for his reaction. His face was cold, but a flash of surprise flickered across Mila's face.

Phoenix stared at the tunnel's worn floor. "She wasn't in the shadows," he said. "She was in the shadows of the shadows. The darkest part of the city's darkest district."

"You really like the dark, don't you, Phoenix?"

"No," he said, shaking his head. "I prefer firelight."

Mila slapped the glow stick against the tunnel's wall. "You girls want to argue all day," she said, "or are you ready to move?"

Phoenix stared at me firmly, his eyes unblinking. "We're ready."

We'd reached a dead end. Another set of metal bars ran up the wall like a ladder. I felt the air in my lungs thin here; the moisture must have been dissipating up the makeshift chimney. "Where does this go?" I asked.

Mila began climbing. "Up," she said simply.

"South Atlantic," said Phoenix.

I shivered, remembering the documentaries we'd watched in middle school about South Atlantic crime rates. In them, drug addicts convulsed on street corners and stores were bordered up with bulletproof glass rather than wood. *The underbelly of Newla*, the documentary's host had called it.

"Don't look down," reminded Mila as we climbed. "Long way to fall."

"Thanks for that," I said. Then to Phoenix: "Is there another city district we could go to instead? Maybe one that's a little safer? A little less sketchy?"

He laughed. "You're crawling out of the ground from a lava tube. I think you can manage a 'little sketchy.'" He had a point.

At the top of the chimney was a landing surrounded by concrete walls. On one side was a black square door, like the wrong side of a bank vault. Phoenix grabbed the glow stick from Mila and twisted a series of black knobs on the door. It sprang open, and the sweet smell of pomegranate incense mixed with lemon—and maybe grapefruit—burned my nose.

Phoenix crawled through the doorway, and Mila and I did the same. A circle of wide-eyed civilians stared in silent awe as we emerged into the back room of a shop covered in tie-dyed fabrics. Phoenix waved off their stares.

"As you were," he said. "You are merely hallucinating. Excellent choice of drugs—very potent. Thank your dealer."

The group nodded, and a guy in a pink bandana promptly fell asleep. Phoenix shut the vault door behind us and covered it with fabric. A woman in red sunglasses stared at a bag of pills she held in her hand. "We've gotta get more of these," she said.

We hurried from the back room into the store's main area. A thin layer of smoke swirled in the air as we moved past chunky lava lamps. The cashier behind the counter stared at us with wide eyes.

"Narnia," whispered Mila in his ear. "It's real." He shut his eyes, nodded, and ran to join his companions. A sign over the register read, in green, yellow, and red letters: *"Dredson's Divine Herbal Incenses."*

Phoenix tossed me a pair of sunglasses and a black poncho from behind the counter, and we exited by the front door. It was nighttime, and the fluorescent streetlights were momentarily blinding after our eyes had grown accustomed to the glow stick's soft light and the Skelewick street lamps. We kept our heads down and merged with the crowds that hurried along the cobbled sidewalks.

On the next street corner, a man groaned and rocked himself back and forth, his arms across his chest and his eyes rolled back in their sockets. I looked away. "Is it always like this—busy?"

Phoenix shook his head. "There's a car show this weekend, and that's where we're headed."

"A car show in South Atlantic?"

"Mostly stolen," he said. "Which is why we're here: no better place for us to get a car. They've already made fake plates for them to put them in the show. If one goes missing again... well, it's not exactly like the new owners can file a police report."

Phoenix always seemed to be one step ahead.

We moved along, following Phoenix, and soon came upon a series of white canvas tents towering over a street blocked off with orange cones. I wondered how far our sunglasses and ponchos would get us, and simultaneously prayed that most of the city's cops were still back at the Morier Mansion fighting the fire. Phoenix slipped a guard at the gates several bills, and we pushed through into the crowded tents.

"Pick a car," said Phoenix.

I pointed to a yellow one on a pedestal, with windshields that slid open in lieu of doors.

"Too high-profile," he said, shaking his head. "Try another. On the floor, preferably."

I pointed to a black jeep in the corner. Its window tint was the same shade as its paint. The car was largely a shadow under the tent's bursting fluorescent lights. Phoenix liked shadows.

"Not bad," he said, turning to Mila. "You see it, Meels?"

Meels had already started toward it, and we pushed through the crowd after her. When we arrived at the jeep, I heard a clank and saw the metal boot attached to the car's front wheel roll off. Phoenix hopped in the passenger side, and I climbed in the back.

Mila adjusted a mirror and glanced back at me from the driver's seat. "Ready?" she asked, and the car's engine roared. I felt a twinge of pride in my chest as its lights flickered on—glad to have been of some use to the group for once.

I shook my head. These two were not my friends; they were murderers. I should have felt no pride in being "of use" to them.

The jeep surged forward, carving a path through the crowd. People ran screaming as we tore through the white tent, swerving around both cars and civilians. There was a concession stand at one end of the tent, and Mila aimed the jeep right for it. Workers dove screaming from the stand as we slammed directly into it.

Mila held her foot on the gas and the engine groaned. Finally, the wooden stand splintered into pieces us as we roared ahead.

A bit farther on sat a stack of metal boxes that flashed and hummed, and Mila crashed right into it. Sparks flew like bolts of lightning, and the jeep moaned loudly as its engine died. I saw bundles of sparking wire hanging along the car's edge, and then the tent's lights flickered and went dead. It seemed we'd crashed into its main power supply. I guessed this was why Mila didn't usually drive.

"Get out," said Phoenix. The airbag hung limply in front of his face. "Now, Kai."

Mila's head lay smashed against the steering wheel. I pushed open the door and climbed out, dodging the sparking wires and twisted metal as I fled. Phoenix quickly joined me, Mila's limp body dangling from his arms.

"Pick a car," he said again. Screams sounded throughout the tent, and engines roared as other cars were freed from metal boots under the cover of dark.

Here and there, cars sprang to life, and their headlights lit the tent, illuminating the chaos that now surrounded us. I immediately pointed to a red convertible in the corner. Phoenix quickly cut its boot and then keyed in. He laid Mila in the back, pointed me to the passenger's seat, and then started the engine. Mila groaned in the back. Cars raced alongside ours as we joined the fray.

I realized then that Phoenix had never intended to drive off in the jeep: the crash had been part of his plan from the beginning. He'd *intended* for Mila to slam into the generators and knock out the power, enabling the other cars to be stolen. These were all just movements in his well-orchestrated symphony. The guards could've stopped one car from fleeing from the tent, but they couldn't stop them all. You couldn't stop a parade. You couldn't stop a symphony. And Phoenix was the conductor.

Away from the tent, we glided along the neighborhood's worn streets, eventually merging onto the highway that led us out of the South Atlantic district, and then out of Newla altogether.

"Where are we going?" I asked.

"Suburban Islands," said Phoenix, his eyes darting back and forth as we weaved through traffic. "We'll have to stop at a border station in Maui. Should be there in a couple of hours. Go ahead and sleep, Kai. Get some rest while you can." Mila snored in the back, and he winked. "I'll keep my eyes open," he said. "For all of us. Don't you worry."

I watched as he ran his hand along the gun's length in his pocket. Rest was not an option. If I was going to live—and I needed to if I was to save Mom and Charlie—then from here on out, I would have to keep my eyes open. To close them would mean darkness—and in Phoenix's world, darkness meant death.

# CHAPTER 29

TRAFFIC IN THE Pacific Southwestern Tube slowed to a crawl at the Maui border station. Unlike the Pacific Northwestern, which contained only subway tracks, the Pacific Southwestern had wide lanes for cars and the commuter traffic that moved between Maui and Newla. A line of cars thirty vehicles deep had formed ahead of our red convertible. Mila cursed under her breath, and I pretended to wipe nonexistent sleep from my eyes. I'd been feigning sleep for the past three hours.

"Sorry," said Phoenix. "It's not usually like this."

"It's fine," I said. I thought of Charlie's face—her smile that wrinkled to one side when she spoke, her big blue eyes that glowed brighter than any other vaccinated person I'd met. "Not like I had anywhere else to be." I lied—I could've been saving Charlie.

"No hot dates? But you're a wanted man, Mr. Bradbury…"

I felt sick to my stomach. Here he was, joking with me, when he knew eventually he'd have to kill me. "Turns out," I said, "the Feds like bad boys more than girls do."

Mila smirked. "Not true."

"Yeah?" I turned in my seat. She had a bump in the center of her forehead from where she'd struck the airbag. "Then how come you aren't back at *Dredson's Divine Herbal Incenses?* Some bad boys there, if I ever saw them."

"Burnouts aren't bad boys," she said. "They're just burnouts."

"Maybe I'll be a burnout one day. Once all this is done."

"Go ahead," she said. "But it'd be a waste of your lungs."

It was the first time Mila had paid me a compliment. "Are you saying I've got good lungs, Miss Vachowski?"

She rolled her eyes, and I grinned. "I'll take that as a compliment."

"Nah," she said, "just a fact."

"It's a compliment," said Phoenix, smiling. I felt sick again.

Suddenly the car behind us slammed into our bumper, and we lurched forward. Phoenix tried to hit the brakes, but the momentum shoved us forward, crumpling our front fender against the car bumper ahead of us. Phoenix gave a signal and we threw on our sunglasses. He jammed his arms against his side door, but it was too crumpled to budge. I tried my handle. Jammed, too.

Phoenix pulled something from his pocket and pressed it against the windshield, which immediately shattered into tiny pieces. We crawled out.

The Tube's familiar glass curve hung overhead. Agents were stepping out of the border patrol stations wearing yellow and orange jumpsuits with X's across their fronts, just below the letters "*M.T.C.*" Agents of the Ministry of Transportation & Commerce.

"Fantastic," muttered Mila. "Absolutely fantastic…" She pulled her poncho's hood over her head and kept her eyes down as the agents approached.

Phoenix glanced at me from the corner of his eye. "*Ministry of TC,*" he whispered. "Also known as the *Ministry of Total Crap.*"

I stifled a laugh as the agents approached a truck driver six cars ahead. We were part of an eight-car pile-up that blocked an entire lane. Around us, cars swerved to stay ahead of traffic.

The agents moved along the line, hopping from car to car, collecting license and registration as they passed. "What do we do?" I asked Phoenix.

"Just keep your head down, and trust me."

A chubby and slightly balding agent approached us. "License and registration, please."

Behind his sunglasses, Phoenix smiled brilliantly. "Of course, of course." He placed a hand on the agent's shoulder. "But you see, my friend, our glove box is jammed."

The agent pushed off Phoenix's hand. "You can't get it out?"

Phoenix reached for his wallet. "I'm afraid the impact was too great." The agent pinned Phoenix's hands behind his back.

"I'll have to take you into custody, then. All three of you, that is. This car could be stolen for all we know," he said as he cuffed our hands. "Just had a big riot down in South Atlantic."

"You don't say," said Phoenix. "Wasn't there a car show there this week?"

The agent nodded suspiciously. "Yeah. Some idiot tried to run off with a jeep. Ended up crashing into a generator. Serves the low-life right, if you ask me."

The agent led us to the Maui border office for the Pacific Southwestern Tube, where he parked us on a bench and then disappeared into the back. The office was littered with pictures of baby seals, tossing their heads as they swam through the water, whiskers drenched and brown eyes wide and saucer-like. Phoenix tilted his head toward the pictures. "Shame they went extinct."

"I always thought there were more farther out at sea?" I said.

Phoenix shook his head. "That's just what they say when they don't want you to know the truth."

I thought of all the things Phoenix had said to me because he didn't want me knowing the truth.

At last the agent who had cuffed us trotted in from the back room. "The commissioner will see you now. And for goodness' sake, take off your sunglasses. We're inside."

Phoenix smiled, but made no attempt to take off the glasses. As we followed the agent into the back room, I saw that Mila still had her head down and her hood up. Silently, I wished she'd take off the stupid hood. The sunglasses were bad enough. The hood raised even more suspicions.

A man in his forties sat at a small table, and pointed toward three folding chairs on the opposite side. "Take a seat," he said. A brown mustache curled around the sides of his nose. He wore the same orange suit as the others, except that his had the word "Commissioner" embroidered along his back. Behind the commissioner sat what I guessed was a two-way mirror.

"Names?" he barked, not even lifting his eyes from his notebook.

"Henry Smith," said Phoenix without hesitation.

"Laura Williams," said Mila just as quickly.

The commissioner looked at her oddly, and she dropped her head. He raised an eyebrow in my direction. "And you are?"

"Uh, Chester." I cursed myself for not choosing a common name like the others. They'd figure me out in a second; Chester would be an easy name to verify as false in the system. Henry and Laura, on the other hand, were much more common, and might get bogged in the system. I crossed my fingers and prayed Phoenix had a plan.

"First name *Uh*," said the commissioner, " and last name *Chester?*"

My bottom lip quivered from nerves. "No, no," I said. "It's Chester Mc—Munchies. Chester McMunchies."

We were screwed. From the corner of my eye, I saw Mila mutter "*Shit.*"

"You get that?" said the commissioner toward the ceiling— the room was miked. He put a finger to his ear and nodded. "Right then," he said. "We're looking the three of you up in the database."

The room was shrinking. My heart felt tight against my chest. The commissioner cracked his neck. "Let's take the glasses off, then, shall we?"

Phoenix feigned a struggle with the cuffs. "I can't," he said, raising his voice to the rich octave that signaled one was a spoiled brat. "It's too *hard.*"

"Christ's sake..." muttered the commissioner. He reached for Phoenix's glasses. At the last second, Phoenix jerked his head to the side, and the commissioner stumbled onto the table. I imagined his colleagues laughing on the opposite side of the window. He pulled himself up. "What the hell was that?"

Phoenix pouted below the dark glasses. "You can't just grab them," he said. "They're *Zwallens.*"

Zwallens was one of the largest luxury brands on this side of Maui. Sunglasses made by Zwallens could easily run into the thousands. The cheap red sticker that ran along the side of Phoenix's glasses told me they were definitely *not* Zwallens, but I doubted the commissioner would know the difference. Zwallens were mostly just marketed to people in their twenties; people the commissioner's age were encouraged *not* to wear them.

The red convertible, the fake sunglasses—Phoenix was creating a persona: that of a spoiled rich kid from the wealthy suburbs of Newla. I wondered if the name "Henry Smith" he'd given was real or fake. Maybe it'd been someone he'd known in a past life.

Phoenix weakly lifted his wrists again. "Maybe you could unlock them? They're making my arms terribly sore, and my chiropractor says—"

"You think I was born yesterday?" The commissioner shook his head. "I've seen kids like you before: spoiled rotten. Think you run the world. Please, spare me your entitlements. You'll wear the handcuffs until we've confirmed your identity, and that's final." He wandered around the table and kneeled in front of Phoenix. "But the sunglasses, well, those have got to come off *now.*" He gingerly lifted Phoenix's glasses, his eyes bright with the knowledge that he was holding something truly expensive.

Phoenix butted him hard in the head, and the commissioner fell to the ground. Mila quickly squatted by his side and fished a ring of keys from his pocket. "See any black ones?" she asked. "Maybe one with an edge like a jigsaw?"

There were at least twenty keys dangling from his keyring. I scanned the bunch as best as I could. "Uh, lemme see... Could you maybe twist them around?" She turned them in the air. "There," I said, "that's better." I turned and tapped a black key with my finger. She grabbed it from the bunch and twisted it toward her handcuffs with surprising dexterity. In seconds, the cuffs fell from her wrists with a clank.

"Who's next?" she asked. Phoenix raised his arms behind his back, and she undid his, followed by mine. I wondered how she knew the keys so well. How had she known that the black ones alone would unlock the cuffs?

Phoenix stared at the commissioner and rubbed his forehead. "God, he's got a thick skull."

Mila rolled her eyes. "Kinda like the guy who hit him." Phoenix grinned. She tossed him the keyring. The keys looked small in his hands, like they weren't real keys at all. I stared at my own hands. They couldn't have been much bigger than Mila's...

"Those things," I pointed to Phoenix's keys, "they look like nuggets in your hands... You know... Because they're small..."

"Dear god," said Mila.

I could've slapped myself upside the head. There was something magnetic about Phoenix. Like, in a weird way, he was a superhero, and even though I knew he was going to try to kill me, a part of me wanted to just shrug it off and say, "Well, that's just how he is."

Phoenix smirked. For a second he didn't look so wise or grown-up. He just looked like a regular nineteen-year-old kid. "You know what they say about big hands..."

"No correlation," I said quickly, and Mila chuckled.

Phoenix turned a key in the door, and it opened with a click. Down the hall, an alarm sounded, and the lights flashed. It was starting to seem like all lights ever did anymore was flash.

I tossed my glasses to the floor—I needed my vision clear if I was going to run—and followed Phoenix's pounding feet. The thump of his shoes against the cold, white tile was drowned out by a familiar voice. *"This is an emergency,"* a woman's voice announced. My chest shivered—I was back in the Tube. The megalodons were circling. Charlie was floating by...

*"There has been a security breach. The building is now on lockdown. Please head to your designated area immediately. This is an emergency..."*

Men in yellow suits scrambled down the hall looking like giant French fries. We raced down the corridor in the opposite direction, hurtling past scrambling T&C agents. One tripped on another's yellow suit, falling to the ground and throwing his hands toward his colleagues, imploring them to save him.

"LEAVE HIM! LEAVE HIM!" another shouted.

There was a window at the end of the hall, and sunlight poured in with little regard for the flashing lights. It was morning—we'd driven straight through the night. A metal gate lowered from the ceiling as the building prepared for lockdown.

"Shit," muttered Mila. "They're really locking us in."

Phoenix didn't stop running. He tore through the building like it was on fire. "Where's the commissioner's office, Meels?"

She shrugged and feigned indifference.

"I know you know where it is. Now please, just tell me."

She squeezed her eyes shut and pointed.

"Does he have a window view?"

"I don't remember," said Mila. "But I think he grew flowers in his office."

Phoenix nodded. "He's got a window then."

We sprinted down the hall. How did Mila know the commissioner? Maybe this was why she'd kept her head down. Maybe she'd been caught before.

The commissioner's office was stuck in the hall's corner, and as soon as we were inside, Mila slammed its door shut behind us. She moved to lock it, but Phoenix shook his head. "We don't have time. I need the keys." She tossed him the set.

The commissioner's office was painted orange like sherbet. Pictures of his dog—a basset hound—lined the walls. On the desk were stacks of books, pens, and paper clips. A large window glowed to the desk's left, and light shined brightly on a pot of pink petunias sitting on its ledge. Even as we stared, bars began to lower themselves across the window.

Phoenix jammed the keys between the lowering bars and the windowsill. They groaned, then stopped altogether. With a shaking fist, Phoenix then shoved the bars back up. They wailed as their circuits burned and died. Phoenix then stuck the keys between his fingers and punched through the glass, his knuckles getting sliced as it broke into shards. He climbed through the window and motioned for me to throw him a hand.

Just then the door slammed open, and the commissioner stood panting in the doorway, his face red with blood and sweat.

"What do we do?" I asked Phoenix. He pointed to a paper clip lying separate from the rest, and then to the commissioner. I grabbed it and held it high in the air. I'd underestimated the power of Bertha's special paper clips before, but not now.

"TAKE THIS!" I yelled. I tossed the clip with a flick of my wrist and braced myself for the eruption of smoke that would follow.

The paper clip bounced harmlessly off the commissioner's chest and fell to the ground. He scratched his head. "What the hell?"

Phoenix grabbed my hand and pulled me through the window.

"It was just a normal paper clip?" I said.

Phoenix nodded. "But it distracted him, didn't it?"

I pretended not to be disappointed, but silently I added paper clips to the list of things I couldn't trust: puddles in public restrooms, door handles, the Lost Boys, and, now, paper clips. I had a feeling the list would grow indefinitely.

Mila crawled through the window after us. As she slipped out, a hand shot out from the office and wrapped itself around her ankle. The commissioner's bloodshot eyes appeared in the window, staring angrily at her as he fought hard to catch his breath. Mila's hood fell back around her neck, and a flash in the commissioner's eyes told me recognized her curls.

"Mila Vachowski," he said, his eyes foggy—distant like those of the denizens of Skelewick. "I *knew* that wasn't your face on the news."

Mila turned and, for the first time since I'd met her, I saw real fear in her green eyes. She tried to pull her leg away, but the commissioner held on even more tightly. "I remember your father," he said. "He was a good man. One of the best we had in the Ministry. We don't get ones like him often."

Mila nodded slightly, her eyes drooped, and her mouth went slack in a breathless gape. The commissioner released her leg. "I hope you know what the hell you're doing." Mila yanked her leg away, and we ran.

The commissioner had known her father—he'd worked for the Ministry of Transpiration & Commerce. *That* was how she'd known about the keys and the layout of the border station—because she'd been there before many times. We ran over a hill that backed up against the side of the station and fled into the city. Mila wiped tears from her eyes.

I wondered, again, who *were* the Lost Boys, and what were they really doing? And, perhaps most importantly: what did they want with me?

# CHAPTER 30

WE STOLE A white minivan from a Bixby & Barnnigan's parking lot in Maui. Phoenix figured it belonged to a soccer mom
and that she'd be in the store for a while, giving us time to run
before she reported its theft to the cops.

Next we drove to a local *Drive-n-Thrive* burger shop, and
demanded that they give us a set of their uniforms (ridiculous
green baseball caps) and pairs of sunglasses. I tried to edge in a
request for a cheeseburger by showing them my socks, but
they hadn't fired the grills up yet and it'd be thirty minutes if
we wanted to wait.

Phoenix hadn't wanted to wait.

In Maui, we drove along the ocean highways (mostly because there were fewer police officers there) instead of taking
the Tubes. The ocean broke along the cliffs and shoreline, its
water dull and gray, complemented by the angry clouds above.

Mila slept in the front seat. She'd said her head still hurt
from the airbag earlier. That, and she didn't want to talk about
the conversation with the commissioner. She didn't want to
acknowledge her past at all. I asked Phoenix what happened

exactly, but he shook his head and said, "She'll tell you in time, kid."

I sort of resented the fact he called me kid. I was fifteen years old, for god's sake—an adult for all Federal intents and purposes. Had I been vaccinated, I could've voted in the fall elections. Instead, I sat there with brown eyes like a child, praying the Indigo pills Phoenix had given me those first few days were still working.

When at last we reached the end of the highway, we had no choice but to merge onto the Atlantic Northwestern Tube. It was much quieter than the Pacific Southwestern, with only three lanes for cars and one track for the subway. Phoenix told me the Tubes that went to the Suburban Islands were really only busy during rush hour, when commuters used them, and that, unlike Maui, border patrol was essentially nonexistent. Sure enough, the man at the station waved us through with a smile. He didn't even stop us to check out our registration.

"Strange that security's so lax here," I said.

Phoenix shrugged. "I guess they figure they've got nothing worth attacking. Better to put the troops near the big cities."

"Did you hear what the commissioner said? About Mila being on the news?"

"Yeah, I remember him saying something along those lines. It can't be helped, I'm afraid. The girl they caught was probably a criminal anyway. I hope they execute her—for *her* sake. Torture would be far worse."

I couldn't believe what he was saying. How nonchalantly he spoke. I felt sick to my stomach, and a lump formed in my throat. "Torture?" I croaked.

"Oh, yeah," he said. "If the Feds catch us, we'd better pray for death. It may seem like a fair trial on TV, but off-screen... you can be sure they'll pull us apart piece by piece, the way a megalodon maims its meals before it eats them. They'd marinate us in our own suffering like a steak in vinegar."

I thought of Charlie's bald head and sunken eyes. I imagined the Feds pulling her apart—using the chopsticks from her bun to cut her into pieces until all that was left were her bright blue eyes. *The girl was probably a criminal anyway.* Phoenix didn't have an ounce of compassion for human life. Death rolled off his shoulders like rain.

"We're here," he said. We sat outside a small two-story house with blue shuttered windows. It was identical to the other houses in its row, a clone, right down to its manicured lawn and rosebush to the right of the driveway. Phoenix tapped Mila's arm to wake her.

"But Sarah," she mumbled, wiping sleep from her eyes.

"Who's Sarah?" I asked, but they'd already climbed out of the car.

Phoenix rapped his knuckles against the white wooden door. "Let yourself in," called a woman's husky voice. It was familiar. I'd heard it before. In my past life—where I hadn't been an enemy of the people, a Lost Boy.

Mila turned the knob, and the three of us entered a living room. A woman sat on a green leather couch, fanning herself with a red paper fan in one hand as she eyed the cuticles on the other. "You can shut it behind you," she said, without looking up.

Phoenix slammed the door. "Neevlor's dead."

The fan fell from the woman's wrist. I saw a burning bird flash across its side as it dropped.

It was the woman from the Tube—the one I'd spoken to the day it cracked. The one who'd told me not to get vaccinated. She laid her head down on her knees. "This is wrong," she muttered. "This is all so wrong."

Phoenix sat next to her on the couch. "Nice to you see you too, Gwendolyn."

"Who's the kid?" she said without lifting her head.

"This is Kai."

I offered her my hand. "Pleased to meet you."

She ignored it. "Pleasure's all mine." She ran her hands through her graying hair.

"Don't doubt it," said Mila, through gritted teeth.

Gwendolyn looked at her, and her eyes watered below her graying hair. Mila moved to the opposite end of the room. I picked up the fan and handed it back to Gwendolyn.

"Thanks," she said. Her eyes met mine for the first time. A look of recognition flashed across her face. "I—I know you," she said. "You were on the Pacific Northwestern Tube the day it cracked. I *thought* it was your face they showed on the wanted posters. I saw your friend's face, too. She's been on the news. Her head's shaved and her chopsticks are gone, but she's still quite pretty. They got it wrong, didn't they?"

I shrugged. "Sorta," I said. "For me at least, I guess the crimes listed on the posters are starting to be accurate."

Gwendolyn shook her head. "They're not accurate at all. You haven't done anything wrong—"

"He's done a few things," said Phoenix.

Gwendolyn ignored him. "And the girl," she continued. "*She* didn't do anything. The press isn't even using her real name. They're saying she's Mila." She turned to Mila. "They're saying she's you."

Mila crossed her arms. "How's that *my* problem?" Her words stung, and my blood boiled.

Phoenix stepped toward me. "You *knew* the girl they showed on TV? And you didn't *tell* me? You acted like she was a stranger!"

"I'm sure there's more than a few things you haven't told me," I said.

He shook his head. "You have no idea what you're saying, kid. You don't have any idea what and who you're dealing with."

"Really?" I said. "Because I think I'm starting to see things pretty clearly."

Gwendolyn moved between us. "My appointment is tomorrow afternoon," she said. She smoothed the wrinkles in her cream-colored dress. "Dr. Howey confirmed it this morning."

Phoenix backed away, but he kept his stare focused on me. "Excellent," he said. "Everything's in order then."

Gwendolyn nodded. "Car's in the garage. You can keep the keys when we're done. Everything else is going to the state. They'll liquidate half the assets and give the rest to charity."

"Ah," said Mila, "the conscience clocks in right at the end."

Gwendolyn pursed her lips and headed toward the kitchen. "I'm not proud of what I've done," she said, wiping dust from the kitchen table, "but I'm doing my best to make amends."

Mila's eyes were hard. "It's not enough. It will never be enough."

"Stop it, Meels," said Phoenix, grabbing her arm. "She's doing the best she can."

"Not all of us can be as brave as Harper," Gwendolyn called from the kitchen. She sliced onions at the sink and stared out the back window.

Phoenix joined her. "You've been brave enough, Gwendolyn."

I followed them into the kitchen, and saw that the table was already set for lunch. Three floral placemats were laid out in perfect symmetry.

Gwendolyn sniffed back tears. I wondered if it was the onions or Dr. Neevlor's death. Probably a bit of both.

"You'll have to excuse me," she said to me. "I didn't know a third person was coming. Placemats are in the cabinet to the left, top shelf."

We ate lunch in silence.

"Good carrots," I finally muttered.

Gwendolyn smiled faintly. "They're from my garden."

I twisted the veggies on my fork. "You don't say?"

The main course was chili. Mila needled her bowl with a spoon, never lifting her gaze from its depths. I don't think she could look at Gwendolyn without getting mad. I wondered what had happened between the two, what Gwendolyn had done to evoke Mila's wrath. I sipped another spoonful of the stew. It was the same shade as Neevlor's blood. I was trying hard not to think about it.

"Spicy," I said.

"It's the onions." Gwendolyn's eyes watered again as she stared at Mila. "Gives it that extra kick."

Mila pushed out her chair and stood. "Well, this is bullshit.'

"The onions?" I asked.

She waved at the table. "This whole thing—this lunch. *Everything*. This whole stupid plan."

"*Meels*," hissed Phoenix. He pushed her back into her seat. "What do you think you're doing?"

She stood again and ran from the kitchen. "I'm going to lie down. I'll see you all in the morning."

I glanced at a clock on the wall. It was two p.m.

"Well," said Phoenix. It was followed by silence.

I pushed the stew around with my spoon. "What's for dessert?" I asked finally.

"Peach cobbler," said Gwendolyn. I pictured Kindred feeling a silent stab in her chest and dropping a bowl of blueberries on the floor. Peach could've killed her.

"Wonderful," said Phoenix, his eyes wandering to where Mila had stood. "That sounds really nice."

"Yes." Gwendolyn nodded. "Did you see I still have my fan?"

Phoenix smiled. "I'm surprised it made it out of the Tube with you. I thought it'd be lost in the commotion. The bombs threw us for a loop."

Her eyes were glassy with nostalgia. "We had our fair share of commotion at the Ministry, too. You don't get to be Director of the Lottery without a hearty dose of catastrophe."

"And a hearty dose of Indigo," muttered Phoenix. I wondered if he was thinking about the Indigo Report—the virus they'd managed to manufacture in the samples.

Gwendolyn passed out cobbler, but I felt sick to my stomach again and couldn't finish it. I resigned myself to pushing it around my plate.

Gwendolyn smiled at me from across the table. I felt bad for her, and for the fact that she lived entirely alone. No family and no friends, it seemed. I wondered how she'd become the Caravan's ally, and how she'd met Phoenix.

"How, uh, how did you know Dr. Neevlor?" I asked. I'd only known Neevlor briefly, but the name still felt thick and not quite right on my tongue. I kept wanting to call her Madam Revleon. It was strange how quickly you got attached to a name. "Did you work at the same Ministry together?"

Gwendolyn shook her head and sipped from her glass of water, patting the corners of her pink lips with a napkin afterward. "Harper and I were neighbors for years. We used to ride the subway on the Tube together. She worked for R&D, and I worked for Health. Different Ministries, but they were only an island apart."

"So she lived in the house next door?"

Gwendolyn nodded.

"Was that before she moved to the Morier Mansion?"

Phoenix pursed his lips and stared at Gwendolyn, watching her with burning eyes. Had he coached her on what to tell me? What was he worried Gwendolyn might say?

She was too busy watching me spoon the cobbler to notice his stare. "Harper lived next to me for twelve years, but that was before she started her investigation... Before she wrote the Indigo Report and tried to get it published. Then everything changed." Her eyes got watery again—the way they'd been when she'd stared at Mila. "They started trying to kill her."

"Who did?" I asked. "The Feds?"

She nodded.

"And you helped her get away," I finished. "She came to you for help, and you helped her get to Newla. That's where you met Phoenix and the Lost Boys. How you became connected to the Caravan."

It was all falling into place. Everything was making sense. Gwendolyn helped Neevlor escape from the Suburban Islands to Newla. Once there, they ran into Phoenix, who'd already staked out the mansion. He'd offered to help hide Neevlor, with the Caravan's support, in exchange for the Indigo Report.

He'd been looking for a way to start a war, and the contents of the Indigo Report gave him just what he needed. Taught him how to contaminate the vaccine with a virus.

"You helped Neevlor get to Newla," I said again.

The secrets were falling into place. Phoenix couldn't hide the truth forever.

Gwendolyn, however, shook her head. "I didn't help Dr. Neevlor at all." She took a deep breath. "I told her to go to hell."

# CHAPTER 31

HACKNER INHALED A final puff from his cigar before he patted Margaret's arm—time for her to go. They'd been lying in his red satin sheets for nearly five whole minutes. It was about all he could stand of the woman once the deed was done.

Her red hair matched the sheets and was sprawled about her head like a wicker basket. "Already?" she asked.

"Yes, yes." He patted her bum to push her out of the bed. "You really are wonderful, darling—and take that as a compliment, because there are two girls I see regularly who I don't say that to. But, you see, there's a nation I must run. A great one— the greatest in the entire world. She is my lady, and I her lad."

Margaret kissed his cheek and slid back into her black velvet dress. "God, I love that you're so patriotic, baby. I shouldn't be so selfish. You're too good a man for me to keep you all to myself."

He waved off her compliment; the patriotic bullshit always got to them. "Don't be silly, Marjorie—Margaret, definitely Margaret," he said. She was too infatuated to notice the slip. "You really are quite wonderful." He slid to the bed's edge and buttoned his pants. "Same time next Tuesday?" She nodded.

"And, please, try to be gentle with the door this time on your way out—no need to slam it, darling. It's old wood."

Hackner tightened his tie before pushing open the mahogany doors between his room and the chancellor's chambers. How long he had dreamt of the chambers being his before he'd actually earned their keys. And they belonged to him now—the keys and the chambers. His rightful jurisdiction as the Federation's chancellor.

"Hackner!" Miranda's shrill voice called from the Con-Synth. He laughed bitterly. The chambers would never be his They had and always would belong to her.

"Hackner!" she called again.

"Yes, Miranda?" He pushed the door shut behind him. The others didn't know—couldn't know—of her existence. It was better for everyone that way. Sometimes, he wished even he didn't know. Wished he still thought the government belonged to the people of the state rather than to her.

"For once," she said, "I'm pleased." Her sinewy figure appeared behind him before flashing onto the chaise lounge.

"And why's that?"

She pointed to a stack of white papers on his—her desk. "Ah," he said. "I see we've begun recycling. Really, I'm surprised this office didn't start sooner—"

"Results, Hackner," she said through gritted teeth. "We've finally got results. They found the Indigo Report, you idiot."

Hackner hated when she called him an idiot. He was the free world's elected leader for God's sake, and it's not like they could've elected an idiot. He lowered himself into his chair and pressed his feet against the back of his desk—against the place where the prisoner named Charlie had hidden. Miranda had been raving about the Indigo Report ever since he'd arrived in office. Bitching about how badly they needed to find it, and how they had to keep it hidden from the public, though she never told him quite what it was.

He scanned the documents on his desk. God, there were a lot of words in these reports. He couldn't be bothered with so many words. He was more a man of action. "Less reading, more rutting," his father always said, and he couldn't have agreed more.

Hackner saw the smugness line Miranda's face like a red gloss. She always thought she was in control—that she knew everything. That she had all the power. At the end of the day, however, she was still tied to a small green orb. He grinned. "Since you're so informed," he said, "I'm sure you're aware of the fire, the explosions at the South Atlantic car show, and the lockdown at the Newla-Maui border station?" He cracked his neck to the right. "Or did you miss those while you were busy panting over the Indigo Report?"

The lift in her brow told him that she had not been aware, though he knew she'd never directly admit it. Couldn't confess that even a second had passed where she hadn't been in total control—where things hadn't gone perfectly according to plan.

He drummed his fingers along the ConSynth's curved glass. "The Lost Boys are moving, Miranda." He paused to let that sink in. "So where's your boy? Where's Mr. Kai Bradbury? Something tells me he's already forgotten about the girl. I suppose the *glamour* of crime got to him."

The chaise lounge sat empty. He heard her breathing behind his throat. Despite the chill that ran down the length of his back, he savored the sweet satisfaction of finally having the upper hand.

"I commissioned the construction of a second ConSynth," she said quickly. "It'll be done by the end of the week. Just a precaution."

"Same color?" he asked. "I do find the green's become tiresome."

She ran her hand over his shoulder. He reminded himself that she couldn't touch him—she was just a hologram, a consciousness suspended by the power of technology, and nothing more. "This one," she said, "is going to be red, darling. I know you like red. And we wouldn't want my dear Hackner to become bored with me, now would we?"

"No," he said, shaking his head. "We certainly wouldn't want that."

She lay across his desk, hanging her bare leg just over his lap. She rubbed her hand along the length of her neck as her lips cracked into a smile. "I'd hate for you to get sick of me, like you have poor old Margaret."

He tightened his jaw. "You were in my room. Again." He wondered how many times Miranda would follow him without him knowing it.

"I'm always with you," she said with a smile. "In the office, the boardroom, the bedroom: everywhere. There is nowhere you can hide from me. Not that you'd want to, of course."

Hackner thought of the prick he felt every so often along his spine. A sure sign she was near—that she was watching.

Miranda kicked her heels on the desk. Hackner didn't mind—her feet weren't really there. "The prisoner in fourteen's acting up again." She tucked a strand of hair behind her ear. "You don't think he'll come for her either?"

Hackner shook his head. "Doubt it. Let's give her to R&D."

"Since that's worked so well in the past."

Hackner shrugged. He couldn't have cared less what they did to things in R&D. From all his encounters with them, he'd come to the conclusion they were about as scientific as eighth-graders pulling frogs apart for the science fair. No real genius, expertise, or talent. It was probably best that way. Made it easier to maintain what Miranda called a "healthy" level of progress. Which was no progress at all, in reality.

"What would you have me do with her?" he asked. "Give her two more weeks with Zane? She's hardly even looked at the rope."

Miranda waved away his suggestion. "I'm afraid she's too far gone for that. I've seen her through cameras. At this point, her brains are like scrambled eggs. She can't even feed herself—Sage does it all."

The blind girl. How Hackner hated her. She'd already betrayed them once by helping Charlie try to escape. And Miranda had let her off easy. She didn't want her precious pet refusing to mix his antidote. She'd only made Minister Zane give the

girl ten lashes. Ten! It was ridiculous. The girl wasn't even unconscious afterward!

He thought of the prisoner in cell fourteen again. "Perhaps
the Ministry of Health, then? They could always use a fresh
cadaver for experiments. And we could bring it to them still
alive."

Miranda grinned and cocked her head to the side like a bird
examining its prey. "You can be brilliant sometimes. Did you
know that, darling? It's no wonder you got elected."

"It's settled, then," he said. "I'll have the guards take her
this afternoon."

Miranda chewed her bottom lip. "Perfect," she said. "And
might I also suggest that the guards who go with her go without uniform? In plain clothes, perhaps?" Miranda's suggestions
were never really suggestions: they were just funny ways of
giving orders.

"Of course," he said. "Whatever you wish."

"We don't need civilians seeing more men in uniforms—
they've already got too much cause for concern. The Pacific
Northwestern Tube has yet to be repaired. They're still shut-
tling Moku Lani citizens back and forth to the other islands via
ferry... Yes, guards in plain clothes will make things look a bit
more normal. Let them blend in and keep things a bit calmer."

Hackner nodded. She didn't want the public knowing the
government wasn't fully in control. That they had no idea
where the Lost Boys were or where they'd attack next. For all
the Feds knew, every city was a target. The bombs could've
already been laid, and they'd have no idea. The thin threads
that had held their society together for so many years were un-
raveling. The world they knew was in jeopardy of becoming
scrambled.

Scrambled. Like the brains of cell fourteen's prisoner, Dr.
Mary Bradbury.

# CHAPTER 32

OAHU'S ONCE WONDROUS mountainsides had given way years ago to an endless crop of hospitals. The entire island was now a field of clinics and—as Gwendolyn soon informed me—waiting rooms.

She typed a code on a keypad to the left of the Ministry's metal doors. "Lord knows I can't stand those things." Even the Ministry of Health's back alley looked sterile. White dumpsters rested on the outskirts of the Ministry's main marble tower.

"Mostly labs," Gwendolyn acknowledged. "But there's a small hospital on the third, fourth, and fifth floors for government officials. No waiting rooms for them, of course."

"God forbid they have to wait even a minute like the rest of us," muttered Mila.

The glass door slid open. Phoenix double-checked the device he'd slapped against the side of the building. I recognized it as the silver box from Bertha's lab. A Video Loop Fractalfyer, she'd called it (also "deep shit").

Phoenix, however, called it a "VLF" for short. He said it disrupted the building's security feed flow, filling it with endless patterns of images from earlier in the day. Like looking through a kaleidoscope of monotony. Since Bertha designed it, I was naturally skeptical of its effectiveness.

"You're sure it'll work?" I asked.

"It's Bertha's," said Phoenix. "It's got to."

"Dr. Howey," said Gwendolyn, "will meet us on the third floor, in the janitor's closet across from the women's restroom."

Mila pursed her lips. "Charming."

We entered the building's receiving zone in its vast warehouse, which occupied the first two floors. Rows of supplies sat on high metal shelves, and rovers ran along their lengths, plucking inventory as they went, racing straight past us with little regard for our appearance.

"Real secure," muttered Mila. "Nice place to keep the world's largest supply of Indigo." She kicked a rover's wheel as it passed. It beeped shrilly, but otherwise paid her no attention.

"There's no Indigo on most of these floors," explained Gwendolyn. "Just the occasional vaccine or two in transit. The reserves are in the building's top six floors."

"And how many floors are there exactly?" I asked.

"Ninety-nine," she said without hesitation. She pressed her right two fingers below her cheekbone in the Federal salute, leaned against the door before us, and pressed her eye against its retina scanner.

"Really?" I asked. "They couldn't make it a hundred?"

The scanner beeped and she removed her head. "It's a metaphor," she explained. "Despite the Ministry's best attempts, the health of the nation is not—and will never be—one hundred percent. The ninety-nine floors remind us of this fact. They remind us to keep trying, keep reaching for that one hundred percent."

"So…" I said. "Budget cut?"

"Yeah, honestly I think they just ran out of funding."

We wandered through the Ministry's floors without so much as a second glance. Gwendolyn told us that once you were in, people would figure you had a reason to be there. For all they cared, you could have a bomb strapped to your chest, and they wouldn't give you a second glance—they were that absorbed in their research, that absorbed in leaving their names hallowed in the building's sacred walls. Since the onset of the Carcinogens, the greatest legacy one could leave was an ounce of new knowledge in the medical sector.

Gwendolyn told us that most people who worked for the Ministry of Health were too busy to watch TV, which explained why they didn't recognize us from news reports. Work was their life, and it stayed that way for most of them until they died.

This Ministry, in particular, made it a point to withhold promotions to positions of power from people with families. The Ministry needed leaders who were completely focused on leaving a legacy in the medical field—they couldn't afford for employees to have distractions. Occasionally a family man slipped through, but even then his childless colleagues typically made it a point to cause him to fail.

A woman in a white coat and thick glasses hurried past us with a clipboard. She smiled at me and I smiled back. It was the first stranger to have smiled at me since we escaped Club 49. I guessed she liked my cheeseburger socks, but I'm sure it didn't hurt that the security alarms weren't going off for once. Bertha's device—the VLF—was working, and for that I was grateful.

When Gwendolyn opened the janitor's closet door on the third floor, I saw that it, too, was oddly sterile. The shelves were lined with packaged dusters and bottled water used for mopping the floors. A man in his forties crawled out from between two shelves. His bald head shined like the Ministry's marbled walls, and his navy suit hung in folds around his slight frame. In one hand, he clutched a leather padfolio.

He eyed us from behind a pair of clear, plastic glasses, and I recognized his face as a vaguely familiar. Had I seen him on TV?

Gwendolyn jumped back, startled. "Marvin!" she cried. "Dr. Marvin Howey, my dear, how are you?" She wrapped her arms around his tiny frame, crushing him between her sagging bosoms.

He straightened his glasses. "I've been better, though it's certainly nice to see you again, Gwen." He extended Phoenix a hand. "And to finally meet you, my good sir, in the flesh."

Phoenix shook the man's hand with a somber look. "A pleasure."

Dr. Howey gave a lopsided smile. "The Lost Boys," he said to himself. "Never thought I'd see the day." He turned to Gwendolyn. "How much time do we have?"

"Enough."

"There's never enough time, my dear," he corrected her. "Never enough."

"Did you read the report?"

He gritted his teeth. "And then burned the copy, like you asked." He stared at the closet's sterile shelves, his gaze muddied for a moment, lost somewhere in the distance. "It was hard."

"Reading the report?"

"No." He shook his head. "Burning it."

"It's a pity you had to. The Feds stole Neevlor's only other copy."

"Oh?"

"They got Neevlor, too. They must've been scoping out the mansion for a while. How else could they have known?"

"Indeed," he said, nodding. "How else could they have known?" There was something in his eyes that looked to me like feigned sincerity, as if he actually *knew* how the Feds had found Neevlor. Perhaps he'd been the rat. I wished Charlie were here. She was the best judge of character I knew. She'd know if the man was being honest.

Gwendolyn sobbed, and Dr. Howey rubbed her arm. "Dr. Harper Neevlor was a good woman," he said. "She'll live on forever through her work. The Indigo Report is monumental."

Not for the first time, I wondered what Phoenix held over their heads to get them to do his dirty work—what it took to get people like Gwendolyn and Dr. Howey to give up their careers and possibly their lives. It didn't make sense. Phoenix was just a kid, not much older than me. What did he tell these people he would do? What were they getting out of helping him? What kind of sick, twisted desires did Phoenix promise them would come true? There had to be something.

I thought about what Gwendolyn said earlier, about how their work was everything to these people. They had no families. No partners. Nothing else, really. Just their work. Their work was their legacy—the only way they could live on forever. Even Dr. Howey said it about Dr. Neevlor and the Indigo Report.

So that was it: legacy. The chance to have their work turn into legacy was what brought people like Gwendolyn, Dr. Neevlor, and Dr. Howey together. Phoenix promised them that history's pages would not forget them. By working with him, they'd be assured to live on forever.

Dr. Neevlor had discovered how to engineer a virus—one powerful enough to control most of the free world—and implant it in the Indigo vaccine. By the time the Report was written, she'd already done it. Her discovery was powerful and dangerous—too much so for the government to let it fall into the wrong hands—so they shut it down.

But she'd kept working at it—kept a copy of the original report—and so they had to have her killed. Somehow, however, she escaped and ran into Phoenix, maybe in the slums, maybe in the Skelewick district, and he promised her sanctuary. A single copy of a report wasn't the sort of thing that left a legacy, but he promised her a revolution—one made possible by her discovery. Together, they could turn the people against the government and begin a new world.

Power and legacy: the kinds of promises that made people like Gwendolyn, Neevlor, and Howey forget who they were in order to find out who they could become, how they would be remembered.

It made me sick.

Dr. Howey led us to his office on the seventh floor. The elevator's doors closed behind us, and I stared at the black domed cameras lining the halls. A placard on one side of the elevator read *"Indigo Reserve Board Offices"* in blue letters. I'd heard of the Indigo Reserve Board before. It was the governing organization that determined distribution of Indigo supplies and directed how to manage the continual shortage of vaccines.

Suddenly I realized where I'd recognized Dr. Howey's face from: he'd been on TV several times since his appointment some odd number of years ago. He was the current chairman of the Indigo Reserve Board—the most influential man in the world when it came to the Indigo vaccines. Only the chancellor's influence rivaled his when it came to Indigo supply.

He shoved a key into a door at the end of the hall, and the door's frame glowed a soft white, beckoning like the Daisies in Club 49. The room we entered was also entirely white, populated mostly by a brilliant chandelier several stories long hanging from a vaulted ceiling. Its glass bulbs glowed brightly, and a plush ivory chair rested beneath it in the room's center. Yet for all its whiteness, the room didn't seem sterile, but heavenly.

"Please, take a seat," said Dr. Howey to Gwendolyn. "We can start whenever you're ready, my dear."

I threw Phoenix a confused look, but he simply stared at the hanging chandelier as Gwendolyn breathed deeply and lowered herself into the chair, her body shaking and glowing beneath the fixture's brilliant light.

Dr. Howey pushed a button on the chair's side and it reclined slowly.

Gwendolyn's blue eyes shined brightly. "I think I'd like some music."

Howey shuffled to the wall and pushed a button. A cello's soft hum echoed in the chambers.

"Thank you," she said. "That's lovely." She shifted in her seat. "What do people usually say, Marvin? What *is* there to say at a time like this?"

He pulled a syringe from his pocket. "It depends on the person, Gwen."

What was he doing? I tried to get Phoenix's attention, but he was still staring at the light. Mila traced her foot against the floor's marbled lines.

Gwendolyn exhaled slowly. "Will it hurt?"

Dr. Howey searched for a vein. "You'll just feel a prick." He plunged the needle into her arm.

She sobbed quietly. "How—how long do I have?"

I felt sick to my stomach. The room's walls were bending. It was the first time I'd ever been present for a euthanization. When Dad's time came, he'd gone in with Mom. I stayed in the waiting room with Charlie. She held my hand, rubbed my head, and somehow made my world a bit brighter despite the despair. I wished she were here now.

Dr. Howey rubbed Gwendolyn's hand. "You've only got a few minutes. It was a strong dose. You'll feel radiating warmth within a minute, and a little euphoria."

"Th-thank you, Marvin," she said, the words catching in her throat. "That sounds n-nice."

Dr. Howey kissed her forehead. "I'll miss my dear Gwendolyn," he said. "I've missed you a lot these past few months. The Lottery's new Director just isn't the same."

"You should know by now not to call it that," she said. "It's no lottery at all. It's not random, just data and statistics. The Longevity Observation Termination Telesis Operative is well named." Gwendolyn turned. "Mila?"

Mila kept her head down, but Phoenix muttered, "She's crying, Meels," and pushed her forward.

Mila wrapped her hands around Gwendolyn's, and the smile faded from the dying woman's lips. "I'm so sorry... This is all disgusting. This whole thing. This whole place. Everything I've done. Don't give me a coffin," she said. "I've already buried myself in regret."

Mila breathed deeply. "You didn't know what you were really doing. You couldn't have known about Sarah, or all the others—they didn't tell you."

Gwendolyn stared at the chandelier. "Ah," she said, "but I think a part of me *did* know. When I saw the names spit out of the system—saw the results of the physicals, the diagnostic tests, and the reports on lung capacity. I saw them—the children behind the statistics—but I was too afraid to do anything."

Mila was shaking. She shut her eyes tight. "There aren't many names that I remember pulling," Gwendolyn continued, "but your sister's was one of them. Vachowski is not a common surname. Her initials, S.V., are the consonants in the word "save." I should've put her name back in the system. I should've saved the girl."

"Then why didn't you? She was too young when it happened."

A tear rolled down Gwendolyn's cheek. "I wish I could have. Trust me—I wish *all the time* that I could have. But her lung capacity was only fifty percent. There are never certainties behind the math, but fifty-percent lung capacity means they'll almost always be dead by ten—usually eight. Your sister was lucky to have made it to nine."

Gwendolyn's breaths were coming in spurts now, like a weight was pressing against her chest. "I th-think it's time for me to go," she said. "E-everything's warm now, and the l-light is s-so brilliant. Maybe I'll be forgiven for what I've done."

I wondered what Gwendolyn had done. What was the Lottery? How were children being killed? Nothing made sense. The more questions that were answered, the more confused I became. Gwendolyn mentioned something about diagnostic tests and lung capacity—she must've meant the results of our annual Federal physicals.

Mila's voice turned soft. "Maybe you will, Gwendolyn."

The woman's head lolled to her side, and Dr. Howey felt her wrist for a pulse.

My mind still raced with thoughts, trying to process what Gwendolyn and Mila had said: the Ministry of Health put the data from our physicals into a system. Maybe they used it to track the nation's health over time, or determine how to allocate vaccines. Maybe there was a way to figure out which children were more susceptible to the Carcinogens, and who could make a recovery with the help of medication. Maybe Gwendolyn had pulled Sarah's name from the system and prevented her from getting the medication she'd needed.

I'd never heard of any medications, other than Indigo, that could fight the Carcinogens, but based on their conversation, it seemed like such medications might exist.

Dr. Howey rubbed Gwendolyn's cheek. "Dead," he confirmed. "Goodbye, my friend."

I felt a pang in my chest. The woman with the phoenix fan was gone—the only other person in the room who'd known Charlie.

Howey pulled another syringe from his suit pocket and jabbed it into his own vein, laughing as he did so. Phoenix ran toward him. "What the hell are doing, Howey?"

The room's door slammed open. A squadron of guards stood in formation on the other side, their guns aimed in our direction.

Phoenix stared at Howey and shook his head. "You double-crossed us."

"It had to be done," he said. "Indigo had to be saved. It's my life's work." He gave a signal, and the guards stepped forward.

I scanned the room for a place to hide, but there were none. It was just vaulted ceilings, a brilliant chandelier, and us.

Phoenix shook his head. "*This* could have been your life's work. What we're trying to do right here, right now. You read the Indigo Report—*it* could have been your legacy. "

"Oh, it will be," Dr. Howey said, laughing. "I'll be forever remembered in textbooks for catching Phoenix McGann and the other Lost Boys. Neutralizing the greatest threat to national security in all of history. You, Phoenix, are my legacy."

"But Gwendolyn—"

"Is dead," Howey finished coldly. "And she was a confused woman. The Indigo Report went to her head in her last months. She was always a numbers person. Ideas weren't good for her head. Our system is perfect. The world is in order. There will be no war."

"Then you'll burn with us," shouted Phoenix. "You've already betrayed your country enough. Mila snagged your badge in the closet. We have what we need to continue. And I assure you, we'll get what we came for. You'll not be remembered as a hero. Not by anyone. The people will want to *forget* your name."

Dr. Howey's eyes fluttered as the euthanasia medicine coursed through his veins. "The people will want no such thing." The syringe fell from his hand. "I'll be d-dead. In a m-minute. And so will y-you, Ph-Phoenix McGann." He gave the guards a final signal as he collapsed to the floor.

Like torrential rain, the bullets poured over our heads.

# CHAPTER 33

PHOENIX KNOCKED ME to the floor as he fired at the ceiling, the bullets from his gun joining the fray. Federal bullets raced past my ears as I slammed against the tiled floor, and overhead, I watched Phoenix's bullets slam into the chandelier's crystals. The fixture rocked in the air. One by one, the crystals the bullets hit fell from the air, raining brilliant light as they broke on the ground.

"MOVE, MEELS," Phoenix yelled. Mila rolled from Gwendolyn's chair, pulling something from Howey's pocket before rolling again to the room's edge. The chandelier shook as Phoenix fired at it again. I crawled to the room's corner, and prayed that the brilliant light pouring from the raining crystals would blind the guards. More crystals fell, and I watched the guards stare, dumbstruck, at the rain.

Mila joined me in the room's corner. "What *is* this place?" I asked.

"Royal euthanization room," she said. She pointed to the ceiling. "Mostly for government officials, hence the fancy chandelier."

Phoenix fired again, and the chandelier moaned. Above us, the ceiling cracked, and the guards stepped back in the doorway. Phoenix fired a final time before joining us. The walls shook as crystals poured from the fixture, covering Gwendolyn's body in streams of light.

Phoenix pointed to the doorway. "Five seconds," he said, pushing us forward. "Move."

My legs burned as we ran. Adrenaline coursed through my veins—Phoenix had saved my life once again. The Feds had tried to end it, but Phoenix had saved it. Why? What fate did he have in store for me? Or was he just raising a lamb for the slaughter?

He aimed his gun at the guards as we charged. The men stared at the ceiling with lowered weapons, dazzled by the brilliance of the falling chandelier. Behind us, I smelled smoke rise and thunder echo as the ceiling's cracks snaked down the walls. The great chandelier was falling. Its light and rubble would erase Gwendolyn's and Dr. Howey's corpses forever.

I heard a loud snap as the chandelier's cords broke and it plummeted from the ceiling. "JUMP!" yelled Phoenix, and Mila and I obeyed without hesitation. The ground shook as the chandelier smashed into a million pieces, and we hurtled past the guards who fell in the wake of the chandelier's shockwaves. Jumping from the ground had saved us from a similar fall.

"Elevator?" I asked, only slightly hopeful, as we ran.

Phoenix shook his head and pointed to a doorway at the hall's end. "Stairs," he said. "Safer that way. Fewer people will see us going to the top."

I braced myself for ninety stories of stairs.

As we ran, I felt a pang in my chest: I missed Gwendolyn. It was hard to believe she was gone. Only a few minutes ago we'd been talking to one another and laughing. She made me think of my own mom. I think it was the chili. Mom always made chili when it was cold outside. Then I felt another ache in my chest: I missed Mom. But I breathed deeply and shook it off—I couldn't think about Mom now. I had to keep running, keep moving with the Lost Boys. That was my only chance of finding her, wherever she was.

We pushed into the stairwell, and stood at the edge of a column of stairs that wrapped around the building's corner. A hollow column stretched high in its center, running from the building's first floor to its top. Mila pulled something that looked like a gun from her pocket. Bertha's invention: the Grappling Gun. She leaned against the railing and fired it toward the highest set of stairs she could see. A grappling hook affixed to a cord launched from its end in lieu of bullets, and a clink echoed as it attached itself to a railing high above. Mila pulled hard on its cord, checking that it was secure. I searched my pockets, thinking I might've been given a similar weapon, but I felt only bundles of paper like lint. I was the only one who hadn't been given a gun for the mission. If I wanted to survive, I was at their mercy.

"Grab on," ordered Mila. I wrapped my arms around the curve of her waist as Phoenix wrapped his arms around her shoulders. Mila pulled her weapon's trigger again, and we shot through the stairwell's hollow center, racing past landings as we rose.

The gun jerked to a stop, and we pulled ourselves over the railing to safety. A placard on the wall read, "Floor 31." Mila fired the gun again, and again I wrapped my arms around her waist. We repeated the process twice more in total. By the end of it, my arms felt sore in their sockets.

"Better than an elevator?" asked Mila.

I puked over the railing's edge in response.

This floor's placard read "Floor 92," and when I looked left of the landing, I noticed the stairs stopped abruptly here. The Indigo Reserves rested overhead, and must have been secured with a separate entrance.

Phoenix ushered us out of the stairwell and into the hallway. "You got the keys?" he asked Mila.

She pulled a keychain from her pocket.

"And the badge?"

She nodded again.

"Let's move, then."

Phoenix scanned the badge to the right of a metal door in the hall's center and pulled a circular device from his pocket. He placed it between his upper and lower eyelids and covered his iris before pressing his face against the door's retina scanner.

"Digital retina duplicator," he said to me as the scanner beeped and the door clicked open. "Sparky hacked the system and downloaded Howey's retina signature last night."

"Couldn't he have hacked the codes from Howey's badge, then?" I asked.

Phoenix shook the badge in the air. "The badge contains a small blood sample. The codes are fragments of his DNA that aren't stored on the server."

"Right," I said, as if storing blood droplets in ID badges made perfect sense.

The room we entered consisted of walled concrete and steel pillars. A single staircase in its center led directly to the ninety-third floor. We climbed, and at the top of this staircase, we found another door and a slab of thick glass guarding the Indigo Reserve room's entrance.

Around us, six women in white lab coats stood flabbergasted at their workstations. The first to recover from the shock pulled a gun from under her desk. Another threw a handful of mints at us. The one with the gun shook her head and muttered, "*Jesus*, Trish."

I've seen many movies where the hero gets shot. Usually, he's breaking into a bank vault at the end of the movie, and some clerk behind the counter pulls out a gun and shoots him in the chest. Despite the blood that pours out of him, he manages to stanch the bleeding, continues robbing the bank, and then sleeps with the nearest blonde before receiving any medical attention. I knew this was not one of those movies.

Phoenix fired his gun twice in the air, and the Federal employee who'd been holding hers threw it across the floor, crying.

I picked the gun up off the floor.

"We need someone to give us an eye," said Mila. "Now."

The group of women gave more watery sobs, and I heard one of them mutter something about Trish giving up one of hers because she had a lazy one. Trish responded to this suggestion by showering the mutterer with a handful of Tic-Tacs.

Mila shook her head. "Oh, for God's sake. You get to keep it in your head. We just need it for a minute."

"Sorry, Trish," muttered a woman.

An employee with black hair hurried toward the stairs and the retina scanner. "But I don't the know codes," she said.

Phoenix scanned the badge again and held his eye to the scanner. "We've got them."

The woman placed her eye in the scanner after him. Five clicks sounded, and the door swung open.

"We needed two different retina signatures," he explained to me as the woman ran back to her colleagues.

Behind the door, a towering warehouse five stories tall loomed. Rows of glass racks stood perfectly aligned, filled with cases of Indigo that sat undisturbed below dimmed lights. The room's refrigeration sent a shiver down my spine as it leaked through the open door.

The vaccines were kept at a constant temperature of fifty degrees to ensure their viability. There were no workers or drones roaming the warehouses' hundreds of rows.

We stepped inside, and the door clicked shut behind us.

Mila shook her head. "This isn't right."

A clock flashed 12:00. The room's power had been recently reset. I wondered if the grand chandelier's fall down on the seventh floor had caused it.

"You got the stuff, Meels?" asked Phoenix. She shoved her hands into her pockets and nodded. "What about you, Kai?" he said. "Check your pockets."

I reached into my front and back pockets, and felt the lint balls I'd touched earlier. "Just these stupid things." I moved to toss them.

"WAIT!" He grabbed my wrist. "Didn't you learn anything from the paper clips?"

"Yeah," I said. "I can't trust anything around here."

Mila rolled her eyes. "I'm pretty sure you thought that before the paper clips."

Phoenix gripped my wrist tight in his hand. "Those are gum wrapper bombs. Altogether, they have a combined force of ten kilotons when detonated."

"Holy shit," I said, remembering Bertha's comment. The others nodded. "And you wonder why I can't trust things around here…"

Phoenix ignored my comment. "We're going to line them along the warehouse's left wall, spacing them equally to make the most of the blast."

"Won't that knock out the Indigo?" I asked.

Phoenix gestured toward my recently acquired gun. "Shoot the rack."

"Uh… what?"

"Shoot the rack," he said again.

I fiddled with the gun the woman had slid me, pointed it at a rack of Indigo, and fired.

Nothing. I tried to pull the trigger again.

Nothing. The stupid gun was jammed. I shook it and tried to fire again. Mila rolled her eyes. Maybe I had the safety on. I slapped its sides with my fingers.

Mila grabbed it. "Give it here before you shoot your brains out."

She fired at the nearest rack of Indigo. The space around the rack rippled, and the bullet dropped to the floor.

"Force fields," I muttered.

Phoenix rubbed the stray hairs on his chin. "Something of the sort."

We lined the gum wrapper bombs along the wall, hid behind a rack farther back, and poked our heads out to watch.

I stared at the line of gum wrappers that seemed incredibly unlikely to explode. "How do we set them off?"

"It's a somewhat scientific process, really," said Phoenix, sucking in a breath. "Significant force must be applied to the wrapper at just the right angle to trigger an appropriate chemical reaction within its solution-soaked paper. The first bomb's detonation will trigger a similar process in the others, instigating a chain reaction, and, subsequently, a series of detonations."

Phoenix was really well read.

Mila shrugged. "I'm gonna shoot one until it blows."

Phoenix nodded. "That works too."

Mila fired at the first bundle of gum wrappers along the wall. An explosion of fire erupted. I jammed my fingers into my ears as I fell to the floor, knocked back by the chain of explosions that followed. Smoke and debris slammed against the rack's side, but the force fields appeared, absorbing the blows and protecting both the Indigo and us. The wall the gum wrappers had been lined against wasn't nearly as lucky: it was blown to smithereens.

My ears rang as the smoke cleared. One side of the warehouse was now exposed to open air, and the cooling system's engines hummed furiously as they fought to keep the warehouse chilled.

Mila pointed to helicopters hovering overhead. *Shit*, she mouthed. *Feds*.

Phoenix shook his head and grinned. *Not Feds*, he mouthed.

Music blared and trumpets thundered as the ringing in my ears gave way to the blistering beat of mariachi music.

Big Bertha was here.

Phoenix stared at the other copters. "Caravites," he muttered through gritted teeth. "Vern kept his end of the deal."

I pretended not to catch the last part. Bertha's helicopter door swung open, and Dove poked his head out, aiming a gun in our direction. I leapt out of the way as he fired. His projectiles hit the ground just below the first rack of shelves. Thin, clear nets with metal prongs rushed across the tiled floor. Phoenix and Mila each grabbed an end and secured them to the racks' sides. As soon as the prongs were secured, they sprouted small metal legs and crawled along the racks, wrapping them in the clear net like industrial-strength saran wrap.

There was a flash of light around the racks, and then Dove held three fingers to the side of his left eye. Phoenix did the same, and the helicopter pulled away. Dove—or more likely Sparky, remotely—must have deactivated the force fields. The Lost Boys salute was merely the signal to go. The racks of Indigo flew from the building in chunks, the Indigo cargo secured by the clear, crawling net.

The other helicopters repeated the process. Nets were fired, prongs were attached to the racks by Phoenix and Mila, and then a signal was exchanged and the racks were carried away. I watched from the corner as a third of the racks disappeared through the hole we'd blown. It seemed too easy. Where were the Feds? Hadn't they felt the chandelier fall? Or the gum wrapper explosions? Hadn't Howey called them?

As Phoenix and Mila clipped the last copter's net to a shelf, a plane dropped from the clouds and knocked the copter toward the ground, pulling the shelf of Indigo with it. Vaccine cases smashed into the ground, and I wondered how many kids would have to go for weeks without their Indigo as civilian screams echoed from below.

Phoenix turned to Mila. "That went better than I expected." She nodded.

I felt sick to my stomach. The thought of crumpled bodies burning in the wreckage of the fallen helicopter made me want to puke. I ran to the warehouse's edge and hurled through the wall's opening.

"I'm sorry!" I yelled below, hoping my voice would carry down with the wind, but realizing that from ninety-nine stories high it was probably futile.

"No need to apologize," called a deep voice from within the warehouse. The chancellor stood at its entrance, flanked by two dozen Federal guards. His lips twisted into a sick smile. "After all," he continued, "we're the ones who are late."

# CHAPTER 34

"HIDE!" SHOUTED MILA as more guards poured in.

"Find the Lost Boys!" ordered the chancellor. The Feds formed two lines along the front perimeter as I stood there, dumbstruck. I pulled up my cheeseburger socks: it was time to be brave.

Mila hit me hard in the side, knocking me to the ground. "I'm starting to think you've got a real death wish."

"If only I had a magic lamp."

What good would it do to try and escape? I was dead either way. The Lost Boys wanted to kill me. The chancellor wanted to kill me. With the exception of Kindred, lately everyone seemed like they wanted to kill me. (Kindred probably just wanted to bake me muffins.) There'd be no escape. In all honesty, my odds were probably best with the megalodons. When it came to killing, at least they were indiscriminate.

Mila dragged me behind a case of smashed Indigo and pointed to the ledge where the copters had once loomed. "We've gotta jump, Kai, and soon." She stared at my socks. "You better pull those socks up so damn high you get a wedgie."

"It doesn't work that way," I said.

She yanked them to my thighs. "Today, my friend, it's going to have to. We're jumping out and diving down."

Blue fluid trickled along the floor. Indigo, gallons of wasted Indigo. Vaccines that wouldn't find their way into the veins of kids who were dying. Outside, the rain poured. The world was crying for the vaccines that were broken and the lives that would now be lost.

The Feds fired a round of projectiles I recognized as Dummy Darts. They hadn't come here to kill us—if they had, they would've brought bullets rather than Dummy Darts. No, they wanted to capture us. Probably put us on trial. I thought about Charlie and her shaved head. Her bright blue eyes, hollowed, and her chopsticks long gone. I thought about jumping from the building. I thought about saving Mom from the Caravites and Charlie from the Feds. If I died, they were both doomed. I shook my head. "I—I dunno if that's such a great idea..."

On the horizon, a fleet of copters formed lines in the sky. The Feds fired another round. Mila narrowed her eyes. "You'd prefer to stay here?" A Dart clattered to the floor next to us, its pseudo-poison oozing from its syringe in thick droplets. I shook my head. "Then it's down we go," she said.

"You don't have a—er—jetpack? In your pants? Or pockets or something?"

"No." She winked. "Just a death wish."

"I guess that's almost as good."

Across the warehouse, Phoenix held his fingers up and counted down from five.

"Hold fire, men," called the chancellor. His voice had a certain silky smoothness to it—characteristic of a used car salesman. He stepped toward the smashed Indigo case Mila and I hid behind. "I think I need a moment with my friends." His leather shoes clacked against the tiled floor as vaccines cracked beneath his toes.

Phoenix held up a one, then gave us the Lost Boys' salute—the signal. We ran. I stumbled over Mila's shoe, knocking the grappling gun she'd used earlier from her belt and to the ground. My legs burned beneath me as it clattered to the floor. We couldn't turn back. Not now. We had to move. We had to run. The chancellor's leather shoes clacked louder behind us.

Phoenix bent his knees and threw himself over the edge, snapping his eyes shut as his face fell forward. Mila nodded slightly: we were to do the same. There was no time to be afraid. No time to listen to the screaming in my chest. I had my cheeseburger socks on, after all. I had the power to be brave. I bent my knees and pushed off the building's ledge as the chancellor yelled behind us.

For a split second, Mila and I were suspended in midair—flying. Just floating as the island of Oahu lay sprawled beneath us, its hospitals and clinics mere specks of sand. My stomach dropped in my chest. I was falling now, and, like Phoenix, I snapped my eyes shut.

Then something clamped around my wrist. I watched as Mila continued falling, and a copter dropped from the clouds. Though its music had stopped, I recognized it as Bertha's, on its way to save Phoenix and Mila.

My shoulder was nearly yanked from its socket. The clamp around my wrist held me in the air as Mila fell below. I hung there, flat against the side of the Ministry's marbled tower. The chancellor's face grinned at me from far above; he held the grappling hook gun I'd knocked from Mila's belt.

I tried to slide the grapple from my wrist, but the chancellor merely laughed. "Pity about the Indigo, Bradbury," he shouted over the thunder and rain. "And about your friend." His lips twisted into a sick smile.

"She'll be fine," I yelled, glancing at Mila as the clouds engulfed her. I wondered why I bothered saying anything to the chancellor. Maybe it was his twisted smile, and the swagger in his shoulders when he walked—his smugness evident even in his step. Dad would've called him a "real politician."

"I'm not talking about Vachowski," yelled the chancellor. "I'm talking about Charlie."

So—he knew the truth about Charlie. And still he was parading her around as Mila. He knew the jury would execute an innocent girl, and he was willing to let it happen, just to prove a point. He was sick. I slammed my wrist against the tower. The cord attached to the grappling hook gun jerked in his hand.

He smiled again, his lips twisting into a grin like the Cheshire cat's. "We could help each other, you know."

"I sincerely doubt you'd help anyone in the world other than yourself."

He grabbed the cord and pulled it up toward the ledge, hand over hand. "I could grant you a pardon."

"Cut me down!" I yelled. "Or Dummy Dart me to hell. Really, whatever you have to do, just don't pull me any closer. Your breath probably stinks like… fish tacos."

Admittedly, not my best insult, but I hoped the confidence I feigned in my voice and the insults I hurled would be enough to provoke him. Get him angry enough to just cut the cord.

The insults rolled off his shoulders "The girl, too," he said. "She doesn't have to die."

I felt my pulse rise and the blood boil in my chest. "It's *your* fault! *You're* the one who wants her to die—you even know the truth!"

"Come, now, Bradbury," he said, shaking his head. "I think we both know it's Mila Vachowski I want dead. I couldn't care less about your friend Charlie. But, unfortunately, the public wants her head served up on a silver platter. And as chancellor, I'm forced to make that happen. Now, if I could serve the *real* Mila Vachowski's head instead… well, that'd certainly make things easier for everyone. Wouldn't you agree?"

I tightened my jaw, and told myself to think of Charlie. Of all the people she'd helped. The young girl on the Tube she'd probably saved. The way she snorted when she laughed, and the way the chopsticks in her hair made people stop and think. "You want Mila?" I said finally. "That's all you're after?"

He grinned again, and the hairs stood on the back of my neck. "I want *all* of them, Kai. Every single Lost Boy. Phoenix.

Mila. Dove. Bertha. *All* of them. *All* the enemies of the state. *All* the terrorists. The ones trying to bring the Federation down."

I felt a small amount of peace knowing he hadn't learned about Sparky or Kindred. Both worked behind the scenes and didn't go into the field. They were safe regardless of what happened today.

I closed my eyes, felt my wrist burn from the grappling hook's pressure, and took a deep breath. "You'd let Charlie go, then? And clear my name? Absolve me of the charges against me?"

The chancellor nodded.

"Why would you do that?"

"Because," he said slowly, "I'm tired of innocent people, soldiers, civilians getting killed trying to find five teenaged felons. I know you haven't been doing this long, Bradbury. Otherwise we'd have had you on the record sooner. The Pacific Northwestern Tube was your first attack. Now, I don't really believe you're a bad man... just confused. And I'm willing to give you a second chance. Please, Bradbury, let me give you another chance."

"How could I get them to you?"

The chancellor grinned. "I'm guessing the Lost Boys have a radio?"

I nodded.

"I trust that if you can hack into the Ministry of Health, you can hack into the Light House's radio signal."

He had a point. I had no doubt Sparky could. I stared into the chancellor's blue eyes—he'd been pulling me higher as we talked. His face was only five feet from mine now as he leaned out the hole in the warehouse's wall.

"And why should I trust you?"

He laughed. "I could ask you the same thing about the Lost Boys: how can you trust *them*?" He pulled me all the way up now, and held his face inches from mine. "Come now, Bradbury. I've done my research. And though you haven't been with the Lost Boys long, I'd have expected you to do the same.

I know who you care about; I know the people you're looking for. I've got Charlie, Bradbury—but who's got your mother?"

My throat tightened, and my heart burned in my chest. "Keep your eyes open, Bradbury. I'll be expecting your call."

And with that, he cut the rope.

The ground hurtled quickly toward me. What did the chancellor know about my mother? Why hadn't he told me more? When would everything finally make sense? I was falling now, like the drops of rain around me. My clothes became damp as I raced through a cloud. In seconds, I'd splatter like an egg on the ground.

A metal prong flew past, and a thin cord spread out across my body like saran wrap—the same type of net used by the Caravite copters to grab the Indigo. A helicopter roared as it turned in the air. Suddenly my stomach settled in my chest—I was no longer falling. I hung from the side of Bertha's copter like a caterpillar wrapped in a cocoon.

Federal copters dropped down from above, hovering over Bertha's blades. They had no guns, no bullets, not even any darts. But still, they hung above us. They weren't trying to kill us. They were just trying to push us down.

Bertha dropped her copter even lower in the sky. I couldn't have been more than twenty feet from the ground. The Feds continued to hover overhead.

Below me, I saw two groups of men fighting against one another. The Feds, in their black and green uniforms, and the Caravites, dressed like ragtag gypsies in all sorts of attire. One group of Caravites stood farther from the rest, away from the outskirts of battle on the ground. The men in that group were tall, like the Federal guards, but lacked the standard black and green uniforms, their casual clothes instead confirming they were, indeed, Caravites. The Federal copters, looming over Bertha's blades, were slowly forcing her in the direction of this lone group. I wondered why they didn't just crash down on us now. I guessed they wanted us alive—wanted to learn more about the virus Phoenix and his team had created.

In the center of the isolated group of Caravites, I saw a single woman. The men hustled her from side to side. Her hair was in matted patches. She smiled and cried at the same time as her lips perpetually babbled and her tongue pushed in and out of her teeth. Her bright blue eyes wandered aimlessly. She was a woman clearly on the brink of psychosis.

One of the men mouthed something. Another put a hand to his ear and nodded before putting a gun to the woman's head. We dropped lower in the sky. My saran-wrapped cocoon swung just a few feet from the woman's head.

For a split second, her eyes stopped wandering, and I noticed her nose was angled sharp from the side. I knew that nose. Her eyes met mine.

Mom.

For a moment, she was lucid. *Kai*, she mouthed.

Then the man with the gun pulled the trigger.

# CHAPTER 35

DOVE'S FACE WAS solemn as he pulled me into the copter. "Balls," he muttered. It was probably the only thing he could think to say. Mila and Phoenix sat facing forward. They stared straight ahead without saying a word.

The Caravites had killed my mother. They'd held her prisoner all this time—tortured her to insanity, held a gun to her head—and now they'd killed her. My neck was damp. Probably all the rain. I wiped it with my hand. My fingers were stained red. Blood. I felt sick to my stomach. I puked in the cabin's corner. My heart was on fire. It burned, and burned like hell. Like someone had torn off a piece of it and then lit it on fire. I knew immediately the burning would never go away. My heart would never feel the same again: Mom was gone.

And if the Caravites had their way, then soon I would be too.

Bertha twisted the controls, and we shot into cloud cover. Apparently she thought we'd lost the Feds, but I knew that they'd never really been chasing us. The chancellor had only wanted to make sure I saw what they—the Caravites and Lost Boys—had done to my mom.

There was something I didn't like about the chancellor—something slimy, a thirst for power maybe—but he'd been honest with me. He'd admitted he'd been holding Charlie to get to me and the other Lost Boys. He'd shown me the truth about Mom. It was horrifying and heartbreaking and scarring, but it was still the truth, and it was more than Phoenix had ever given me. Phoenix was right, after all: the lies chewed you, but the truth devoured you whole.

Now we raced home to New Texas. I wondered where they'd dropped the nets filled with the Indigo cases, but I wasn't really in a position to ask. I sort of figured they'd passed it on to the Caravites somehow. I guess it didn't really matter. Not now. Not anymore. The Feds would get it all back soon, anyway.

Bertha broke the silence. "Well," she said. There was more silence. She fiddled with the controls. Mariachi music blared. Mila pounded the back of Bertha's seat. "TURN THAT SHIT OFF!" Bertha muttered curses under breath and turned off the music. More awkward silence followed.

Dove sighed. "Balls." He breathed against the copter's windowpane and drew a frowny face in the fog that was left. Underneath he wrote "*Sory Kai.*"

The poor guy was at least eighteen and he still couldn't spell—but it was a nice gesture in his own way.

It was too late for gestures, though. My resolve had already hardened. I'd known from the beginning not to trust them—that everything they'd told me was a lie. Especially the stuff they'd said about Mom. They *knew* the Caravites had her this entire time, and they'd lied to me about it, hidden the truth.

"You can't think about it," said Bertha finally, still staring at the controls. "Thinking about it won't make it easier. Not now at least. Better to pretend it didn't happen—"

"Come on, Bertha," said Dove. "Let the little man grieve for a minute."

Her nostrils flared. "For Christ's sake, Doveboat, there are worse ways to die than by a gun—"

"And how would you know?" I asked. My blood was boiling. "HOW THE HELL WOULD YOU KNOW?"

For once, Bertha fell silent. Everyone was silent. We just stared at the gray horizon. At the clouds that never went away—that just sat there, floating. Hanging, and would continue to hang until the end of the world.

Today of all days, however, *my* sky was a bit more gray.

It wasn't easy when Dad died. I guess it's never easy to say goodbye. It doesn't matter how long you know it's coming. When you watch someone get on their train, and they leave you standing at the station, it's hard not to feel the rain.

Euthanizations weren't easy. They were manufactured goodbyes. Cold and artificial. But they were still goodbyes. They didn't feel like this—like someone had pulled apart the threads of your heart's fabric.

The five of us stayed silent as Bertha landed the copter next to the New Texas fort. Dove squeezed my arm. Bertha caught my eye, sighed, and frowned. Phoenix and Mila did nothing. I guess they were still planning when to kill me. Probably would try to throw me out in the ocean. Make it look like an accident or something.

"We should've told him," Bertha whispered to Phoenix as we walked toward the fort.

"Told me what?" I said.

"Nothing," snapped Phoenix. "We don't have anything to tell you, kid."

"Is it time for my pill again?" I asked, wondering how long it'd been since I'd taken the last one. "When do I get my pills again?"

Phoenix frowned. I was pushing his buttons. Soon, he'd have no choice but to reveal his intentions.

"Since I'm apparently never getting vaccinated," I continued, "don't you think it's about time for me to get them again?"

Bertha's eyes widened, confirming my suspicions. The pills they'd given me were bullshit, like hormones they gave to cows to sedate them before slaughter. Never meant to be a lasting solution to the Carcinogens—just a temporary one to keep me quiet until they pulled the gun.

I ran into the fort. Why had they needed me at all? Why had they kept me around? Why had they insisted I go into the field with Phoenix for every mission if they were just going to kill me in the end? I closed my eyes and thought about the look on Mom's face, her lips as they'd mouthed my name, the book I'd seen sprawled open in the Caravan's library...

And suddenly, everything clicked: they'd been after Mom all along. The moment they had me in their hands and realized who I was, it became all about *her*. It was never about *me* at all. They'd been using me as a way to keep her cooperating, working on whatever sick plans they'd hatched for the megalodons. There was a reason the megalodons appeared whenever the Lost Boys got in the water. They were controlling them, some way, somehow. Just another one of Phoenix's ways to start a revolution, I guessed. Mega sharks and microscopic poisons. God, what a guy.

As the others filed into the fort, I ran to the control room. I had to call the chancellor and stop whatever plan Phoenix was hatching. I didn't trust the chancellor, but I trusted the Lost Boys even less. And, if I helped Hackner, there might still be a way to save myself and the nation. And Charlie.

Sparky swiveled in his seat as I entered the room. "KB!" he shouted. "You're back, and you're alive! Kindred and I were worried. We wondered if—"

I grabbed a gun from the table, and Sparky hesitated. He pulled Tim from his neck and stood. "Easy there, KB... Feel free to put that gun down at any time..."

I fidgeted with the trigger and fired a round at the floor. Darts bounced off the tile in lieu of bullets.

"Dummy Darts?"

Sparky nodded and stepped back.

"How strong?"

He stepped back again. I pointed the gun at his chest.

"Pretty strong," he said. "Bertha added sedative to them. One Dart would knock you out for a few hours—maybe send you back a day or two." I pictured Phoenix and Vern with several rounds of Darts in their chests. Tongues out, eyes dazed, brains scrambled—Fryers.

I kept the gun pointed at Sparky's chest. "Show me how to work the control panel."

He shook his head. "I just—I don't think so, KB."

I fired a Dart at Tim. He rolled from the panel to the floor. Sparky rushed to help him.

"Show me how to work the control panel. I need to know how to work the radio."

Sweat collected on Sparky's forehead and he nodded. He showed me how to work a few buttons. This one blocked the Feds' transmitters. That one hid our signals on the network. This one could broadcast a message to any receiver in the Federation.

He glanced nervously at the gun I still aimed at his neck. "It's kinda—uh—nice showing someone around up here. Dove and Bertha are the only two even remotely interested in learning. Bertha usually just slams the controls and starts pressing buttons. And, well, Dove—bless his heart—he's a little *slow*, if you haven't noticed. Nice guy—loyal to a fault—but doesn't take the time to ask questions. He leaves those to Phoenix. Probably why they get along so well. Honestly, I'm not entirely sure he even knows how to tie his own shoes. I think Kindred does it—"

I fired a Dart into Sparky's neck and tightened my jaw. I didn't have time to listen to him babble. I needed to get out of here, to save Charlie while I still had the chance. I remembered the news report I'd seen in the mansion. Two days had passed since then. There wasn't much time left before she was sentenced and executed.

I rolled Sparky under the table and wrapped Tim's unconscious body around his neck. The door flew open. Kindred ran in, her eyes a flurry of tears. Her outstretched arms offered me sheets of muffins. "OH MY GOD, DEAR," she sobbed. "I AM SO SORRY ABOUT YOUR MOTHER. I DON'T EVEN KNOW—"

I squeezed my eyes shot and fired a Dart into her neck—
the Dart guns were easier to fire than their bulleted counter-
parts. She stared blankly at me, set the muffins on the table,
and fell to the ground. I felt awful. I knew she wasn't in on
Phoenix's plan—she was too nice—but I couldn't let her get in
the way. I rolled her under the table next to Sparky, praying
that even if the Feds got the others, they wouldn't find these
two.

I cleared my throat and pressed the button Sparky showed
me earlier. I typed in *"Chancellor's chambers,"* and the computer
connected me to the appropriate radio network. "This is Kai
Bradbury," I said into the microphone, "declared enemy of the
state and alleged Lost Boy. I'm tired of running. These people
are not my allies or my friends. I want to surrender the coordinates of New Texas." I paused. "Over."

The radio went fuzzy as the chancellor's voice came in.
"This is Chancellor Hackner." I could almost hear his twisting
smile. "You have my full attention, Bradbury. You remember
the conditions of our deal, I trust?"

I nodded. "You've got Charlie there?"

"Yes," he said. "She's with me right now. Go ahead and say
something to your friend, Miss Minos."

My heart pounded in my chest. My ears felt hot and my
hands got sweaty.

"Hey there, Kai-Guy. I guess it's probably not the best time
to tell you I got a hell of a haircut."

For a brief moment the numbness that had nestled in my
heart vanished. I knew it would come back later, but when I
heard Charlie's voice, a flame replaced the dull burn in my
heart.

I think it was love.

Crap.

The Lost Boys didn't matter. They had never mattered. It
was just Charlie and me. Soon, the nightmare with the Lost
Boys would be over.

I took a deep breath and read Chancellor Hackner the coordinates.

# CHAPTER 36

I SHOVED CHAIRS in front of the table where Kindred and Sparky lay. If I was lucky, they wouldn't wake until after the raid was done, and by then we'd all be gone, and they'd think it was still morning. They'd still be waiting for us to get home from the Ministry. Hopefully they'd stay safe and hidden. They were both vaccinated. Maybe one day they could join the general population and start new lives as honest citizens.

I imagined Sparky working at a computer store, and Kindred opening her own bakery. It'd be less exciting than the world they were used to, but it might be enough. They'd be alive and safe, and that was all that really mattered.

I shut and locked the door to the control room and wandered down to the kitchen. Mila stood slumped over the sink, refusing to make eye contact. I guessed it was better this way. Better not to look in her in the eyes again before the Feds took her.

"Sorry," she said finally. She turned to face me.

I ignored the weight that sat on my chest. "It doesn't matter."

Her bright green eyes were different than any others I'd ever seen. Like me, she hadn't been vaccinated. I thought of Bertha's big brown eyes peering out of the windshield and realized she wasn't either. Were their deaths a part of Phoenix's plans, too?

Mila took a deep breath. "No," she said, "it *does* matter. It probably matters more than anything. We never should have told you she was dead."

I clenched my jaw. "But you did."

"I think," she said, slowly, "I think—what we all thought, what we all knew from the beginning... was that she was already dead."

"But she wasn't." *I could have saved her*, I thought.

"No, fortunately—or rather unfortunately—she wasn't dead, and she probably suffered for a long time because of it."

I felt sick again. I couldn't look at her. I reminded myself that the chancellor and his men would be here soon. To take her away. To take all the Lost Boys away. The real monsters had never been in the water. They'd never been the megalodons. They'd always been the Lost Boys.

Mila ran her fingers along the sink's porcelain edge. "We try not to take in kids who've still got reasons to be alive. Kids who have their families. Kids who have their friends. We know what happens to these people when they join our crew— they're tortured and killed.

"But what were we supposed to do with you, Kai? You grabbed my leg. It was all over then, even if I managed to kick you off. To the Feds, you were already one of us. Was I supposed to leave you in the water to die? From the moment we learned you weren't an orphan, we knew they had your mom. The second you grabbed my ankle, she was already gone." Mila sounded detached. I guess she was trying to distance herself from what the Caravires and the Lost Boys had done.

"Right before you regained consciousness," she went on, "we all made the choice to tell you that your mother was dead. We decided that as a group—and even Kindred agreed." I thought about Kindred shaking her head ever so slightly— looking out for my best interest from the start. "We didn't want you to feel guilty about not looking for her—or worse, do something dumb to get her back.

"It wasn't an easy decision, but we all knew it was right. We've all watched our parents die, and we all live with those deaths every single day... There's a reason we call ourselves the 'Lost' Boys, Kai."

I nodded, but I knew she couldn't understand. Wasn't capable of understanding. The way she talked—it sounded like she was reading off a flash card.

But soon the Feds would take her away forever, and I still hadn't got the truth. I decided it was worth a shot—to be honest, asking *anything* at this point was worth a shot. She might not want to tell me who she really was, but it was the last chance I'd get to ask.

"How'd the Commissioner know your father, Mila? Why do you still mumble about your sister, Sarah, in your sleep? Why are you *really* stealing Indigo?"

It was the second question that appeared to catch her off guard. "Sarah," she muttered, her eyes watery. The way most kids our age acted when they thought about the last day of summer.

"Sarah died when she was eight years old. The year she died, Gwendolyn Cherry was the director of the Longevity Observation Termination Telesis Operative—the 'Lotto.' Sarah was in the thirty-three percent of kids who don't make it to fifteen to receive their vaccination—the group that falls victim to the Carcinogens' effects. The group the government tell us would be saved if there wasn't an Indigo shortage."

"So now you steal it," I said. "You collect the thing that could've saved your sister."

"Indigo couldn't have saved Sarah," Mila said, shaking her head. "She was doomed from the beginning. She had weak lungs—you heard Gwendolyn.

"Every year at Sarah's Federal physical, they told us the odds weren't good she'd make it. They told us that, but we never believed them. We didn't think it would really happen. I don't think you can ever believe that sort of thing. Mom used to say the rational heart refuses to accept bad news... I guess it's true."

"So how—how'd it happen?" My head was spinning. I didn't understand what was going on. The more I learned, the more questions I had.

"It happened in class." Mila swallowed hard. "Sarah went to write something on the board—she was a good student like that, better than I ever was—and she had these big glasses. Probably two sizes too big for her head. I think my mom bought them that way on purpose. Thought she might grow into them. That if we bought something as dumb as big glasses she would have no choice but to live long enough to grow into them...

"They shattered when she hit the floor. The doctors told us her lungs closed up, and then her heart just sort of stopped. It had all been painless, they assured us. They said she was lucky to have avoided the seizures most of the other children had when it happened. I didn't think she was all that lucky.

"Mom took it the hardest. I'd come home from school, and she'd just be sitting there in her rocking chair, frantically gluing together the shards from Sarah's broken glasses. She'd glue them together, and then pull them apart to try again. I think she thought if she glued the pieces perfectly, Sarah would come back to get them. Like Death itself would be reasonable and allow Sarah to go back for her glasses, and Mom could see her one more time. Grief makes people believe crazy things like that."

My legs were shaking. I leaned against the kitchen counter to hold my weight. Why was Mila telling me this now? Why hadn't she told me anything before?

"Once Mom lost it, Dad did too. You know he worked for the Ministry of Transportation & Commerce—the commissioner in Maui gave that away. Dad probably could have had his job if he hadn't had Sarah and me. But he did, and you only have so much time—the clock's always ticking off your fifty years.

"So one day, about a month after Sarah's death, I came home from school, and they told me they were going for a drive. They were all dressed up. Mom wore her pearl earrings—the kind all moms wear on special occasions—and Dad had on a red tie. I asked if I could come with them, but they said no, they'd be back soon. And Mom took Sarah's glasses with her. That's when I knew something was wrong."

I thought of Phoenix's parents, of how he told me they were attacked at home. I'd thought he'd made the story up. But when I saw the tears in Mila's eyes, I knew her story was true. She wasn't the mushy sort. I wanted to give her a hug, and tell her it'd be okay. I guess I wanted someone to do the same for me.

"My parents never came back. They never came home. They drove themselves off a cliff." I felt my knees buckle. I was going to be sick again. "The detectives guessed they died on impact, but they said we'd never know for sure. The sharks got to their bodies before anyone else could." She stopped, and looked me right in the eyes.

I just shook my head. "I—I dunno what to say."

She snorted. "Now you know how I've felt all day." She put her hand on my shoulder. "I'm sorry about your mom, Kai."

"Then why'd you do it?" I asked quietly. "Why'd you kill her?"

"WHAT?" She stepped back. "What the hell are you talking about? Who put that idea in your head?"

I stood silent, and she shook her head. A moment of realization flashed across her eyes.

"You talked to the chancellor. On the roof, after the raid... That's why you took so long to fall. You were hanging there, talking to him."

"I saw books lying around in the Caravan," I said. "You were studying all her research—trying to figure out all the information you could squeeze from her—"

"Kai—"

"I saw the Caravites holding her down before she died. One of them fired the gun that killed her." I stepped away from Mila, trying not to think about her sister, or what she'd been through, and just focus on what was at hand. "I know who and *what* you people are. I know what you're trying to do here. I figured it out a long time ago—and it makes me sick. I'm sick of all these lies and all this *bullshit*."

I pushed a tin of muffins to the floor. Mila grabbed my arm. "You don't know anything," she said. "You think you know, but you have *no idea* what's really going on here. We didn't kill your mom, Kai! We never had her. Neither did the Caravites, and I mean, really? Those idiots can barely keep their own damn boats together. I think hiding your own mother from you is a bit of a stretch."

She squeezed my arm hard. "And what made you so certain they were Caravites? Because of their clothes? You think Feds always wear uniforms? That the bad guys always announce themselves with gunshots or explosions or—I don't know—mariachi music? You think the Caravites would kill your mother right in front of you—for what? To deliberately turn you against them? Does that make ANY sense?

"Open your eyes, Kai—the Feds killed my sister. They ran some bullshit diagnostic tests, and then Gwendolyn Cherry—on behalf of the Federation—decided she was in the weakest thirty-three percent and pulled her name from the system.

"They *poisoned* her, Kai. *They* did. Not the 'Carcinogens,' but the Federal government. And then they pretended it was an accident. And you know *how* they do it? They manufacture viruses. Custom viruses, tailored to target only specific individuals' DNA. They put them in our water supply, and the viruses find their way to their victims.

"There ARE no Carcinogens, Kai. There's nothing in the air. The only thing killing kids around here is *people*. And our enemies aren't Girl Scouts—they don't have to wear stinking uniforms."

The room was spinning. I remembered Mila's conversation with Gwendolyn, and Gwendolyn saying something about seeing the names behind the statistics, the children behind the names. The initials S.V. The legacy of regret she was leaving behind.

I remembered what Dr. Howey had said after she died: that the Indigo Report went to her head.

What was in the report again? I tried hard to remember, but it was difficult when the room was spinning. Something about viruses and genetics... Everything was blurry now—it was too much. What was I doing? What had I done? What had really been in the Indigo Report? If the Carcinogens weren't real, then what was Indigo?

"But Indigo," I said, my whole body shaking. "There has to be something in the air—there's gotta be *something*." My lips were quivering. "Maybe—maybe it's too complicated for them to tell us. There's gotta be something... because we have Indigo. The vaccine's a miracle." The words felt stale in my mouth. "It's saved millions of lives. It's the reason we can even exist..."

Mila stared at the ground and fiddled with her fingers—she might have been crying. I thought I saw tears roll down her face. I felt my cheeks. They were wet. The tears were mine.

Phoenix stood in the doorway, shaking his head. "Indigo has never saved a single life. It's never saved anything."

God, now not only was the room spinning, the world was shaking. When would it stop? When would the world stop? The Feds would be here soon. Their helicopters would break the horizon, and everything would be over. Charlie would be here. Things would make sense for the first time in a long time. I could forget everything I'd learned. Forget the truth.

Who needed the truth?

"I'm afraid Indigo didn't save humanity," said Phoenix. "It destroyed it. It's not a real vaccine at all—it's a *virus* that delivers a slow acting poison, Kai."

"But the euthanizations—"

"Are a way to cover up dosage discrepancy. Like any pathogen, people react differently to the Indigo virus. Some die immediately after the virus awakens from its thirty-five-year incubation period. Others hold on to life a little bit longer while their sanity dissolves, the unleashed poison wreaking havoc and driving them to erratic behavior. Before euthanizations, some people even committed murder as the neurotoxins dissolved their will to live and think rationally. The mandatory euthanizations returned order to the whole thing—stopped Indigo from being so messy. I know it's hard to believe, Kai, and for that, I'm sorry."

His words hit me like bullets—I had had it wrong all along. He sucked in a breath and said it again: "Indigo *is* a virus."

# CHAPTER 37

MIRANDA MORIER DECIDED she'd wear a red dress tonight to celebrate the Lost Boys' capture. She was thinking of a strapless one with ruffled chiffon fabric draped around its hem. She'd add a blue brooch, think her hair a foot longer (a perk of existing only as a hologram), and wrap her shoulders with her favorite mink shawl.

Pouring her consciousness into the ConSynth had its advantages: she could appear and disappear in a room whenever she wanted, and change her appearance by simply imagining a different version of herself. A single thought could change her hair, shirt, or height in seconds. Her physical presence in the room was just a projection of her own imagination—a hologram cast from the ConSynth's glowing green depths, which stored the electrical composition of her former brain. It was like she'd put her soul in a box.

Sage rapped her knuckles on the chambers' door.

"Come in, darling," Miranda called. Sage hurried into the room with a package and plopped it down hard on the desk. Miranda cocked her head to the side. "Heavy, was it?" Sage nodded.

Miranda sprawled herself across the room's chaise lounge, then took one look at the box before shaking her head. "Just shove it under the desk, darling. I don't need it after all."

Sage poked a finger at the box. "What is it?"

"Now?" Miranda smiled. "It's just a hell of a paperweight." She was lucky the blind girl was so dim—the poor thing had no idea what she'd carried down the hall, the power and possibilities that could be found within the machine's depths.

Miranda watched as Sage rubbed her fingers against the green ConSynth's surface, the oils from her fingertips leaving a filmy resin. Miranda pursed her lips—she hated when people touched the ConSynth. It was too close to them cupping her actual soul.

Miranda decided she'd had enough of Sage. The girl had been useful for a time, but now it seemed she was beginning to develop her own ideas—helping Charlie try and escape, for example. She was becoming bold and restless, and Miranda simply couldn't afford the risk any longer. The girl would need to be executed, and soon.

Next month, she decided. That would leave her enough time to train a new girl. She would start with a younger one this time. The younger ones were always better workers. Not as ornery, and more willing to accept another's authority. Miranda would have Hackner take her to H.E.A.L. in a few weeks, after the Lost Boys had been tried and executed, and she could find a suitable replacement there.

Miranda looked up and found the blind girl staring at her, her glazed eyes hard and relentless. It was unnerving. What was she thinking?

Not much, Miranda decided.

Sage chewed her lip and rubbed the ConSynth. "It's another one, isn't it?"

Miranda flew across the room. What had the girl said? What did she know? She tried to brush off the question with a laugh. "What did you say, darling?"

Sage's eyes widened and she shook her head. "Nothing."

For a split second, Miranda thought the girl was on to something—that she knew about the ConSynth. About both of the ConSynths, now. Maybe she was scheming. Planning a way to kill her.

"The box is another paperweight," said Sage quickly. "Isn't it?"

Miranda released a sigh of relief—the girl had no idea. She was far too dim. Delightfully so. "Yes, darling... another paperweight. You're so clever!"

Miranda thought she saw the girl let out a deep breath. Perhaps, she *was* on to her, after all? Miranda would have to accelerate the execution—maybe in a week or two.

"Unfortunately, darling," she said, smoothing the edge of her sapphire suit, "I don't think the paperweight is going to be to my liking after all. I'll have Maintenance take it tomorrow."

Sage reached for the box. "I can take it."

Miranda cleared her throat. "That won't be necessary. You've already done so much. I'll let Maintenance get it in the morning, don't you worry." Sage nodded. "You should probably be off, darling. I'm feeling exhausted."

The girl turned to the box once more before nodding and exiting. Oh, yes—something needed to be done about her, and soon.

Miranda would have Hackner schedule a trash pickup with Maintenance for tomorrow morning. She wouldn't need the extra ConSynth now that the Lost Boys had been found. There had never been any real threat. She'd just been overly cautious. The extra ConSynth could be safely destroyed. After all, she couldn't have anyone getting any ideas, trying to pour their consciousness into an orb and achieve immortality like her.

She sighed. She had to admit, a part of her was disappointed. The Lost Boys had fallen more easily than she'd expected. She'd hoped for a bit more blood, maybe a few more bombs. They always needed extra justification for the Ministry of Defense & Patriotism's exorbitant budget.

She eyed the papers sprawled across Hackner's desk and reminded herself she was lucky the girl was blind, or else she could've learned the truth. The Indigo Report was not the first of its kind—not by a long shot. There were always idiots in R&D who figured out the system— people who put two and two together and realized what was really happening. They were always killed, of course. Except for Neevlor—the one who got away. Found Phoenix and the pesky Caravites and started this whole mess. The other ones hadn't been so lucky. They'd found their ends in the megalodons' mouths instead.

Miranda was lucky the beasts were always hungry.

Well, not lucky really, but genius. After all, she'd had them engineered to be that way.

# CHAPTER 38

WE WERE STILL standing in the kitchen when the first wave of bombs dropped. The first thing I saw through the window were helicopters swarming on the horizon, and then the window's glass pane shattered into a hundred pieces from force of the explosions. Mila shoved me down, but Phoenix remained standing in the doorway.

"It doesn't make sense," I said as my chest hit the ground.

He pulled me up. "Of course it doesn't." Another bomb exploded on the beach. "Sense would imply that what I've told you is both reasonable and comprehensible, and I'm personally of the opinion that it is neither."

The ground shook as the Feds dropped another round of bombs on the island. I imagined the plastic shoreline breaking off in pieces.

Phoenix flicked a speck of dirt from my shirt. "Have you ever entertained the possibility of a world without aluminum cans?" He'd lost it: the Feds were bombing the island and he was sitting here musing about aluminum cans.

I shook my head and glanced at the shattered glass on the floor. "Uh, not really?"

"And do you know approximately how long aluminum cans have been around?"

I shrugged. "Do you?"

"No idea," he said, nodding excitedly, "and that's precisely my point. We, as a society, have managed to invent television screens that can bubble, fizz, froth, shimmer, and sparkle like a bottle of champagne, but further innovation of something as common and simple as an aluminum can has evaded us."

Mila glanced nervously out the window, scattered glass crunching underneath her shoes.

"What's your point?"

"And the common cold? Let's consider the paradox surrounding the common cold—a virus as old as mankind itself—and our inability to create a vaccine to eradicate it in even the loosest sense. We pride ourselves on maintaining the highest health and research standards—yet we're completely unable to eradicate even the most common of viruses.

"And despite all that, the Feds expect us to believe that one day we were confronted with a wholly new and unfamiliar enemy—radioactive Carcinogens—and that they were able to concoct a mixture to stave off its effect in record time! Rather remarkable, don't you think?"

I didn't know what to think.

"If we're seeking truth," Phoenix went on, "perhaps we ought to look no further than the terminology itself. 'Carcinogen' is the absolute vaguest term the government could've provided. By definition, a carcinogen is any agent involved in causing cancer, which—when you think about it—is quite literally *anything*. Doesn't *living* cause cancer? Each day you're alive and healthy increases your risk of procuring cancer. But it's not the *cancer* that kills children—it's the Carcinogens. Are they viruses, bacteria—what are they, Kai Bradbury? Those are the sorts of questions the Feds don't want you asking. Because then, you'd realize they don't really exist... that there is no such thing as the Carcinogens."

More bombs dropped, and the fort shook. Mila ran from the kitchen to get the others.

"It's an illusion, Kai. Everything you know, everything you think you know, everything they've ever taught you, is an illusion. Because wouldn't it be *inconvenient* if people lived past fifty? If they had time? Time to question things. Time to think about things. Time to think about the man behind the curtain.

"Because isn't it *convenient* that every single person born with blue eyes had a genetic weakness to the Carcinogens? That the gene which made a person more resistant to the Carcinogens—allowed a person to survive instant death after exposure—*happened* to be on the same chromosome as the one for eye color? That, with Indigo, the government could pick out from a distance who had been vaccinated and who hadn't? Doesn't that seem convenient, Kai?"

More bombs. More explosions.

A bomb landed a little too close, and Phoenix pulled me into the other room as a kitchen wall was blown apart. "There was no natural selection—there was a deliberate genocide. And there's another one happening today. Happening right at this very moment. Only this time, it's different. It's not a single group of people they're after. No, that would be simple. They've already done that. They've already won that war. Every person who was ever born with blue eyes is dead. They killed them to make the 'Carcinogens' look convincing.

"No, now they're after something bigger. They're trying to eliminate something greater: the truth. They're driving the truth to extinction."

Mila appeared behind us and grabbed Phoenix's hand. "We've gotta go, Phoenix. We've gotta get out of here—New Texas is toast."

"Where are the others?"

"Bertha and Dove are getting ammunition. I can't find Kindred and Sparky..." She was silent. "I—I think they're gone."

"Gone?" Phoenix choked.

Mila glanced at the ground. "We—we lost the left wing."

"And you checked the control room?"

"Empty."

Phoenix shook his head. "They've got be here somewhere. They have to be."

Mila chewed her lip. "I don't know how they found us. How the hell they found us in the middle of the Pacific Ocean."

Phoenix stared at me: he knew. He always knew everything. I bet he wished he'd already killed me. *I* sort of wished he had, too.

"It doesn't matter," he said, still staring at me. He turned to Mila. "Go help Bertha with the guns."

"But—"

"We'll find Sparky and Kindred, Meels. I promise you."

It was all coming to me in flashes now. The pages of the Indigo Report, the books in Neevlor's library, the Chairman's comments about a perfect system and an ordered world. The confused look Kindred gave Phoenix that first day, when he asked her to get me Indigo pills. There was no such thing. They'd probably given me sugar pills. And there was a reason he'd never had Mila or Bertha vaccinated, even though they had the supplies. He wasn't killing them—he was saving their lives.

"Why didn't you tell me sooner?"

In the midst of dropping bombs and explosions, Phoenix laughed. "Would you have believed me? You hardly trusted me when it came to a paper clip."

He had a point, but I still shrugged. "You could've tried."

"We tried with Bugsy."

"But it didn't work." I remembered his conversation with Vern. "So you killed him."

"We didn't *kill* him! I can't believe you'd even suggest that. I don't know who you think we are, but we'd never kill one of our own. We did things differently with Bugsy than with you. We told him the truth about our world—the truth about Indigo and the Carcinogens—too soon. He became unstable. Started screwing things up on missions. Forgetting where he was in the middle of raids... To be honest, I don't think he died by accident during the Pacific Northwestern Tube's accident. I think he... killed himself."

"He wasn't ready for the truth," I said slowly.

"It devoured him whole." Phoenix's eyes got watery. "I don't think he could admit Indigo's reality to himself. He wasn't ready to look away from the light and see the darkness that was around us all along. It was easier to keep pretending things were all right. The truth—it broke something inside him."

The fort was burning. Chunks from the ceiling rained down around us. Phoenix knocked me to the ground to get me out of the way.

"Why did you tell Vern you'd kill me?"

Phoenix stared at where the ceiling patch had fallen. "You heard that? I *thought* someone was there... You were in the contact closet, weren't you?"

"Contact closet?"

"Blue things, they look like eyes. Contact lenses. All along the shelves. The closet door was cracked open, but I thought I saw it shut quickly when Vern and I entered the hall." I nodded, but still wondered what exactly a contact lens was.

"The Caravites wear contacts instead of getting vaccinated," he explained. "It used to be that when the Feds caught an unvaccinated adult, they could see immediately that he was a Caravite, which assured they received a slow, tortured death. So the Caravites started wearing blue contact lenses to avoid that outcome. As long as a person has the blue eyes, the Feds don't know the difference, and they receive a quick death. Bullet to the head, best-case scenario. The Federation doesn't have room for 'vaccinated' criminals. But brown eyes in an adult—that's a sure sign of terrorism. And terrorists are tortured for a long, long time when caught."

Bertha barreled into the room, cuddling a shotgun in one arm and a rocket launcher in the other like babies. "Oh, for Christ's sake. Are you two just gonna sit here and braid each other's hair over brunch? Or do you wanna—I don't know—help us fight and LIVE?"

Phoenix smiled. "Brunch sounds lovely, thanks." Bertha nudged him with the butt of the shotgun. He pointed to the door. "Go ahead, Bertha. A merry welcoming party awaits you." He ran a finger over the shotgun's barrel. "Sawed off the end, did you? A woman after my own heart."

She grinned and ran out the door. I watched her fire into the sky. A helicopter plummeted into the ocean. She fired again at the burning rubble that floated on the water. Phoenix looked on like a proud parent. My heart still pounded in my chest.

A projectile struck Bertha from behind and she fell. I pulled Phoenix's arm. "They shot her! We have to get out there before they kill her!"

He crossed his arms. "Doubtful. They're almost certainly firing at us with Dummy Darts. We can't stand on trial if we're dead, and they'd like to make this whole affair look remotely democratic." He paused. "How many of us does he think he's getting?" he said quietly.

He knew I'd talked to the chancellor—that I was the one who'd given him the coordinates.

"Four," I said, wiping the sweat from my forehead.

"Kindred and Sparky are safe, then?"

"I hid them in the control room."

"The control room's walls are made of reinforced steel. There's maybe a fifty-percent chance they'll make it even with the explosions."

"That's reassuring," I said weakly. A copter landed on the beach and soldiers leapt out to wrap Bertha's limp body in a cellophane net.

Phoenix watched as they dragged her away. "I'm not mad at you, kid. You did what you thought you had to do."

"But I—I was wrong."

He glanced at my ankles. "You're wearing cheeseburger socks... Not the kind of kid I would expect to make every shot he took."

"I thought you liked the socks?"

He winked. "Only on you, kid."

God, he was cool.

Dove and Mila hurried to join us in the hall, armed with more of Bertha's guns. They peered out as the men dragged Bertha's body into their copter's cabin.

Dove aimed his gun. "Balls," he said, clicking off its safety.

Phoenix pushed Dove's barrel down and shook his head. "We're done."

"WHAT?" Mila shouted. "What the hell are you talking about, Phoenix?"

"We're done, Meels. Put your hands up and your head down when you walk out."

"But—"

"C'mon, Meels." He pointed toward the door. "Hands up."

The Dummy Darts struck her and Dove almost instantly. I felt sick to my stomach. *I* had done this to them. I was the one responsible for their deaths.

Phoenix put a hand on my shoulder. "Well," he said, offering his hand, "this is it. I'm the last one left. They won't stop bombing the fort until I'm gone."

I watched as another copter with black and green stripes landed. "You don't have to go, Phoenix. We—you—could think of plan, and we could escape."

"Revolutions aren't fought with elegant plans, Kai. They're fought with instincts."

"Instincts?" What was he trying to tell me? What did he want me to do?

He nodded. "Revolutions are fought with instinct, not eloquence," he said again. "You followed your instincts, and now I'm following mine." He gave me a small smile. "Good luck, Kai Bradbury." He stepped toward the door. "I'm afraid you don't have much time left to save your girl. For that, and many other things, I apologize."

My face went white. "How—how'd you know about her?"

He laughed. "It was the look on your face when Gwendolyn asked about her."

Crap. "Was it really that obvious?"

"Painfully so, I'm afraid. Fifteen-year-olds aren't particularly renowned for their ability to mask their emotions."

The bombs stopped, and Chancellor Hackner stepped out from black and green copter. He strode past the destruction toward the fort.

"Besides," said Phoenix. "I've known for a while that you were searching for something. After the incident with the megalodon, you seemed determined to stay with us. I should've known from the beginning it had to do with a girl."

I laughed nervously. "Er—doesn't it always?"

The chancellor was gone from the beach. Phoenix looked me in the eyes. "I hope he keeps his word."

"What are you talking about?"

"I hope the chancellor keeps his word and gives you the girl."

"How did you—?"

Phoenix smiled. "Because that's what you want most." He held his left hand to his eye. "The Lost Boys' salute," he said. I held my hand to my eye—my thumb resting on my jaw's corner and my index and middle fingers against my brow—in response. "It reminds us to keep our eyes, ears, and hearts open when seeking the truth."

"You're not terrorists," I told him. "Or anarchists. Or even Indigo Thieves. You're revolutionaries."

He grinned. "I'm glad you think so, too." He started toward the door. "And, kid—I know what you heard me tell Vern, but you should know I never meant it. It was just something I said to get the Caravites' help with the raid. I was never planning to kill you. Not in a million years."

"Because I'm one of the Lost Boys?"

"Because you're one of my friends." He glanced at my ankles. "And because nobody deserves to die while wearing cheeseburger socks."

A Dummy Dart lodged itself in Phoenix's neck. He crumpled to the floor and convulsed. Chancellor Hackner appeared in the kitchen's doorway wearing his trademark twisted smile.

"Ah, Bradbury," he said, offering his hand. He kicked Phoenix's body against the wall to reach me. "Truly a delight."

I stepped back. "Where's Charlie?"

He caressed his gun's trigger and grinned. "Let's be reasonable, Bradbury."

My whole body shook—he'd promised he'd bring her. "Where the hell is she?"

Hackner licked his lips. "Come now, you didn't really think I could let her go, did you? I mean, her mug shot's been plastered across the Federation for nearly a week now. What would the press say? What would the people think?"

I balled my fists. "You gave me your word. You *promised*."

"You're a bright kid, Bradbury." He shoved the gun against my neck and breathed in my ear. "You should've realized by now that a politician's promises are worth less than dog shit."

Phoenix was right. He was right about everything. *I* was the one who'd been wrong all along. The Feds had never been on my side—they'd never been on anyone's side. There had never been a way to save Charlie.

Chancellor Hackner breathed in my ear again. "But I'll make you a deal."

"I'm done with your deals."

"That's unfortunate," he said, "because I'm afraid you really haven't much of a choice."

Three of his men darted into the kitchen and wrapped Phoenix in a net like the others, then dragged him toward the beach. When they were gone, the chancellor continued.

"Because you've been so incredibly helpful, Bradbury, I've decided to let you go."

"Let me go?" It was a trap. It had to be a trap.

"Yes," he said slowly, "but only on the condition you promise not to come look for the others. I will allow you to run off, change your name, start a new life. We can burn your file and tell the courts you died in a megalodon's mouth while resisting capture."

"Why would you do that?"

"Because," he said, his lips twisting into a smile, "the thought of you spending the rest of your life alone—knowing you are single-handedly responsible for the death and slow torture of all your friends—would give me great pleasure. I don't like arresting criminals, Bradbury—I like seeing them punished. I like to watch a man with fire in his heart smother his own flames to keep his soul from burning. So, what do you say?"

I resisted the urge to spit in his face and tell him to go hell. He was sick. There was something wrong in his head. Maybe he had no soul. I squeezed my eyes tight. I had to slow down for a second and think. And not the way I was used to thinking—my kind of thinking was what had gotten me into this mess in the first place. No, I had to think differently. I had to think like Phoenix. To Phoenix, there were always other options, other opportunities. There were two days before Charlie stood trial. Two days before the courts ordered her execution. There was still time.

Chancellor Hackner would take the other Lost Boys to the Light House—to the same prison that held Charlie. I could rescue them all. I thought about Sparky and Kindred, both of whom still lay unconscious upstairs—they could help me. Together, we could save everyone. There was still a way.

I buried my face in my hands. "Oh, god." I paused for dramatic effect. "Oh, god. Oh, god." I pretended to wipe away tears from my face before shaking his hand. "It's—oh, god—it's a deal."

My acting was bad on a good day. In the third grade, I was cast as a peach in the school play. I had one line in the entire show—the farmer asked, *How ya doing?*, to which I responded, *I'm just peachy*—but even that was cut when I got so nervous each time that I literally wet my pants. I prayed the chancellor was too self-absorbed to notice.

He flashed me another sparkling smile—yep, he was definitely too self-absorbed—and ran his fingers through his silky hair. "I think you'll find," he said, sliding his gun back into its holster, "that I'm really a generous man at heart."

"Too generous," I agreed. "Far too generous." His promises might've been dog shit, but so were his brains.

The soldiers who were waiting on the beach, eager to shoot me down, stood baffled when the chancellor walked away from the fort empty-handed. They exchanged looks: he was letting a Lost Boy get away? But the chancellor merely waved them off, and I heard him mutter something about him having a larger brain—among other organs.

I was left standing in the fort's ruins as the copters took off from the beach. The chancellor may have left my hands empty, but he left my heart full of a yearning for vengeance.

Phoenix's instincts had told him this would happen. He knew the chancellor would betray me. He knew I'd want revenge. And he knew I'd come to save them—and Charlie.

There was still time to act. There was still time for one final raid.

# CHAPTER 39

BOTH KINDRED AND Sparky were surprised when I woke them—the Dummy Darts had made them forget the entire incident. Tim, however, looked moderately pissed. Apparently the solution wasn't nearly as effective on sloths.

When I explained what happened, neither Kindred nor Sparky were very happy—unsurprisingly. Kindred wept when she heard the others had been taken prisoner, and Sparky actually punched me in the cheek. Hard.

"What the hell were you thinking, KB?" I let the force of his blow carry me to the ground. I'd never seen him so angry before. I guessed I'd have been just as mad if he'd done the same. I shut my eyes tight and lay there for a minute. Tim crawled onto my chest and slowly slid his claw across my cheek like a slap.

"That's enough, Tim." Sparky pulled him off my chest. "C'mon, get up, KB. Get up already. We don't have much time."

"So you'll go with me, then?" I asked. "To save them?"

Kindred dabbed tears from her eyes with a tissue. "It's not like we really have a choice, dear."

"But it's a suicide mission."

She straightened the edge of her floral dress. "They're all suicide missions." She had a point. "Once in a while," she continued, "I'd like one less risky. Something simple. Like getting a stick of frickin' *butter*. We're almost out," she added. It seemed that Sparky wasn't the only one who'd been slightly unhinged by the news.

Sparky typed something on the computer, then shook his head. "It looks like they've beefed up Light House security since the Ministry of Health raid. From what I see, it looks like they've got guards guarding guards. They know you're coming. The entrances are impenetrable. There's no way we're getting in."

"I'm not planning on getting in," I said. "I'm planning on getting under." Sparky looked confused. "Never mind, just— do you think you could get us to Newla?"

"Affirmative. Only trouble is getting us back."

"We'll have Phoenix by then. He'll figure it out."

Sparky smiled and stared at the screen. "I admire your optimism."

"Optimism's all we've got at this point, isn't it?"

"Affirmative."

~~~~~~

Kindred had insisted we all wear black. "It's the proper thing to do," she'd said matter-of-factly. Sparky and I had come out covered in matching black tracksuits to find her in yet another floral dress, topped with a speck of black in the form of a beanie. Even Tim wore a black sweater.

An extra set of Wet Pockets got us to Newla. This time we set them to take us to the Sewage Treatment Facility. I doubted the Feds expected to find me in the same place twice.

It was nightfall when we arrived. The drainage pipes had been covered in scaffolding since my last visit—the fire drill floods appeared to have damaged them badly.

We used the scaffolding to pull ourselves from the water, then ran through several of Newla's neighborhoods. The news of our capture was everywhere, blasted across the city's bubbling screens: *LOST BOYS DOWN—THE FEDERATION IS SAFE!* The captured vigilantes' mug shots accompanied the news. Mine, however, was conspicuously absent. The only evidence that I'd ever existed was an occasional variant on the usual headline: *LOST BOYS CAPTURED—ONE DIES DURING RAID.*

To the press—to the world—Kai Bradbury was a dead man. It seemed incredible, but evidently the day the press declared someone dead was the day the world stopped looking. It had taken less than a day for the Hawaiian Federation's entire population to learn my face, and it would take even less time than that for them to forget it. People just didn't have time for things that weren't of the utmost urgency. They never had time.

We were lucky that neither the Feds nor the public had ever come to know the faces—or even the existence—of Sparky Stratcaster and Kindred Deer. It was fortunate that they had always stayed back at New Texas.

The Skelewick district's yellow lights welcomed us with open arms, the denizens with their familiar blank stare. It was only now that I realized the poles' metal feet were rusted, the haunting light not the only thing betraying the neighborhood's age. I saw the gates of the Morier Mansion looming at the end of the street, and then, on a nearby corner, I saw the man with the trench coat and the glowing watches, gazing at a street lamp from atop his barrel.

At this point, my soul was as lost as anyone's had ever been. I gestured toward my wrist. "You got the time?"

Kindred pulled me toward the mansion. "I think he's a bit busy, dear."

The man's eyes turned from the lamp and stared me in the face, the yellow light catching in his blue irises. Before turning away, he tossed me a silver watch on a chain.

Kindred eyed it suspiciously. "Uh—*dear*," she hissed, "what is *that* for?"

"It's for the lost soul," I answered.

The man nodded from his barrel. I threw the chain around my neck and ran toward the mansion.

Kindred panted behind me. "Care to explain what just happened?"

"I—I think it's a metaphor," said Sparky.

"Oh," she sighed, "well—in that case—don't bother. I haven't the head for that sort of thing. You only have so much gray matter, you know. I've got to save all of mine for the recipes."

"Because those muffins won't bake themselves," I said.

She smiled. "Neither will the poisons." It seemed there was still much about Kindred I didn't know.

I was somewhat surprised to see that the Feds had set the gates and fence back up after knocking them down in the earlier raid and fire. Signs had been posted as well: "WARNING—TREPASSING IS A FELONY." I guessed this was government property now.

I quickly clambered over the iron gates. Kindred and Sparky both struggled to follow, and it was clear why Phoenix had never brought them in the field. Tim bested them both by several minutes in a true testament to their speed.

The smell of smoke still wafted from the building's charred remains. Only the outside shell of the place remained, and that hadn't escaped unscathed either. It was like the building had become a red apple—rotten to the core.

But the building wasn't our destination. We headed straight for the banyan tree, which was far enough away from the house to have been largely undamaged by the fire. I quickly shinnied up a hanging root and settled myself along a low branch. Sparky and Tim joined me, but Kindred remained on the ground, shaking her head. Together, Sparky and I grabbed her arms and pulled her up onto the branch with us. Tim helped by snagging her beanie. It looked better on him than it did on her.

I struggled to find the keypad in the tree's mass of branches, then struggled to remember how exactly Phoenix had gotten its center to slide open. Why hadn't I paid more attention? I couldn't believe our brave rescue attempt might get stopped before it had even started.

At last Tim crawled past me, and I heard a few beeps on the keypad—followed by a crunching sound. The trunk's center slid open and Tim crawled down, the keypad's wired remains hanging from his mouth.

Well, there's always another way.

We lowered ourselves into the tunnel as scattered moonlight bounced through branches and lit its depths. Then the tree's trapdoor resealed itself with a click, and the little light we'd had was gone.

I took a deep breath. "So... anyone got a match?"

"Negative," said Sparky.

"You can't be serious, dear."

I hadn't gotten this far in my head—the extent of my planning had stopped at getting to the tunnel, and even that had been a stretch to begin with. For the first time, I realized what a miracle it was that Phoenix was always so prepared. I had packed some dynamite borrowed from Bertha's room, as well as some snacks—I'd be a dead man before I forgot to bring some snacks—but a flashlight had been the last thing on my mind.

The silver watch felt cool against my chest. I thought back to my first encounter with the watch man, and the way the watch faces had glowed from within his trench coat. Would this one glow, too? I fiddled with a button on the watch's side, and its silver shell slid open—revealing a glowing face It wasn't much, but it would do.

We made our way down and through the tunnel until we reached the fork I'd seen earlier with Phoenix and Mila. I stared at the branch we hadn't taken the last time, and remembered Phoenix's words: *They say it goes all the way to the Light House's cellar.* I wondered if he'd known I'd come back this way. He probably had—this was Phoenix, after all.

It was a long shot, but it was the best shot we had. I followed the unfamiliar path, and Sparky and Kindred followed.

We'd been walking for at least half a mile, and I was beginning to wonder if this part of the tunnel would ever end, when my face slammed into a brick wall and I crumpled to the floor. For a brief second, I wondered how many times I'd crumpled to the floor in the past few weeks. It seemed like every fifteen steps I took, my legs had an obligation to hit the ground.

"Next time," Sparky laughed, "*watch* where you're going, KB."

The pun was almost worse than hitting the brick wall. I guessed I deserved it for the Dummy Darts.

My nose burned where it had hit the wall. I put my hand to it and felt blood pooling in my palm. Kindred made me lean forward to drain it. We didn't have much time. We had to keep moving. Bloody nose or not, we couldn't stop.

"Can one of you—uh—just get the stuff from my bag?"

Kindred pulled out the dynamite. "Oh, dear... spicy."

"Affirmative." Sparky nodded.

The three of us lined the dynamite sticks against the brick wall. A pit formed in my stomach when I remembered we'd forgotten the matches. We were stuck. We couldn't go any farther. The mission was a failure. I shook my head. "We've gotta go back into the city. I don't have the matches. The watch won't cut it this time."

Kindred pulled a sparkly pink lighter from her pocket. "We can just use this."

"Kindred! Why didn't you give me that earlier? When I was searching for a light?"

She stared at me blankly. "You didn't ask for it, dear."

"I asked for matches!"

Kindred rolled her eyes. "I think we can both agree this is hardly a match."

So this was why Phoenix didn't let her into the field.

I grabbed the lighter and straightened the dynamite along the wall. Sparky fiddled with the fuses, configuring them so they'd all three go off at once, like Phoenix had done with the gum wrapper bombs.

When everything was set, I said, "Get as far away as you can."

Kindred and Sparky started running. I heard rubber slap against concrete, and flashed the light toward Kindred's feet. She was wearing flip-flops. Pink flip-flops.

And this was why Phoenix didn't let her into the field.

I lit the fuses, then hurried after the others, back down the tunnel from which we'd come. I wasn't sure how long those fuses were, so I ran like hell. Soon I was passing Kindred. She pulled off her flip-flops, held them in her hands, and hurried to catch me. Both of us ran together toward Sparky in the tunnel's black abyss. Kindred panted next to me. My lungs burned, but I knew I could run faster. I pushed myself harder.

Kindred's footsteps slowed behind me. I reached back and grabbed her hand. "D-do it," I said, my breathing coming in spurts, "f-for the muffins."

Her sprint matched mine again. The dynamite sounded. The resulting explosion lit the tunnel and lifted our feet off the ground, throwing us airborne. I twisted to my side as I fell in an attempt to soften the landing. Kindred flayed her arms to the side and hit the floor in a belly flop.

Around us, the tunnel shook and moaned—it was going to collapse. Its walls were too old to handle the explosion. Again, I wondered who'd built the tunnel, and if it had been the Moriers. Why had they been so eager to get to the Light House?

Sparky's footsteps echoed—he was running back toward us. "Get up! Get up!" he yelled. I shined my watch's light in his direction. "The whole tunnel's coming down! The ceiling's falling in chunks—the blast destroyed its whole damn infrastructure."

We got to our feet, and ran again—but this time, back toward where we'd set off the explosion. The air was hot and smoky, and smoldering concrete lined the walls. When we got back to where we'd set the dynamite, the brick wall previously blocking our path was nothing but a pile of rubble. We pushed through.

Above us, ceiling chunks crashed to the ground. The walls shook again. I prayed that Phoenix was right—that this branch of the tunnel led to the Light House. The only other alternative was death.

We sprinted for what seemed like another mile. Every few seconds, the ceiling would crack and concrete would rain down around us. By now, I was sure the way back was blocked by fallen rubble. There was no turning back, only moving forward. Toward the Light House, the Federation's capital building.

The air grew damp and musty as we ran, smelling like stagnant water and rotten eggs. The tunnel's walls narrowed, and the ceiling above us ceased its cracking. This area seemed unaffected by the explosion. When my hands felt the tunnel's flat walls give way to evenly spaced pillars, I stopped for a moment and shined my light between the pillars.

Stacks of skulls stared back at me.

I stumbled backward. The watch flew from my hand, throwing its light across the tunnel

Kindred sobbed. "Oh—oh my god."

The tunnel's walls were no longer lined with concrete, but skulls. This tunnel didn't lead straight to the Light House at all.

It led to catacombs.

Phoenix's words echoed in my mind: There was a genocide.

So this was where they'd stored the bodies—where they'd buried the millions of blue-eyed people who'd died all at once. The ones that they'd told us were "killed" by the first wave of Carcinogens in the months following the Final World War's end. These skulls belonged to the people who were sacrificed in order to bring about the impetus for the creation of the Indigo vaccine. Their deaths had caused a mass panic, which in turn had led to Indigo's miraculously rapid development.

In school, we were taught that the bodies of the first batch of Carcinogen victims were sent out to sea. They'd lied. *Here* were the real bodies. The real corpses. Not out at sea, not burned, not buried. No, the people who had done this must have wanted something more—something symbolic. So they'd built the empire's capital on catacombs created from the victims' corpses. They built the Light House on top of the bodies—as a symbol, to those few who knew, that the Federation was standing not because of the people it saved, but because of the people it killed.

The Federation didn't rely on Indigo at all—it relied on the careful cultivation of fear, lies, and the deaths of its people.

Footsteps echoed in the hallway just ahead. I lifted the light and saw a girl my own age, her head cocked to one side. Her eyes stared back, unblinking and glazed—she was blind.

I raise a finger to my lips, hoping Kindred and Sparky were smart enough to remain quiet. The blind girl might not even notice we were there. We could escape.

"Well, hello there!" Kindred called to the girl. "What's your name, dear?"

This was why Phoenix didn't let her into the field.

The girl leapt toward Kindred and pressed a knife against her neck. "You have three seconds to explain how you got in here before I slit your throat."

# CHAPTER 40

"THREE SECONDS," the girl said again. Blood appeared where the knife dug into Kindred's throat.

"Kindred Deer!" she shouted. "My name's Kindred Deer! Put the knife down—PLEASE—sweetie. I don't mean you any harm."

"Don't call me sweetie," said the girl. She cocked her head in our direction. "And the others?"

"You can hear us?" I asked. "But we didn't say anything."

"Well, you just did. I had a feeling someone was there."

Sparky slapped my arm. "Nice going, KB."

The girl smiled. "There's two of you?"

I punched him in the shoulder. "Nice going, Sparky."

The girl shrugged. "I could hear you breathing anyways." She pushed the knife harder against Kindred's throat. "Now, names."

"Sparky Stratcaster."

"Kai Bradbury."

The girl shook her head. "Not possible—he's dead. The Feds got him yesterday. Your real name?"

Kindred coughed. "Could you—uh, dear—loosen the knife a wee bit? It's a bit sharp on my throat and you see—ah, perfect, thank you, dear—his real name *is* Kai Bradbury. He's the one and only. He's got the cheeseburger socks to prove it."

To our surprise, the girl suddenly lowered the knife. "Friend," she said, stepping in my direction. Kindred ran and hid behind a pillar, then jumped back when she realized she was pressing herself up against human skulls.

Again, the girl spoke to me. "Friend."

I stepped back. "Uh, friend?"

She nodded. "Charlie said you'd be my friend."

Something leapt in my chest upon hearing someone say Charlie's name again.

"She said her friend Kai would be *my* friend, too."

Charlie was still alive, and this girl knew her—she'd know where to find her and how to get us there, too. I wrapped my arms around the girl's shoulders. She patted my back.

"Friend," she said again.

I nodded. "Friend." The girl might've been blind, but she knew how to navigate the darkness. In Phoenix's world, that was a good thing. If we were going to save Charlie and the others, we'd need this girl's help.

I grabbed Kindred's and Sparky's hands and put them into the girl's. "They're friends, too." Tim smiled and pressed one claw against the girl's hand. Her eyes widened in surprise, but she took it and shook it gently.

"Wow," she said. "S-so many new friends. So many new friends at once." She caught her breath and muttered quickly. "I can burp my ABC's."

I had no idea what to say, so I just sort of smiled and nodded.

"How excellent!" said Kindred. For the first time, I was glad she was in the field. "Perhaps you can tell us your name, too?"

"Sangria Penderbrook," the girl answered, "but I prefer Sage."

"Then we shall call you Sage!" said Kindred triumphantly.

"Before today, I only had one friend—Charlie Minos. But now I have four—or, uh, five"—she clearly wasn't sure yet what to make of Tim's handshake—"and I think that's quite a lot." Then she closed her eyes and started to burp. "A—B—C—"

"Excellent start!" interrupted Kindred. "You will definitely have to show us more later, dear. But first, make us wait. Suspense makes everything better, wouldn't you agree?"

Sage sort of nodded. Evidently, she wasn't used to people interrupting her, or maybe just listening to her in the first place.

"We're searching for our other friends," said Kindred. "Maybe they can become your friends too? How does that sound? You could have four more new friends for a grand total of nine friends. Now wouldn't that be extraordinary?"

Sage nodded—she was shaking. The thought of having nine whole friends was too much for her. She might have been my age, but whatever they'd done to her in here must have stunted her maturity.

"But we'll have to be careful," said Sage. "They'll kill you if they see you. People aren't supposed to be down here." She paused. "Should I continue my ABC's now?"

"No, no, dear," said Kindred, shaking her head. "Suspense—that's where the real show is. Keep us in suspense, dear! And while we're letting the suspense build, we can get you some more friends."

Sage nodded, and without another word, turned and headed down the tunnel. The rest of us looked at each other, shrugged, and followed.

Sage clearly knew the layout of the catacombs well. As she guided us along, she explained that she'd been through them many times. Once, she told us, they made her bury someone down here, but she was young, and started crying. After that, they hadn't asked again.

Eventually Sage led us to a brick frame and a metal door, which in turn led to a series of mazes and corridors. We were lucky Sage had found us. We'd never have made our way out if she hadn't.

Sage's room was on the Light House's lowest floor—the basement, between the kitchen and the hall that led to the catacombs. The room was the size of a closet, with only enough room for a cot wedged between two walls. Before we moved on, I turned on the extra VLF I'd borrowed from Bertha's workshop and prayed it would work as well for us now as it had in the Ministry.

"The kitchen staff is asleep," Sage explained. "There won't be any guards until we get out of the basement. Charlie's on the eleventh floor, in the holding cells."

"And the others?"

"If they didn't come here by choice," she said, "then that's where they'll be too."

We snuck past the first floor's guards with surprising ease—Sage knew their routines well. She had us avoid the elevator and take the stairs, saying it was less likely we'd run into guards that way. But just as we reached the second floor's landing, two guards pushed their way in. Sage hurried up the steps ahead of us, but Kindred, Sparky, and I were caught at the landing.

The first guard, a fat man, eyed us up and down. "What's this? You fancy a stroll?" he asked.

His friend, a tall, skinny man with a thick mustache, tilted his head. "Yer wearin' all black..." His breath stank like liquor. He pulled a flask from his pocket and took a swig. "Whaddya doin' that fer?"

I saw Kindred taking deep breaths to calm herself. Sparky eyed the stairs that would carry us back to the basement.

The skinny one squinted at Kindred. "Yer not lookin' so good..."

Kindred's face went white, and she curled her hands into fists.

"Knuckles," she said, "prepare yourselves!" She couldn't be serious—she was still wearing the pink flip-flops, after all.

What did she think she was doing? "For today," she continued, spinning her fists in the air, "we serve knuckle sandwiches."

With a single jab, she smashed the skinny guard in the face, and he crumpled to the floor. Immediately, she clutched her hand. "Mother—"

"Kindred!" I said.

She blushed. "Sorry, dear."

Before the other guard could react, she decked him too. He fell harder than the first. As we stole their guns, I noticed that the fat one had a headset shoved in his ear—he was miked. The rest of the guards had surely heard our encounter, and would come looking for us. There wasn't much time.

We ran up the stairs after Sage, who seemed to know every step and turn of the building by heart. How long had she lived here? At the fifth floor's landing, we heard guards pile into the stairwell from the third floor's landing, swarming like bees as they climbed.

Sparky turned toward Sage. "What floor is Security's main office?"

"Fifteenth floor."

"Think you can hack it?" I said.

"Affirmative. I suggest we implement a bomb threat procedure."

"A lockdown?" I asked.

He nodded.

"What good will that do? We'll be trapped."

"The alternative," he said, "is letting the reinforcements, which they'll inevitably call, take this building by storm. And they'll be armed with things far worse than these guns. Just look at the walls," he said. "The Light House is like a giant bomb shelter: if we can't get out, they can't get in. It'll be better if we take this fortress from the inside out."

I nodded. Better to be locked inside with the building's existing defenses than allow the entire might of the Federation to be brought in.

When we reached the eleventh-floor landing, I stopped, but the others kept going. "But, Charlie—"

They shook their heads.

"She'll be here when we get back," said Sage. Guards were still bursting onto landings on the floors below. They were only one floor behind us now—we had to keep moving. "C'mon, Kai."

Sage seemed to have realized that what we were doing involved far more than just making her a few new friends, though she didn't seem to mind. I nodded, and followed her up the stairs.

At the fifteenth floor, the door to exit the stairwell was secured with a retina scanner. Just below us, more guards burst onto the fourteenth floor's landing, joining their comrades who were, at this point, breathing raggedly. One groaned something about "NEVER. TAKING. THE STAIRS. AGAIN."

I grabbed one of the guns we'd stolen from the guards and fired at the retina scanner. The bullet ricocheted right off it. One of the guards in the fray yelled: "OH MY GOD, CRAIG! MY SHOULDER!"

The lights in the stairwell began to flash what was by now a very familiar red. The woman's voice came on the speakers: *"This is not a drill."*

Firing at the scanner had sent the building into lockdown. I smiled weakly at Sparky. "At least we don't need the security office."

He shook his head. "Negative. External systems can override normal lockdown procedures from the outside: the reinforcements can still get in. The bomb threat protocol can be activated only from the central security office. It's the only procedure that can prevent them from getting in."

"And you know all of this, how?"

His face flushed red. Tim patted his cheek. "Er—I might have hacked the security system a time or two before they activated the new protocols. I've got a lot of free time, okay?" I guessed never sleeping would do that for you.

Just then, the door to our landing was kicked open, and six guns were immediately pointed at my face. My chest tightened.

"Well, hey," I said, trying to keep things casual. Sage curled into the space between the door and the wall, hiding in the shadows. "It's nice of you guys to—uh—help us out... in a weird way."

Kindred shoved her gun in a guard's face. "ON THE GROUND!" She fired a round of bullets in the air. "ALL OF YOU! GET ON THE GROUND!" She took a deep breath. "Dears," she added quickly.

Three men turned their guns toward her. "DROP YOUR WEAPON," one shouted.

Kindred's hands shook as she dropped her gun. She pulled off a pink flip-flop, and tore its strap. A crumbled gum wrapper fell into her hands—one of Bertha's bombs. If she set it off, the whole stairwell was going down.

*Like a giant bomb shelter.* If the bomb exploded, the Light House's walls would absorb its force, and the building would implode, collapse in on itself. The guards exchanged confused looks, but kept their guns focused on her chest.

Kindred held the wrapper in the air. "Two kilotons," she said. "At least, that's what they tell me."

"Horse shit," muttered one of the guards.

"It's your choice, dear." She moved to slam it against the ground. "Not like *I* have a wife and kids... What do I care if we die?"

"WAIT!"

Kindred smiled. "Hand over the guns, dears, or we're all dead." They passed them over without hesitation. She pushed past the men into the hall. "Now, if you'll excuse us..." We moved past the guards, slammed the door shut behind us, and hurried down the hall, now fully armed.

Outside the central security office, more guards waited, but again Kindred led us through. A giant 360-degree screen wrapped the central security office's walls, showing footage from cameras across the fortress. Sparky immediately pointed to one image—reinforcements closing in. The Light House was surrounded. Within minutes, the reinforcements would be inside.

Sparky ran to a keyboard in the corner and clapped his fingers on the keys. The massive screen went black, then a flood of green scrolling ones and zeroes appeared. Sparky was hacking the system. Occasionally, Tim slapped a claw on the keyboard and Sparky gave an approving nod.

Suddenly the screen flashed to an outside view of the building. Guards hurried toward the fortress, but before they could get there, sheets of metal slammed over doors and windows. Sparky had activated the bomb threat protocol. The guards threw themselves at the doors, calling for backup.

Sparky stared at the guards. "No use calling your friends," he said. "I've blocked all signals within a one-mile radius." He smiled at the keyboard. "This thing's got some wicked controls."

Kindred nodded. "It's wicked, all right." She raised the gum wrapper bomb in one hand. "I say we still take this place down."

Sage nodded. "To the ground."

"But first," I said, not wanting them to forget about Charlie, "the others."

We were so close. I'd see her in minutes.

"GET ON THE GROUND!"

A guard stood in the doorway, his gun aimed at Sparky, his finger caressing the trigger. Sparky started spinning in his chair—a feeble attempt to dodge the bullets, I guessed.

The guard fired.

Kindred fired too.

The guard fell to the floor. Blood pooled around his limp body.

"Oh—oh my god," said Kindred. "Oh, dear." She threw a hand over her mouth and sobbed as she stared at the man she'd killed.

Sparky hung forward in his seat. I ran over to him. In the folds of his arms, I saw Tim—bleeding.

"He—he was hanging on my chest," said Sparky. "I—I thought if I spun, the bullets might miss me." Tim's eyes were closed. "They did," he said. "But one got Tim... caught him in the arm. Caught him real good."

"We don't have much time," said Sage quietly. She might've been blind, but she saw us falling apart better than anyone. "They'll kill them if we don't get there fast enough. Once they figure out the building is in lockdown, they'll realize there's no escape. And they'll kill all of them." Her blind eyes bore into mine. "Charlie, too."

I grabbed Kindred's flip-flop, and she placed the gum wrapper bomb in my hand. Her eyes were still trained on the man she'd killed.

"The twentieth floor," said Sage to Kindred and Sparky, though I wasn't sure either was listening. "Meet us at the twentieth floor. In twenty minutes," she said. She pulled me out the door. I ran toward the stairs, but Sage shook her head. "Too many guards out there. Probably all waiting for us in the stairwell still. We'll have to take the elevator."

The elevator came only seconds after she called it. It seemed too easy, and a pit formed in my stomach. Something bad was going to happen. We climbed into the elevator, and I pressed the button for the eleventh floor.

Toward Dove, toward Bertha, toward Mila, toward Phoenix.

Toward Charlie.

The elevator chimed, and its doors opened.

Red sniper dots lit its back wall.

The guns fired.

# CHAPTER 41

SAGE SHOVED ME to the ground as bullets poured in. They'd known we were coming. I slipped Sage a gun as we ducked to the elevator's side, and we both fired back at the guards. Sage handled the gun almost better than I did.

The red dots disappeared, and the gunfire ceased. We jammed the "Hold Door" button and waited for another round of retaliation, but none came. I poked my head out past the elevator's door. Ahead, a desk sat empty in a corridor. Behind it, a door sat propped open and a retina scanner screeched. Where were all the guards who'd been firing at us?

Sage pointed ahead. "This way."

As we hurried down the hallway, there was no one in sight—the guards were gone. Sage pushed past an empty desk and a screeching scanner, and I followed. We hurried down the line of cells. A door at the end of the hall stood open.

"FOR CHRIST'S SAKE." It was Bertha's unmistakable voice, shouting through the barred slots of one of the cell doors. "IT'S ABOUT TIME—"

Sage slammed the slot shut as she passed. She continued running down the hall and I followed her lead. Bertha and the others could wait. First, we had to find Charlie.

Sage ran straight for the open cell door, and cursed when she reached it. She wrapped her fingers along the doorway's cold metal frame. "They got her," she said quietly.

"What? What do you mean?" I scanned the room. My heart sank in my chest. No one was there. The cell sat empty.

"They must've taken her to the chancellor's chambers," said Sage. "They've been carting her between the two for a couple of days now."

Now I understood why the guards had ceased fire—and why we had so easily avoided being shot. They hadn't been trying to kill us at all; they'd merely been stalling us while they took Charlie hostage. My chest felt tight again, and I swallowed. "Where are the chancellor's chambers?"

"One floor above us," said Sage through pursed lips.

"We just rode past it." Sage nodded. "We'll—we'll find her," I said, hoping Sage didn't detect the uncertainty in my voice. "Let's get the others first."

Bertha slapped me hard when Sage finally unlocked her door.

"Ran right past me!" she muttered. She grabbed the pink flip-flop I still held in my hand and slammed it across my chest. "And I have absolutely *zero* doubt you laughed about my flip-flops too... Probably thought Kindred was wearing them for sport." She turned the sandal in her hand and examined its torn strap. "You get the bomb out?"

I nodded, and placed the bundle of microscopic explosive in her hand. She assessed its crumpled sides before slapping me again with the flip-flop. "Now let's get the others."

Mila stared at me hard when her cell door swung open. Her jaw tightened. "You."

I stepped back. "Uh—er—hey, Meels?"

She stormed past me. "Don't call me that."

Bertha passed her the flip-flop, and she smacked me upside the head.

"Are we even now?" I asked.

"Not even close," Mila said. She gave me a small smile, and then hugged me.

Dove was staring idly at the wall when we got his cell open. "Dove," I said, waving my arms in his direction. "Dove Malone! Earth to Dove Malone!"

He shook his head and looked confused. "Whoa, whoa— uh, sorry," he said. "Sorry about that. I was sorta daydreaming... You know... like when you're dreaming... but you're also awake."

I patted him on the back. He still looked stunned. "Right, then," I said, grateful he hadn't slapped me. "It's good to see you too, Dove."

He narrowed his eyes. "Wait a minute... You're the reason we got sent here." Bertha offered the flip-flop, but he declined. I breathed a sigh of relief.

"Balls," he said, and then kneed me in the groin.

"I—I guess I should've seen that one coming..." I moaned.

Phoenix's cell was farthest from the others. The Feds had known he was our ringleader, and so they'd punished him accordingly. I ran my hands along the cell's painted black numbers. *Cell 14.*

Sage unlocked the door and pulled it open. Phoenix lay curled in a corner. His body was shaking and his eyes stared blankly at the ceiling. Mila and I ran to his side. Bloodstains wrapped themselves around his forearms, and a fresh scar ran parallel to his collarbone.

They'd been torturing him.

Sage stood quietly in the corner. "He had a visit from Minister Zane last night."

Bertha shuddered. "*Don't* say that name."

Sage nodded quickly. The worried look that flashed across her face told me she knew she wasn't doing a great job of making friends. At least she still had Charlie. We both still had Charlie.

Mila rubbed Phoenix's back. "Snap out of it," she said. "Come on, Phoenix. We—we really need you right now."

Drool rolled from the corner of Phoenix's cracked lips, and his blank eyes stared at the ceiling. He grabbed my arm and pointed above.

*W*ritten on the ceiling in red—dried blood, I guessed—was a single word: *Kai.* My name was circled with a heart.

I recognized the handwriting. It wasn't Charlie's.

Phoenix pointed to the wall next to him. *Mary Bradbury* was scribbled in the same red.

It was Mom's.

"I keep thinking," said Phoenix, "about the things they've already done to me, and the things they *say* they'll do—"

Mila shook her head and sucked in a breath. "Stop, Phoenix—"

"And I think about how long your mother was here. And the things she endured. The pain that strikes you like lightning. Everything gets foggy. Memories. Places. People. Everything. It's like I'm looking at them through water, and they twist and turn with each ripple of pain. It's like I don't belong to life anymore. Like I'm *this close* to being unable to connect the names and faces ever again.

"Your mom must have felt like this, too—like she was standing in the middle of oblivion. But somehow she still saw your face, remembered your name, and wrote it on the ceiling…"

I buried my face in my hands. My eyes felt damp. I couldn't let the others see me like this. I had to be strong. I pulled my cheeseburger socks up above my ankles.

Phoenix stood. "It's a testament to her strength, her courage, and her love for you, Kai. She stood there in the middle of oblivion, and still carried you in her heart." He paused. "I am so sorry. For everything. For all the shit I've done. I don't want to lie to you anymore. You'll only get the truth from me, from here on out." He looked at my feet. "For starters, I hate your cheeseburger socks."

I laughed. "Maybe you don't have to give me *all* the truth."

He grinned.

"Well," I said. "I guess it's time for me to be honest, too. I hate that you think you know everything. And worse yet, I hate that you probably do."

He shook his head. "Not everything."

"Bullshit," Mila muttered. "You know everything."

Bertha clapped her hands. "All right! That's enough of this crap. Group hug, and then let's go kick some ass."

We hugged. It was cheeseburger cheesy and wonderful. We weren't Lost Boys—we were a family.

Sage stood in the corner. Bertha motioned for her to join. "C'mon on over here, Paige."

"It's *Sage*, Bertha," I muttered.

"Quiet, Car Battery!"

Sage joined in on the hug. I thought I saw tears form in her eyes.

At last we separated, and Phoenix cracked his neck—back to business. "I take it we're in lockdown?" he said.

I nodded. "Bomb threat protocol."

"Excellent." He glanced at the gum wrapper Bertha held in her hand. "You've got a bomb?"

Bertha mimicked Sparky's voice. "Affirmative."

"You and Dove take it to the basement. Can you rig it to detonate after a few minutes?"

She put a hand on her hip. "Do you even know me, Phoenix?"

He grinned. "Right, then." He pointed to Sage. "She can show you the way."

Sage shook her head. "I'm staying with Kai Bradbury. We've got to find our friend."

Phoenix nodded, remembering now why I'd come all this way. "Well," he said, "can you give 'em directions? You know this place better than any of us."

Sage nodded.

"Meels," Phoenix continued, "you're coming with me. We're finding the chancellor, and teaching him a lesson. Then we'll figure out how to get out of this place."

"The chancellor will be in his chambers," said Sage. "That's where Kai and I were headed—I'll show you the way."

Phoenix nodded. "We'll meet back on this floor in fifteen."

"No, meet on the twentieth floor instead," said Sage. "It has the helicopters and the hangar. Sparky and Kindred are already meeting us there." It wasn't often someone corrected Phoenix, but he seemed grateful rather than irritated for the help.

"Listen to her," he said to Bertha and Dove. "The twentieth floor in fifteen minutes—set the bomb to detonate in twenty, then."

We passed a few guards on the way to the chancellor's chambers, and fired a few rounds at them. They didn't put up much of a fight: Sparky's system hack had cut them off entirely from all communication, and like worker bees lost from the hive, they were aimless and unsure.

The chambers' doors creaked as we entered. Inside, the dimly lit room was empty. Charlie wasn't here.

Phoenix put a hand on my shoulder. "I'm sorry, kid."

I turned to Sage. "She was supposed to be here—you said she'd be here."

Sage wandered around the room, seeming lost for the first time since I'd met her. "I—I thought she would be. I guess—I just—I don't know."

Phoenix put an arm around her shoulder. "C'mon. Maybe she's with the chancellor. We'll find him and get them both." He paused. "We don't have much time until we have to meet the others."

Sage nodded, still lost. "I guess." She took a deep breath. "Let's go, then."

As the rest of them ran out into the hall, I hung back in the room, entranced by the glowing green globe on the chancellor's desk. Strangely, it reminded me of the Skelewick district's hypnotic lights.

Mila popped her head back into the room. "You coming, Kai? We've really gotta go…"

"I—I don't think so," I said. "I think I should wait here. Maybe Charlie will show up. I—I just need a minute. I'll meet you at the top."

Mila nodded—she understood. She knew what it was like to hang your hopes and dreams on a person. She'd done it with her sister. The door slammed shut behind her.

I ran my hands along the dark room's walls, and hit a switch. The room lit up. I wandered to the green globe and pressed my fingers against its curved glass. Gases swirled around my fingertips, and the sphere hummed.

And then I saw her. She was lying flat on the ground beyond the desk, her eyes shut, her arms folded across her chest. After all this time, I'd finally found the girl I'd been searching for.

I'd found Charlie.

# CHAPTER 42

ON THE OUTSIDE, I was standing still in an ordinary room, but on the inside I was flying. Charlie lay there on the floor, her chest rising and falling in spurts. Since I'd last seen her, her cheekbones had gotten sharper, her eyes more sunken in her skull, and her long blond hair had been replaced by her bald head's soft sheen. But she'd never looked more beautiful to me. It was like my heart hadn't known a part was missing until it was found again. For the first time in a while, it remembered why it was still beating.

I brushed Charlie's cheek with my hand, and she yawned and smiled. Her eyes cracked open, the same brilliant blue I'd remembered. "Hey—hey there, Kai-Guy." She winked. "I think I'm ready for my close-up."

I laughed and rubbed her cheek. "Of course you are." I pulled her to her feet.

"I apologize," she said, only sort of laughing, "for looking like a hardboiled egg." She glanced at her legs—they were thin. "Correction," she said, "for looking like a hardboiled egg on sticks."

"But in a good way," I said. "Like a classy hardboiled egg on a stick—the kind they'd serve as an appetizer in a fancy French restaurant."

She chuckled—that familiar laugh. "A French appetizer, huh? I suppose that's mildly reassuring."

There was a fire in my chest. I wanted to kiss her and hug her and take her out to have a Cotton Candy Cocktail. I saw two pencils resting on the chancellor's desk, and I offered them to her. "Like chopsticks," I said.

She rubbed her bald head. "For my hair?"

I shook my head and grabbed a pencil from her hand. I held it to my head.

She smiled. "Unicorn."

"Almost," I said. "Narwhal."

"Heard they're extinct." She put her hand on my shoulder. My palms got sweaty.

"You never know. I saw a dolphin."

"A real one?"

"Yeah," I nodded. "And I broke into a ministry." Girls loved a bad boy.

"Really?"

"Not the one for education either. That one would've been pretty lame."

"You could've gotten yourself a lifetime of abacuses..."

I pretended to nonchalantly flick dust off my shoulder. Pieces of lint just stuck to my sweaty palms. "I broke into the Ministry of Health."

She shrugged, but I could tell she was impressed. "That's nothing," she said. "I learned how to burp my ABC's."

"Really?" I teased. "I don't believe you."

"It's true." She breathed deeply. "*A—*"

I was madly in love with Charlie Minos. I knew it right then—right at that moment—without a doubt. She was the only girl in the world who could've burped the ABC's and had me at A.

"Sage taught you," I said. My heart was beating fast. I tried to catch my breath.

"Yeah, she did. You've met her?"

"She's how I found you."

Charlie smiled. "She's pretty unusual—a man-riding-the-subway-wearing-a-bag-of-peanuts-as-a-hat-and-declaring-himself-a-king kind of unusual—but I love her just the same."

"You love everybody, Charlie."

"At the risk of sounding as clichéd as every girl, in every movie, ever: I really missed you, Kai."

I should've kissed her then, but I was too nervous. Instead, I did the only thing I could think of: I put the two pencils between my teeth and clapped my hands. "WAL-RUTH!"

Charlie laughed. "SOMEBODY GET THIS MAN A BAG OF PEANUTS—he needs to get on the nearest subway and wear it as a hat."

A woman in a sparkling sapphire suit appeared in the corner. I jumped back. How had she gotten in here? "Who's your friend?" she asked Charlie.

Charlie breathed hard. "We gotta get outta here, Kai."

The woman stepped toward us. "He's cute." She eyed me up and down, stopping at my socks. "Well... maybe not yet. But you can tell he's going to be. If you squint your eyes a bit and turn your head to the side."

Charlie grabbed my hand and laced her fingers with mine. It was nice. I wished we'd done it before. "Come on, Kai."

"Guards are outside," said the woman. She stared hard at Charlie, begging her, daring her to try and escape. "If you walk out now, you'll both be killed. Why not stay in here with me? It'll be just the three of us. Just for a bit."

Charlie's arm was shaking, and ragged breaths rose from her hollowed chest. I stepped toward the woman. There was something familiar about her—like I'd seen her before. The desk's green globe glowed brightly. "What do you want from us?"

The woman spun away from me and into the center of the room. "Everything," she said with a small smile. "I want everything."

Charlie was still shaking. I had to be brave. I had to re-member my cheeseburger socks. "Well," I said, "you can't—uh—you can't have it. You can't have—er—everything. You need to... share. And stuff."

She narrowed her eyes, amused. The way a twisted kid's face got when he shook an ant farm. "Choice words. Who writes your dialogue?"

I frowned. My hands were shaking now too. There was something abnormal about this woman. "Uh, I write it myself. I think."

The woman turned to Charlie. "Really?" she asked. "Really, honey? *This* is the best you could do? C'mon, darling. You were so cute when you still had your hair."

I stepped toward the woman. "She's still cute."

The woman just laughed.

Charlie's hollow eyes stared at the floor. I squeezed her hand, and realized mine had gotten sweaty again. How did it always get so sweaty? I wanted to pull it away and wipe it on my shorts. What was I supposed to do? God, these were things they needed to teach you in school. Forget calculus.

The woman's gaze met mine and I stared straight into her blue eyes. They weren't the usual blue or the Charlie-blue—they were a gray-blue. The color of rain-stained concrete. I knew those eyes. I'd seen them before, in a picture, not long ago.

"Do you know who I am?" she asked.

Charlie shook her head no, but I kept staring at the woman. I had to be sure before I said anything.

"But are you afraid?" she asked Charlie, and Charlie nod-ded. She smiled. "Good. You're a smart girl. You *should* be afraid. You should be absolutely terrified."

She spun around the room in circles. As she whirled, differ-ent dresses replaced her sapphire suit in flashes of color. At last she stopped, just inches from my face, and her dress settled into place as a blood red ball gown. She smiled, and it melted into a puddle of blood on the floor, revealing a black and green jumpsuit beneath.

"*I* am the reason," she said slowly, "the Hawaiian Federation exists. I am the creator of Indigo. I am the one who destroyed the world and saved it in a single swoop."

"That's not possible," I said. "The Indigo vaccine has been around for too many years."

Her lips curled into smile. "It's quite possible, obviously," she said, "because I'm still here. Indigo must have saved me."

I balled my hand into a fist. "Indigo has never saved anyone—not a single soul. All it does is kill people. Exterminate them, and the truth."

The woman cocked her head to the side, like a bird that's spotted prey. I noticed the cleft in her chin, and then I was sure. She was the woman from the Morier Mansion's picture frame. The one with the sisters. She was the one in the middle.

"You were in the Morier Mansion," I said.

Fear flashed in the woman's eyes before being replaced with something more sinister: desperation. She didn't want to be recognized.

I stepped toward her. "You were in the Morier family portrait. I recognize your eyes and the cleft in your chin. You were the one in the middle. Your name is... Miranda." I stepped closer. "Those were old pictures," I said. "The colors were bleeding and everything. How is it possible that you were alive for those pictures?"

Miranda cleared her throat. "For a minute there, I thought I was feeling something. Was it—dare I say it—mercy? But now, well, now it's gone. I suppose mercy is like love." She flashed her eyes toward Charlie and then back to me. "Ephemeral. Fleeting. In the palm of your hand one moment—gone in the next."

She was close to me. Close enough that I could reach out and touch her. I stepped closer again, but my shoe caught on its laces and I fell forward. I threw my hands out—and slid right through her. My face hit the ground.

Miranda stood above me, looking down. My arms had plowed through her nonexistent torso.

Charlie sucked in a breath. "Oh—oh my god."

Miranda wasn't real—at least not really *there*. She was a ghost, a projection, a hologram, like the ones shouting jingles from Newla's skyscraper balconies. But she was a damned good one.

She stepped over my fallen body and smoothed the creases of her black and green jumpsuit. "This was not supposed to happen. This was not a part of the plan. You've doomed yourself, now. HACKNER!" she called. "HACKNER! GET IN HERE!"

"You're not real," I said slowly. Charlie pulled me off the ground. "You're not really standing here. You're not really alive."

Her eyes spun in their sockets. She threw her head back and laughed. "Oh, I'm real all right. I'm more real than anything you could ever imagine."

"No, you're not. You're an illusion—a hologram. You're nothing."

Something in her gray eyes had been set on fire. "Just because something is an illusion, doesn't mean it's nothing. You have no idea what *nothing* is, boy—but in a minute, I'm going to teach you."

The door flew open, and the chancellor entered with a revolver in his hand. He pointed it in my direction, but Miranda shook her head. "The girl." Hackner's lips twisted into his Cheshire grin.

Miranda circled us, disappearing and reappearing in the room's corners. "I've been in love before," she said. I wrapped Charlie's hands in mine. Something told me to kiss her—right now before I lost my chance.

"Years ago," Miranda continued. "I felt the thickness—the drunkenness it brought to my blood. The way your heart boils in your chest. It was intoxicating—like good wine. But it was *too* intoxicating. Drink too much wine and it becomes a poison. Too much wine kills you."

"I'm not drinking wine," I said. "I'm not drinking poison."

The chancellor lowered his gun.

"Love," said Miranda, "is a poison. Too much love kills you."

I thought of how far I'd come: the places I'd seen, the friends I'd met, Mom's death. The way my life had changed in an instant. Charlie was still shaking, but when she squeezed my hand, my heart was warm—I wasn't afraid of anything.

I stared at Miranda. "It saves your life, too."

She laughed hysterically. So hysterically that even Hackner seemed alarmed. "You think I can't get to you?" she said. "You think I don't know how to take *everything* from you? Make you feel like nothing? Make you *become* nothing? You think I don't know how to stop your pathetic heart, you little shit?" She glanced at Hackner. "I could have him shoot you in the chest right now, Kai Bradbury."

"Go ahead," I said. "I'd still be standing."

Hackner scratched his head. "How's that?"

"Because," said Miranda, her voice shrill and mocking, "*his heart*—everything that matters to him—isn't in his chest at all. Isn't that right, darling?" Her body shook with laughter. "Your heart beats outside a body that's all your own. It doesn't beat in your chest at all anymore, does it?" She pointed to Charlie. "It beats in hers—in the girl you tore up half the Federation trying to save.

"But I'm afraid you'll soon realize that from the moment you brought her on the Pacific Northwestern Tube, you doomed her. You," she spat, "not us, *you* are the one who has done this to her. You are the one who will be responsible— perhaps the only one responsible—for the death of Charlie Minos. You're the one who killed her. Aim at the girl, Hackner. Aim at the girl and fire."

I moved to block the bullet, but I was too late. Hackner pulled the trigger.

# CHAPTER 43

SAGE HEARD THE gun go off before the others, and knew instantly where the sound had come from. She turned and ran back down the hall toward the chancellor's chambers.

She smashed right into Chancellor Hackner, coming the other way down the hall. "Outta my way," he growled as he pushed past her.

Sage heard screeching wheels roll by—a trunk, she thought—and a familiar voice. "Bye, darling," Miranda's voice called to her.

"Miranda? Where are you going?"

Miranda laughed, her voice echoing back down the hall. "Ah, darling," she said. "You really were a dumb bitch."

Sage curled her hands into fists. She knew now, for certain, that she'd been lied to all these years. Manipulated by a heartless woman who dribbled out feeble acts of affection. And she'd foolishly gobbled it up. After all, it was the only affection she had known for a long time—until recently.

Sage had figured out some time ago that Miranda wasn't really there. It had taken her a while, granted, but eventually she'd deduced why the woman never touched her, why she kept her distance. Why the woman needed her help mixing the antidote in the first place. Why, no matter how close Miranda got to her, Sage never felt her breath, her body heat.

The blindness had actually helped her with this. Since she couldn't see, she had grown accustomed to feeling a person's presence—their heat, their smell, the subtle air currents as they moved. But with Miranda, she'd never felt anything but coldness.

Miranda was a ghost in a box.

Sage had never said anything, of course. She didn't want to invoke Miranda's wrath. And it was useful to her that Miranda think her stupid. But she knew far more than Miranda could have imagined.

She'd even figured out where Miranda's consciousness was housed: in the globe on the chancellor's desk. Sage had gone out of her way to touch the globe from time to time, and noted Miranda's irritated reaction. Yes, she was pretty sure. And she was willing to bet that if that globe ran out of energy—even for a split second—then Miranda's consciousness would be lost.

She'd heard the people, too—the ones that went wailing in-to the chambers and came out, weeks later, in bags. Strong and husky when they went in, thin when their corpse came out, their life energy burned away. The machine sapped their souls like lamps sapped electricity. Sage had a feeling there'd been a body in the trunk Hackner dragged as he ran by. Food for Miranda.

Sage had a theory that Miranda had wanted to use Charlie as a battery. The girl was skinny now, but Sage still felt her energy, and she guessed Miranda could too. It explained why they'd carted her back and forth between the chancellor's chambers and her cell: they were prepping her for the procedure.

When Sage reached the doorway of the chancellor's chambers, she heard Kai's sobs emanating from within. She quickly joined him on the floor, and found that he was huddled over a body. Charlie—it had to be. The shot Sage heard must have been fired at her. Warm blood coated the floor—she was bleeding out.

Sage turned to Kai. "Does she still have pulse?"

Kai only moaned, inconsolable.

Sage squeezed her eyes shut tight. She didn't have many friends to begin with, and she wasn't about to just sit here as one died in front of her. "Does she have a pulse?" she asked again.

"It's—it's weak," he whispered. "Soon, she'll be—" His breath caught in his throat.

Sage jumped to her feet and searched the desk, hoping she hadn't yet destroyed it. Nothing—it wasn't there. She quickly reached her hand underneath—and there it was. The cardboard package—the other "paperweight." Miranda hadn't yet had a chance to destroy it.

It was a long shot, but Sage didn't have any other choice. She lifted the orb from its box.

Just then the other two Lost Boys entered the room. They must have finally figured out where Sage had run off to.

"Oh my god," said Mila. "Oh—oh my god—"

"I need help over here," Sage said. Phoenix ran to her side. "Check the box for directions," she instructed.

Phoenix sighed. "They don't put directions in the boxes."

"How do you know?"

"I just—I know." She heard him grab something from the box. "But we'll need these clips, and these metal nodes. They've got special salve on their backs. They'll need to go on Charlie's temples after we've attached the battery."

Sage wondered how her new friend knew so much about it, but she was glad he did. She nodded and moved over next to Kai.

Mila was breathing hard. "She—she's dying, Phoenix." Sage could hear the hesitation in her voice.

"We can save her, Meels. Sage, hand me those cords attached to the ConSynth." Sage passed him the two cords. They were hollow like tubing. "One for the current battery," he said, "and one for when the battery needs replacement. The Con-Synth can never be without power."

Sage's arm brushed his shoulder—she could tell he was strong. "How—how do you know all this?"

"Look—we don't have much time. We have to find Charlie a battery. Are there guards in the hall?" Sage got the feeling he wanted to avoid the subject of how he'd known about the ConSynth.

There were no guards in the hall—they'd all disappeared. Gone to the roof, probably, to assist with Hackner's escape copter. There was no more time. If they wanted to save Charlie, they needed a battery.

Sage felt along the length of one of the cords Phoenix had handed her. One end led to the globe—the ConSynth, Phoenix had called it—and the other end led to a needle wrapped in plastic packaging. Like an IV of sorts. But this kind didn't feed you, she knew. You fed *it*, and it drained you to the bone.

She touched Charlie's hand one last time, and then slid the needle into her own vein.

Phoenix grabbed her arm. "What the hell are you doing?"

Sage felt sleepy. She shook her head. "We both know there are no guards outside. This has to be done." She'd failed Charlie once already, when they'd tried to escape. She wouldn't do it again.

She'd lived a decent life. She'd had her share of sorrow, sure, but she'd also had joy and—now—hope. That was something that Charlie had helped her to see. It was all right, now, if this was how she spent the rest of her life. Sage was prepared to save her friend; perhaps because she knew her friend had already saved her.

Phoenix took her hand and pressed it to his head, holding two of her fingers and her thumb spread against the side of his face, her wrist turned outward, not inward like the federal salute. This was something different—something good.

"The Lost Boys' salute," he told her. "Open eyes, ears, and heart. I salute you, Sage."

She smiled. A tingling sensation rushed up the length of her arm and filled her insides. She felt warm, the way she'd felt the first time she met Charlie. When she knew she'd made a new friend. Miranda had never known Sage at all. Sage wasn't dumb. She was brave. And she had friends.

This was enough. This was more than anything she'd known in a long, long time. Her body was tingly and warm as the ConSynth's drugs washed over her like a wave. It felt like she was being lifted in the air. Like she was basking in the sun's warmth on a Kauai beach. Like Charlie was touching her hand against Sage's cheek. Her whole body radiated warmth. There was a splintering moment of joy.

Rapture.

And then, nothing.

# CHAPTER 44

PHOENIX SLID THE metal nodes over Charlie's temples, and I watched as her body convulsed and Sage's went limp. Charlie's head rolled back and her mouth foamed, her whole body shaking.

Mila pressed my face to her shoulder. "Look at me," she said. "Don't think about anything else. Just look at me."

What were they doing to Charlie? Oh, god, what were they doing to her? We were inside, but somehow it felt like it was raining. Everything in my world was falling down, like concrete chunks from the tunnel's ceiling. I'd missed my one chance to kiss Charlie, and I'd never get it again. Soon, she'd be gone—if she wasn't already.

A guttural moan escaped her lips and her chest lurched. She quivered and shook, then fell back to the ground, her skin cold and gray. Mila squeezed me tight against her shoulder. I reached for Charlie's wrist. There was no pulse.

She was dead.

It felt like the floor had fallen out from under us. My heart plummeted in my chest. Miranda should have killed me. I guessed she sort of did. The glass orb glowed red next to Sage's limp body. Swirls danced beneath its rounded glass.

The word *CALIBRATING* flashed across the sphere. A clock appeared amid its swirls, and it blinked *72:00*. I watched Phoenix peel the metal nodes from Charlie's forehead.

"What—what did you do to her?" The words caught in my throat and I fought hard to swallow tears.

Phoenix lifted Sage's body in his arms. "Sage saved her. Charlie's going to be all right."

The heat had gone out from the room. I looked at Charlie's body: cold, lifeless. I pressed my hand against her cheek, caressed bones that stood out so easily. Her eyes were shut tight and her face looked peaceful, as if she'd merely dozed off for a brief nap. I'd never see her Charlie-blue eyes again.

Phoenix grabbed my arm. "We've got to get out of here, Kai. The others are meeting us at the top."

I couldn't stop staring at Charlie. Phoenix put his hand on my shoulder. "She'll be okay," he said. "She's in here now." I rubbed the red glass orb and stared at its blinking clock. "You've got to trust me, Kai."

I nodded and tried to ignore the weight that settled on my shoulders like an iron coat.

"Check the desk," said Phoenix to Mila. "Do you see anything?"

"Phoenix—we don't—there's no time."

She, too, had been rattled by Charlie's death. I glanced at Sage's body, hanging limp in Phoenix's arms. Her cheeks were rosy, her lips parted in a brief smile.

"Check the desk," said Phoenix again.

Mila flipped through stacks of paper. "Memo, memo, magazine, memo, analytics report, oh god—" She held up a familiar book that was now bound together by brass rings. "The Indigo Report."

Phoenix nodded. "Take it with us."

I glanced one last time at Charlie's body and stroked her hand with mine. Her spirit was no longer there; only her physical body remained. And Charlie had always been so much more than just a body. I had to trust Phoenix. She was okay. Somehow, she was okay.

Together, we ran through empty halls toward the elevators. Phoenix carried Sage's limp body, her chest rising and falling with shallow breaths. I gripped the red orb, the ConSynth, between my hands, the red swirls spinning around my fingertips in shapes that looked like hearts.

The elevator chimed when we reached the twentieth floor.

"Get down," I said to Phoenix and Mila. We all threw ourselves against the sides and dropped to the floor. Bullets pounded the elevator's back wall the minute the doors opened. I slid Mila a gun across the tiled floor, and she threw a hand out and fired into the fray.

Her gun froze and she showed me her cartridge. "Shit," she muttered. "Outta bullets."

Through the open doors, I saw the row of guards shift their guns toward another elevator as it, too, chimed. They fired several round in its direction.

Who was in there? Kindred? Sparky? Bertha? Dove? Did they know to duck? Were they hit? I glanced at Sage's limp body. When was this all going to be over?

A voice thundered a poor rendition of the mariachi classic: "*DAW-DUH-DUH, DAW-DUH-DUH, DAW-DUH-DUH! DAW-DUH-DUH, DAW-DUH-DUH, DAW-DUH-DUH! DAW-DUH-DUH! DAW-DUH-DUH, DAW-DUH-DUH! DUH-DAW-DUH-DAW-DUH-DUH-DUH-DAW!*"

Big Bertha was here.

She fired back at the guards, knocking them one by one to the ground. Her bullets made a piercing sound, unlike normal bullets, when they struck flesh. She must've rigged something from old weapons she'd found in the basement.

The guards stared at the doors, stunned, while she reloaded.

"DAMN IT, CRAIG!" shouted an injured guard curled on the floor. "MY OTHER SHOULDER!"

We ran past the group as they continued to stare, dumbstruck, at Bertha's elevator. Glancing around, I noticed this floor was different than the others. Like the Indigo Reserve at

the Ministry of Health, it was more of a warehouse than anything else, equipped with massively high vaulted ceilings that
reminded me of airplane hangar. Racks of supply-filled shelves
lined one side of the room, rows of helicopters the other.
Hordes of men were piling into the copters. The chancellor
and Miranda had to be among them.

"Anyone see Sparky?" said Phoenix as we ran toward the
safety of the shelves. There were at least two hundred guards
in the room. Even without working radios, they flocked to this
floor like bees to a hive.

"Not yet," said Mila. "How much time do we have?"

Phoenix shook his head. "Don't have a watch."

I reached down into my shirt and pulled out the glowing
watch. "Five minutes," I said, and we ducked behind a row of
shelves.

Phoenix admired the watch's white glow. "Where'd you get
that from?"

"Skelewick neighborhood."

His lips turned up in a small smile. "You used the tunnel." I
nodded. "I thought you might have—it was the sort of crazy
thing I would've tried."

Mila pulled cardboard boxes off the shelves. "Bullets," she
said, reloading her gun.

The guards closed in on Bertha's elevator—a few had broken from the line and pretended to wander the shelves, searching for the group of intruders who'd run past them so easily.
But as soon as they felt they'd made a good show of it, they
took off toward the copters to escape.

Bertha's singing had quieted now—she must be running
out of ammo. Mila charged.

As she fired at the line of men, a few fell to the ground, but
a couple of them made a dash straight for Bertha's elevator,
guns swinging across their chest as they ran. Bertha was done
for.

A copter lifted off the ground at the massive room's other
end. Its blades sliced through the air like butter, creating gusts
of winds like hurricanes as it lifted toward the room's high

vaulted ceiling. I squinted and saw two figures plummet from its side, abandoning ship.

Phoenix had seen the figures too. "Sparky and Kindred," he said.

The helicopter slammed into the ceiling, sparks flying from its blades as they cut through the warehouse, its burning wreckage lighting the other helicopters as it fell.

The room broke into chaos. The guards running toward Bertha's elevator turned and headed for cover. Bertha, and now Dove I saw, took advantage of the opportunity to dash from their elevator toward the shelves. I waved to them, and they joined us in the shadows.

Bertha looked at Sage's limp body and frowned. "What the hell happened to her?" Her eyes followed the cord from Sage's arm to the orb in my hands. "Wait—where's Charlie?"

I stared at the ground and took a deep breath.

Bertha stepped back. "Oh," she said quietly amidst the chaos. "I'm—I'm so sorry, Kai."

"It's okay," I said. I glanced at the red orb. "Phoenix says Charlie's in here."

"In a big-ass Easter egg?"

"Well—it's not an egg, exactly," I explained. "It's an orb."

"Right," she said. "An orb." Dove still looked confused, but Bertha whispered in his ear, "Already cremated her," and he gave me a sympathetic nod.

At the other end of the aisle, I saw the shadows of Sparky and Kindred. "Over here!" I yelled. "Hey! Over here!"

More copters burst into flames like fireworks. Men were on fire, and ran like screaming torches. Kindred and Sparky limped over to where we stood. Sparky clutched Tim's body tightly to his chest.

"You two all right?" said Phoenix.

"Affirmative," said Sparky.

Mila grabbed Tim from Sparky's arms—a tourniquet had been wrapped around his wound. The sloth stretched his uninjured arm toward her face and stuck out his tongue. Mila wiped tears from her eyes and laughed.

"How do we get out of here, Sparks?"

"I coded a glitch in the system," said Sparky. "When the bomb goes off, the computer will reset itself. The restart should disable the lockdown, and open the building's doors and windows as it recalibrates security settings."

Phoenix nodded. "You're a genius, Sparky. We can hijack a helicopter and be out of here in less than a minute. Simple."

Through the shelves, I saw guards swarm the few remaining helicopters. Apparently having decided it was every soldier for himself, they fired bullets at each another and jockeyed for the limited spots, scrambling to get away from the stronghold that had become a prison. As one copter lifted from the ground, guards below threw themselves at its landing skids. It teetered in the air, the extra weight throwing it off balance, and then it slowly lowered back to the ground, its blades ripping into two other copters, lighting them into oblivion.

Phoenix was wrong—this would not be simple.

The building shook, and we were knocked to the ground. Supporting columns moaned and shelves fell like dominos, crashing into each other as the room continued to shake. We jumped out of the way as the shelf we hid behind toppled.

Bertha's bomb must have gone off. The ceiling was falling down around us in chunks. Screams saturated the air as falling shelves crushed guards.

There wasn't much time. The entire Light House was crashing to the ground.

# CHAPTER 45

"GIVE ME YOUR GUN," Phoenix said to Bertha as we ran. She tossed him her weapon, and he caught it between his neck and shoulder, reminding me again that he was more Hercules than man. "You take Sage," he said to Dove, and passed the girl over to him. "Don't let her get far from Kai, or the cord will come undone."

Phoenix fired a test shot from the gun, and the bullet hissed as it left the barrel. "What the hell are these?" He turned to Bertha. "Some sort of dart?"

She smiled. "Not darts—nails."

"Nails?"

"Rusty ones," she said with a twinkle in her eye. "Only thing they had in the basement."

No wonder the guards had fallen so quickly—the nails had broken into shrapnel as they flew from the barrel.

Dove scrunched his nose. "God, did it stink down there! Worst smelling basement I've ever been in!"

I shook my head. "It wasn't just a basement, Dove. There are catacombs down there."

Bertha's face looked queasy, but Dove nodded, unfazed. "Ah, *cat*acombs," he said, knowingly. "I thought it had something to do with cats. Litter boxes smell terrible."

Kindred patted his arm. "Bless your heart, dear."

We ran toward the burning chaos, entering the fray as guards killed one another, too preoccupied with their own survival to pay any attention to us. Phoenix fired nails at any guard foolish enough to get in our way. We ran to the warehouse's other end, toward an area where the ceiling slid back into pockets, revealing open sky.

Behind us, guards clawed at one another. Fingers gouged eyes, feet crushed ankles, and blood coated the floor like syrup. Phoenix pointed to the closest copter. Its engine was already humming, and its blades fired up. Guards swarmed it, attracted to the engine's hum like bugs to light.

Bertha whacked a guard with her pink flip-flops, and then spun them in the air like a pair of nunchucks, knocking more guards to the ground. Phoenix and Mila fired their guns, and nails and bullets flew through the air.

Kindred rubbed the glass orb in my hands. "I'm so sorry, dear," she said. "But it is a lovely vase."

I shook my head. "Charlie's in here."

She smiled knowingly—like it made perfect sense. "How wonderful, dear!"

We pushed through to the revving copter, Phoenix and Mila taking out most of the guards with their guns. A young man in uniform, however, remained in the pilot's seat. Bertha elbowed past him, and he pointed his gun in her direction. Her hair stuck out to the sides in patches and her eyes were wild.

The young man snickered. "A *girl* in the pilot's seat? Just crash the copter now, why don't you?"

Bertha beat the shit out of him with her flip-flops, then tossed his abused body to the ground and slammed the door shut behind him. She wiped snot and sweat from her face before settling into the pilot's seat.

Dove threw up his hands. "WOO!" he shouted. "GIRL POWER!"

Mila rolled her eyes. The ground shook again. The floor below the copter was cracking into pieces.

"Get us in the air, Bertha!" shouted Phoenix. "Now, preferably!"

The landing skids lifted, and we hovered. The floor we'd rested on moments before crumbled into pieces like bread. Men threw themselves at our landing skids, a few successfully grabbing on, and the copter rocked from the extra weight. But Bertha flicked the controls, and the men fell into the growing abyss.

Another copter hovered near ours, and its rotor caught our skids, jerking us in the air.

Bertha sucked in a breath. "Fasten your seat belts, boys and girls." She glanced back at the cabin. "And sloths. Tim—I'm looking at you... I can wait."

"BERTHA!" Phoenix yelled. "The whole building is going down!"

"JUST LIKE THE LEVEL OF RESPECT IN THIS COCKPIT!"

She flicked the controls, and we sailed up and out of the warehouse. Rising copters crashed to the ground, falling into an abyss of fire and smashed rotor blades.

As our copter hovered in the air, a few others joined us. Below, I saw the supply shelves plummet through the floor as the Light House's insides were consumed by fire.

At last, one final copter darted out the opening, billows of smoke erupting from the tumbling ruins behind it. It hovered near the others for a moment, then darted toward us. As it approached, its door swung open, and we were greeted by Chancellor Hackner's twisted grin. Beyond him, an orb glowed green in the cabin.

He waved at me through the open door, his smile so white it burned through our fogged glass. There were other men in his copter I didn't recognize—probably ministers, council members, or other corrupt politicians.

I glanced at Mila. "Pull the door open."

She gave me a look. "You're kidding me."

Phoenix threw it open and tossed me his gun. I leaned out the door while he held my legs.

"Pity about the girl," the chancellor shouted. "It was never my intention for you to have to live without her. If I had my way, you wouldn't have lived at all. You will forgive me, though, won't you, Bradbury?"

"GO TO HELL!"

I aimed at his throat and fired. A nail flew out in shards, bouncing off the side of his copter.

His lips twisted into another grin. "You can't be serious, Bradbury," he laughed. "This is too rich." I fired again. The nails struck empty air. He laughed harder. "You're killing me, Bradbury. God, this is good—your mother's *drool* had better aim."

"Aim high," said Phoenix. "Just above his head, brace the butt of the gun against your shoulder, and lean with it when it kicks."

I tightened my grip on the trigger. Hackner grabbed a gun from his cabin and aimed in my direction. I fired again.

A nail drove through the palm of his right hand. The gun fell from his grasp. He howled in pain, his eyes wild, and blood streamed down his arm.

"YOU LITTLE SHIT!" he snarled. "YOU'RE DEAD, BRADBURY! THAT I PROMISE YOU! I WON'T REST UNTIL YOU DIE WITH MY HANDS WRAPPED AROUND YOUR SKINNY LITTLE THROAT!"

A pink flip-flop flew from our copter and slapped him across the cheek. Mila gave me a wink. "Someone had to do it."

Chancellor Hackner slammed closed his copter door. Through the tinted glass he mouthed: *I will kill you, Bradbury.* And then his copter tore off into the clouds.

Bertha pushed onward through the sky.

I turned to Phoenix. "We're gonna let them get away? After all they've done?"

Phoenix shook his head. "Today is not our day."

"The hell it's not. We just brought down the Federation's capital building."

"What would you have us do?" he asked. "Kill them all right now? Maybe get a few of ourselves killed in the process?"

"Then why did you give me your gun?"

"It was too far for a kill shot, but he deserved to have someone to shut his mouth. And you deserved to taste vengeance," he said. "They're not getting away, Kai. We can always find them. They're just people."

I looked at the clouds the chancellor's copter had cut through. "Some people are more than just people," I said. "*Those* people are more than just people."

"And we're more than people," said Phoenix. "We're the sun breaking after years of rain. We're the revolution. But killing off a few government officials won't make the Federation's people realize that. It will make them hate us for telling them everything they know is wrong. Killing the chancellor will just make him a martyr, and the people don't need a martyr just yet. They need the truth."

I shook my head. "I don't need the truth anymore. I just need Charlie. Mom and Charlie." Kindred rubbed my back and squeezed my shoulder. "Mom had this dip in her nose," I continued. "Like a dimple—you could really see it when she smiled."

"I bet she smiled a lot," said Kindred.

I nodded. "Yeah, she did." A pit formed in my stomach again. "It's strange to think I'll never see her again."

Kindred shook her head. "You'll see her again, dear."

I forced a smile. "Thanks, Kindred." I stared out the window at the sprawling sea. It started raining. "I wish you could've seen Charlie's chopsticks. They always stuck straight out from the back of her bun. Sometimes, when she was in class, a pencil joined them. Occasionally a toothbrush, if she'd had a rough morning. Mom joked she even wore her chopsticks to sleep."

Phoenix squeezed my shoulder. "Hang in there, kid."

I glanced at the numbers swirling in the red orb. They flashed and changed to *71:00*.

"Seventy-one hours," said Phoenix. I just sighed and nodded.

Phoenix rubbed the ConSynth's edge. "Take us home, Bertha," he said at last.

# CHAPTER 46

SPARKY SAID OUR names were all over the news. According to the radio stations, there was a nationwide manhunt—the largest in the new world's history—for the surviving Lost Boys. Boats scoured the seas, searching. Apparently, they even showed our mug shots before the movies. I, of course, was exempt from the coverage. The Feds were sticking with their story that I was dead. Charlie, too. Phoenix said, however, that it was just stuff for the press. The chancellor and Miranda were searching for us, yet they were also developing a plan. He said we should be doing the same.

They gave me a room in the New Texas fort, right next to Sparky's. The whole island was pretty damaged, but its bones were still good, and, in time, they said it'd be fully repaired. And now I was officially a member of the team—an orphan, like the others. A real Lost Boy if there ever was one.

Kindred had put Sage in the bed I was in when I first arrived, and Phoenix had created a plan to get Sage an IV and keep her fed with fluids—he said as long as we fed her, she'd stay alive. We had a raid planned for a Newla hospital later that week, to stock up on the medical supplies she would need. We all agreed we wouldn't let go of one of the bravest girls we'd ever met: our new friend, Sage.

I was sitting in the fort's basement, running my hands along the ConSynth, when its countdown clock flashed *24:00*. The red ConSynth felt warm beneath my fingers, like it generated its own heat, and maybe its own heartbeat. I heard feet on the ladder. Bertha and Phoenix join me in the basement. The air smelled vaguely like muffins.

I smiled. "Kindred's cooking."

Phoenix nodded. "She's making a cake."

"Blueberry, I assume?"

He grinned. "Wouldn't doubt it."

Bertha put her hand against my back and gave me an odd smile—the kind you give to your dentist when he says he's glad to see you.

"All right," she said, removing her hand. "I'm terrible at this shit—I just feel creepy." She pointed to the ConSynth and held her face in her hand. "I'm really sorry about all this—about all these dead people you really liked."

In a weird way, I was touched. Bertha wasn't good at dealing with her emotions, but it was nice to see that she cared enough to try.

I patted her on the back and turned to Phoenix. "I've been meaning to ask you something."

"Go ahead," he nodded. "Anything you want, and you'll get the truth."

"Why me?" I said. "I mean, I get that I probably would've died and maybe been tortured if Mila had left me to drown—but still, even after that, there were so many times you could've let me slip away. The first time I woke up and tried to kill you all—perfect chance to let me die. I dove right into a megalodon's mouth, after all—it would've saved you a lot of trouble. Why would you want to worry about dealing with someone else? Someone who caused more problems?"

"First off," he said, "if someone is crazy enough to dive into the mouth of a live megalodon—to let the ocean's most *horrifying* monster eat them whole—then that's a person I want on my team. The kind of person I *need* in order to make this revolution successful. Crazy people are, perhaps, the only individuals with enough bravery and foolishness to change the world. The meek might inherit the earth, but only after the fools have tamed it, transformed it, and made it their own."

"The megalodon... that was nothing. I wasn't even thinking."

"And that's a good thing," Phoenix said. "Revolutions aren't about thinking—they're about instincts. A caterpillar doesn't think about becoming a butterfly. It just trusts its instincts, and it does."

"You're the one," said Bertha in a hushed voice. "The one we've been waiting for. The one we've been waiting for, for a long, long time. You're the one who will save us all." She grabbed my cheeks and bore her brown eyes into mine. "The one who will take back the world. You're the one from the prophecy, Kai Bradbury. The boy the elders said would come!"

"There's a prophecy?" The room was spinning. Everything got blurry. "This is... all part of a prophecy?"

Bertha broke into laughter. "Christ, Car Battery! You think I'd believe that bullshit?" She punched me in the shoulder. "I'm just screwing with ya. There's no prophecy."

My heart was still pounding. "Good thing we all promised to be honest with each other..."

She pointed a finger to Phoenix. "*He* promised you honesty; I didn't. I'm gonna keep screwing with you until the day you die."

I turned to Phoenix. "And when exactly will that be?"

He hesitated. "I—I thought we established I wasn't trying to kill you..."

"I know," I said, "but what comes next? When do I risk my life next? I mean, we've got the report, and we've got tons of Indigo. What's next?"

Phoenix smiled. "Patience, grasshopper."

Kindred poked her head into the basement. "Excuse me, dears!" She held a cake in her outstretched arms. "Cake here for Mr. Bradbury!"

"What?" I said. "What for?"

Kindred passed it to Bertha and climbed down the ladder. "Your birthday, dear. We never celebrated it properly."

"Ah." I smiled and glanced at the cake. "Let me guess... blueberry?"

"Heavens no!" Kindred looked disgusted. Bertha breathed a sigh of relief. "It's strawberry."

Bertha groaned.

Kindred passed me the cake. "Have a look, dear."

Painted on a layer of white frosting was a crude picture of me and the Lost Boys, in a circle, holding hands. In red icing, someone had written, "HAPPY BIRTDAY, KAI!" and below that, "FAMILIE."

Bertha shook her head. "Jesus, Dove..."

"Wow," I said, still staring at the cake. "I—I don't know what to say. Except thank you." My eyes felt damp, and I wiped them with my hand. "It—it means a lot, guys."

Kindred smiled. "We've got something else for you too, dear."

Mila climbed down the ladder and passed me an envelope. "For you, Kai."

Inside the envelope was a picture of my mom. Her black hair was pinned up, and her face was turned to the side. It was a mug shot, obviously, but it was still Mom. It was the only picture I had of her now. Kindred was right: I did get to see her again.

I sucked in a breath. "Wow." I wanted to say thanks, but the word caught in my throat.

"I grabbed it from the desk when we were running from the cells," said Mila. "I wanted to surprise you."

"You did," I said. "Thank you." I glanced around the room. "Would this be a bad time for a group hug?"

Bertha started to grumble, but Phoenix shot her a look, and she nodded. "Bring it in, then, I guess."

Something was missing.

"Where's Dove and Sparky?" I asked.

*"HAPPY BIRTHDAY, DEAR KAI-I!"* their voices trailed in from above. They climbed down the ladder wearing red party hats decorated with pictures of cheeseburgers.

*"HAPPY BIRTHDAY TO YOU!"* they finished. Tim was hanging from Sparky's neck, his arm still bandaged where he'd been shot. He, too, wore a party hat.

"Did we miss it?" said Dove.

Sparky glanced at Bertha's red face and shook his head. "Negative."

"JUST BRING IT IN ALREADY!"

We wrapped around our arms around each another, and Dove led another round of "Happy Birthday." Bertha nursed the cake in the center, and Tim fought to sneak in occasional licks. The whole event was strange and bizarre and wonderful. The Lost Boys weren't terrorists, anarchists, Indigo thieves, or even revolutionaries. Now, they were simply my friends.

In that moment, I felt oddly like Sage Penderbrook, standing there, marveling at something as simple as friendship. Somewhere in the midst of all their lies to me, and all my lies to them, we'd unearthed something impossible: the truth.

The world was changing—maybe it always had, and always would. There were more stars in the sky than photosynthetic bacteria in the ocean. There was more light than dark. There was truth and freedom, and the people of the Federation would soon know both.

Indigo was poison meant to keep people in invisible cages. But revolution was coming, and Phoenix was leading the way. A new republic would rise.

And the Federation would fall.

# CHAPTER 47

THE GLASS CASING of the ConSynth hummed in my hands. Today, its red glowed brighter than ever before. Its countdown clock flashed *00:03*. No longer was it signaling hours, but minutes. It would soon be fully calibrated.

Sage's body twitched on the bed, and I rubbed my hand against her wrist. She fell still again. I massaged the wrinkles that lined her forehead, and her breathing steadied.

Soon I'd see Charlie. She'd be right here, in this room, like nothing had ever happened. My hands were already getting sort of sweaty.

A part of me wondered if the ConSynth would work. If we'd even hooked it up right. If synthetic consciousness was even possible...

But I'd seen Miranda Morier. I'd seen the way she moved. The way she spoke. The way she was very much alive. The ConSynth could work. It had to.

Still, had we done it right? Phoenix and Sage had hooked it up while I'd sat in a puddle of tears like Frosty the Melted Snowman. Was Charlie's body supposed to have seized up like that? Like she was going into cardiac arrest?

I shook my head, trying to clear away the negative thoughts. I couldn't think like this. It didn't do any good. Phoenix and Sage did the best they could, and that was all I could've asked of them.

The clock flashed *00:02*.

I'd told the others I wanted to be alone in the room when the time ran out—that I wanted alone time with her if it worked, or alone time with myself if it didn't.

I'd slicked my hair back and worn one of Phoenix's ties. He'd offered me a jacket too, but I passed. When I tried it on, I looked like a Girl Scout swimming in shoulder pads. I guessed it was yet another testament to his size and my pubescent blooming, or lack thereof.

Of course, Bertha said that fifteen years old was probably a bit late to be blooming. She said some flowers never bloomed, but just sat there on the vine as buds for a while before wilting.

I told her some flowers should learn to mind their own damn business.

Phoenix had been in touch with the Caravites. He explained to me that they'd never really just been stealing Indigo vaccines—they'd been destroying them. That's why it hadn't mattered when they'd fallen from the sky. They were just trying to prevent the virus from getting injected into the veins of children. Captain Vern reached out to Phoenix after we escaped from the Light House. He finally admitted running was no longer an option, and—with the capital building being blown to the ground—war was the only path left. The Caravan didn't need its plates polished anymore. Now, it just needed people.

Phoenix and Vern were planning a raid on the Ministry of Research & Development in Kauai. They said it'd be the toughest yet, with reinforcements increasing security twofold as Indigo production rushed to clear shortages and meet demand. I'd already agreed to go with them. Turns out, I wasn't half bad in the field.

Now, children were dying from the "Carcinogens" more than ever before. Phoenix suggested we start recruiting kids from the street as Lost Boys, and Kindred agreed to head the efforts. We'd learned that she was okay in the field, but after shooting the guard, she admitted she didn't have it in her to kill more people. Recruitment, however, was different, and she decided it would suit her quite well. And she'd already started developing materials. Mostly blueberry muffins.

The ConSynth's clock flashed *00:00*. The orb glowed a brilliant red, and the numbers disappeared among swirls, the machine humming louder than ever, then abruptly going silent.

I pressed my fingers against the glass. "Hello?"

No response.

There was no one in the room. I was still alone. I shook the orb a bit. "Anybody in there? Charlie?"

Nothing.

The sphere's swirls settled. I held my eye to the glass and squinted—a part of me wanting to believe I'd see a tiny version of her in there.

I felt someone staring at me from behind. I turned—and saw her standing on the opposite end of the room.

Charlie.

The room's dim light lit only her face. Her body was still cloaked in shadows.

Somehow, it was a different Charlie. Not the Charlie I'd seen in the Light House—the one who'd been starved and tortured and lay dying with her bald head pressed against the chancellor's floor. No, this was a different Charlie.

This was the old Charlie—the girl I'd grown up with. The girl with the bright blue eyes and chopsticks shoved in her perpetually messy bun. The girl whose blue eyes were a shade all her own. Not gray, like Miranda's, but Charlie-blue.

She smiled and waved at me from across the room.

My hands were sweaty. What should I do? What should I say? Again, I was reminded of all the things they didn't teach you in school—the stuff they should've taught instead of calculus.

I just grinned and waved back. "Hi, Charlie."

"Hey there, Kai-Guy." She smiled. "I've got something to show you."

She glanced down. My heart was melting. What was she wearing? Lingerie? A purple prom press? A chicken suit? What was happening? What was I supposed to do? Nobody had prepared me for this moment. Megalodons were easy. Girls were hard.

She stepped from the shadows and pointed to her feet. She wore a pair of red cheeseburger socks.

The world made sense.

Charlie was there. Everything would work out. I took a deep breath.

Things always worked out when you wore your cheeseburger socks.

# AUTHOR'S NOTE

Dear reader,

Thank you for reading *The Indigo Thief*. I have loved writing about Kai, Charlie, Phoenix, and all the other Lost Boys over the course of the past year. Things are certainly not finished with the Lost Boys and the Hawaiian Federation.

If you're so inclined, I'd greatly appreciate a review of *The Indigo Thief*, posted on amazon or goodreads. Whether you loved it or hated it, I'd just enjoy your feedback.

Reviews these days can be tough to come by, but you, the reader, have the power to make or break a book with them.

Thank you again for reading *The Indigo Thief*, and thanks for spending time with me.

In gratitude,

Jay Budgett

# ACKNOWLEDGEMENTS

First, I would like to thank Ruthie Berk. There is no other person who had more influence on this book than you did. Without your support I doubt I would've ever finished it. Thank you for teaching me about life, love, and all the things in between. If every author had a Ruthie, there'd be more books in the world. Thanks for being my Charlie.

Chris Okawa—thanks always for your excitement, encouragement, and kind words. There is no person whose opinion and insights I respect more than yours. You are one of those incredible people who can look at other's fragile dreams and see the strong realities that they can become.

Thank you Mom for keeping me grounded and for humoring all my crazy ideas. Dad—thanks for your belief, support, and words of encouragement.

Thanks to Lindsay Gregory for believing in my story and for your early critiques—they helped shape the story more than you'll ever know. Susan Faurer, thank you for being my "eagle eye." I am so grateful for your enthusiasm to read and improve this story. Your zeal for life is truly contagious.

I am fortunate to have had many teachers who, in one way or another, helped shaped my belief in myself to tell stories, as well as my ability to do so. Thanks Blair Biederman for giving me the opportunity to finish my first piece of writing way back in high school. It gave me the courage to keep writing. Thanks Gregg Maday for teaching me more about shaping stories than anyone I've ever met. You've got an incredible eye for stories and a gift for teaching others how to tell them.

Lastly, I'd like to thank my phenomenal editor David Gatewood for helping me transform this novel from what it was to what I'd always wanted it to be.

# ABOUT THE AUTHOR

Born and raised in Phoenix, Arizona, Jay Budgett is a senior studying business at Arizona State University. In his spare time, he enjoys travelling, swimming, coffee drinking, and scuba diving. He is also the playwright of a comedy titled *Greener Pastures*. Jay loves to hear from his readers. Connect with him at: jaybudgett.com.